Valentine's Day is truly a time for love. Three talented Arabesque authors share passionate love stories that are sure to warm your heart, body, and soul . . . and leave you absolutely breathless.

BOOK YOUR PLACE ON OUR WEBSITE AND MAKE THE ARABESQUE ROMANCE CONNECTION!

We've created a customized website just for our very special Arabesque readers, where you can get the inside scoop on everything that's going on with Arabesque romance novels.

When you come online, you'll have the exciting opportunity to:

- View covers of upcoming books

- Learn about our future publishing schedule (listed by publication month and author)

- Find out when your favorite authors will be visiting a city near you

- Search for and order backlist books

- Check out author bios and background information

- Send e-mail to your favorite authors

- Join us in weekly chats with authors, readers and other guests

- Get writing guidelines

- AND MUCH MORE!

Visit our website at
http://www.arabesquebooks.com

TRULY

Geri Guillaume
Adrienne Ellis Reeves
Mildred Riley

ARABESQUE

BET BOOKS

BET Publications, LLC
www.bet.com
www.arabesquebooks.com

ARABESQUE BOOKS are published by

BET Publications, LLC
c/o BET BOOKS
One BET Plaza
1900 W Place NE
Washington, D.C. 20018-1211

All Kensington titles, Imprints and Distributed Lines are available at special quantity discounts for bulk purchases for sales
promotions, premiums, fund-raising, and educational or institu-
tional use. Special book excerpts or customized printings can
also be created to fit specific needs. For details, write or phone
the office of the Kensington special sales manager: Kensington
Publishing Corp., 850 Third Avenue, New York, NY 10022,
attn: Special Sales Department, Phone: 1-800-221-2647

First Printing: January 2001

10 9 8 7 6 5 4 3 2 1
Printed in the United States of America

CONTENTS

STOLEN HEARTS

Geri Guillaume

This is for all the hearts that have helped me. For Robert, the one closest to mine. Thanks for all of the encouragement. For Donna, who kept my other little hearts out of my hair so I could write. For Caroline's humor and Bruce's how-to. Thank you all!

Prologue

Houston, 1969.

"Come on, baby. You can do it!"

"No, I can't . . . I can't. Please don't make me, Xavier. Just give me a little something to take the edge off."

Xavier X patted his lady and winced when her slender hand squeezed hard enough to almost crush the bones of his flat, stubby fingers. He knelt beside her, trying to relieve his own discomfort as well as hers. "Baby, you know I can't do that. You made me promise that no matter how much you begged, you didn't want me to give you anything. Remember? You made me swear."

"But it hurts, Xavier X. It hurts so much. It's got me out here pretty bad. I'm shaking all over."

"I know, baby. I know. But you're almost through this, Thelma. Hang in there a little while longer."

"Tranquility!" she snapped back. "I'm Tranquility X now, damn it! Don't you ever, ever, *ever* call me by that racist, slave-mentality name again." She squeezed his hand to emphasize her point. This time, Xavier was certain that he heard the third metatarsal of his right hand snap in two.

"Oh, yeah. I forgot. Sorry, honey. You're right," Xavier X soothed.

"And don't you dare tell me you know! How in the hell can you know? Are *you* sitting in a pool of ice-cold water, feeling like you're about to pass a twenty-pound bowling ball through your guts? Are you? *Are you?!*"

"Warm the water up, Chastity," Xavier X directed at the combination part-time live-in, part-time lover, midwife, and mystic guide. "Can't you see she's shivering in there?"

Tranquility grabbed two fistfuls of Xavier X's dashiki and pulled him to within inches of her contorted face. Beads of perspiration popped out on his forehead at the menacing image of his once peace-loving lady's face with teeth bared and flecks of foam collecting in the corners of her lips. Her kohl-lined, big brown eyes narrowed to nearly slits as she hissed at him. "Stop messing around and get me something, Xavier X, or so help me, I'll strangle you with those love beads around your neck."

Xavier X looked to Chastity for support. Nothing happening there. She seemed more interested in watching the swirling smoke from the purifying incense. Chastity finally shrugged. Though she and Xavier X sometimes had a thing going when it was Tranquility's time of the month or when she'd gotten too big to want it anymore, she wasn't about to get involved in this two-way struggle.

"But Tranquility, baby, if I leave now, I'll miss it. Do you know how long I've been waiting for this?"

"Oooohhhh, let me guess," Tranquility purred. "Something like nine freakin', ankle-swelling, back-aching, bean sprout-craving months!"

"But we talked about this," he protested. He had to speak loudly as his beloved Tranquility's voice reached a deafening crescendo.

"What do you mean 'we', Negro? Do you see a freakin'

'we' in this tub? No. It's me, me, *me*. And me, myself, and I are telling you now that I can't take much more of this pain. You can't imagine what this is like.''

"Oh, I don't know about that," Xavier X groaned as he extricated his fingers from her death grip. As he dipped his shoulder and leaned toward her, he told himself it was a show of solidarity and sympathy for her pain. That wasn't exactly the case. He was trying to relieve some of his own. As long as Tranquility continued to suffer, so would he. It didn't take a genius to figure out that it was in all of their best interests if he helped her.

With his other, pain-free hand, he reached for a dark-green bottle chilling in a bucket of ice beside the birthing pool. For the past hour, he had been feeding Tranquility ice chips. Each time a contraction hit her, her teeth ground the chips down to water in no time. The last time she clamped down, Xavier suspected that she got an unhealthy dose of molar in the last swallow.

He stuck the top of the bottle into his mouth and pulled the cork from it with his teeth. He'd planned to toast the birth of his child with this. The way Tranquility was glaring at him now, he couldn't wait that long to crack open the bottle.

Together, he and Tranquility had home-brewed the boysenberry wine. They'd harvested the fruit under the light of a full moon, making love in their backyard vineyard that same night. It was only fitting that the wine be there to celebrate the birth resulting from that union. Everything about the wine was all natural. No chemical fertilizers or pesticides. If he gave her a little to ease her pain, it wouldn't pollute her body. It couldn't hurt the baby. If it helped her to relax, surely it could only help the process. What could a sip hurt? But he wanted to be sure. They'd stayed clean for over a year in anticipation of this moment—without as much as a bromo to put in their bodies to cure a stomach ache.

"Is it all right, Chastity?" Xavier asked the midwife. She

hunched her shoulders again and blew softly on a stick of musky incense until the tip glowed bright red.

"Give me that drink, Xavier X!" Tranquility snatched the bottle from him and raised it to her lips.

"Not too much, baby," Xavier X warned just as another contraction hit her.

Tranquility cried out and doubled over. Dark-red wine spilled over the white tunic she'd made with her own hands and stained the water where she sat. The red stain spread outward like an omen of the pending birth.

"Oooohhhh, wowwww, man!" Chastity said in awe, tilting her head to follow the wake of the spilled wine. "This is like some kind of sign. Like one of the plagues of Egypt."

"Do something, Chastity," Xavier X insisted. The midwife placed the heels of her hands against Tranquility's shoulders and pressed her back into the tub against a plastic-covered pillow. "Take it easy, Tranquility. Breathe in. . . . Breathe out. That's it."

"I didn't know it was going to be like this," Xavier muttered. "Maybe we should get her to a doctor, huh?"

"I'm not going anywhere like this," Tranquility clutched his arm. "And certainly not to some overcrowded free clinic. I'd rather have my baby in the bushes. Just get me something to take the pain way. Please, baby. Please!"

"Why don't you go see Augie?" Chastity suggested. "He's got some stuff that'll help. She could give birth to an elephant and never feel a thing."

"Augie?"

"Yeah. He's got a crib above a tire shop over on Mesa Road. Tell him you've got a killer headache and that I said you know what's good for it. Augie knows me. You could say that I'm one of his regulars." Chastity giggled and waved the incense stick in the air. Xavier looked at her dubiously. Lord only knew what she was really seeing in the gray trail of scented smoke.

"I don't know," Xavier X hesitated. "We worked so hard to keep pure."

"Do you want to see your lady suffer? Remember that everything she's going through, your baby feels, too."

"But I don't want to miss the birth."

Chastity rolled up her sleeve and stuck her hand into the icy pool, ignoring Tranquility's yelp of discomfort when she checked the baby's progress.

"Hardly even dilated. You've got time, Xavier X."

Xavier looked at his woman—the only woman in his life as far as he was concerned. Chastity lived there, too. And he had to admit that her willingness to share his bed when Tranquility didn't want to be bothered had almost made him ask her to become a permanent part of his life a few times. But he always came to his senses as soon as he left her bed and slipped back into his life with Tranquility. He and Tranquility "loved" there, in every sense of the word. It was more than the quick fix that Chastity offered him. He couldn't bear to see Tranquility like this. This was supposed to be a joyous, blessed event. But with each look, Tranquility was damning him further and further into the pits of flaming hell.

"All right. I'll go," he said reluctantly. He gently wiped his palm over Tranquility's forehead before kissing her. "Don't let our baby come before I get back, Tranquility."

"It's not as if I have a say in the matter," she panted but still looked up at him with grateful eyes.

"Cross your legs," Xavier X teased.

"If you'd thought of that nine months ago, I wouldn't be in this mess, Xavier X!" Another wave of pure, unadulterated pain hit Tranquility, followed by a stream of obscenities that Xavier had not heard since the time he and Tranquility were dragged away by the local police from a lunch counter sit-in at the downtown Sears.

Xavier jumped into his VW bug and cranked up the engine. The sputter of the engine couldn't drown out the sound of Tranquility's cries. He turned on the radio and hoped the soulful rips of P-Funk would drive her voice from his head.

By the time he returned, it was the absence of noise that

bothered him even more than Tranquility's screeches. He catapulted himself out of his car and into the house, shouting her name.

"Tranquility? I've got something for you." He stopped in the front room where the birthing pool had been set up. It was empty. "Tranquility? Chastity?" he called out. He rattled the brown paper bag, knowing that the sound was like the ring of the dinner bell to the starving. Chastity emerged from the back room, wiping her hands on the hem of her sundress. "You're back. I'll take those now."

Xavier X held the bag out of her reach. "I didn't bring these for you. Where's Tranquility?"

"I moved her to the back room. She was making too much noise. I didn't want anyone to call 'The Man' on us."

Xavier X followed Chastity to the back bedroom. "Tranquility? I'm back. I brought something for you."

Tranquility's eyes fluttered open—red-rimmed and barely focusing. "And I got something for you, too, Xavier X." She pulled the covers back and unveiled two mewling bundles.

"Wha . . . wha . . . what—" his mouth worked, but he couldn't quite complete the sentence. He whirled on Chastity. "I thought you said that I had more time!"

"What do I look like to you—a cuckoo clock? It's not my fault that you took your own sweet time getting back."

"Nine months," Xavier croaked. "Nine months. I'm gone for twenty minutes. You couldn't keep her plugged for twenty minutes! What was I supposed to be paying you for? I could have done what you did."

"Xavier, come hold your babies," Tranquility said, trying to sit up, then falling back weakly. "All of them. All six of them healthy and strong. All except the one with the purple squiggles and the yellow eyes. I ain't keeping that one. I told Chastity she could have that one. It matches the inside of her van."

Her words startled him. "Tranquility? Baby, are you all right? Chastity what did you do to her?"

''Nothin'. I didn't do nothin' to her. What are you blaming me for? It was your wine.''

Xavier X peeled back Tranquility's eyelids. Her pupils were dilated to almost the size of dimes. ''Yes, you did. What did you give her?''

''Nothin'. It's just the wine kickin' in.''

''You're lying. She's on some kind of serious trip. Tranquility, wake up, baby. Wake up and talk to me.'' He knelt beside his lady.

''Pay the rest of the money before you get all caught up in the family moment,'' Chastity said. She may have dropped out of college to discover herself, but she was no dummy. If she didn't get her money now, as soon as Xavier X put his hands on those babies, there would be no collecting.

''You're not getting a freakin' thing from me,'' Xavier X declared. ''You come up in here, with your birthing pool and your incense and your wind chimes. You gave her something, and now she can't nurse. It's poisoned her blood. It'll kill the babies.''

''I had to give her something. She almost kicked my teeth in when I went for the forceps.''

''You used those torture devices on my babies? I told you— no drugs, no tools. It was just supposed to be you, me, and Mother Nature.''

''Well, you weren't here, and Mother Nature split when Tranquility punched me in the face and called me a clammy-handed bitch. You owe me thirty dollars for my troubles, Xavier X. I need that green, man. Pay me.''

''Get out!'' Xavier flung the bottle of wine at her.

Chastity squealed and ducked. ''What's the matter with you? Are you on some kind of trip, man? Because you'd better come down off your high and pay me before—''

''You could have killed them! You could have killed my family, my baby . . . what do we have anyway?''

''What do you see?'' Chastity gritted through clenched teeth.

Xavier X's expression softened. "I see girls. Two beautiful baby girls."

"What you see is what you get," Chastity said angrily. "Are you gonna give me my dough or not?"

"Not. You almost killed my family."

"But I didn't."

"You won't get the chance. Get out, Chastity."

"You owe me, Xavier X."

"Yeah? Well, as long as I owe you, you'll never be broke."

Chastity closed her eyes, held her hands palm upwards and chanted—the sign that she was about to go into the trance that used to enthrall and entice Xavier X.

"It's not going to work this time. I don't want you here. Pack your stuff. I want you gone in one hour. And you'd better make sure you only take what's yours."

"All right, all right. I'm splitting. I'm outta here. Just remember, Xavier X, that you called it."

Chapter One

"I'll get it! It's for me!"

A streak of purple and blue was all Justin Malloy saw of his nephew Emeril as the lanky teenager went streaking down the hall. Justin stared after him with a puzzled expression. Had the phone rung? How could he tell with all that loud racket coming from his room? Justin followed the trail of crushed potato chips ground into the carpet and sloshed strawberry soda against the walls to the guest room that Emeril had taken over for the week. He pushed open the door and opened his mouth to complain against the near hit-and-run, then shut his mouth with an audible click. His jaw worked back and forth, grinding his molars. *Oh, my dentist is going to love me on my next visit.* He tried to remember the last words his brother had told him before dropping off the boy. *Count to ten. Count to ten. Count to ten.* He repeated the mantra in his head in sync with the music coming from Emeril's stereo. *No, not radio,* Justin mentally corrected himself. *Public address system. Nothing that loud and that obnoxious could be called a simple radio.*

Seeing what he was seeing now, Justin was beginning to

regret his decision to give the boy his space. He hadn't been in the room since Emeril had moved his stuff in. When he'd agreed to watch the boy for his brother while he and his second wife (her third marriage) took off on their honeymoon, he wasn't quite sure what he was getting himself into. They'd given him a list of 'do's and don'ts.' But that had been at the last minute as they scurried to finish packing. The scurrying heightened to a frenzy as the taxi's meter kept ticking away.

His brother and his wife could have written him an entire manual, and it still wouldn't have prepared him for this. The boy was the product of his new sister-in-law's first marriage. It was bad enough that Emeril had to deal with yet another new stepfather. Before he could get acquainted, he was thrust on a total stranger, loosely called 'family.' It was a tense situation all around. Justin did what he could to make him feel at home. How could he do that when even his own home wasn't looking like home to him now?

He hardly recognized his guest room. What happened to his one-of-a-kind art pieces? Autographed prints by Kathleen Wilson and Harry L. Davis lay stacked against the wall like rummage sale rejects. And what had taken their places? Pin-up glossies of humans on steroids, slicked down with enough glycerin to slide off the poster. Who in the world were "The Rock" and "Stone Cold"? These so-called pro-wrestlers and their equally muscle-bound female counterparts adorned his wall.

What happened to his hand-stitched down comforter? His grandmother had made that for him as a going-away-to-college gift. He just knew that Emeril couldn't be sleeping on that tattered, fringed, food-stained haven for who knew what kind of germs. When Justin saw Emeril lying with his head at the foot of the bed, his feet propped up on the wall with his U-boat–sized tennis shoes, he was ready to hit the roof.

"Emeril," Justin began. When he received no response, he put two fingers between his lips and whistled sharply.

The boy spun around and regarded him with all of the wide-eyed innocence of a newborn panda. "Wha . . . ?"

For a moment, Justin was instantly transported back in time. Having no parenting skills of his own, he felt the spirit of his father descending over him and taking possession of his throat.

"Don't 'what' me, son. Get off that phone right now and clean up this mess. I want it sanitary by dinner time. That gives you a running head start of three hours. Think it's possible?"

"Come on now. Don't be that way." Emeril complained loudly. Then he covered the mouthpiece of the phone with his hand and said, "Please, Uncle . . . uh . . . Uncle Justin. Just five more minutes. I promise I'll get it cleaned up."

Justin's eyes narrowed suspiciously. Who could be talking to Emeril on this line? It was an unlisted number. It shouldn't have rung for him. He shouldn't be giving that number out. Justin considered snatching the phone away and putting the party on the other end through the third degree. But, when he spotted a well-creased photo tacked to the headboard, he checked himself. There was something so familiar about Emeril's situation—something about his expression that struck a chord with him. So poignant. So puppy-doggish. Emeril was in lust. At that young age, Justin didn't dare call it love.

Justin clucked his tongue in silent sympathy. He'd complain about the pinhole in the custom-made, cherry-wood headboard later. He had to admire the boy's taste. The girl in the picture was quite attractive, and—Justin suspected—a few years older than Emeril's fourteen years of age. No wonder the boy had been so moody, so reluctant, to leave the comforts of his home, family, and friends. Here he was, dumped in the home of a virtual stranger, having to satisfy himself with a crumpled photograph and a few stolen moments on the telephone. Relenting, Justin held up his hand and spread his fingers, indicating the amount of time Emeril had left to talk on the telephone.

Emeril rolled his eyes, so Justin reluctantly held up the other hand, doubling his time limit. Emeril grinned at him, then turned his back on his uncle. Muttering, Justin went back to his office. He closed the double-glass doors behind him without much confidence that the thin insulation would block out the sounds of unadulterated youth coming from his guest room. He didn't need to go back to act as timekeeper for Emeril. Justin had barely settled into his work when the boy came tapping on his glass.

He made a show of checking his watch. "Two minutes, that must be some kind of a record for getting a teenager off of the phone."

"Can I come in?" Emeril asked.

Now, this is a switch, Justin mused. The boy usually barged in without much regard for what Justin was in the middle of. Conference call or catnap, it didn't matter. Seeing the panicked expression on Emeril's face, Justin used this moment to exercise what his brother called his "puny patience muscle." He wasn't used to having his work flow interrupted so many times a day.

When he'd opted to operate his one-man, web design business from his home, he made certain that every conceivable interruption to his creative process was taken out of the equation. He had multiple phone lines installed—a DSL line for his computer for the quickest connection to the Internet and regular land line with an unlisted number for his personal calls.

"What is it, Emeril?"

"We gotta go out," the boy said.

"We?" Justin raised a sardonic eyebrow. Unless Emeril was talking about his crew that he'd left behind, Justin didn't think the word 'we' was in his nephew's vocabulary. "What do you mean, 'we'?"

"I'm in trouble."

"What kind of trouble?" All sarcastic comments drained out of Justin's head. Take one sullen, lovesick teenager and one overdeveloped 'round-the-way girl wannabe—and Justin's imagination conjured up at least a hundred loaded connotations for the word "trouble."

Emeril didn't have to try to read his uncle's mind. It was

written all over the uncomfortable creases of Justin's face. "Not *that* kind of trouble."

"Whew!" Justin blew out an unexaggerated sigh. "I thought I'd have to sit down and have 'the talk' with you, son. It wasn't something I was looking forward to."

"You still have the number to my mama's hotel in Cozumel, don't you? You could have called her, if you were so scared."

Justin's face brightened. "Yeah. I almost forgot about that. That's one long-distance bill I don't mind forkin' over the dough for if I didn't have to—"

"Can we get back to *my* problem now, Uncle J?"

"Yeah ... yeah ... sorry about that. What is it that you need, Emeril?"

"A Valentine's Day gift for my lady."

"Your lady?" Justin echoed, trying not to smile. The boy was deadly serious and probably wouldn't appreciate having his tender affections trampled on.

"I promised her that I'd get her something nice. She's not too happy that I had to miss out on her party by being stuck here. That is ... uh ... I mean, since we get to spend all of this quality time getting to know each other like family should."

"Uh-huh," Justin grunted. "Ease up on the sucking up, son. How much is it going to cost me?"

"Not a dime. I've got some money saved up from my allowance. Mama was supposed to take me shopping before she left."

"Don't take it too hard. Your mama was a little preoccupied before she left, Emeril."

Emeril smacked his lips and said. "Hold up, Uncle Justin. You don't run a child psych game on me, and I promise to go easy on the sucking up."

"Deal," Justin said, holding out his hand for a shake.

"So are you going to take me out or not?" Emeril ignored it, so Justin folded his arms under his armpits.

"Where do you want to go?"

Emeril shrugged. "I dunno. Somewhere I can get something

nice, that doesn't cost a lot of money. But I don't want it to look cheap, you know?''

"I guess that old saying about it being the thought that counts doesn't apply here?''

"My lady's got expensive tastes. I can't have my lady lookin' raggedy. Not if she's gonna be seen with me.''

"If she's got expensive tastes, maybe you need to get a job,'' Justin suggested in all seriousness.

"You know, Uncle J, that's the same thing my mama said about you.''

"What do you mean I should get a job? I have a job!'' Justin's voice echoed after the boy as he retreated to the guest room to pick up his wallet.

"Surfin' the net?'' Emeril scoffed. "What kind of job is that? Have you got benefits?''

"Yeah,'' Justin retorted. "One of my most prized benefits is having the flexibility of watching over you while your mother and my brother take off on a honeymoon I helped to pay for with my 'no-job' having self. Yeah, son. I get great benefits.''

"I didn't ask you to take me in. I could have stayed with my friends.''

"And miss all of this wonderful bonding time?'' Justin retorted. He half smiled to ease the sting of his sarcasm. His expression softened as he said, "I wouldn't miss this opportunity for the world, Emeril. I don't mean to say anything against your mama. It's just that I get a little irritated when people talk about my work. I work at home, but I work hard at what I do. Half the new web sites put out there were developed by guys just like me,'' Justin said proudly. "Next time you dot-com yourself to some cool site you point all of your friends to, think about what your mama said, then think about what you've seen while you've been staying with me. Now get your stuff.''

"Where are we going?''

"You said you wanted a gift for your lady, didn't you? I've go to make a run on the other side of town. We can do your shopping over there.''

* * *

How did that old saying go? *You can take the boy out of the 'hood, but you can't take the 'hood out of the boy.* Justin imagined that some of his friends would take issue with that. Driving around in their sports-utility vehicles and setting up tee-off times with the boys from other virtual offices, some of his friends pushed away their neighborhood roots with more vehemence and enthusiasm than an umpire and coach confrontation at a baseball game. And though he ran with some of the same boys, his footsteps always took him back to what he would always consider to be his home base.

Justin took his foot off of the gas pedal, approaching the familiar exit for the northeast side of town. He could almost finish the trip with his eyes closed. He knew every rut in the road, every bump. It seemed as if he recognized every soda or beer can littering the access ramp. He could almost close his eyes and let the car continue the rest of the way. But he didn't. He knew better than that. He knew that this was a notorious trouble spot. Even as he exited the freeway, there would be at least six eighteen-wheelers trying to get on the freeway, heading for the ship channel and beyond. Those big rigs wouldn't be thinking about a tiny, drop-top Mercedes cruising along memory lane. If he didn't snap his mind back, he would be a blood-red pebble caught in the treads behind some pistol-packing, Yosemite Sam, dirt-encrusted mud flap.

"Where'd you say we were going again?" Emeril stared out the window with undisguised irritation.

"To a friend's house."

"A woman?"

"None ya," Justin replied, meaning that Emeril should mind his own business. Emeril looked curiously at his uncle. Somewhere between the exit from Highway 290 and the jaunt over the 610 loop, his uncle had been replaced by someone he didn't recognize. His body language, his speech patterns—nothing about him was the same.

"How long is it gonna take?"

"As long as it takes. Relax, E," Justin looked over and grinned at him. "I'll get you to the stores before they close."

E? Emeril mouthed. "I know you're not taking me out over here," Emeril said incredulously. "What am I supposed to pick up for my lady? A fifth?" The profusion of liquor stores dotting every other corner competed with the number of churches resting on the alternate corners.

Justin turned the wheel hard, making the U-turn past the sign that welcomed him to THE GARDENS. He smiled to himself, reliving a memory. The sign was up today, but it was Friday night. Traffic was starting to get heavy. And judging from the traffic trying to get to the liquor store on the opposite side of the road, the sign didn't have a chance. A careless or drunken driver would knock the sign down before the weekend was over.

He passed the brightly lit combination gas station and fast-food restaurant and wondered about the church that once stood near that corner. He could still hear the gravelly voice of the minister, fervent and static-filled, bellowing out his sermon over the loudspeakers.

After passing three more side streets, he turned right at the corner at the house with the cyclone fence and the ever-present string of Christmas lights. Mid street, he whipped a fast left and pulled into a crushed gravel drive. A black-and-tan rottweiler lay in the middle of the drive, with her pups scampering around her. Justin tooted the horn—not so much to make the dog move as to announce his presence so that she wouldn't respond with aggressive surprise when he got out.

He climbed out, tapped his horn again, and called out, "Faizon! Yo, Faizon! Come on out and get this man-killer off of me!" He looked over his shoulder at Emeril still sitting in the car. He'd hunkered down as if he didn't want anyone to recognize him. The mama dog hadn't paid Justin any attention. She yawned, showing huge yellow teeth, and rested her head on her mammoth paws.

Moments after the call, the solid oak door of the white frame house with mint-green trim opened, followed by the creak and slam of the screen door. The largest man Emeril had ever seen stepped onto the porch. The wooden floorboards creaked and groaned under his weight. Emeril suspected that at any moment the man would go crashing through the floor. At one time, he might have been a candidate for Mr. Universe. Emeril could see remnants of thick muscles in his biceps and thighs from his cut-off shorts and muscle shirt. But what may have been a barrel chest at one time had succumbed to the ravages of gravity and one too many chopped-beef barbecue sandwiches. Emeril took him in with one long gaze—from the top of his bandana-covered head to the bottom of his flip-flop covered feet.

"What do you want?" the big man rumbled, gesturing with a can of Bud Light at Justin.

"I'm the rent man," Justin called out. "You're six months past due."

The big man belched, long and loud, making the mother dog sit up and take notice. "Like hell I am. I talked to your sister, and she said I don't have to pay. In fact, I ain't six months late, son, I think she is."

Justin pointed a finger at the big man—and not a very nice finger, either. Emeril couldn't tell by the big man's expression if he should dive under the car for cover, crank up the engine to make a quick getaway, or run to find the nearest phone to call the police. He got out of the car, edging closer to Justin, ready to snatch the keys if he had to.

Suddenly, the big man started to laugh. He threw his head back and displayed a wide, gap-toothed smile.

"It's about time you brought your narrow ass out here, Butter."

Butter? Emeril mouthed and tried not to laugh. That was a nickname given to lighter-skinned blacks. His uncle's complexion was medium brown. But he supposed in comparison to Faizon's dark tones, his uncle would seem that way.

"Mama's been wondering when you were going to come

by. She's been holding that peach cobbler for you since the last time you stopped by. It's got mold and crap all over it and I think a family of rats have moved into the pie pan. But what the hell? Throw a scoop of ice cream over that bad boy, and it's all good."

Justin threw his arm around Emeril's shoulder and said, "Come on in."

"You have got to be kidding," Emeril said out of the corner of his mouth.

"Wha?" Justin returned, mimicking Emeril's tone.

"Who's that you got hiding behind you, Butter?" The behemoth took another swig from his beer and leaned back to stare at Emeril.

"This is my nephew, Emeril. He's part of the family now."

"Yeah, I heard that Gideon had gotten married again."

"How come I didn't see you at the wedding?"

Faizon shrugged. "Had things to do. You know how it is."

"Yeah, I know how it is," Justin said easily enough. He dropped the subject when he saw an uncomfortable expression cross Faizon's face.

"How you doin', little man?" Faizon turned to Emeril.

"Hey," Emeril lifted his hand in return.

"Don't 'hey' me. When you come into a man's house, you shake a man's hand."

Emeril didn't want to, fully expecting Faizon to crush his hand—even though, with each passing moment, the man was turning out to be more of a gentle giant.

"That's right," Faizon said in approval. "Good strong grip. That's how a man is supposed to act. You want a beer, little man?"

Emeril looked at Justin, his expression hopeful, excited.

"Don't even think about it, peach fuzz. You're not *that* much of a man, yet."

Faizon's laugh boomed as he ushered them inside. The interior was surprisingly better kept than the outside would appear. A huge, dark-green leather sectional dominated the front room.

The wide-screen television was probably connected to a satellite dish. A girl, about seventeen years old, held a remote in her hand and was flipping through channels faster than the human eye could follow. Emeril knocked some of the dirt off of his feet before stepping onto the green, white, and burgundy oriental rug.

The girl looked up, and, with an ear-piercing squeal of delight, dropped the remote and launched herself off of the couch and right into Justin's arms. She flung her arms around Justin's neck and kissed him on the cheek, leaving bright-pink lipstick that matched her six-inch long nail tips.

"Hey. Back off my sister, Butter, or I swear I'm gonna have to cut you." Faizon bellowed.

"How are you doin', Chantal? Are you staying out of trouble?" Justin asked.

"Straight A's in school," she replied. She held out her hand. "Hand it over, Mr. Justin, You promised me five dollars for every A."

"I want to see the report card."

She whirled around and snatched it from the corner of a picture frame. Something told Emeril that she had the report card ready so that she could run the same lines on everyone who walked through the door.

Justin pulled out his wallet. "I'm telling your mama that you're jacking me for my last dime. By the way, where is Miss Tansy?"

"Mama's gone for her dialysis treatment. She'll be back in a couple of hours."

"Dialysis?" Justin's brow furrowed. "How long has she been sick?"

"About three months," Faizon responded.

"I didn't know."

"See, you ought to come out more than every blue moon," Chantal said, pocketing the money. After she'd gotten what she wanted from Justin, she cast a curious glance at Emeril—

who was a little tall for his age but was showing potential for filling out nicely.

"Who's this, Mr. Justin?"

"This is Emeril, my nephew. Gideon's stepson."

"Hey," she said, eyeing him up and down.

Faizon put a huge, ham-handed palm on top of Chantal's head and spun her around toward the television. "Don't even *think* about it."

She smacked her lips at him, then resumed her perch on the couch.

"Say, Chantal, where's a good place around her to pick up a present? Emeril needs to buy a Valentine's gift for his girlfriend," Justin asked.

Chantal raised her eyebrow at Emeril. "The way Faizon's acting, you'd think that you were too young to be going with anybody," Chantal asked. "You're not too young, are you, Emeril?"

"She's not ... not really my girlfriend ... yet," Emeril stammered, distracted by the purse of Chantal's pink lips and the strained stretch of cloth over her pushup bra. "We're just talking."

Justin leaned over and muttered to Faizon. "An hour ago, she was his lady and had to be taken care of in the worst kind of way."

"Oh-ho," Faizon replied.

"You could try Karimah's," Chantal answered. "They just opened up another store on this side of town."

"Karimah's," Justin echoed.

"A chain of boutiques run by a couple of sisters," Faizon supplied.

Chantal reached under the couch and pulled out a glossy flyer that advertised the store's opening.

"Good idea," Faizon said. "Me and one of the sisters are real close."

"Like you getting out of paying the rent?" Emeril piped up.

"That kid's got a real mouth on him, Butter."

"Who are you telling?"

"If you're going, you'd better go now before all of the best stuff gets picked over," Chantal encouraged.

Chapter Two

"Call it in the air, folks. Heads or tails?"

Kallista Hart turned to address the stocky young man sitting beside her. She twirled a shiny, new gold-dollar coin between her nimble fingers. The muted light radiating from several security monitors cast an odd shadow on her face, and Brandt, the junior member of Kallista's loss-prevention team, could not tell if she was kidding.

Deandre, the third member who rounded out the crew working this shift, was the senior member of the team. She'd known Kallista for three years, ever since she'd signed on to help monitor Kallista's sister's first upscale boutique—"Karimah's." Deandre had helped to establish the security procedures for the second store. And now that they were about to have the grand opening ceremony of the third, Deandre was starting to get a handle on Kallista's personality.

Kallista never kidded about money, that much was certain. There must have been something else going on. Deandre followed her gaze to the scene playing itself out on the monitor, then chuckled. She leaned over and whispered to Brandt. "You'd better take tails, junior."

"Heads," he said, ignoring the tip. Brandt was a new addition

to the team; the ink on his bonding paperwork was barely dry.
He was new to the security game, and he still had a lot to learn.
He was allowed to make mistakes as long as he didn't make
them twice. At his interview, he'd convinced Kallista that what
he lacked in experience, he made up for in enthusiasm. Wherever and whatever she needed him to be, he could be. Kallista
had hired him because of his youthful exuberance as well as
his "Generation X" looks. He looked young for his age. He
walked the walk. He talked the talk. Put him in a room full of
teenagers, and he could be just as delinquent. He could canvass
the boutique floor, without the "just-browsing" crowd picking
up on the fact that he was an undercover agent.

Kallista kept twirling the coin. Seconds later, she tossed it
up. Deandre caught it in midair, snatching it away from Brandt.

"You call it, D," Kallista said admiringly. She picked up
the bag of corn chips that Brandt had dropped in order to catch
the dollar. Then she popped a handful of chips into her mouth.
"You lost the call, you pick up the ball."

"Your turn to be the tail, junior," Deandre said, indicating
the monitors.

"I'm on it. Miss H, remember, I've got the two-way on me,
so I'll know if you eat up all of my chips. I'll be able to hear
you crunching loud and clear."

"Yummy! Finger lickin'!" Kallista said, sticking out a small,
pink tongue to lick the reddish-orange salt from her fingertips.
"These are corn-roasted, barbecue flavor. Sorry, Brandt. You're
not getting this bag back. Your chips have got about as much
chance as that poor idiot who just tried to hide three silk scarves
in his pants pocket." She dusted her fingers off on her pants
leg before pointing to the screen. "As if anyone would believe
he's got that much going on down there."

"If he had, he wouldn't be here trying to buy himself some
love," Deandre scoffed.

"I should have called tails," Brandt surmised. All this time,
Kallista and Deandre had been playing a game, trying to guess
where the shoplifter would try to hide the merchandise. Cameras

that were strategically positioned around the store constantly swept the area.

Suddenly, Deandre burst out laughing. "Ooh, ooh, boss, let me take this one. Please!" She jumped up and down and raised her hand as if she were in grade school. "I want the woman at the perfume counter."

Brandt concentrated on the monitor, trying to figure out what had tipped Deandre off.

"How did you—" he began.

"Unless I miss my count, she just sprouted a third breast," Deandre tapped the glass.

"She *is* a little young to be swinging so low," Kallista remarked.

Deandre shook her head. "There's no 'wonder' in that bra. She's packing."

Kallista chuckled, despite the seriousness of the events playing out before her on the monitors. She knew that there would be trouble today. No way to avoid it. It was as if some giant, unseen hand in the sky was stirring in all of the ingredients for a perfect, destruction-of-faith-in-humanity kind of day. Combine a pinch of petty larceny, a pound of merchandise set out in open displays, and a dash of a false sense of anonymity. Mix well. Bring to a low boil for a twelve-hour, opening-day sale and what do you get?

"The holding room is going to be full to bursting. Just to be safe, I think I'll call for a couple of uniformed officers from the storefront down the way," Kallista mused aloud.

"I don't know if we should do that," Brandt hesitated. "This is Miss Karimah's big day. I don't think she'd like a bunch of uniforms standing around, making customers nervous."

"She's gonna like it even less if half of her merchandise winds up walking out the front door," Kallista countered.

"The real headache is going to be processing all of those out there slick enough to try to walk out of here with the merchandise," Deandre said confidently.

"Speaking of slick. Take a look." Deandre pointed to another strategically placed camera. "Does she really think we're going to believe that's her natural color? Oh, no. Blondie over there is going to have to be picked up on sheer nerve alone."

"You take her, Deandre. I'll keep monitoring from here. With you tailing and me keeping an eye on tape, we should be able to build some pretty airtight cases that will stand up in court."

"See you in a bit, boss."

"Not if I see you first," Kallista said, repeating their favorite standing joke. She canted her head in the direction of the security monitors to indicate that she would be keeping a close eye on them. Her security team wasn't bothered by the statement. They knew that she was watching out as much for them as she was for the blatant thievery going on in the store. Deandre closed the door to the "Command Center," as they liked to call Kallista's office.

Kallista sat back in her chair, propped her feet up on the table, and crossed her sneakered feet at the ankles. She picked up the bag of chips once more, munching contentedly and following the explosion of crunch and salt with a swig of grape soda.

To the outside observer, she appeared totally blasé about what her loss-prevention team was about to do. In fact, it was just the opposite. She was very concerned. She wasn't going to move from that spot until every one of the team members had picked up their tails, processed the ones they had to, and joined her back in the security booth.

In order for a shoplifting charge to stick, the suspect had to be in sight at all times—preferably by the agent making the stop. If by some chance the suspected shoplifter turned out to be an honest citizen making an honest mistake, then Kallista would call it a good day's work. One less person she had to drag into her office to show them the offense tape. One less person she had to see burst into tears or deny that it was her or him on the tape.

She didn't care if shoppers stuffed items in every available crevice as long as they stopped by the cash register located near the entrance. Even though each pick-up might have seemed routine, it wasn't. Not that she didn't trust her team to do their job—she did. She had to. She had handpicked both of them. She'd chosen them as much for their senses of humor as their abilities to do their jobs. They'd chosen a thankless job. It was a job filled with accusations of incompetence, snitching, and outright lying. It wasn't much fun sitting in the security booth, day after day, looking for a reason to distrust people. With the all-seeing camera eye trained on potential shoplifters—even the most indignant customers—her team remained assured in the face of counter accusations.

They went out, knowing the routine. Each one would trail the suspected shoplifter. Not too close, not too far, nothing conspicuous. They wouldn't move in, not even if the suspect was busy cramming articles so far in and around their bodies that their own mothers wouldn't recognize them. As long as they didn't destroy property trying to take it, the security force wouldn't move in until they'd left the store. Moving any sooner than that was just asking for trouble. As long as they hadn't left the store, anyone could swear up and down that they were going to pay for the item before they left.

Kallista kept her eyes glued to the monitor. She propped her chin on her fist, suddenly interested in a particular area. Her sister, Karimah, was making her rounds. Even though the picture had no sound, Kallista could almost hear her sister's throaty and somewhat loud voice directing the focus of energy.

Karimah was a showstopper. Kallista had to give her sister that. When she walked into a room, heads turned. That went for men *and* women. Karimah possessed flawless, dark, smooth skin and almond eyes with chocolate-brown irises. Her thick, sooty lashes curled without benefit of chemicals. Karimah wore her hair natural, with thick cornrows interwoven with tiny white shells or mother-of-pearl beads. Her arms were decked out in an array of silver, gold, and copper bangles. Large hoop earrings swung from her lower lobes, but several gold studs dotted the remainder of her ear, almost as far up as the cartilage could hold.

Kallista couldn't help staring at her. Karimah was the most beautiful, even though they were twins—identical twins, two siblings spawned from a single egg. Kallista knew that she couldn't compete with her sister's striking looks. Didn't want to. She had stopped trying a long time ago. She never had to ask her parents to stop dressing them alike; they had never started. From the moment the two girls had drawn their first breaths after birth, their parents must have seen enough difference in them to want to keep their identities separate. They didn't have to wear nametags or bracelets to distinguish them. One look at Karimah's beaming face, and they knew which one she was.

Kallista always gave the obligatory smile in family pictures. But it couldn't compare to Karimah's. How could it? It was like looking for a single point of light by staring through the corona of the sun. As they grew older, Kallista remained in Karimah's shadow. *It wasn't such a bad place to be,* Kallista mused. After all, it must take a lot of energy, so much effort, being so beautiful all the time. When Karimah stepped out to face work, every hair was in place, her makeup was earthy and flawless, her clothing was impeccable.

Kallista told herself that she was glad that she didn't have that kind of pressure. There was something to be said for being able to roll out of bed, toss on some jeans, slap on a cap, and then call the grooming regimen done. She kept her nails short and glossed. She didn't have to worry about bimonthly trips to the manicurist to touch up or replace six-inch nail tips or worry about the dreaded threat of nail fungus. There was also something to be said for not having to bother with the gossip of hair salons or the inconvenience of stripping so that perfect strangers could beat and knead her body in a so-called massage. She didn't want to have to pay to sweat in the sauna of a fancy-schmancy spa. She was a shadow walker, and that's the way she liked it.

Chapter Three

Justin moved around the store, stopping first at one display, then another. Half of his mind was on keeping an eye on Emeril as the boy window-shopped for a gift for his lady. The other half was looking for a way to turn this unscheduled trip into a business opportunity for himself. He was more than a little surprised that he hadn't heard of this place before. Not that he made it over to the northeast side of town very often. Faizon's family's reaction on seeing him was enough to let him know that he needed to stay in touch more often. But he wasn't *that* disconnected from his roots. Maybe he shouldn't be surprised. The outside of the place was deceiving. At first glance, it spoke of cheap-looking but overpriced items.

Yet there was a steady flow of customer traffic in and out of the store, which seemed to offer a little bit of everything for all kinds of tastes—jewelry, fragrances, artwork, clothing, books, and music. The closer he examined some of the merchandise, the more impressed he became. He paused at a display for ladies' lingerie and grinned at the headless mannequin.

"Hey, Butter, check this out," Faizon said, pointing to the mannequin. "Sister girl is looking good in that red."

"Faizon, if that mannequin's looking good to you, you need to get out of the house more often." Justin shook his head in mock sympathy.

"You think she'll go out with me?" Faizon stood up on the platform and wrapped his arm around the mannequin's waist, which swayed precariously on the dias. Faizon used the opportunity to hug it even closer to him.

"She doesn't have a head," Justin pointed out.

"That mean she can't say no. No head, no mouth. Cheap, quiet date. No shelling out for food she'll eat off my plate and hers."

"She's wearing that outfit, but she has no arms, no head, no mouth. Why do you want to ask her out again?" Justin ticked off on his fingers as he pointed out for Faizon the disadvantages in his choice of women.

"Oh, come on, Faizon, you can do better than that!" said a woman's voice.

Faizon looked over Justin's head at the woman approaching them. He quickly cleared his throat and stepped down from the dias. Justin knew by his friend's expression that something was up. He resisted the urge to look over his shoulder. Something told him that he should walk away. He ignored the voice inside of him, intrigued by the woman addressing his friend.

"Don't stop now, Faizon. The show was just starting to get interesting," she continued.

Justin turned around at that. The voice, lightly teasing, piqued his curiosity.

"That's all right, Karimah. That relationship wasn't going anywhere."

"Sounds familiar," the woman remarked dryly. Justin thought he actually saw Faizon blush, a considerable feat since the man's skin was dark as midnight. If he'd had an infrared scanner, he'd swear that he could see waves of heat coming from Faizon's cheeks.

"So, who's your friend, Faizon? And I'm not talking about the mannequin."

"Oh . . . uh . . . this here's Justin Malloy. A friend of mine from back in the day. Butter . . . I mean, Justin, this is Karimah Hart. I was telling you about her."

"Pleasure," Justin said, extending his hand.

"Malloy . . . Malloy . . . seems like I know that name. Say, are you any kin to Corbin Malloy?"

"You know Corbin? He's my first cousin."

"Really? Isn't this a small world. How is Corbin? I remember I used to have the biggest crush on him in middle school. Even then, that boy was fine. I sure was sorry to see him move out of the neighborhood. Is he still here in Houston? Next time you talk to him, tell him that Kari Hart said hello."

"He's married with four kids, a dog, and an SUV," Faizon said, a little too quickly.

Justin squashed his grin. He wasn't exactly sure what was going on between Faizon and Karimah, but he could guess. She said "tease" in every word, every nuance. Faizon's case of puppy love equaled Emeril's, if not surpassing it.

"Married? That's too bad. Tell him I said hey anyway. You never know. Things happen."

She then patted Faizon's cheek to drive home the fact that she was only teasing him. Cruel teasing, given the state he was in, but highly effective. It had his attention. In fact, Justin noticed just in the few minutes that she was standing there, they'd attracted quite a bit of attention. Something about the woman drew a crowd.

"So, what brings you to Karimah's?" she asked Justin.

"I'm here for my nephew. He's looking for a gift for his little girlfriend."

"Oh, puppy love is so sweet," Karimah said, once again casting Faizon a sidelong glance. Faizon shifted uncomfortably. "When he finds something that he likes, tell the cashier that I said to take an extra ten percent off." She pulled a business card out of her pocket, wrote the discount amount on the back, then scribbled her initials on the card.

"You don't have to do that," Justin said.

"You better take the discount, Butter. These prices aren't cheap," Faizon advised.

"This isn't your run-of-the-mill wig shop," Karimah said with pride. Now it was Justin's turn to avoid her gaze. He admitted that he had been thinking that when he first pulled into the parking lot. "Wig shop" was a loose term for all of the little shops that sprung up around town that sold everything from hair extensions to formal wear. You would usually see them coupled with either a barbershop or nail salon, or tucked in the corners of neighborhood grocery stores.

"Speaking of which, I'd better go see how Emeril is doing," Justin said. He excused himself to give Faizon a chance to be alone with Karimah. As soon as he left, the press of customers surrounding Karimah swelled. They'd heard her give Justin a discount and were hoping for some of the same royal treatment.

"How's it going, Emeril?" Justin said, coming up behind the boy.

Emeril blew out a frustrated breath. "I see a lot of things I want to get, but it's a little out of my range, Uncle Justin."

Justin couldn't tell if the boy was fishing for a loan or not. "How much have you got?"

"Twenty bucks."

"Well, I just met the owner of the store. She said take an extra ten percent off of whatever you pick out."

"Are you serious?"

"I wouldn't joke about a thing like that."

"Cool," Emeril said. He waved to get the attention of the young woman behind the counter.

"Need some help picking something out?" Justin offered.

"Naw. I think I got it, Uncle J. I know what my lady likes."

Justin held up his hands and moved aside. "It's your show. You handle it."

His attention was diverted to a display of books and CDs,

laid out on a table draped with vibrant Kente cloth. A CD player was sampling sections from the music on display. Justin picked up a CD case, reading the cover material to find out more about the artists.

"Local artists. They're very good."

A voice he'd only recently heard, but which was already etched in his memory, spoke softly into his ear. Justin half-turned, surprised to see Karimah Hart standing next to him. He wondered how she could have sneaked up on him. He supposed that, if he hadn't been so concerned about Emeril, he would have sensed Karimah's presence sooner. There was nothing subtle about the woman. He took a step sideways, presumably to browse more of the selections on the table. In truth, he needed to re-establish the personal space she had invaded.

"I think I went to high school with this guy," Justin said uneasily, tapping the cellophane-covered CD case.

Karimah regarded him curiously. "You didn't go to high school on this side of town. I would have remembered you."

"Just like you remembered Corbin?"

She nodded.

"Do you have a photographic memory or something, Miss Hart?"

"It's not as if it was that long ago, Justin Malloy. I'm just very in tune with things that suit my fancy. And don't call me Miss Hart. You make me feel so old. Call me Kari."

"Kari," he echoed, giving her a nod. "When my father got promoted, my family moved when I was in junior high. We moved out to Fort Bend county."

"I thought so."

"What is that supposed to mean?"

"What do I mean?" Her eyes were wide and innocent. "I was just moving the conversation along. You sound like you've got a problem with where you live."

"Sorry if I sound a little defensive. It's just that I don't like talking about my past."

"You mean not to certain people," she said perceptively.

"Folks who might think that your folks sold out when they moved out of the neighborhood. I get the opposite reaction. People ask me why am I still living in the house where I was born when I can afford better."

"Why did you stay?"

She shrugged. "I live where I live. My friends are here. My business is here. Why would I leave it? It's obvious to me that you haven't left altogether yourself. You're still hanging around with that gangster Faizon."

"Faizon is good people," Justin said in his friend's defense.

"When he's not in and out of the county jail. That's one reason why I couldn't hang with him. I got tired of wondering if this would be the last time I would ever see him. One of these days, he's going to get into real trouble. They'll put him away for life or strap him to a chair. I don't want to be around to say 'I told you so.' "

Justin shifted uncomfortably. He knew that he had fallen out of touch with his long-time friend. So much that he was only vaguely aware of the events that marred his life. He suspected that Faizon had only recently gotten out of trouble. Otherwise, he couldn't think of a good reason why he would not have shown up at his brother Gideon's wedding.

"You look like I just killed your best friend," Karimah said, noting Justin's expression. "Maybe I should change the subject, turn it back on you. Faizon tells me that you're some kind of designer?"

"Not clothes," he explained. "Though, the way your customers are snapping up those outfits, I'm starting to wonder if I didn't pick the wrong profession."

"What do you do?"

"Web design work."

"Oh, are you into that e-commerce, dot-com stuff?" Karimah said, raising her eyebrows.

"Trying to be, anyway."

"Are you any good?"

"I make enough to keep the bill collectors happy."

Karimah screwed up her face and laid an empathetic hand on his shoulder. "I know what you mean. It looks like I'm doing pretty well today. I've got all six registers running. But when it's all added up and everyone's been paid off, I'll barely turn a profit."

"Maybe you ought to look into other ways of generating sales," he suggested, fighting the urge to physically remove her hand from his shoulder. Her hand was pleasantly warm, but it felt like a brand to him—indelibly imprinting her mark on him.

"Uh-oh. I feel a sales pitch coming on," Karimah said, stepping back and holding up her hands as if to ward off an unspoken evil.

Justin breathed a mental sigh of relief. He couldn't remember the last time he was so affected by one woman. Grudgingly, he thought that maybe he should heed the advice that he had given Faizon. Maybe he should get out more often. "I'm not going to harass you, Kari. I was just moving the conversation along."

"Well, don't move too far. I might be interested in what you have to say."

"Really?" Now he was sounding as puppy-doggish as Emeril.

"Really," she repeated. "Do you have a card or something? Maybe I can call you later to set up a private demonstration."

Justin fished out his wallet and handed her his business card. "Here you go. Call me anytime."

"You can bet I'll take you up on it." She backed away from him. "I guess I'd better get back to the store before they send a search party after me."

"Good luck with your opening. And thanks for helping my nephew out."

"I expect that you'll return the favor soon enough," she predicted. She lifted her chin, pointing at a section of the store across the room. "Is that your nephew? Looks like he's trying to get your attention."

Justin looked back to see Emeril wave at him. A small, gold gift box was clutched in his hand.

"In a minute," Justin mouthed to him. He wasn't quite ready to leave yet.

Emeril made a face, then called out. "I'll be waiting by the car." He spun around, heading for the front of the store.

Apologetically, Justin shrugged and said, "He's got a little girlfriend who he's trying to get back to."

"But *you're* not in a hurry," Karimah asked. The unasked question of whether or not he was involved with someone hung heavy in the air.

"No. I'm not in a hurry," Justin replied, taking a step closer to allow her back into his personal space.

"Good. Then you can expect to be hearing from me."

Chapter Four

Kallista couldn't hear a word that was being said. The closed-circuit televisions used to monitor the store's activities provided only visuals. But she had a pretty good idea. Karimah had reeled in another one. By the way she seemed to be going after that one, he must be offering her something special. Kallista didn't think that anything could tear her sister away from Faizon once she found out that he was in the store.

If Karimah had a weakness, it would have to be Faizon. She couldn't get enough of that big man—even though they had both traded opportunities to crush each other's hearts. It was trouble from the moment they met. Faizon, with his penchant for expensive but ill-gotten gains couldn't keep up with Kari-mah and her yen for attention. He couldn't acquire enough items to shower her with the attention she thought that she deserved. It just wasn't enough for Karimah.

Kallista thought back to the running tally she kept on Kari-mah's conquests. There had to be at least five already this week. Something about the grand opening of her third store charged Karimah, made her ten times more vibrant—if that was even possible. Karimah's charm had gotten them the extension on the loan they needed to complete the store's preparation. Her smooth talking convinced a couple of their clothing distributors to throw in some extra, hard-to-find items. Her melodious voice, coming from the airwaves of the local radio station, drew in customers who would normally settle for flowers or a box of chocolates for their significant others at this time of year. Kallista didn't know what this latest conquest would provide, but she knew she'd find out soon enough when Karimah came to gloat about who and what she'd snapped up. She watched her sister leave the CD display to head back toward the lingerie area, where Faizon still browsed.

Kallista muttered a curse under her breath. She hadn't meant to be so caught up in what her sister was doing, who she was talking to. She'd meant to keep an eye on Faizon. She'd heard that he was rehabilitated. But old habits died hard. It would be just his brand of humor if he snatched an item out of Karimah's own boutique to later give to her as a gift. The man was sweet, but he couldn't help himself. He liked pretty things. Sometimes, Kallista wasn't sure if his attraction for Karimah wasn't part of this affliction.

The camera panned, and in the far corner, she saw Deandre diligently working the lingerie section. *Good for her!* Kallista thought. She had chosen well. Because Deandre had been with the store for several years, she knew all about Faizon. And— Kallista was reasonably sure—that Faizon would recognize her. There would be nothing walking out of the store that day.

"Excuse me, sir. My name is Brandt Collins. I'm a loss-prevention agent for Karimah's boutique."

Justin paused in the middle of keying in the code to open the doors of his car when a young man dressed in baggy jeans and a Hawaiian shirt approached him.

"You're a what?" Justin asked.

"He's a snoop," Faizon interpreted for him.

"What do you want with me?" Justin wondered if this was a way for Karimah to draw him back into the store. He'd gotten the impression that she had a skewed sense of humor. If this was a joke, it wasn't funny.

"Would you please follow me back into the store, sir." Brandt reached for a chain around his neck. Dangling on the end was a white, plastic card with a picture identifying him as an agent for the store.

"What's this all about?" Justin demanded.

"Just follow me, sir."

"Look. I'm tired, and I'm ready to leave. You'd better tell me what's going on because I'm not taking another step until you do."

"Sir, I believe that you have something that belongs to the store. I'd like to talk to you about the necklace this young man here has in his possession."

"Karimah herself gave us a discount," Justin said, comprehending the man's implication but not liking it one bit.

At that assertion, Faizon started to laugh. "Man, are you trying to say we took a five-finger discount? You must be drunk or crazy. Do we look like we need to steal?" He spread his arms and stepped up to the young agent, knowing fully well what effect his wide girth would have on him.

Though concerned about Faizon's reaction, Brandt stood his ground. He was no slouch himself, about five feet eleven and heavily built. Still, he knew he was no match for Faizon. If it came down to a physical confrontation, he would rather let them go. His job was to get the merchandise back without incident. Nothing in his contract was said about him getting crushed to a creamy pulp in the process.

"Come on, Uncle Justin. Let's go," Emeril said, reaching for the handle of the car door.

Brandt reacted without thinking and broke Kallista's cardinal rule of loss prevention—he was never allowed to initiate contact. He was only allowed to defend himself. Deandre was the one with all of the self-defense classes. She was the one who was trained to subdue a violent customer. If things got too rough, she was the one that Brandt was supposed to call on.

But, since he was new to Karimah's, he was equally motivated to prove himself. Not to mention that it was a blow to his pride to have to call on a woman to back him up. Brandt didn't consider himself sexist; in a fight, he wanted Deandre on his side. This was about him being able to handle his own jobs. He had been trailing the boy for a while. When he saw him pick up the necklace, then leave the store, it was his opportunity to prove to Deandre and Kallista that he was worth his paycheck.

"Hold up a minute there, son," Brandt used his most official tone. He reached out and placed his hand on Emeril's arm.

Emeril reacted strongly, jerking his arm back, his fist balled. "Take your hands off of me, you stupid rent-a-cop."

"Don't touch him," Justin said, interjecting himself between Emeril and Brandt. He hitched his shoulder, thumping Brandt in the chest.

"Back off!" Faizon said, adding to the heat of the moment.

"Look, Mister, I'm just trying to do my job," Brandt placated. Things were starting to get ugly. They were attracting unwanted attention. He wanted to get control of the situation.

"What is that? Gang up on young boys?" Justin countered.

"We have him on tape, sir." Brandt said stiffly. "If you just come back to the office with me, I'm sure all of this will be cleared up."

Justin turned to regard Emeril with eyes as hard as agates. "You'd better start talking, Emeril."

"I don't know what he's talking about," Emeril insisted.

Justin canted his head in the direction of the boutique. "I want to see the tape."

"You gonna take his word, Butter?" Faizon asked, referring to Brandt.

"I don't think I have a choice, Faizon. The camera doesn't lie." He then turned to his nephew. "For your sake, son, you'd better hope that it's someone who looks a hell of a lot like you on that tape.''

Justin sat in the security booth, his hands folded tightly across his chest, his fingers gripped his forearms so tightly that he was sure he'd have permanent grooves etched into his skin. He did so knowing that, if he released his grip, his hands would instinctively, uncontrollably, and irrevocably choke the life from his ward.

"So what happens now?'' Justin gritted. He avoided asking the question for as long as he could, choosing instead to review the tape no less than ten times to be certain that he'd burned the image into his brain.

"Karimah's has a zero-tolerance policy, Mr. Malloy. I'm sure you've seen the signs posted around the store. The policy states that we prosecute all offenders.''

"But he's a minor,'' Justin objected. "You can't arrest him.''

"Then the liability for his behavior could fall to you. The final word will have to come from Miss Hart to decide what happens next.''

Justin, Faizon, and Emeril exchanged glances. A look of relief flooded Emeril's face. He had it covered on both ends. Faizon said he knew Karimah Hart. And Emeril had seen the woman going after Justin. By the way she had been all over him, he was as good as free. No trip to a juvenile-detention center for him.

"If you'll just take a seat, she'll be with you in a minute,'' Brandt assured him.

Faizon clamped his hand down on Emeril's shoulder and said, "Hang tough, little man. It's going to be all right.''

"Don't go giving him false hope, Faizon. If your friend doesn't try to kill him for ripping off her store, I will.''

"All I wanted was a gift for my lady,'' Emeril insisted.

"And that's supposed to make me feel sympathetic?'' Justin snapped.

"Ease up on the kid, Butter."

"I don't thinks so. Today, it's a thirty-dollar necklace. Tomorrow, who knows what? Son, I don't think your mother is raising you to be a thief. Certainly not a petty one."

Emeril stuck out his jaw, and turned his face away. Why was he always dragging his mother into this? It was obvious to him that she didn't care what happened to him. She'd married that man after knowing him for less than a year. She'd broken her promise to take him shopping for a gift for his lady. And then she'd dumped him off with this uptight computer geek. It wasn't fair! He didn't care if she was upset with him for pulling a stunt like this. Maybe it served her right for ignoring him.

"If you wanted to get the necklace for your friend, why didn't you come to me and ask?"

Emeril threw his hands up and stalked away from his uncle. "Like you really would have given me the money. You should have seen the look on your face when I asked you to take me somewhere."

Justin circled around him, grabbing the boy's chin and lifting it so that their gazes locked. "I might have given it to you. You'll never know now because you didn't ask."

"I'm not a begger," Emeril declared, jerking his head away.

"No, you're a thief," Justin countered,

"Justin!" Faizon's voice rang out sharply. "That's enough. Have a care, man. You could be branding little man here for the rest of his life. Those kinds of words stick . . . they stick hard. Take it from me, Butter. I know."

"He's lucky I don't give him the beat-down of his life. I can't believe he'd put me through this hassle for a thirty-dollar trinket."

"Would it make you feel better if I told you that I was going for the three-hundred-dollar one?" Emeril said snidely.

"You're pushing it, little man," Faizon warned.

Justin glanced at his watch. "How long are they going to keep us waiting?"

Faizon shrugged.

"This is not good," Justin predicted.

"I don't think Kari is the type to punish a kid for a simple mistake."

"I'm glad you have that much confidence in her. I can't say that. I don't know her as well."

"It's not as if you didn't try," Emeril muttered, glaring at Justin. Justin glared back.

"What's that supposed to mean?" Faizon asked.

"Nothing," Emeril and Justin said in unison.

"Do you want me to go talk to her?" Faizon offered.

"Do you think it will do any good?"

"What could it hurt?"

"The way I'm feeling right now, Faizon, you really don't want me to answer that." Justin threw up in hands in a mingling of disgust and despair. If this was the kind of headache and heartache he had to look forward to being a parent, he'd rather hold off as long as he could.

"I guess we've kept them waiting long enough," Kallista said, checking the monitor once more. The man Brandt had identified as the minor's uncle was wearing a trench down the center of the small waiting room with his pacing. Every so often he would stop, look as if he was about to say something to the boy, then think better of it. How, in that small waiting area, he managed to appear as if he was keeping a good two miles distance away from the boy, she didn't know. She supposed it was by necessity. He was beyond angry. His tightly controlled gait was in complete contrast to the easy stance he'd adopted when speaking to Karimah just half an hour before. With each passing moment, he became more and more agitated.

Kallista hadn't meant to keep him waiting that long. It wasn't standard operating procedure when it came to processing shoplifters. It was her experience that the sooner she met with them and explained to them the store policy, the easier it was to get through the difficult phase of having them arrested. When she reacted quickly, she had the element of surprise and shame on her side. Most of the people they picked up were embarrassed about being caught. They wanted to get the ugly ordeal over with. If they handed over the merchandise without incident, she would usually relent. She might let them go, hoping that the ordeal had scared them enough that they wouldn't try it again. At least not in her store. This only happened when she was dealing with adults.

It was a different matter when dealing with children. She waited so long to talk to the kid and his uncle because she wasn't quite sure what she wanted to do about him. He was a minor, so he wouldn't be sent to jail. A judge in a juvenile court might sentence him to some kind of community service. The brunt of the punishment would probably fall to his parents. Or, maybe it would fall to the uncle, since the boy was in his care. During Brandt's interview, Justin was quick to point out that he was a temporary guardian. He could not be held responsible for Emeril's actions. Kallista grimaced at that. She couldn't see Karimah taking it very well.

Yet she couldn't just set him free. What kind of example would that be to the other young customers coming into the store? If they got wind they could come, take what they want, and not face the consequences, they had another thing coming. Then again, everyone makes mistakes. What was a human being but a collection of mistakes and corrections?

"You ready, Miss Hart?" Brandt prodded her gently. He couldn't understand why she was taking so long to act. Everyone who worked here knew that Kallista didn't suffer a thief for very long. Once the intent to steal was well established, she swooped in on the swift wings of justice to set the matter right.

For a moment, Brandt toyed with the idea that maybe Kallista hesitated because she didn't want to come down hard on the boy's uncle. He had seen how her sister Karimah had taken to him. Would it be too much of a stretch for Kallista to be just as interested? He quickly squashed that idea. *Nah! It couldn't be that.* Kallista didn't lead her life by emotion. *Just the facts, ma'am.* And the fact was, the boy had stolen. She wouldn't let anything deter her from making him face the consequences of his actions.

"All right, Brandt. Let's go," she said, picking up her clipboard. She crammed the last few corn chips into her mouth, then took a swig of soda to wash it down.

"Here," Brandt said, offering her a small piece of chewing gum.

"Thanks, junior."

"Too bad about the kid, huh?" he said, fishing for a reason behind her hesitation.

"I sure hate to see that kind of behavior in one so young," Kallista agreed.

"If it'll sway you at all, Miss H, I'd like to put my two cents in. I don't think he's a bad kid. A little misguided, maybe. Remember that when you go in."

"I'll take that into consideration."

"And something else, too. He's got a mouth on him."

"Don't we all?" Kallista cracked. "I promise I won't let him hurt my tender feelings, Brandt," she said, fluttering her hand over her heart. She'd seen enough of the smart-mouthed kind who came through there. Some of the younger generations cursed more and talked louder than she would have ever been allowed to do when she was that age—even with hip parents.

She grasped the door handle and pushed the door open. Her gaze immediately went to the man who'd identified himself as the uncle, who was standing on the far side of the room. She was distracted for a moment. Watching him from the security monitors didn't quite match seeing him in the flesh. As he stood, arms folded, face tense, Kallista felt an unbidden instinctive response to him. *Run!* The word came unbidden to her mind. *Run away, quickly,* she told herself.

He had the look of a predator—lean, sleek, and ready to pounce. Since he hadn't mauled his nephew yet, he turned blazing eyes to Kallista. His black T-shirt conformed to a well-muscled frame. Not tall, but not short. Five-ten, maybe. Five-eleven? No jewelry. His tastes were simple. The well-worn leather band on his watch was clipped to his belt. As he stood regarding her, his dark eyes narrowed slightly as he took her in as well. Something was bothering him. The crease between his eyebrows told her that. Something he was trying to figure out. *Ah, yes!* She remembered now. He'd met Karimah first. Although they were twins, their personalities resonated differently. Karimah—warm and flowing. Kallista—cool and reserved. Neither Faizon nor Karimah must have told him about her.

Kallista stepped toward him, holding out her hand. "Sorry to keep you waiting, Mr. Malloy. I'm—"

"I know. I know. We've already met," Justin interrupted impatiently.

"No, sir, we haven't," Kallista began with the same long-suffering tone she used when she had to explain herself. "I'm not Karimah. I'm the other—" *I'm the shadow-walker.* The words echoed in her head so clearly, she thought she'd said them out loud.

Before she had the opportunity to properly introduce herself, Kallista was interrupted by a burst of static and a series of chirps from the combination cellular phone/two-way radio clipped to a belt at her waist. She snatched the phone to her ear, holding up her hand to stop Justin's next questions as she concentrated on the voice at the other end.

"Say again, Deandre?" she raised her voice, pressing the finger of her other hand into her open ear. Deandre's voice came back louder and clearer.

"I said you'd better get out here, Miss H. Some so-called ladies from the North-side crew and the East-side *vatos* have just untruced their truce right in the middle of the women's wear section."

"Uh-oh," Brandt muttered under his breath. He threw a worried glance in Kallista's direction.

" 'Uh-oh' is right," Kallista snapped. "I'm on my way," she assured Deandre. She whirled around, suddenly forgetting about the petty larceny committed by Emeril. Right now, rival gangs were gearing up to stake a claim to this territory—her business—at the worst possible time.

No time was a good time for a turf war. But certainly not on opening day. Not when they had worked so hard to build their reputation. Not when representatives from their suppliers would be watching their every move. She had to get out there fast and calm things down before they got out of control. She whirled around, pointing to Brandt and indicating with a gesture toward the door for him to follow her.

"Aren't you forgetting something, Miss H?" he reminded her. She looked over her shoulder and snapped, "Stay here."

"Wait a minute!" Justin called out. "What about—" But she'd already slammed the door behind her.

"Screw this," Justin muttered. "They've got my address. If they want me, they can find me. Come on, Emeril, let's get out of here before we become a footnote in the six o'clock news."

Emeril bit back his grin, trying to appear serious and contrite for his uncle's sake. Justin wasn't fooled by the token expression. "Don't think you've gotten away with anything, E." He clamped down on Emeril's shoulder, causing him to wince and try to jerk his shoulder away. Justin was torn between clamping down harder and cracking the boy's clavicle or releasing him and giving the boy more space. He wasn't sure what to do with all his college education, he still couldn't figure out how to handle one fourteen-year-old.

Faizon certainly wasn't much help, calling the boy "little man" and treating him like he could run things. Where was *he*, anyway? Justin thought that he had gone to work on Karimah Hart to get her to go easy on him. Either he didn't get the chance to get to her, or things were worse between Faizon and Karimah than either one of them let on.

The woman who had entered the waiting area didn't look as

if she had a sympathetic bone in her body. All business. No chance for her relenting in the zero-tolerance policy. Then again, the woman who'd come to greet them said she wasn't Karimah Hart. She was the other one. The other what? The other manifestation of a split personality? The woman who'd greeted them was as far from the warm and welcoming Karimah Hart as the North Pole was from the South Pole.

Then it hit him. That *wasn't* Karimah. It must have been her sister. An identical twin? No, not identical. He felt the difference between them from the very moment she stepped into the room. She carried herself all wrong to be Karimah. He couldn't explain it. He couldn't imagine that one chatting him up, teasing him, flirting with him. If Karimah had the looks, then the other sister had the backbone. *What was her name?* Justin wished he'd gotten it before she went charging out of there.

"Can we go now, Uncle Justin?" Emeril complained.

"Yeah, yeah. We're going now," Justin said distractedly. His eyes scanned the area, partially looking for Faizon and partially interested in the disturbance going on to his left in the women's wear section of the boutique.

Two uniformed police officers had interjected themselves between two groups of girls. Justin wondered if their presence was an excessive show of force. The girls couldn't have been more than sixteen or seventeen, just around Chantal's age. Justin resisted the urge to laugh. What was going on? What was all the commotion about? Judging from the look of concern on Kallista's face, he thought that World War III was about to break out in the middle of the boutique.

The look on Kallista's face, however, was no laughing matter. She was trying to remain calm and professional even though one of the girls screeched at her in a mixture of Spanish and English. *Mentirosa. Puta.* Liar. Whore. Justin was able to pick up a couple of the names because of his few trips south of the border while sowing his one wild oat during college. He started to move on, unimpressed by the pubescent display of aggression. He imagined that this must have been some kind of gang initiation that went wrong. Come in, steal a few items, and get out. Go back to the gang family, and show how slick you were to get away with it right from under the nose of all the security. Something obviously went wrong. Someone had gotten caught and now had to pay the price—literally. If this was what all the fuss was about, he wouldn't wait around to see the outcome. He was out of there.

The girl came out of nowhere, launching herself at Kallista. The uniformed officer barely reacted in time, stepping between Kallista and the girl, to redirect the force of the attack. From there, the situation got tense. The screecher's boyfriend thought the officer got a little too free and rough with his hands. He signaled to someone out of Kallista's field of vision. She may have missed who the sign was directed to, but she didn't miss the sign.

"If you've got backup, you'd better call for it now," she urged. "Something tells me the party's just getting started."

From across the floor, Emeril, who'd also been watching the exchange with amusement, turned desperate. "Come on, Uncle Justin. Let's book out of here," he said, grabbing Justin's shirtsleeve. "This isn't funny anymore."

"I know," Justin said. "This is going to get ugly really fast." He moved toward the nearest exit, not surprised to see several other patrons following his lead. Some didn't bother to drop the unpaid merchandise. Justin almost thought that he could read their minds. As long as the store security and police were concerned about the mini turf war going on inside, who was going to bother with them? The store sensor alarms went off on cue. Several pieces of walkaway merchandise had exploding dye packs on them. Those who thought they'd gotten away clean were unpleasantly surprised to find the merchandise and themselves suddenly covered with bright red dye.

Justin felt a pang of conscience bite into his gut. What did he think he was doing, slinking away like some kind of low life? What did he have to hide? Emeril had made a mistake. If he allowed the boy to leave without facing up to what he'd done, that would be two mistakes. His would be the worse of the two sins for not shouldering his responsibility for keeping the boy out of trouble, as he had promised Gideon. As if yanked by a chain around his sense of morality, he stopped short.

Several steps later, Emeril realized that his uncle wasn't with him anymore.

"Uncle J?" Emeril asked.

Justin only had to jerk a thumb back in the direction they'd come. Emeril groaned. He was almost home free. He hung his head, muttering a curse under his breath.

"Watch your mouth," Justin said sharply. By the time they made it back to the main floor of the boutique, the shouting match had escalated into a full scale, knock-down, drag-out fight.

"Daaamn!" Justin exclaimed, drawing out the word for emphasis. Emeril stared at him with a "How come you can say it and I can't" look.

Justin started across the floor, not quite sure what he could do, but not liking the odds. Kallista saw him heading toward her and shook her head to wave him off.

Kallista rolled her eyes. She didn't have time for this. Female gangbangers were about to tear her store to the ground and sticky fingers were whisking merchandise out from under her nose. She didn't need an irate uncle bugging her about some sass-mouthed kid.

Her attention was diverted for a moment—but it was enough. Someone grabbed her from behind, pinning her arms to her waist. The screecher jerked free from the uniformed officer and slammed her body into Kallista, who groaned and tried to double over, the air forced from her lungs with a vengeance. She thought that she was going to be sick. She wretched, her eyes tearing. When the girl drew back her fist to smash into her face, Kallista raised both legs and kicked, sending the girl flying into a rack of clothing.

"*Puta!*" the one who held her shouted in her ear.

Kallista tensed, then went completely limp, letting gravity do her work for her. Her attacker wasn't expecting the sudden drag of weight and slumped forward with her. From that moment, it wasn't hard for Kallista to perform a quick tuck, sending her attacker rolling over her shoulder.

Justin headed for the center of the confrontation, then stopped short when he saw Kallista disengage herself. He didn't know what to do to help her. From the looks of things, it didn't appear as if she even needed his help. But he kept moving forward anyway. Her attacker hopped up, a look of surprise and humiliation mingled with grudging admiration on her face. The uniforms had their own problems to worry about. When the loverboy looked as if he was going to charge Kallista again, Justin stepped between the two of them.

They sized each other up for a moment. More uniforms were pouring through the door. The boyfriend had no weapon; he'd left his piece out in the car to avoid being caught by the metal detectors coming into the store. Maybe it was the fact that he'd let that woman throw him. Maybe it was the cold glow of protective determination smoldering in Justin's eyes. Or even still, the small, handheld, eighty-thousand-volt stun gun that appeared as quickly as the numbing jolt it promised that gave him pause. He backed off, submitting to the escort of the security officer.

Justin turned to Kallista, just in time to see her pocket the nonlethal weapon.

"And just what were you going to do with that?" he demanded.

"What do you think?" she retorted. She started to move away, then grimaced. The anger and the adrenaline rush caused by the scuffle had worn off. When she moved, she felt the twinge of a pulled muscle in her right shoulder, which was competing with the throbbing of her abdomen where the screeching girl had rammed her.

"Hey, are you all right?" Justin asked.

"I don't know," Kallista groaned, rubbing her stomach. "Is my stomach supposed to feel like I'm carrying a thirty-pound bowling ball in the middle of my naval?"

"This is one hell of a way to move merchandise," Justin commented, taking her arm. He swept aside items on top of a table loaded with reduced merchandise for sale. The table was a little high, and Kallista had to hop up in order to sit down. When he saw her sitting on the edge, her feet dangling over the side, Justin felt another surge of protectiveness come over him. She looked delicate, almost childlike. It was in total contrast to the woman who'd tossed the gangbanger over her shoulder and made him back down with a handheld taser.

"This?" Kallista laughed shakily. "This is nothing. I've seen one-day sales at Macy's with more action."

Justin almost smiled. Maybe the twins weren't so different after all. They both used humor in difficult or uncomfortable situations. This one's sense of humor had an edge, but it was one he could appreciate.

"So, tell me, Mr. Malloy. What were you going to do if our friend over there had decided to push the issue?" She nodded at the one she'd flipped over her shoulder. "He's got you by at least twenty pounds," Kallista remarked on Justin's physique. Up close and personal, he looked better and better all of the time.

"What do you think?" he retorted, sitting up straighter and puffing out his chest.

"Scream and cry like a girl?" Kallista lifted a teasing eyebrow at him.

"Bleed first," he elaborated, "then after I came to, cry like a girl."

Kallista gave him a reluctant smile. "Thanks anyway for coming to my rescue. You didn't have to. You could have cut and run like the rest of them."

"Not a problem, Miss Hart."

"No," she said on a long, drawn-out breath. "But what we're going to do about your nephew still is."

"Oh yeah. I'd almost forgotten about that. I guess it's up to *you* what happens to him."

"Don't think that because you stepped in with that Sir Galahad routine I'm going to go easy on your nephew."

"I wasn't asking for any favors, Miss Hart," Justin said stiffly. Though, in the back of his mind, he wondered what kind of woman could still be so hard on him after he'd just risked life and limb for her.

"Good. Because I wasn't giving any," she assured him.

"Good," Justin said tightly.

"Good," she repeated.

"Fine," he said, wanting this last word to end the uncomfortable cycle. He was even more glad when Emeril crossed the floor.

"Uncle J, are you crazy? Going up against one of the Eastside *vatos*. Those boys don't play."

Justin raised his hands, then let them fall limply to his sides again. What was he supposed to do? Let that punk attack her? He turned to face her. He still didn't know her name.

"I'd better go start the paperwork," Kallista said uneasily. Despite her bravado, Justin Malloy had risked more than he should have under the circumstances. He didn't know her. She was ready to push the issue to prosecute his nephew. He had no reason to want to do anything for her. Yet, he had. That sort of selflessness didn't come along every day.

"You'd better go." Kallista dismissed them. "I know where to find you if I need to get a hold of you."

Justin almost breathed a sign of relief. She said "if." That meant she still hadn't made up her mind.

She paused for a moment, giving Emeril a long, hard stare. Emeril stared back for as long as he could, then lowered his eyes to avoid her gaze.

"Emeril," Kallista began.

Oh, great, here it comes. The speech. Emeril's expression spoke volumes.

Kallista continued despite being able to read the words in his face. "I don't know you. You don't know me. I don't know why you'd pick my place to steal from. I don't care why you made the decision. The one thing I do care about is that you made the decision. And everybody in here knows that it wasn't a smart one. I want you to go home and think about that choice. Think about where you might be if you keep going down that road."

Her gaze swept the store, the milling customers, the uniformed officers taking names, the looks of sullen resentment from those who had been caught. She stepped close to him, so close that no one could hear her next words but him. "I can tell by the stuff you're wearing that you've got it good. You've got a good life. You want to keep it? Do you want to keep your life? Think about it."

Chapter Five

I want you to go upstairs and kill that boy!

Justin chuckled out loud, then turned the sound down on his CD player. That line from one of Bill Cosby's comedy routines cut a little too close to home for him. Since leaving Karimah's boutique three days ago, there had been a constant clash of wills between him and Emeril. Everything he tried seemed to make matters worse.

If Justin spent all day cooking a meal that he thought Emeril would appreciate and enjoy, the boy pigged out on junk food. Emeril cranked up his music, and Justin snatched the plugs from the wall outlets. Every word between them was a harsh one, every glance between them was a glare. If Justin thought he could lock the boy in his room for the next week without the boy digging an escape tunnel through the walls, he would. Maybe things wouldn't be so bad if he weren't so edgy. This waiting for one of the Hart women to call him was driving him to distraction.

If he wasn't wishing for Karimah to call him to tell him whether or not he'd gotten the web design job, he was wanting the one who was not Karimah, the other Hart, to call him to tell him whether or not she was going to press charges against Emeril. *What* was *her name?*

Brandt, the loss-prevention agent, had said they had a zero-tolerance policy. He didn't say how long the store would take to enforce that policy. He wondered if petty thievery had a statute of limitations. By the time they got around to processing him, Emeril would have long forgotten that sixteen-year-old girl that he'd stolen for.

Justin turned back to his work and increased the volume on his CD player to finish listening to the Cosby routine.

"Turn that whacked crap down!" Emeril shouted, banging on the walls with his feet. It was as close to imitating Justin as he could come when Justin demanded that he turn off his Busta Rhymes.

"That's it!" Justin shouted back, banging on the connecting wall. "I'm calling your mother!"

"Snitch!" Emeril shouted back.

"Snot!" Justin countered. "Ungrateful little heathen." He had every intention of tracking down his brother and new wife. He didn't care if they were living and loving in a garden paradise. Their son was the spawn of Satan, and it wasn't fair that he was thrust on him without as much as a warning or a hint of what to expect. He was going to call them and give them a piece of his mind, Lord help him. Emeril was as good as gone. That is, as soon as he took this other call. Stupid, ringing phone. It was getting in the way of his getting rid of the biggest headache he'd had since the time he was four years old and had his head stuck between the rails of his grandmother's back porch.

"Hello!" Justin snapped, cradling the phone between his shoulder and ear while he searched for his brother's travel itinerary.

"May I speak to Justin Malloy?"

"Speaking," Justin was still terse until something in the

quality in the voice on the other end of the line caused him to pause.

"Mr. Malloy, this is Karimah Hart."

"Oh, Miss Hart . . . uh . . . hello." Justin shifted mental gears. For days, he'd been waiting for this call. Now that it had come, he was at a loss for words.

"Don't tell me you don't remember me, Mr. Malloy."

"Yes, Ma'am, I remember you."

"Well, that's certainly good to know. A woman doesn't like to think she's *that* forgettable."

"I promise you, that's not the case."

"Do you know why I'm calling, Mr. Malloy?"

"I thought we were on a first-name basis?" he reminded her. The laugh coming from the other end was deep, throaty, and much too enthusiastic. He wasn't that witty. He was still surprised that she'd called him. He was beginning to think that she'd throught better of her decision to seek him out.

"Did I say something funny?"

"No, I guess I just heard something funny. Or maybe I should say 'misheard'?"

"All right. I'll bite. What did you hear that I didn't say?"

"I heard you say that we'd gone to first base."

"Now there's a term I haven't heard in a while."

"Haven't heard in a while or haven't *been* in a while?" she teased him.

"You know I'm not going to answer that."

Again the laughter. "You know, Justin, when I didn't hear from you, I was starting to think that little altercation in the store scared you off."

"Who me? Nah! I eat brawls like that for breakfast."

"I guess there's no telling what a man will put in his mouth these days."

"So to what do I owe the pleasure of this call?" Justin felt uncomfortable with the turn in the conversation. He knew how Faizon felt about this woman. At least he *thought* he knew. The jealous look that had crossed his face when Emeril mentioned Justin was going after her, too, confirmed his suspicions. Faizon wanted her. But to hear Karimah speak of him, she couldn't or wouldn't return the sentiment. The way she was laying it on now, he didn't think Faizon was anywhere in her thoughts.

The silence that hung in the air after Karimah's last comment was heavy and uncomfortable. Justin was afraid to ask her why she'd called. He was afraid of an offer—one that had nothing to do with helping her build her business through Internet exposure. If she made him an offer, literally one that he had to refuse for Faizon's sake, where would that leave him for getting future business in the area? He know how rumors got started. The business community had the most efficient grapevine he had ever encountered. Rustle the wrong leaf, and his business would die on the vine.

"I was thinking, Justin, that we could meet to discuss your plans for launching Karimah's on the web."

"I see," Justin said noncommitally. "Karimah, I really haven't had much time to pull together anything formal for you."

"That's not a problem. How long will it take? One or two hours?"

"If I'm thorough with my research, how about one or two weeks?"

"I'm not sure I like the sound of that. Since we talked a couple of days ago, I've had a lot of time to think. The more ideas I come up with, the more excited I get. I'm anxious to get the ball rolling."

Justin spoke very clearly, choosing his words carefully so that, if this conversation ever came up again, he could say with certainty that he had nothing but business on his mind. "Let me visit some more stores in the area and see what they're doing. That way, I can give you some apple-to-apple comparisons. We can meet to discuss my proposal in a couple of days."

"Sounds like a winner. How does Wednesday sound?"

"All right, then. I'll see you on Wednesday. At the store?"

He made the suggestion first before she could offer to meet him somewhere less conducive to business—like her home or a fancy restaurant with a cozy table for two.

"At the store, ten-thirty."

"Ten-thirty AM, Wednesday, February fourteenth," Justin recited as he entered the information in his personal calendar.

"Almost right. I don't like getting up before noon. This time, I have to make an exception since I'm coordinating all kinds of specials at all three boutiques. I'll be so busy, we won't have time to have any kind of meaningful conversation. That's ten-thirty PM on Wednesday the fourteenth. The store will be closed by then, and all of the employees will be gone for the evening. Nothing to distract us."

Nothing to stop us, either, Justin thought ruefully. Heavens knew that he didn't want to be alone with Karimah Hart. She was too eager, too persuasive. She'd honed the skill of getting what she wanted to a mighty fine weapon. He didn't trust her. But worse than that, he didn't trust himself.

"So, will anyone else be at the meeting?" Justin asked, trying hard not to sound hopeful.

"Anyone else? Who else do you think needs to be there?"

He shrugged, then realized that she couldn't see him over the phone. "Oh, I don't know. Your sister perhaps? I was just wondering how many copies of the proposal to bring to the meeting."

"I think two will be adequate," Karimah said. "If Kallie wants to know what's going on, I'll fill her in later. This type of meeting really isn't her thing."

"Kallie?"

"My twin sister Kallista. You remember her."

"Yes, I do," Justin said quietly. How could he forget the interesting mix of woman warrior and maternal mentor? Whatever she'd said to Emeril left a very deep impression on him. "I just didn't catch her name. It won't be a problem bringing an extra copy for her."

"She asked about you, you know," Karimah said.

"She did?" He was surprised about that. "What did she say about me?"

"It really wasn't about you, per se. She said for you to give the boy a break."

"Oh," Justin replied.

"You sound disappointed."

"Do I?"

"What were you expecting her to say?"

"I wasn't expecting her to say anything at all. I'm concerned that she hasn't gotten in touch with me about what she intends to do about Emeril."

"Oh, I can tell you that, Justin. She can't do anything. We have no solid evidence against the boy."

"What do you mean? I saw him on tape taking the necklace."

"But he didn't have it on him when we searched him. No necklace. No proof. We'd look foolish going to court. Our case would crumble. Courts don't like it when you waste their time with frivolous suits."

"I can always torture the information out of him," Justin said grimly.

"Don't do that. Kallie seems to think you've got a good kid on your hands. My guess is that he couldn't go through with it. If we search hard enough, I'm sure the necklace will turn up in the store."

"You'll let me know, one way or the other?"

"Count on it. See you on Wednesday, Justin. You don't know how much I'm looking forward to this."

"See you then."

"See? I told you he'd go for it, Kallie. Now pay up." Karimah hung up the phone, a self-satisfied grin planted on her face.

Kallista looked up from her magazine. Her expression was as bland as Karimah's was boastful. "Not yet," she said. "I'll pay up when he shows up."

"What were you thinking, making the sucker bet with me, Kallie? Did you think he'd let a little thing like a gang turf war get in the way of sniffing out an opportunity to make some money off of us? Money aside, why would he pass up the chance for a shot of this?" Karimah said. She stood, raised her hands, and strutted up and down the room as if striding along a model's catwalk. "He'd have to be out of his mind."

"Or just not interested in women," Kallista suggested nastily.

"No . . . no, he couldn't be. You don't think he's gay, do you?"

Kallista shrugged. "You can never tell these days."

"Nah, I don't believe it. Faizon isn't the type to hang out with those with a little sweetness in their blood."

Kallista raised her eyebrows.

"I know that look. You're trying to say that Faizon might be that way, too?"

"I'm not saying a word." Kallista made a show of zipping her fingers across her lips.

"I don't believe it. Not the way he was all over me the other day."

"Oh, is that where you two were when I was almost beat down by the East-side crew?"

"You can handle yourself, Kallie."

"Thanks for your sisterly concern," Kallista said wryly. "If you and Faizon are so tight, why are you going after his friend so hard, Kari?"

"Faizon is pleasure," Karimah dismissed the idea of her and Faizon with a multi-ringed hand. "But he's old news. This is different. That Justin Malloy is all business. Serious business."

"You just make sure that he doesn't give *you* the business. Don't sign anything. Don't give him anything until he's proven that he can do the work."

"Yeah, yeah, yeah. I know the drill. Don't trust him until he's proven his worth."

"That's right."

"Good grief, Kallista. When are you going to ease up on the human race? You say that about everybody."

"That's because I don't trust anybody," Kallista declared. "If I want to keep the boutique finances in the black, I can't afford to."

"Not even me? Your own sister?"

"I love you like a sister, Kari," Kallista said, patting her twin on the cheek. "But I don't trust you as far as I can throw you. I know better than to let you have carte blanche with the checkbook."

Karimah leaned across the desk and kissed Kallista on the forehead. "I guess it was me that Daddy dropped on the head, 'cause Mama sure didn't raise any dummy in you."

"And you can take that to the bank."

"I promise not to sign anything without letting you give it your typical, eagle-eyed, nickel-and-dime-the-contract-until-it-hurts going over."

"You sure you don't want me to sit in on the meeting?"

Karimah made a rude noise. Justin Malloy was just a little too eager to be in contact with Kallista again. Her sister must have really made a big impression on him. "You are the last person that I want there," she said, her vanity stung. She continued on a more sensible note. "You'll get us all bogged down in the details, crossing every 't' and dotting every 'i'— this is a strategy meeting, a planning session."

"I know what your strategy is, Kari. You want me out of there so you can put your horny little paws all over that Malloy. You're not fooling anybody, especially me."

"Is that a note of jealousy I hear in your voice, Kallie?" Karimah teased.

"Now, you know me better than that," Kallista countered, avoiding her sister's gaze by pretending to thumb through an art catalog.

"Sometimes I wonder," Karimah said thoughtfully. "Don't you ever get tired of people mistaking you for me?"

Kallista laid down her magazine. She took a deep breath, choosing her words very carefully. "Kari, we're as close as any two human beings have a right to be. We share the same house, we work in the same place, we can even swap mono-grammed towels without incident. The reason why we haven't gotten on each other's nerves before now is because we know our boundaries, our limitations. I know my place. I know who I am. I don't have to compete with you for anything. Not attention, not acceptance, and certainly not over a man. You can have any man you want. If the flavor of the day is Justin Malloy, then I'm happy for you. My concern is that you don't let your fun get in the way of making a sound business decision. Because when you've moved on, decided that he isn't as much fun for you anymore, I will still be here. I want all the work we've put into this business to still be here, too."

"This is only business, Kallie. I don't want him."

"Uh-huh." Kallista was not convinced. "I'll tell you what. I'll stay out of your way until eleven-thirty, and then I'm busting up that party. Past that and with too much wine, there's no telling what you'll agree to."

"I am so hurt that you don't trust me to handle my own business."

"Hey, you remember the last time I left you to handle the business by yourself."

"Oh, I can't even believe that you would bring that up. Let it go, Kallie."

"I can't. We almost went completely bankrupt."

"A nine-year-old selling Kool-Aid on the curbside can't go bankrupt," Karimah scoffed.

"You gave away all of our stuff to one boy, Kari, just because he let you squeeze his—"

"Lemons," Karimah interrupted. "You're still holding that against me? I was just curious about the boy."

"And you haven't gotten over it!" Kallista's tone was accu-satory. "I'll head out to Conroe in the afternoon. There's a little artists' community out there. I think I can work out a deal for some of the artists to become regular suppliers for Karimah's.''

"You go work your deal, baby sister, and I'll work mine.'' Kallista stood up, planted her hands on her hips, and swayed from side to side. "Work it, girl! Work it!''

"You know, you've got to stop hanging around that Deandre so much. You're getting awfully street these days.''

"I can switch it on and off if I have to," Kallista insisted.

Karimah snatched the brochure that Kallista had been reading with intentions of swatting her with it. "What is this? The Artists' Alliance? Wait a minute, Kallie. Is this from that group of wackos who joined together to live in some kind of harmony with nature?''

"They are not wackos. They're just a group of people who want to be left alone to live their lives and create their art, without being bothered.''

"Sounds like a bunch of nutcases to me. Tofu-eating, tree-hugging, sixties rejects. Hello! It's the new millennium. Nobody needs to be walking around with mile-high afros and love beads, chanting and choking on a toke.''

"See, you don't even know what you're talking about. There's nobody in these brochures wearing a 'fro.''

"Where did you get this catalog?''

"I don't know. It's not yours?''

"I wouldn't be caught dead with that borderline cult material.'' Karimah sniffed disdainfully.

"I guess it doesn't matter where it came from. I think I'll head out there. If I like what I see, I'll be striking my own deal.''

"As long as you don't come back talking like a hippie chick, I'll see you at home when you get back,'' Karimah said, making certain that Kallista knew exactly what she meant. She didn't want Kallista busting up her late night date with Justin Malloy. Kallista was too levelheaded, too prone to want to hammer out the nuts and bolts of the deal before they had even begun to get creative. They'd be bored to death before they were halfway into the meeting.

Karimah didn't mean to imply that Kallista wasn't imaginative. She was. She was very creative—when she was excited about something. It was her vision that formed the basis for the present-day boutique.

When they'd purchased the property and had gone to inspect it, it was Kallista who stood in the middle of the floor, which was littered with the last tenant's junk. She was able to imagine the racks of designer clothing, the aisles of books, the cases filled with custom jewelry. With her hands held out in front of her, thumbs linked together, she moved frame by frame throughout the former warehouse. The more pictures in her mind she created for Karimah to see, the more excited Karimah became—even to the point that she was impulsively ready to rush right out and sink every penny into local advertising for a store that didn't exist yet.

"Behave yourself, Kari," Kallista said in warning.

"You know me," Karimah said innocently.

"That's right. I *do* know you. Take it easy on that poor, unsuspecting computer geek."

"He's kind of cute in a nerdy kinda way," Karimah said, wrinkling up her nose. "When I first met him, I didn't think I could go for a man like that. But the more I talked to him, the more I thought, hey . . . maybe."

"What do you think it was that made you look at him twice?" Kallista asked curiously. She had her own reasons to be surprised by her reaction to Justin Malloy. During the skirmish, when she'd captured him out of the corner of her eye heading for the exit, she'd felt an odd sense of disappointment. His nephew had been caught stealing. Why wouldn't he stay around to make sure the boy got his due punishment? Didn't he think stealing was a serious crime? Something about that didn't ring true. He must have known how serious it was. She could see that by the way he'd paced the room, reacting with barely controlled fury to everything his nephew said to him. Why she'd watched him and allowed him to wait for so long was still a mystery to her.

All the regs said that when a shoplifter was caught, it was better to get the arrest procedure over with quickly. But she didn't jump quickly to put this culprit away. She'd allowed them to wait, hoping that the psychological impact of getting caught, coupled with the uncertainty of punishment, was enough to throw a scare into Emeril. Watching Emeril on tape, she had every reason to believe that he was not a repeat offender but rather a rank amateur.

The more years she spent becoming an unofficial student of human nature, the better she became at judging. It was not Justin's and Emeril's reaction to getting caught that surprised her but also her own reaction. Even with all of the evidence before them—from the initial theft caught on tape, to Brandt's tailing, to the final confrontation outside of the store—she'd hoped to find Emeril innocent. Because he was a minor, she'd hoped that the conversation with Justin Malloy would be brief but pleasant.

At the onset of the confrontation between the rival gangs, she was surprised and disappointed to see Justin scramble for the exits like everyone else. Then, he did a one-eighty on her, literally. He'd stepped between her and that girl as if he were invincible. This contrasted sharply with the same air of vulnerability she'd sensed when she'd heard how disappointed he was in Emeril. That made him worthy of a second look. Maybe even a third.

But, then, Karimah announced her intentions of going after Justin herself. That alone was enough to make her curb her own curiosity to get to know him. It wasn't a matter of not going after someone else's object of interest. It wasn't even a question of not wanting to compete with her sister. There *was* no competition. The rules of the game of their lives strictly stipulated that, if Karimah went left, Kallista veered right. If Karimah preferred black, Kallista took white. Karimah basked in the sun; Kallista howled at the moon. The two worked together and lived together, but they did not share lives. Their spheres of influence ran in different circles. Kallista never wondered what would happen if the two spheres ever overlapped. She never cared to know. Her life was full and satisfying as it was. She wasn't going to let a man she didn't know disrupt it. Let Karimah have him.

Chapter Six

He wanted her. At least, Justin believed that's what Karimah Hart wanted him to think. She'd laid on the innuendoes pretty heavily during their conversation a few days ago. He'd prepared his proposal, bearing in mind that he'd have to walk a very fine line. He had to get her to keep her mind and hands off of him enough to listen to the merits of his proposal. At the same time, he didn't want to turn her off with an outright rejection of her advances.

Justin didn't think it was a question of her finding him all that irresistible. He had no illusions about himself. In high school, he was always the skinny kid. He was the brain. He was every girl's best friend—worthy of telling their secrets to, but not jock enough to be the subject of their secrets. In college, he was always the one who wound up holding the jackets and purses while the girls and the other guys in the group dates went out dancing. He was the one all the girls called to borrow homework answers, only to forget his number when it came to being invited to a Saturday night party.

As Justin put the finishing touches on his presentation, his fingers flying over the computer keyboard, he had to stop and give thanks for all those reclusive Saturday nights. While his fellow seniors were studying the ways of getting into the panties of freshman girls, Justin was exploring the wonders of the World Wide Web. He could be himself in an Internet chat room—the self that few seldom saw outside of the confines of the classroom. Online, he was funny, smart, and intuitive. He didn't have to create a false identity. All he had to do was tap into the one he was too insecure to display on campus.

After he'd gone to grad school and found that he had a headstart in taking advantage of this new way to communicate, the rest was ancient history—along with the names of the girls who wouldn't give him the time of day. He had to tip his hat to them, too. They had also taken a hand in making him what he was today—self-sufficient and successful. If it wasn't his looks that drew Karimah to him, surely it was his keen business sense and his confidence in being able to take her business to the next level.

His business was fledgling but successful. If he didn't get Karimah's business, it wouldn't hurt him. But if he hurt her by turning down any offer but a business one, she could certainly kill him. More than the fear of losing his hard-earned business, he was afraid of losing the friendship of Faizon.

Though he felt a twinge of guilt about it, he hadn't told Faizon about his meeting with Karimah. What would that accomplish? It would only serve to get Faizon all worked up. He didn't want that. He'd known since they were kids that you didn't want to work Faizon into a frenzy. The results were not pretty.

So what if she asked to meet him after hours? So what if it would only be the two of them? So what if he was meeting a very attractive, seemingly willing woman on supposedly the most romantic day of the year? So what? What did that prove?

Justin had purposefully avoided looking at himself in the mirror when he made those assertions. He knew that if anyone—including himself—had said those words to his face, he wouldn't be able to keep from responding with a wisecrack.

He checked his watch. It was a full six hours before his meeting with Karimah, and he was already starting to get the heebie-jeebies and talking to himself. No, he was rather warning himself about the consequences of making a wrong decision. He had no intention of taking her up on any offer that didn't involve setting her up with her own web site. So, why did he feel like he was submitting his application to be the poster child for the morally bankrupt? How he wished there would be someone else at that meeting tonight. Anyone. He would even accept that loss-prevention agent, Brandt. He turned off the part of his brain that wondered why Karimah would not want her sister there at the meeting. In fact, she'd seemed suspicious when Justin had asked about her. He didn't know why. The question had been an honest one, a logical one. The fact that she wanted no one around sealed it for him: there was no mistaking her ulterior motive. There was only one thing he could do. He picked up the phone and dialed Faizon's number.

Interstate 59 was surprisingly clear for a Wednesday during the heart of rush hour. As Kallista traveled north, making a mental note to visit some of the outlet stores along the way, she tried to keep her mind focused on her task. She wanted to come back with no less than three verbal contracts from the Artist's Alliance. She'd called several of the names listed in their brochure. Despite Karimah's assertion that they were all social drop-outs and drug addicts, she was impressed by their warmth and willingness to do business with her. To become a supplier for all three of Karimah's boutiques was a prolific artist's dream. No waiting for tourists to stop by to rifle critically through their work. No waiting for overcrowded art shows or fighting for prime space during sidewalk festivals. Here was someone who was willing to come to them, willing to establish a long-term, mutually beneficial relationship. It was as close to having their work displayed in a gallery as some would ever come. They would welcome her with open arms.

As Kallista strolled around the compound, she tried to ignore the odd looks. People would pass her, then stop. Some would back up and circle around to get a better look.

"I'm not her," Kallista said in an automatic response, "I'm the *other* sister."

Her explanation seemed to satisfy them, until the next people she met. She turned that part of her mind off—choosing not to respond at all. Obviously, this place wasn't so taboo for Karimah. She must have been here and made quite an impression in order for Kallista to be getting the reaction that she was getting. Karimah never went anywhere without making sure that everyone knew who she was before she left. Resolutely, Kallista crossed her arms. Well, she wasn't here to put on a show. She was here to conduct her business and get back before Karimah let Justin Malloy completely twist her head around.

As she strolled through the rows of sculpture, paintings, jewelry, and tapestries, she could see why Karimah would want to visit a place like this. The way Karimah dressed and acted, you'd think that she'd never want to leave here. Among all of the artisans pulling every trick in the book to get you to notice them, Karimah would be in ultra-compete mode. This would seem like a second home to her.

With her nondescript daily wear of just blue jeans and a T-shirt, someone could think that it would make Kallista chafe to be seen in a place this. She couldn't blend in. She couldn't be a shadow-walker and remain unnoticed. The open looks from both browsers and artisans told her that. She wondered why she felt just the opposite. Walking around the compound made her feel oddly comforted—despite the odd looks. What was it that gave her a sense of familiarity? It wasn't exactly the clothing. There was nothing in the way these people dressed that said anything *but* comfort. The clothes were utilitarian and functional, yet comfortable. Maybe that's what it was. It was a sense of being comfortable with who and what you were, no matter what was going on in the outside world, that struck Kallista as so familiar. She had found an entire community of shadow-walkers. The more she walked among them, the better she felt.

Her feelings completely drove away the sense of apprehension she'd experienced while driving out here. Yeah, she was irritated that Kari only wanted to get her out of her hair. And, yes, it bothered her that her sister didn't think enough of her business acumen to want her involved in a meeting that might possibly have a huge impact on the business. She could even get over *that*.

What she really didn't want to admit was that she hated missing the opportunity to see Justin Malloy again. She could tell herself that it was only because they had unfinished business between them. But it was more than that. This was the first time she remembered having someone occupy her thoughts for a long time. She wondered so many things about him. That her mind would linger long over those unknown details was in itself wonder.

The facts that she did know about him were from the paperwork he had to fill out during the theft. He lived on the northwest side of town, in one of those master-planned communities, which had winding roads and well-kept cul-de-sacs with names of mystical landmarks like "Whispering Pines Way" or "Languishing Lake Lane." Kallista almost chuckled at the irony of living in such a place. No wonder the pines were talking among themselves and the waters were crying themselves a river. The first thing that developers did when creating those communities was to destroy the natural surroundings. Then, they had the nerve to go back and stick in a few shrubby plants, some mulch, and a few water gardens—and call it "natural landscaping." She supposed it was just snobbery making her turn up her nose at Justin's choice of residency. She and Karimah still lived in the house where they were born, in the Settegast community. Their family had added on to and improved the house, but they still remained rooted in the community.

Justin Malloy's cultured tones didn't fool her. He still hung around with Faizon, and that man was straight up out of the 'hood. Any other man who presented himself as being more than what he was would have immediately turned her off. Not this time. Justin wasn't pretending to be someone that he wasn't. He was a man who was becoming a person he had the potential to be.

Her fascination with him struck up a memory, long buried but slowly reaching for the surface. She and Karimah must have been nine years old, maybe eight, when they found a butterfly cocoon attached to a branch outside of their bedroom window. She had wanted to bring the cocoon inside, to study it under her ever curious magnifying glass. Karimah had stopped her, warning her to let Mother Nature do the job. Through the rainy fall and the mild winter, they waited for that butterfly to emerge. Kallista thought that she would never forget the day the butterfly struggled from its chrysalis. She and Karimah had been sitting under the tree—waiting. Then, it started. Kallista had done her research. She had all of the facts of butterfly migration and gestation periods and species that were indigenous to Texas. When the cocoon began to swell and contract, Kallista shook her sister.

Who could explain why a child would become so fascinated and transfixed by a simple act of nature? It happened all of the time in the trees of little girls' backyards all over the world. But Kallista held on to the belief that something magical was about to happen. She could barely breath, as she squinted up at the tree.

Time stood still as the cocoon cracked open and the vestiges of saffron wings emerged.

"I told you it wouldn't be a monarch butterfly," Karimah crowed triumphantly. And so the argument had gone all through the fall and winter, into spring. Kallista didn't mind being proven wrong. She had only cared to see the ugly brown cocoon turn into something wonderful.

"It's so beautiful," Kallista murmured. She had barely gotten the words out of her mouth before the inevitable had to happen—the butterfly had to leave. If they wanted their summer to be filled with more beautiful flower blossoms, it had to go. But she wasn't prepared for her changeling to leave like this. Not like this.

From out of nowhere, the mockingbird that had tortured them, driving them from the shelter and shade of the large oak tree in the front yard to the mimosa tree in the backyard, swooped down out of the sky. In the span of a heartbeat, the butterfly was gone. It had been months in the making, surviving through rains and unexpected freezes. It had survived kites stuck in trees and curious kittens looking for adventure. All of that preparation, and like that, it was gone.

"Oh well, I guess that's the end of that," Karimah said, shrugging her shoulders. "Wanna play jacks?"

But Kallista could not move. She stood, staring at the empty shell. Her mouth pressed shut, but tears pooled in her eyes. She blinked once, flushing them down the crevices of the hollows of her cheeks and down her chin. Her chest felt so tight. It had nothing to do with the allergies she'd suffered from the mimosa pollen. It was anger building inside of her, anger at the unfairness of it all. That butterfly had worked so hard to *become*. All it wanted was a chance to *be*. It was one of God's creatures, her mother had told her—as unique and as precious as she was. It had barely begun to do God's work, and look what happened? That old mockingbird swooped down and gobbled it up. If one of God's most special creatures didn't have a chance in the world, what chance did she have? She was a poor copy of one of God's creatures. Poor, plain, brown Kallista. While the Karimahs of the world were allowed to flutter free and beautiful, she was destined to be the husk that was left behind.

Kallista wasn't sure how the rock got in her hand. She certainly didn't remember throwing it at the grim foreteller of her fate. She didn't remember throwing that rock, or the other rock, or the other, or the other. She acted on pure impulse—wanting to hurt the mockingbird as much as she'd been hurt. But Kallista did remember the one that went crashing through the kitchen window. And she remembered the punishment afterward. The spanking and the grounding to her room were soon forgotten. The lesson in nature and the effect it had on her until her adult years remained with her. She would never forget that lesson. For almost thirty years, she had been living in a plain, brown shell, afraid of being gobbled if she showed her true colors.

She loved her sister. Heavens knew she did. But she was tired of being mistaken for her—even when she did her best to separate herself from her in dress and speech and choices of friends. The annoyingly familiar looks from perfect strangers had shown her that it wasn't enough. For once in her life, she wanted to be the butterfly that flew. For once, she wanted to be able to spread her wings to the sunlight, to let someone bask in the glory of her natural beauty. She knew that she had the power within her to break free.

A few moments in conversation with Justin had shown her that a man could look at her and not see Karimah. Even though he had mistaken her at first for her sister, Karimah's insistence that she stay away from her meeting let her know that there was something going on beneath the surface. She never before had to go through such effort to separate their friends. The no-compete, rule—remember? For the first time in their lives, was there something worth competing for? For the first time in her life, did she want something worth fighting for? She wasn't sure. But she would never know if she remained in the shadows.

She spun around, jostling the elbow of a woman carrying a large, earthenware bowl. The woman cried out as the bowl went crashing to the ground. "Great! Just my luck!"

"Excuse me," Kallista said distractedly, hardly noticing the commotion she was causing.

"Hey!" the woman called out after her. "Hey, wait a minute.

That bowl cost me thirty bucks!'' She hurried to catch up to Kallista. "Lady, you owe me thirty dollars.''

For a fraction of a second, Kallista considered blowing the woman off. She wanted to hand her a business card and offer her a comparable item from the boutique. She changed her mind when she saw the woman's companion trying to put the broken pieces back together again. It wasn't just the money, it was the item itself. Kallista wanted to find the artisan who could create an item that held its value—even when the piece was destroyed.

Kallista dug into her front pocket for her wallet. "Thirty dollars?'' Kallista echoed. "For that much money, that bowl had better cook my meal and clean up after itself.'' She handed the woman two twenty-dollar bills. "I am sorry about the bowl, miss.''

The woman took the offering, then started fishing around in her oversized purse. Moments later, she pulled out a couple of crumpled bills. "Here you go. Ten dollars.''

Kallista held up her hand, waving it. "Keep the change.''

"I said thirty dollars,'' the woman replied, insistently, pressing the money back into Kallista's outstretched hand. Kallista was surprised by the response. She worked in a business where people often wanted something for nothing. The fact that the woman would turn down free money surprised her.

"Where did you buy the bowl?'' Kallista wanted to know.

"From CeCe.''

"CeCe?'' Kallista repeated.

The woman shrugged. "That's what everybody around here calls her. She's got a potter's wheel set up on the other side of the commune. She gets a kick when people watch her work. She says that it gets her 'mystic artistic muse' going. I saw her make this one. I guess that's why I took it so hard when you broke it.''

"I apologize for making you drop the bowl.''

"Not a problem. I probably would have used it to collect junk anyway.''

At that admission, Kallista did take out her business card. She signed the card *Kallista Hart,* and wrote a percentage discount. "If you're ever on the north side of Houston, stop by Karimah's Boutique," she offered. "If you're a collector, you might find something that you like. And it won't be junk, either. We specialize in designer items, one-of-a-kind, local artists."

" 'Karimah's Boutique.' I just might pay you a visit. Thanks. Are you heading over to CeCe's now?"

"I was thinking about it."

"Me, too. There was this urn that I had my eye on. At the time, I couldn't choose between the bowl and the urn."

"Looks like I made that decision for you," Kallista said, with just enough apology in her voice to make the woman smile.

"No hard feelings, Ms. Hart."

"Call me Kallie." Kallista didn't question why she'd taken an instant liking to this woman. She was working on instinct. Though she'd come to the Artist's Alliance with a list in mind and a schedule to keep, she pushed it aside to go with the flow of events around her.

"Jacynth Metcalf. My friends call me Jacie," the woman offered, holding out her hand. She nodded over her shoulder toward the direction of her companion. "The one still trying to put together the pieces over there is my brother, Ulysses." Then she cupped her fingers to her mouth and shouted, "Just put it in the trash, Uly. I'll meet you back at the car in a bit."

"Your parents got creative with names, too, huh?" Kallista said, grinning at her.

"I guess that was just the sign of the times back then. Something about that fifties and sixties generations. I'm lucky that I'm not a 'Moonflower' or 'Sunbeam' or something *groooovy* like that," Jacie said.

Kallista looked askance at her. She could have been somebody's love child. She fit in perfectly with the scenic atmosphere of this community—with her John Lennon-style shades, sandals on her feet, and tunic dress.

"It could have been worse," Kallistra remarked.

"Like how?"

"We could have been born in the generation when all of us were named 'Brittany' or 'Courtney' or 'Tiffany.' "

Jacie burst out laughing. "I've got six girl cousins, and two of them are named 'Brittany.' What are the odds of that? Come on. CeCe's booth is this way," Jacie said enthusiastically, taking Kallista by the arm and pulling her along. "Wait until you see her collection."

Chapter Seven

A small crowd had gathered around CeCe's booth by the time Kallista and Jacie wound their way to the opposite end of the compound. Even though most of the booths were closing down for the evening, Kallista couldn't tell because of the air of hushed expectation surrounding CeCe's booth. They were too intent on watching the artists to notice the other vendors as they took down their tents, furled their banners, and packed their wares in straw, wadded newspaper, or Styrofoam peanuts.

"I see what you mean about spectators," Kallista mused.

Jacie pursed her lips thoughtfully. "Something must be going on. I've only been out here a couple of times, but this is more people than I'd seen in both of those times put together."

"I wonder what the deal is?"

As they edged up to the crowd, Jacie nudged a spectator. "What's going on?"

"CeCe's trying to beat her own record," he whispered back. Jacie leaned over her shoulder and relayed the message in a whisper to Kallista.

"Why are we whispering?" Kallista whispered loudly and distinctly in jest. It wasn't as if this was a chess tournament.

"If CeCe can finish this last piece, that'll make ten molded pieces for the day. But she's gotta finish before the last vendor takes down their signs. The place is supposed to shut down by eight o'clock."

"Oh," Kallista said, nodding her head. She checked her watch. Not much time. She hadn't realized that she'd been out here that long. By now, Karimah would be well on her way to setting up the meeting with Justin.

"What happens if she beats her record?" Jacie asked.

"We've all pitched in a little cash. If she makes it, she gets almost three-hundred dollars."

"Three-hundred dollars. Are you kidding?"

"Ten bucks a piece," the man responded. "If she doesn't make it, we all get to pick something from the table and name our own price—without dickering."

"She charged you thirty." Kallista nudged Jacie with her elbow.

"Don't remind me." Jacie grimaced.

"I want to see this famous CeCe in action," Kallista said, edging a little bit closer. She was almost at the front of the crowd. As she moved up to the front row of the spectators, something caught CeCe's attention. Maybe it was the motion of the crowd, or a feeling. Maybe she looked up to check her progress against the other vendors.

In the race against time, CeCe didn't appear overly concerned. Her long, gnarled fingers continued to smooth up and down the reddish-brown clay. Every so often, she would reach for a small, clay-encrusted plastic cup and dip it into a pail of water beside her. Slowly—as if in reverent libation—she poured the water over the item that was slowly taking shape. The clay became slicker between her fingers as the wheel continued to spin. The item morphed several times, going from a column of indistinguishable clay to a slender, cylindrical vase, and then to a short, squat bowl—all within a matter of minutes. All because of the slight shifting of her palms and fingertips.

CeCe raised her shoulders to swipe at an errant, blondish-gray strand of hair that had worked loose from her hastily constructed bun. In doing so, her glance fell on the crowd.

"Back so soon?" she called out in Kallista's direction. "That was quick."

Kallista half-turned, thinking that perhaps she was talking to Jacie. After all, the girl had just left her booth with the ill-fated bowl.

"Did you get that . . . uh . . . package from Augie?" CeCe asked. She picked up what appeared to be a small metal pick and touched it lightly against the sides of the new bowl. The effect was instantaneous. Small, serpentine grooves magically appeared around the bowl, from base to lip.

Again, Kallista glanced around.

"What? Are you deaf? I'm talking to you. If you've got it, I could really use it right now." CeCe raised her voice over the whine of the potter's wheel and the growing noise of the crowd as they made their predictions about whether she would be able to beat her record.

Kallista pointed to herself and mouthed, "Me?"

"Yeah, you. Who in the hell do you think I'm talking to? Hurry up and bring me a glass of water so I can take my . . . uh . . . vitamins."

Someone in the crowd snickered. A few knew of Augie and his special "vitamins." CeCe was at her most creative and most productive when she'd had a few of Augie's under-the-counter and above-the-law concoctions. It played havoc with her body when she wasn't sculpting. But for now, there were three-hundred dollars on the line. That bought an awful lot of "vitamins."

Kallista stepped forward, almost directly into one of the last spotlights remaining on to accent a vendor's wares. In a few more minutes, the merchant selling hand-hewn sandalwood-bead necklaces would have packed away the last display. After that, she would no longer need the light. If CeCe hadn't finished molding the tenth piece by the time she'd closed the last crate, CeCe would lose the bet and lose face with the crowd who'd gathered before her.

"I think you've made a mistake . . . uh . . . CeCe," Kallista said. "I'm not who you think I am. Maybe you've gotten me confused with my sister."

Once she spoke up, CeCe's head snapped up—her full attention on Kallista. In the dim light, Kallista saw a look that she had never seen cross the woman's face. It was hard to explain. Kallista thought, for a moment, that CeCe was going to be sick. All of the color drained from her face, leaving it the color of campfire ashes. Then it turned crimson. CeCe's hands clenched convulsively around the bowl, and it became a misshapen lump, wobbling on the wheel as it slowed to a grinding halt. She stood up, her goo-covered hands clenching and unclenching as if she was breathing out her rage through her hands.

The resulting cries of satisfied cheers twisted Kallista on the inside as badly as the lump of clay on CeCe's wheel. She didn't know CeCe. She'd never seen the woman before today. But just by stepping into the light, she had cost the woman three-hundred dollars. Kallista didn't blame her for being angry. She'd be upset, too, if the situation were reversed.

"Come on," Jacie whispered tightly, grabbing Kallista's elbow. "Let's get out of here."

"Oh, I feel awful about this," Kallista lamented. "Maybe I should go and talk to her." She started forward, but the remaining crowd had already surged around CeCe. They were lifting items off her table and slapping money down in their places. Kallista didn't think the money offered was anywhere near what the items were worth. She wanted to do something, but she wasn't sure what. She felt bad about CeCe not making her quota, but she didn't want to feel responsible for CeCe making the bet in the first place. On the other hand, three-hundred dollars was three-hundred dollars. She had to do something.

Pushing her way through the crowd, Kallista got to within inches of CeCe.

"I am so sorry, CeCe," she started. "I didn't mean to break your concentration and make you lose the bet."

The woman glared at her. "Who are you?"

"My name is Kallista Hart," Kallista said, holding out her hand. CeCe shoved her hands deep into the pockets of her frock.

Kallista pulled a business card from her wallet. "I came out here looking for art vendors to help me stock my boutique. My sister and I own a chain in Houston."

After saying that piece of information, Kallista wouldn't exactly say that CeCe had entirely forgiven her, but it did make her raise her eyebrows in interest. Her red-rimmed, watery-gray eyes narrowed with sudden understanding and appreciation of the opportunity.

"A chain of boutiques, did you say?"

Kallista nodded.

"And you're looking for someone to stock you?"

She nodded again.

"Looking for anyone in particular or anything in particular?"

"You seem to meet the qualifications. Good and fast."

"But not cheap," CeCe said, pointing a shaky finger at Kallista. "I do quality work. If you want cheap, I can put you in touch with a few people."

"Sounds like a good place to start talking," Kallista agreed. "Is there somewhere we can go talk?"

"I'd invite you back to my place, but it's a mess right now," CeCe said uneasily. "Why don't you meet me at the Ice House back out on I-59 in about an hour."

"Sounds good," Kallista said. She glanced at her new friend. "Wanna go?"

"Sure," Jacie said, grinning at Kallista. "As long as you don't make me drop my beer, too."

* * *

"Can I offer you something to drink, Justin?"

Karimah brushed past him as she made her way to a ceiling-to-floor wooden cabinet. She pulled open both doors, revealing a television/VCR/stereo combination, as well as a refrigerator and a library.

Justin whistled low with appreciation.

"Thank you," Karimah said.

"You do understand that I was remarking on the entertainment center, don't you?"

"I take my compliments were I can get them, Justin," she said lightly. "So, name your poison."

"I'd better stick with water, Karimah. It's late. I still have a ways to drive back." Justin figured it was a good excuse for why he needed to keep his head clear tonight. He didn't want to return to Faizon's to pick up Emeril with the smell of liquor on his breath.

Karimah looked over her shoulder at him and smiled as if to say: "I don't expect you to drive back tonight."

Justin read the look perfectly. "Just water," he reiterated.

"All right, have it your way." She handed him a small bottle of water, brushing her fingertips over his hand as she passed it to him. She then gestured for him to sit down on the leather couch. "I appreciate your coming all this way to meet with me, Justin,"

"I take my business where I can find it," he echoed her sentiments. "When I saw how well your pre-opening day sale was received by your customers, I smelled an opportunity."

"You mean you smelled money."

"My nose rarely makes the distinction."

"I hope the rest of your senses are more acute," she replied. "What about your sense of touch . . . or taste?" She raised a small hors d'oerve to her mouth and took a dainty bite. When she held out the remaining piece to him, he shook his head no.

He shifted uncomfortably. He'd better speak up now, before they got too deep into the meeting, and he got too deep into something—or someone—else.

"Karimah, I'm going to be honest with you. You are a very attractive woman."

"That's so sweet of you to say."

"I can see where a man could lose himself trying to find out more about you."

"I'm not that complicated a person. My wants . . . my expectations, are simple."

"So are mine. My expectation is this: If you invite me over here to discuss business, then that's what I'm going to do. I don't mess around with the people I work with. It gets too . . . what's the word? Messy. Let's just keep this meeting strictly business."

"I thought it was," she answered, sounding convincingly surprised, throwing in a little pout, to show that her feelings were hurt.

Justin wasn't quite sure what to make of her assertion. Either she'd been flirting so long that she didn't realize what she was doing, or she was really good at getting what she wanted by messing with people's minds.

"I'm not going to sleep with you for an opportunity to work with you," he said slowly and distinctly.

"Sleeping with you was the furthest thing from my mind," she said, lifting her chin. He caught a glimpse of the rhythmic pulse at the hollow of her throat, which warmed the exotic scent of her perfume. That heady scent crossed the close distance of only a single couch cushion to reach him.

"It . . . uh . . . ," Justin began distractedly. "It never occurred to you that you and I could . . . that is . . . we would—"

"Wind up having sex?" she asked bluntly. "Of course it occurred to me."

"And?"

"You made it clear where you stand, Justin. I'm not going to push. What do you think I am? Hard up?" Karimah crossed her legs, drawing his eye along the bronze curve of her calf, all the way up the side of her skirt where a split showed a healthy portion of thigh, as well.

"No, that wouldn't describe you at all," he replied. A description of *himself,* on the other hand, was something else altogether.

With the way she looked at him, the way her perfume smelled, the subtle way her skirt rustled when she walked, what kind of cold fish would he be if he hadn't considered what it would be like to touch her? To taste her? But this was business. He'd put his stake in the ground and now he had to stick to it—no matter how unmercifully the full lines of her breasts beckoned to him when she raised her wine glass to drain it of its contents.

"So tell me what's on your mind," she encouraged.

"What?" he asked, not caring if she knew that his mind was wandering.

"For Karimah's. My chain of stores. What can you do to help the business?"

"Oh," he gulped down half of his water to ease the dryness of his mouth. "What you need is greater exposure."

"I see," she said, then laughed. "And what kind of exposure would that be?" When she leaned forward to refill her wine glass, Justin's eyes zeroed in on the back of her neck and down the row of buttons of her blouse. His head swam as if *he* had just downed two glasses of wine.

"The numbers of people who are willing to step out of their busy lives and into stores is shrinking daily," he said. He recited the words from his presentation, focusing his mind on the business at hand. "We're fast becoming a nation where everything you want is literally at your fingertips."

"Just a point and a click away," Karimah intoned.

"Exactly. If I set you up with a web site, you can compete with the biggest and best of the department stores. If we build a virtual boutique, with distributors from here to Hong Kong supplying your store, your customers will never know the differences while they're browsing through the online catalog pages.''

"Ummm . . . sounds interesting,'' she conceded. "But you're forgetting a couple of things."

"And what's that, Karimah?"

"Most of my customers don't even own computers. They don't know e-mail from emus. How am I going to reach them with this fabulous store of the new millennium?"

"If you're talking about your local folks, you've already got them by word of mouth, grassroot sales. Local flyers and a few radio ads will more than bring them in. I'm thinking outside of Houston, outside of Texas, even outside of the United States. An online market is a global market, Karimah. If a woman down the street is interested in the kind of necklace my nephew tried to swipe from you, don't you think a woman half the world away would be interested, too?"

"Why would she want to buy from me, if I'm half a world away? What's to stop her from going to *her* local boutique where they know her, know her tastes. There's something to be said about the personal touch, Justin,'' Karimah reminded him by touching him lightly in the middle of his chest with her index finger.

"What makes people from Rodeo Drive in L.A. want to fly all the way to New York's garment district? What brings people to the runways of Paris looking for that unique look? I'll tell you what, Karimah. It's vanity. It's human nature, the selfish privilege of being able to say that you got something from somewhere and no one else on the block has it. If we promote your store as the place where everybody who's anybody goes to shop for designer one-of-a-kinds, I can help you get Karimah's up there with names like Chanel or DK or Tommy Hilfiger. It's all in the exposure.''

"You talk a good game, Justin Malloy.''

"I don't play,'' he responded.

"Then, what do you suggest we do first?"

"Get you set up with an ISP.''

"A what?"

"An Internet service provider. From there, we can get some space on their web server to set up your site."

"How long will that take?"

"Not long. A matter of days. We'll start small, just put the site out there to see how many hits we get. We'll put out some pictures of merchandise. Maybe the first one-hundred people or so who e-mail you will get an in-store discount. After we build up some heavy traffic, we'll see about setting up an ordering system so they can actually purchase the items they see."

"Since my merchandise changes on a weekly—sometimes daily—basis, who's going to keep an eye on my web site to make sure the customers aren't looking at merchandise I don't have anymore?"

"That'll be my job to start off with. I'll need to work closely with whoever controls your inventory to make certain I keep accurate records."

"That would be Kallie," Karimah said, sitting back on the chair. It was the first time her name had come up all evening. Karimah felt a twinge of guilt. Maybe she should have asked her sister to the meeting, for all the good it did being alone with Justin. She had been so sure that Justin would have jumped at the opportunity to become intimately acquainted with her. She'd thrown herself at him at every available opportunity. Yet, he had dodged her nimbly, as if she were throwing huge, clunky bowling balls. "She knows every stitch of clothing, every gemstone, every statuette that has ever come through all three stores. I swear, her mind must be photographic the way she holds things."

Chapter Eight

"Oooh. Oh, my! I gotta go!" Kallista said, quickly jumping up from her seat. She held onto the cigarette-burned tabletop to steady herself. She and Jacie were perched in a corner booth at the Ice House, waiting for CeCe to show up. After an hour-and-a-half—and three beers later—Kallista was starting to get restless. Where was CeCe? Why wasn't she here yet? Had her instinct been that inaccurate? She thought that surely CeCe had been interested in striking a deal.

"They always say that you rent beer, you don't buy it," Jacie said, lifting her bottle to salute Kallista.

"That's not what I meant. I've got to get back to Houston. I'm late for a meeting that I shouldn't have missed . . . that is, I shouldn't have been there. I mean . . . hell . . . what *do* I mean?" Kallista said, pressing her hand to her eyes to stop the slow throbbing at her temples.

"Are you sure you're okay to drive, Kallie?"

"Of course I'm okay . . . now where did I put my car keys?" She patted her jeans pockets.

"If you don't remember that, you don't need to be driving,"

Jacie observed. "I'd take you home myself, but I'm already three sheets to the wind."

Kallista stopped patting, her face crumpled in concentration. "What does that mean, anyway? 'Three sheets to the wind.' Why does it have to be sheets? And why does it always have to be three? How come it isn't four blankets to the wind or seven pairs of socks to the wind or even to the sun?"

"You are a very, very, philo . . . philo . . . philosophical . . . prolifical . . . ," Jacie giggled, then hiccuped. "Very deep-thinking drunk."

"I am not drunk!" Kallista insisted. "I don't drink much."

"Which is probably why you're seven socks to the sun now," Jacie said solemnly.

Kallista tried to take a step, then wavered. "Oh, Jacie. I think you're right. I think I've had too much. I'm not driving all the way back to Houston like this."

"Yep. You'd be throwing up before you got to the other side of Conroe."

"I'm going to be throwing up before I get to the other side of this sawdust-covered floor," Kallista predicted. Maybe she should have passed on that second order of buffalo wings. It was certainly starting to pass her up now. She clamped her hand over her mouth and sped to the ladies' room.

Jacie shook her head in silent commiseration and a tad bit of envy. She wouldn't reach the throwing-up stage until tomorrow. That meant she had longer to anticipate the pending suffering. For now, she still had a good buzz going. She didn't want to leave the Ice House. She didn't want to leave her new friend. But it was getting late. Uly would probably start to wonder about her, even though she had called him earlier to let him know when she was going to be home. He had long since caught a ride home with some of his friends. She didn't think he'd take too kindly to having to scare up a ride at this time of night to come and get her and Kallista.

"Oh, I know. I'll call a cab. No, can't do that. Spent my last thirty dollars." She took another swig of beer, expecting the mellow liquid to clear, rather than cloud, her thinking. "Maybe I'll call somebody else to come get us," She dug her cellular phone out of her large purse and put the phone next to her ear. "Hello? Hello? Stupid battery must have died."

She slapped a hand on her forehead. *Duh!* She had to dial a number first. But who? She looked through her purse again, searching for her phone book. Instead, she ran across the business card that Kallista had given her. She dialed the store number. It rang forever before someone finally answered.

Jacie stuck one finger in her ear and yelled to be heard over the noise at the Ice House. She gave directions to the person on the other end of the line, then clicked off the phone satisfied that she had done her duty as an honest citizen to keep two obvious menaces to society like themselves off of the roads.

When Kallista returned, looking shaken and full of chagrin, Jacie shouted at her. "I called Karimah's, and they're coming out to get us."

Kallista grimaced and clamped her hands over her ears. "Jacie, why are you shouting?"

"So that they . . . you . . . that is . . . so I could be heard over all of this loud music, silly. That was a very unphilosophical question."

"Jacie," Kallista snapped back. "There is no music playing. The band played their last set twenty minutes ago."

"Then what's this music I hear in my head?" Jacie asked, just before her forehead dropped and hit the table with a loud *thunk*.

"You sure you don't want to go with me?" Justin asked, picking up his presentation materials and car keys.

Karimah stretched languidly. The nearly empty bottle of wine dangled from her hand. "Trust me, Justin. You don't want two tipsy twins on your hands."

"You're pulling my leg again, right?" At any other time,

this was exactly what he'd want. In fact, he imagined it was every man's fantasy to have twin sisters at his mercy.

"You wouldn't let me pull anything else." She grinned up at him. "You go and bring my sister back here. I know you've been dying to hook up with her again, anyway."

"What makes you think that?" Justin was genuinely surprised.

"Come on, Justin. I'm drunk. I'm not blind. You've been watching that clock and the door for the past four hours, hoping that Kallie would come walking in."

"Not just Kallista," Justin was stung into saying. "I would have welcomed anybody."

"Anybody?"

"I just didn't trust myself to be alone with you, Karimah."

Karimah rolled her eyes and said comically, "I don't think you have anything to worry about. You behaved like a perfect gentleman."

"I'm far from perfect."

"Perfection is in the eye of the beholder. From where I'm sitting, sir, you're looking pretty close to perfect to me."

"Thanks for the compliment. So, once I get her, what do you want me to do with her?"

"You really are a goody two-shoes, aren't you?" Karimah asked in awe. "Twice in one night, you get to hook up with two beautiful, accomplished—and dare I say—willing women. And you have to ask what to do? I hope you show more initiative and creativity in your business life than you do in your love life, Justin Malloy."

"I'll be back as soon as I can," Justin said dryly. "Then I'm taking you both home."

"Every man's fantasy." Karimah yawned as the empty wine bottle finally fell to the carpeted floor.

At two o'clock in the morning, the freeway was almost deserted—except for a few eighteen wheelers pulling out of Houston for Dallas and other points north. Justin made fast time once he left the boutique. Even without the directions from the woman who'd called him, obviously tipsy but clearly adamant that someone come and pick Kallista up, he knew where he was going. The Ice House was a popular hangout. He couldn't imagine what Kallista Hart would be doing in a place like that. It was too loose, too relaxed. She didn't seem like the type of person who would relinquish that much control over her body. Then again, he shouldn't make such rash judgements after knowing her barely one hour.

As he drove along, watching for his exit, he wondered what he was getting himself into. He hadn't recognized himself for the past few weeks. His life was not his own. He wasn't equipped to handle a fourteen-year-old boy. He didn't have that kind of patience. Yet, when his brother Gideon had asked, he'd jumped at the chance—without an argument.

He'd used business as an excuse for not seeing his old friend Faizon. Truth was, he was worried about the serious stuff that Faizon was getting into. The man was too old to be getting teenager-type kicks out of stealing. Justin couldn't be certain, but he suspected that Faizon was rapidly escalating from doing it for fun to making a career out of it. He'd gone over there to perform his own personal intervention. What had started out as a friendly visit to an old friend turned into an encounter in the Twilight Zone once they were at the boutique. He wasn't the type to mix it up with gangbangers, so what did he think he was doing going up against a kid almost twice his size? But he'd done it. Just as Gideon had needed his help, Justin was certain that Kallista needed it, too.

The thing that really got to him was that he knew he shouldn't be making late-night meetings with attractive, oversexed clients. As much as he wanted his business to grow, he wasn't used to rushing foolhardily into a situation where he didn't feel as if he had total control. It didn't make good sense—business or common.

Even though he berated himself for rushing into action before thinking this through, here he was still going on in the same vein. Every bone in his body was telling him to beware. He'd just extricated himself from one sister.

Justin exited the freeway, then cruised down the two-lane access road. There weren't many lights on the road this far out; only the yellow-and-white reflectors dotting the center line and the border between the road and the ditches kept him from veering off the road.

The Ice House was about a quarter of a mile up the road. He could see the parade of taillights exiting the parking lot— a sure sign that the place was closing down for the night. Small pockets of last-minute stragglers around the entrance, making sure they were all right to drive, climbing into cabs, laughing, puking, and promising to meet again for another round of revelry.

He slowed to a crawl, searching the sea of faces for a familiar one. He'd been staring at Karimah's all night long. He had that face indelibly imprinted in his mind, so he knew what he was looking for. He spotted her standing against the wall. The beams from his headlights must have temporarily blinded her, but— for Justin—they set her off in the most appealing light. He could see every detail with crystal-clear clarity. She wore a two-piece denim outfit of form-fitting, acid-washed jeans and a cropped jacket covered with buttons of all shapes, sizes, and slogans. Her hands were tucked into the pockets of her jeans. To the casual observer, she might have been hiding them to keep them warm from the cool, February chill. Justin suspected that she might just as well be keeping a firm grip on that mini stun gun that she had been known to brandish.

Kallista's left knee was bent, with her foot planted against the wall. Hints of brown skin showed through a thinning space in the knee where the denim was stretched to its limit. Her gaze was focused on some point beyond him, and her eyes tracked the sporadic progress of cars out on the main highway. She seemed to be searching, too. For Karimah, maybe? Or for that security agent, Brandt? Each time a car passed that she didn't recognize, Justin thought he saw her proud shoulders slump a little more. He could see indecision on her face, too. Should she go back inside? She glanced over her shoulder at the entrance. Or should she wait a little longer? Her gaze turned back to the road.

This was no place for a lady who was all alone. He wondered where that tipsy friend of hers was—the one who'd called to come rescue Kallista. *Come to think of it,* Justin mused, *this is no place for a man all alone, either.* He found himself wishing for the hulking presence of Faizon. But Faizon was keeping an eye on Emeril. When Justin had called him and told him that he would be later than expected, he could hear the tightness in Faizon's voice. Then he'd explained how he was going after the other sister, and Faizon became friendly again. Friend or foe, Justin could have used that big man right about now. He tooted the horn once, then twice, to get Kallista's attention. She ignored the sound at first. Too many horns had already gone off. He considered whistling for her, then heard his grandmother's voice reminding him how to treat a lady. He would simply have to walk up to her to let her know that someone had finally come to her rescue.

The last group of hard-core stragglers stumbled out the door. Kallista was so still, so quiet, that she hoped they would pass by without noticing. Once they were gone, she intended to duck back inside and call Karimah once again. She'd already dialed the store several times but didn't get an answer. She'd called the house, but the answering machine picked up. She and that Justin Malloy must be having one hell of a strategy meeting. Kallista checked her watch. Almost three o'clock in the morning. Maybe they'd gone off to have an early breakfast—IHOP or Denny's or something. She wished that she didn't feel this way, but she really hoped that they were out somewhere in public.

When she checked her watch again, the sudden movement caught the attention of some stragglers. Like a chain reaction in a domino rally, first one turned, then another, then another. She could feel their eyes on her—bloodshot, curious, crazy. They were a little too juiced up to let the night end on such a disappointing note. She could almost see the drunken brains thinking, planning. They were twisting themselves up for one more party, with her as the star performer. Kallista lifted her chin, meeting their stares. She hadn't accepted any invitations to join them all evening, and she certainly wasn't going to accept now—when she had even less control over what could happen to her.

In retrospect, Justin would realize that the events that were unfolding at this moment happened in only a matter of minutes. But for now, time seemed to move agonizingly slow for him. He would later remember every detail. He could see Kallista's reaction to those men—beauty marred by belligerence. Later, he would wonder why he'd chosen that moment to think of her as beautiful. Later, he would wonder why he continued to think of her at all. Yet, here he was, early in the morning, answering the call of gallantry. For the second time, he was charging to her rescue. Her predicament awakened feelings of protectiveness and possession that no sane human being should feel—considering the short time he'd known her.

Emeril had questioned his sanity. Maybe he should question it, too. She had given him no reason to foster these feelings for her. She had not smiled at him in any special way. She had not flirted or chased or made overtures to give him any hope that she would want him. There was nothing he could point out with certainty that made him think that she wanted him or needed him at all.

Or had she? Had she, just being Kallista Hart, given him everything he needed to pursue the possibility of a relationship with her? Had her very essence beckoned to him? Justin was imaginative and fanciful when he had to be, especially when it pertained to his work. In his daily life, he was Mr. Practical.

Was that backwards? Perhaps so. But, up until now, it had served him well. It had helped him gain a measure of success. He saw no reason to change this outlook. Until now.

Now would be a really good time to show up, Kari! Kallista thought in irritation as several men ringed her in. She regretted turning down that ride from Jacie's brother. When she saw how tired and bleary-eyed he had been, she didn't have the heart to ask a stranger to drive her back home. Someone she knew was coming for her if she could just wait a little longer. Kallista gripped her taser, using whatever sense of security it offered her.

Come on. Where are you?

She'd even welcome that Justin Malloy right now. *Even though he probably wouldn't be any use to me,* she thought. She told herself that it was the annoyance at her predicament that made her so testy. She ignored the tiny voice inside her that said it might be jealousy, and she fast-forwarded past the images of Karimah and Justin making love. After Karimah had finished working him over, he'd be too sated, too languid, to fight off any aggressors.

Justin increased the length of his stride as he walked up the cobbled path leading to the bar's entrance. As he walked, he prepared himself for a confrontation by building an impenetrable wall around himself—a bad-ass wall that said ''Don't mess with me.'' His Italian suit said that he had money for lawyers to buy him out of trouble. His hardened expression warned anyone of writing checks their behinds couldn't cash. By the time he'd reached the fringes of the straggling, slobbering drunks who'd ringed her in, he was projecting an attitude that cut through the stench of their breath.

To dispel any doubt of who he was and what he was there for, Justin snaked his arm around Kallista's waist. After uttering an apology for lateness that everyone could hear, he leaned forward to lay a possessive kiss on her lips. Was it the adrenaline flowing through him in preparation for a fight? Was it the suppressed sexual stimulation for the sake of keeping it all business with Karimah? Or was it the mingled look of surprise, relief, and suspicion on Kallista's face? Justin wasn't sure what made him kiss her initially. But he knew one thing: it was her reaction to him that caused him to hold, and even push the bounds, of the kiss. What had started out as a display for the sake of getting her out of trouble turned out to happen for his own benefit and pleasure.

An acerbic acknowledgement of his presence died before it ever reached Kallista's lips. Pure sensuality sprang to life. The witty wisecrack disappeared when he coaxed her lips open and touched his tongue to hers. She should have been yelling at him for keeping her waiting for so long, but she found herself soundlessly giving in to nonverbal cues that instead made her welcome him.

She'd forgotten that she was secretely mad at him for staying with Karimah so long. She'd even conveniently forgotten that she'd belittled him, thinking that he was too weak to get her out of trouble again. She should have known better. There was nothing weak about this man. Not his words. Not his ways. And certainly not his kiss. If she'd known that computer geeks were like this, she would have hung around the programmer's lab in college. Maybe it was all the typing on the computer keyboard that put the unique mixture of strength and finesse in his hands. There was no fumbling, no guesswork. He knew exactly where to touch her. When his palms caressed her along both sides of her spine, she arched her back, leaning into him. If she had been a cat, she would have purred.

Justin encircled her with both arms, inviting her into the warmth of his embrace. Time stood still, and everything about her crystallized in his mind: the thud of her heart against his chest, and feeling the warmth of her thighs pressed against the length of his would remain in his memory. He expected a moment like this to be awkward and forced. There was so much working against them: brevity of time, the influence of alcohol, business ethics. If he wanted to, he could come up with at least a hundred reasons why he shouldn't be kissing her. The truth was that he didn't *want* to come up with those reasons. He simply wanted to kiss her. And he wanted her to kiss him back. It was a simple wish—one that Kallista fulfilled with more enthusiasm than he would have thought possible from her.

"Get a room!" someone yelled, tapping Justin on the shoulder.

The interruption was like a cold dash of reality. He broke apart from her, fumbling in his pocket for a handkerchief to wipe the traces of the kiss from his lips. As he backed away, he said something about it being a long, late night.

Kallista cleared her throat and muttered something about having one too many beers. The wall of forgetfulness and disregard of convention came tumbling down around them. If she didn't say something quick to ease this horrible tension, it would be one very long ride back home.

She looked up and said the first thing that popped into her mind. "Happy Valentine's Day, Malloy."

Justin paused in his tracks. He'd almost forgotten about that. This was the most romantic day of the year, and here he was backpedaling as fast as his feet could carry him. What was the matter with him? This was worse than college. Hadn't he had enough of letting "the good ones" pass him up? He looked at her, the one Hart he'd been more than happy to rush out to get. Throwing caution and convention to the wind, he took her hand in his.

Chapter Nine

Justin and Kallista held hands during the entire drive back to Houston, until he pulled up to the boutique. When he cut the engine, an unspoken cue caused them to also cut the physical connection. Kallista withdrew her hand from his and folded both hands primly in her lap.

"We're here," Justin said unnecessarily.

"I'll ... I'll just go inside and see if Karimah's ready to go," Kallista said quietly and slowly unbuckled her seatbelt.

"Okay," Justin responded. What he'd been anticipating—agonizing about—was here. The awkwardness he didn't want to experience with her was crowding in. When had it started? He couldn't be sure. Where was that vibrant, intelligent woman who'd fired all kinds of questions at him about his plans for their business during the drive back?

She had asked things like: How much space would they need on the ISP's server? Could he suggest a billing company that could handle high-volume online purchases? What was the best encryption software to protect their customers against hackers and credit-card fraud? She'd done her research and expected definitive answers from him.

He hated to admit it, but he'd kept his proposal to Karimah simple because he didn't expect she wanted to know the details. Listening to Kallista, he regretted not including her in the meeting. But, if things had worked out that way, he wouldn't have shared that kiss.

He glanced at her now. She was acting as if the events of the night had never occurred. A quiet, reserved imitation of Kallista had somehow appeared. When she glanced up at the door, he thought he saw something in her face. Apprehension. Reluctance. She didn't *want* Karimah to join them. For reasons that mystified yet pleased him at the same time, she didn't want to share this moment, this man, with her sister.

"I'll be back in a minute," Kallista promised.

"I'll be right here," he said easily. But he was starting to get a very uneasy feeling inside. He couldn't explain it. His grandmother would have called it a premonition. He felt like he should gear up for another fight. But, unlike the stragglers at the Ice House, he couldn't identify this foe. He glanced over his shoulder, feeling the proverbial hairs on the back of his neck stand on end.

"Wait a minute, Kallista. I'm going with you," he called out to her.

After Kallista smiled encouragingly, he wasn't sure what was going on inside of that head of hers. He wasn't sure what was going on inside of his *own*. He was only certain of what he felt in his heart. Something told him that if he let her walk through that door to be eclipsed by the flaring energy and personality of Karimah Hart, he would never get his Kallista back. That sister would consume her. Kallista would find some reason for regretting the kiss. She would find some way of snatching back the pieces she had shared with him. He couldn't allow that to happen.

He had told Karimah that he knew a good opportunity when he saw one. He'd adopted that attitude to keep him from being afraid of risking whatever it took to get his business off the ground. Now, he was presented with a golden opportunity of a different kind. Kallista was that opportunity—offering him something more to his life than work. He wasn't going to let her walk away from him.

"Hold up, Kallie," he repeated, then said almost shyly, "I don't think you should go in there by yourself at this time of night."

Kallista was more pleased by his use of her nickname than by his chivalrous offer to escort her inside.

"You don't have to worry about me."

"Yes, I do," he countered. Justin wasn't quite ready to reveal his reasons for not letting her out of sight.

She opened the door and stepped inside, reaching for the control panel to deactivate the motion sensor alarm—and saw that it had already been deactivated. If Karimah were still here, she wouldn't have set it. She could never remember how to configure the box so that it would only monitor the parts of the store she had no intentions of roaming. The upstairs offices were usually monitored only by cameras when someone was working late. It was easier to just move around without worrying about setting off the silent alarm.

"Kari?" she called out.

When she received no answer, Justin offered, "She must still be in her office upstairs . . . asleep."

"Yeah. Right. Asleep," Kallista said, giving her sister the benefit of the doubt. "Passed out" didn't sound as kind, but it was probably closer to the truth. She started toward the stairs leading to the upstairs offices. "Kari? Are you up here?" She raised her voice.

"Do you think she went home?" Justin asked.

"We tried to call there, remember? No answer. Besides, she said she'd wait for you here."

"It's almost five o'clock in the morning," Justin said, amazed that he was still awake. "Maybe she got tired of waiting."

''Kari's not the most patient person. But I thought she'd still be here . . . you know, really worn out after you and she, that is . . . after your meeting.'' Kallista had trouble looking at him.

Understanding dawned on Justin. No wonder she'd been so reluctant to go inside. She didn't know what state she expected to find her sister. Drunk? Disrobed? Just what kind of meeting did she imagine he had with her? Probably the same one that Karimah imagined that they would have.

''What we did at the meeting shouldn't have tired her out that much. It was strictly business.'' He took both Kallista's hands in his own. ''Trust me,'' he said, earnestly. He knew she would never come right out and ask whether or not he and Karimah had slept together. And he would not embarrass her by insinuating that she'd jumped to the wrong conclusion. The best that he could do was allay her fears. He tilted her chin to look him directly in the eyes. ''Do you?''

''Trust you?'' she echoed. ''That's a hard question, Justin. I have no reason to. I mean, we've only known each other a couple of days. Your nephew wanted to steal from me. You've spent way too much 'quality' time with my sister. And you're asking me if I trust you?''

''Will you?'' he pressed.

She nodded her answer, then said, ''Call me crazy.''

''Positively certifiable,'' Justin teased, leaning toward her. Kallista closed her eyes and turned her face up to meet his kiss once again.

''Well, well, well! What do we have here? Love birds finally come home to roost?''

For the second time that night, their perfect moment was interrupted, not by strangers, as they had been at the Ice House, but by Karimah. Kallista felt like cursing. Why couldn't she have stayed absent for a few more minutes?

She'd come around the corner, her arms laden with a pile of vibrant outfits. She paused at the bottom of the stairs, staring up at Justin and Kallista embracing. The strangest expression Kallista had ever seen crossed Karimah's face. Shock and disbelief registered first. Then, her face hardened to a mask deeper and darker than any of the statues Kallista had seen on her visit to the Artist's Alliance. The expression startled Kallista, making her want to pull away from Justin as if she'd just been caught doing something terribly naughty. Kallista hadn't felt so guilty since the time her mother came scolding from the back door, waving the rock that Kallista had thrown in one hand and broken dish in the other. She didn't move, but she must have somehow communicated her intention to Justin. He responded by tightening his grip on her hand.

"Hail! Hail! The gang's all here," Karimah sang mockingly. "So this is how you come back to me. If a thousand people would have sworn on a stack of Bibles a mile high, I would have never guessed it. My own sister . . ."

"Kari, let me explain—" Kallista began, but she stopped when Karimah brought her hands up, scattering the clothing.

"Save it. You don't have to explain anything to me. It's perfectly obvious to me what's going on. You're a cheating little tramp. You sneak around, hiding from me, taking what— by all rights—should be mine. What's there to explain?"

"Karimah, settle down," Justin interjected when he heard the gurgle of surprise from Kallista. "You're not making any sense. I told you from the beginning that you and I were business."

"You stay out of this. This is between my sister and me."

"You don't want him, Kari!" Kallista protested. "You said yourself that you and Faizon were better suited for each other."

"Faizon who?" Karimah spat.

"Look, it's late. We're all tired. Let's all go home and talk about this tomorrow when we're all thinking clearer." Justin tried to inject some sanity back into the situation. No matter how far off base Karimah Hart was, she had been right about one thing. He didn't want to deal with both sisters at the same time.

"Maybe you'd better go, Justin," Kallista began.

"Yeah, Justin," Karimah mimicked nastily. "Maybe you'd

better go. Sister dearest and I have some things we need to talk about.''

''Karimah, you'll feel better after you've had some rest,'' Justin suggested.

''You're the last person I'd want advice from,'' Karimah snarled. ''You're just another dog sniffing around, trying to take away what's rightfully mine.''

''Just how much did Kari have to drink?'' Kallista murmured out of the corner of her mouth. Karimah was giggly when she'd had a little too much. She got sleepy and, in the right company, frisky. She'd never seen this side of her before. Then again, this was the first time they'd ever been faced with having to share something they both wanted.

Justin threw Kallista a worried glance. He didn't like what he was hearing. He didn't like the fact that she was pouring all her venom on her sister.

Squeezing Kallista's hand in his, he led her down the stairs past a glowering Karimah. ''You're coming with me,'' he said firmly, for Kallista's ears only.

''Wait, Justin. I think we need to—'' Kallista began to protest.

''She's not going to listen to you, Kallie. She's not thinking clearly. Give her some time to calm down, to sleep it off.''

''I don't know,'' Kallista hesitated.

''I do. The sun's coming up. My eyes are going down. I'm exhausted. You must be, too.''

''Looks like Kari's got her second wind.''

''Let her blow and blow and blow the house in,'' Justin said with forced levity. ''These little piggies aren't hanging around to watch.''

''I don't want things to get so bad between us that I can't talk to her. We live together. We work together.''

''There *is* such a thing as too much togetherness, you know. You said you would trust me. Now's the perfect time to exercise that trust.''

''Where are we going?''

"To Faizon's house. I've got to pick up Emeril."

"I hope you're right, Justin. Kari and I have never fought like this before."

"My brother and I used to fight all of the time. Now we're best friends. I've never heard of siblings who didn't fight."

"Kari and I are more than siblings. We're twins," Kallista said, as if that explained everything to him. "Try to imagine this. All our lives, we've shared everything. We shared the same womb, then divided equally between us all our mother had to give. We drew our first breaths just moments apart from each other. There wasn't anything I wouldn't do for her, give to her. I believed that she felt the same about me, Justin. Nothing should change that. No wine—no matter how potent—should have made her look at me the way she just did. For a minute, I thought she despised me."

"Karimah doesn't hate you, Kallie," Justin soothed. He pressed his hand to her cheek. "And you don't have to feel like you have to give everything up for her. Cut the cords, honey. You're out of the womb now. If you don't put some distance between the two of you, she's gonna suck you dry."

Kallista closed her eyes. For the first time that she could remember, someone was asking her to step out of the shadows. She had taken a chance by reaching out for the warmth of Justin's caring. She was afraid of getting burned. What if it didn't work out between them? When her other relationships had not gone as she had hoped, there was always Karimah to go back to. If she cut herself off from the only one who had always accepted her for who she was, what would she do? Who would she be? Kallista didn't know.

Kallista awoke, not quite sure where she was. She tried to stretch. Her foot collided with the rails of a bed that was not her own. She cracked open an eye and peered around. This was definitely not her room. Bubble-gum pink was not her color. The huge, fluffy pillows and a canopy overhead made her feel as if she was floating on a big, pink, digustingly cheery cloud. Instinctively, she hated it, closing her eyes against the saccharin assault on her senses. The very thought of floating brought an unbidden nauseousness to her stomach. Remnants of beer and buffalo wings made her groan in anticipation of another round with the toilet bowl.

"Are you awake now?"

A young girl's voice, in between smacks of chewing gum, addressed her.

Kallista raised up on one elbow and responded carefully. "I think so."

"Good. I'll tell Mr. Justin. He's been waiting for you to wake up. He told me not to disturb you, but by the way you were moaning and talking in your sleep. I told him that you were already disturbed."

"What time is it?" Kallista asked, sitting up quickly. She immediately regretted that she had.

"If you're gonna puke, the bathroom is that way." The girl pointed the way with a neon-pink fingernail.

"Thanks." She swung her feet off of the edge of the bed. "I think I'll be all right."

"You'll feel better after you get it all out of your system."

"I'm working on it." Kallista smiled wanly. "I just want to do it on my own terms."

"I'm Chantal, Faizon's sister."

"Pleasure to meet you. I'm—"

"I know who you are. You're Kallista Hart."

"Did Justin tell you?"

"Nope. In fact, I told him," Chantal boasted. "I told him about you. That is, about you and your sister's boutique. If it weren't for me, he would never have brought Emeril to you."

"So fate is an eighteen-year-old girl," Kallista sighed.

"Seventeen," Chantal corrected. "I set some clothes out for you. We're about the same size. Except I think my breasts are bigger than yours. That's all right. Mr. Justin is crazy about you anyway."

"Really?" Kallista said bluntly, trying not to crack a smile. The girl's honesty was refreshing, if not entirely appropriate.

"He hasn't stopped talking about you."

Must be a condition of the household, Kallista thought wryly as she hauled herself off the bed. The girl kept talking, even when Kallista closed the door to the bathroom to start her shower. She was still talking, without a noticeable break, when Kallista came out fully clothed. She had no trouble picking up on the one-sided conversation.

Though she appreciated Chantal's generosity, her room, her clothes, and her youthful musings and observations, she wished for a little piece and quiet. Her mind was busy enough on its own. How in the world was she going to smooth things over with Karimah? She had been so angry last night, so vindictive. If it had been anything else with the potential to come between them, there would have been no question in her mind. Kallista simply would have let it go. Nothing was worth fighting her sister about. *Nothing.* She'd said it with bravado before, and she would say it again. As she stared at herself in the mirror, she practiced the smile that would make Justin believe that she was feeling better. Everything would be all right. But there weren't enough smiles in the world to make herself believe it.

"Mama's putting lunch on the table. You'd better come on out before Faizon eats it all," Chantal warned.

"I'm right behind you," Kallista promised.

"Here she is, Mama!" Chantal sang out.

"Chantal, honey. I told you not to go bothering that woman." A female version of Faizon pushed through the swinging door of the kitchen.

"She was no bother," Kallista said and mentally crossed her fingers behind her back. The girl meant well. She couldn't help it if her entire personality screamed "Pink!"

"Hello, honey. Welcome to my house. I'm Tansy Francone."

"How do you do, Ms. Francone," Kallista said, holding out her hand.

"Everybody 'round here calls me Mama Tansy. You do the same."

"Yes, ma'am," Kallista said, compromising.

"Sit down to the table, honey. I'll have lunch for you in just a minute."

"Oh, I'm not that hungry."

"Hush now. You look like a good wind could blow you away. Faizon! Butter! You bring those plates out here and set the table, now."

Faizon came in from the kitchen first, carrying a stack full of plates between his hands. Justin followed, balancing the flatware, several tall glasses, and a pitcher of iced tea. Kallista couldn't help noticing how good he looked. He didn't appear at all as if he'd only had a few hours sleep. Only the dark five o'clock shadow against his light brown skin gave any evidence that he was any worse for wear. He wore only his dress shirt and slacks. His tie and suit jacket were laid carefully against the back of the couch when they'd come in. How could he look so good when she felt she must have looked like hell? Worry lines creased between her eyebrows, and she had bags beneath her eyes from her troubled sleep. And worse, she was dressed in the style of a seventeen-year-old.

To Justin, she couldn't have looked more beautiful. "No worms in your diet," he said, grinning at her. Kallista smiled back shyly. She was conscious of the eagle-eyed gaze of Mama Tansy, the curious looks from Chantal, the suspicious looks from Emeril, and the sly looks from Faizon.

"Everybody sit down now. Sit to the table before the food gets cold."

Protectively, possessively, Justin took Kallista's elbow and guided her to the table. "How did you sleep?" he whispered solicitously.

"Like there was a pea under my mattress," she responded.

"Better than a log," he said, making a comical face. "Faizon sawed his all night long."

She burst into real, hearty laughter this time. From that

moment on, she felt a little more at ease. The conversation was pleasant enough. Justin and Faizon were teasing each other like old times. Chantal and Emeril eyed each other across the table. Mama Tansy kept everyone's plate and glass filled. She chattered along, too, covering every subject under the sun. But Kallista had the distinct impression that there was a lot more to her than talk. Once, when Kallista fell silent, thinking about how she was going to break it off with Justin, she felt warm brown eyes on her. Not Justin's. They were Mama Tansy's. Kallista quickly lowered her eyes, pretending to be interested in the garnish on her plate. She had to look away to keep that woman from peering deep into her soul.

"Ready to go back?" Justin asked, reaching for Kallista's hand.

She nodded glumly, wordlessly. She didn't have to say anything. Justin felt the change in her as easily as he would a change in the wind. For a moment, he thought it was a reluctance to go back to face her sister. Things could have gotten pretty ugly last night. But when she pulled her hand from his, Justin experienced a moment of panic. It was something more than that. She was ready to go all right. She was ready to leave him. He shook his head, denying what he was starting to read in her eyes. *No.* He wouldn't let her go!

Mama Tansy stood up abruptly. "I've got more food than I can keep fresh in my old Frigidaire. Why don't you let me fix you and Kallie some plates to go, Justin. Come give me a hand in the kitchen."

It was a summons if ever Justin heard one. He smiled encouragingly to Kallista, then followed Mama Tansy back.

Chapter Ten

"Hand me that plastic wrap over there, Butter," Mama Tansy said, breaking the uncomfortable silence. Her back was to him as she laid out paper plates, dill pickle slices, and hero sandwiches. "That's a dear," she murmured when he handed her the package. "Do you think this will be enough for the two of you?"

He didn't want to talk. He didn't think he could force words over the lump in his throat.

"How 'bout some pie? I made me a couple of sweet potato pies last night. Just had me a taste for it. You take one of them back with you when you go."

"Yes, ma'am," he managed to croak.

"Anything else you think you might like, Butter?"

He shook his head no. This time she turned to face him. "Are you sure?"

"You trying to fatten me up, Mama Tansy?"

"No. I'm trying to smarten you up. That's a really sweet girl you've got out there, Butter. You sure you're not wanting her?"

Mama Tansy canted her head in the direction of the kitchen-ette. When she sat down, she rested her huge forearms on the wood-grain veneer top. When she leaned forward, the table creaked. She took Justin's hand and patted it. "Son, I've seen a lot of things. I'm old, and I'm sick. I'm not long for this world."

"Don't say that, Mama Tansy. You're going to bury us all."

She smiled. "I ain't afraid to die, Butter. What little time I've got left, I want to do all I can to make this world a little better place when I leave it. Now, you know that I've never been one to meddle. Maybe if I'd mothered less and meddled more, my Faizon wouldn't have been a guest of the County so many times. I love you like my son. When you let me, I'm gonna watch over you like I do my own. I'm gonna say this, then I'm gonna let you go . . ."

"What's that, Mama Tansy?"

"Justin, don't you let that woman get away from you."

He opened his mouth, ready to deny knowing what she was talking about.

She raised her finger and placed it to his lips. "I know she's kin to that woman who nearly drove my Faizon crazy trying to get things for her. And I know she's probably dealing with her own issues. But if there's anything else I know, I know this—you two belong together. You need her. She needs you. Nothing else—no one else—in this world matters. Don't be no fool. You take her hand, and don't you ever let go."

"Are you sure you don't want me to go with you, Kallie?" Justin asked, taking Mama Tansy's advice to heart. Kallista had insisted that he drop her off in front of the store and leave her there. She had to face Karimah on her own terms, on familiar grounds.

"Trust me this time, Justin," she said. "You being there would be like waving a red flag in front of a charging bull.

This is something we sisters need to work out. Thanks for being so sweet and wanting to rush to my rescue again.''

"I'll be there if you need me."

"I know. I'll keep that in mind."

"Say, Miss Kallista. You gonna eat that?'' Emeril asked, gesturing toward the lunch Mama Tansy had prepared for her.

"No, you can have it.'' Kallista made a small face that was no reflection on the food itself. She climbed out, taking a deep breath to steady herself. The thought of arguing with her sister was tying her stomach up in knots.

Emeril propped his elbow on the door and called out as they were pulling away. ''If she gets too rough, Miss Kallista, you could always juice her with that oversized bug zapper!''

"Watch your mouth, E!'' Justin cautioned, for the sake of being the responsible adult. But, he turned a comic look to Kallista as if to say, "Not a bad idea!''

"I'll call you,'' she mouthed to him, catching his eye in the rearview mirror. Then, on impulse, she blew him a kiss. As soon as she walked through the door, she ignored the odd looks from the employees. Brandt was making his rounds in the music section. He caught her reflection in one of the huge, hanging security mirrors. He started toward her, but Deandre read the ''do not disturb'' look on her boss's face. She grabbed his arm to hold him back. Later, when Kallista remembered the distance everyone gave her, she would be grateful for the perception and their wide berth of serenity they offered her. For now, she was feeling anything but serene. When she grasped the stairs where hours before she had argued with Karimah, her palms felt slick with sweat.

She took slow measured steps as she went over her prepared speech. She would say that she was sorry. She would tell her sister that she didn't want to fight. It wasn't worth it. She hoped that Karimah could forgive her. Even as she prepared to grovel, she wondered if she could forgive herself for backing down. She had been shadow-walking all of her life. This one time that she stepped into the light, the results were disastrous.

Karimah was in her office. Music was blaring. She must have had lunch delivered. Wafts of steamed vegetables, rice noodles, and shrimp-fried rice came through the crack of the door. Kallista paused. That was Karimah's "morning after" lunch. She only ordered it when in a good mood. Maybe this conversation wasn't going to go as badly as she feared. Kallista rapped once, then twice, with her knuckles before going in.

Karimah looked up, her expression pleased. "Oh, there you are. Come help me with these." She was sorting two stacks of clothes into piles by color, then by function.

"What's this, Kari?" Kallista asked, using work as an excuse to ignore the looming questions hanging heavily in the air.

"You tell me. I found them in a pile on the floor in one of the store rooms. I thought you had pulled them out to set up another display.

Kallista shrugged, then shook her head. She hadn't.

"I'm surprised to see you here," Karimah said, lifting one dress up to the light to examine its texture and craftsmanship. She hung a coordinated scarf around the hanger, then nodded in satisfaction at her creation.

'Why? Did you think I'd stay away after last night?''

"That's exactly what I'm talking about," Karimah said. "You and Justin must have had quite a night last night." Her expression was sly. "I'd say that I was jealous, but that wouldn't be true. More like greedy. I guess it doesn't make sense. I can't have them all."

Kallista blinked in total surprise. Her sister's tone and expression was almost gleeful.

"You're . . . you're not mad at me?" Kallista stammered.

"Mad? Why should I be mad? I told Justin to go after you."

"You told him to go after me?"

"Are you hard of hearing or something, Kallie? *Duh!* How else did you think he wound up at the Ice House? I sent him. You two are better suited for each other, anyway. As soon as I started talking to him last night, I thought 'Geez, this is just like talking to Kallie.' ''

"I don't get you, Kari."

"What's there not to get?" Karimah said, tossing a jacket to her sister, which came down and covered Kallista's face. "It's obvious you belong together. When you didn't show up last night, I figured that you'd figured that out on your own. So I called Faizon to come and get me."

"Whoa! Hold up a minute. What did you mean when we didn't show?" Kallista asked, snatching the jacket off her face. Had she heard right? "We came back for you just like Justin promised he would."

"Faizon took me home last night, Kallie," Karimah insisted. "Just how much did you drink last night?"

"I said the same thing about you. I'm not the one having the memory lapses."

"There's nothing wrong with my memory." Karimah denied. She put her hands on her hips and glanced around the clothes strewn about the room. "Now what was I going to do with these again?"

"So, you sure we're cool about Justin and me. You're not going to pull that web deal out from under him?"

"No more going out drinking with the girls again." Karimah wagged her finger in warning.

"No more. I swear." Kallista raised her hand. "I swear. I'm off the sauce for good."

"What about this one?" Kallista suggested, holding up a small vial of perfume.

"No. Not that one." Justin immediately dismissed it.

"Why not? What's wrong with it?" She hid the edge in her voice. As much as she was enjoying Justin's company, she was ready to call it a day. It had been a hard day today. For every shoplifter who easily gave up the goods, there was one they had to physically subdue. Brandt was out with a broken arm. Deandre was working their South-side store. All day long, she had been dealing with people who knew their jobs, but who didn't know her and how she liked to operate. The officers at the substation teased her, saying that they were going to move their storefront to her boutique if she kept calling them for backup support.

"You want to have your site pegged and registered for pornographic material? Blocked for children eighteen and under?" Justin teased her about her choice.

Kallista took another look at the vial. This was going to be harder than she thought. When she offered to help Justin find the items for the photo shoot, she hadn't expected all fun and games. But she hadn't expected this, either. The man was *very* serious about his work. Everything had to be just so. Now that Emeril had returned to his parents, Justin could throw himself wholeheartedly into his work. The only person more picky about what merchandise should be used to represent the store was Kallista herself. She didn't think there could be a tougher character than herself. But Justin was giving her a run for her money. Grudgingly, she admitted that she'd met her match in Justin Malloy—in more ways than business.

She had been attracted to the perfume vial because she knew the scent that was contained inside. It was one of her favorites. She wasn't thinking about the packaging. Justin took it from her hands and placed it back on the counter with a definitive thud. "We put a shot of that on your web site, and you'll get more hits from deviants than your counter can handle."

"Maybe you're right," Kallista said reluctantly.

"Trust me on this one, Kallie," Justin said, moving past her to search for more items.

Kallista picked up the item. "I still kind of like this one," she insisted. She held the vial up, fascinated by the way it caught the muted light from the store and reflected it in a kaleidoscope of colors—reddish purple, bluish green, even white light sparkled through the prism of the carefully crafted glass. "What's wrong with it? I think it's pretty."

"There's nothing wrong with the glass. Or even the scent of the perfume itself. It's the topper I object to. Or maybe I should say 'topless'?'' He raised an eyebrow to indicate an *Akua-ba* doll, a fertility figure from the Ashanti culture. The female adorning the top of the perfume bottle was bare to the chest and, to represent and celebrate womanhood, had been given obviously oversized breasts.

"What planet are you from? This is the first time I've ever heard a man complaining about an overly endowed woman," Kallista teased him.

"I'm an equal opportunity complainer," Justin said as he gestured toward the male version of the fragrance. "I'm not snapping pictures of *that* either."

Kallista bit her cheek to keep from laughing out loud. "What? I don't see anything wrong with that." The male figure was just as well endowed.

"Now I know what to get you for Christmas," Justin said with a wry smile. "Come on. What about that emerald-colored atomizer over there? Place it against the black, velvet cloth with that faux emerald and diamond necklace. That will make a pretty good shot."

Kallista fished her keys from her pocket and opened the case to retrieve the necklace. She paused. Memories of what had brought Justin to Karimah's in the first place caused her to turn and ask.

"So how is Emeril doing these days, Justin?"

"Better," Justin supplied. "He's seeing a child counselor to help him deal with the upheaval in his life."

"He really is a good kid."

"I know. If I didn't believe that, I wouldn't have offered to keep him for a few weeks this summer."

"Will you bring him to the store?" Kallista asked.

"Don't worry. I'll keep a better eye on him this time. He won't be lifting any more of your merchandise."

"I wasn't implying that . . . ," Kallista began, then closed her mouth. That's exactly what she was implying. It shouldn't bother her that he could read her so well. But it did. In the weeks after their first Valentine's Day kiss, they had steadily grown closer. There were times when it seemed uncanny. He could pick up on nonverbal cues, which only Karimah could read before. Either she was becoming more transparent, or as Karimah had told her, they really were soul mates.

"You know he's welcome here any time, Justin. After all, he really didn't take the necklace."

"But he wanted to."

"But he didn't," she countered.

"Yeah, but he . . . oh, never mind. I guess he's working through his issues of why he wanted to take the necklace in the first place."

She spread the velvet cloth over the counter as Justin instructed, then arranged the necklace and perfume bottle against it as he set up his tripod and spotlight.

" 'Bout ready?" Kallista asked over shoulder. Justin waved his hand to indicate that he'd heard her. He had his face pressed into the lens, concentrating on adjusting the camera position.

"Just about," he said.

As soon as Kallista moved out of the way, he snapped a few experimental shots. He then removed a disk from the digital camera and inserted it into the drive of his portable computer. His fingers flew over the keyboard, bringing up the images he'd just taken within seconds.

"What do you think of these, Kallie?" he asked.

She moved alongside him, peering at the images.

"These look really good. I'd move the necklace a little closer to the perfume, though. Maybe rearrange the stones so they don't look so magazine-ish. I want to give the impression that this could be any woman's dressing table. I know how my dressing table looks. Not nearly this neat and . . . arranged."

"You're no slob," Justin said appreciatively. Her style was simple, understated, utilitarian. She matched him in his penchant for wanting everything in its place.

"Well, if I had jewels like this, I would probably lay them out like so."

Justin nodded, appreciating her point of view. He didn't

consider himself a professional photographer. His forte was getting the pictures online. But he had enough knowledge of the process to know when something was working and when something wasn't. And at the moment, he just wasn't feeling it. He just wasn't getting excited about the shot. He supposed he was a little distracted. Hell, more than a *little* distracted. He couldn't keep his mind on what he was doing. All the employees were gone after hours. Karimah was off with Faizon somewhere. Why were they talking about jewelry when there was something more precious they could be discussing—Kallista herself. If he had to discuss jewelry, there was another piece he wanted to talk about, something marquise-cut, about one carat, and burning a hole in his pocket for the past three days.

After snapping a few pictures, Justin indicated that he was ready to move on to the next display. But Kallista wasn't quite ready. She was still in a strangely teasing mood. She held up the necklace.

"You sure you aren't part crow?" Justin asked. "Aren't they fascinated by shiny, sparkling things?"

"Maybe I am," Kallista conceded. "When I was a little baby, my father made this mobile for my bed. As the story goes, my mother had this lamp she had bought at a garage sale. It was an ugly thing, black and white, with fake, glass teardrop gems hanging from the lamp shade, which was lined with faux fur."

Justin made an oval with his mouth, expressing his opinion without words.

"My mother adored that lamp—my father hated it. One day, my father was vacuuming in the front room, and the lamp just mysteriously wound up in pieces all over the floor. The base of the lamp was smashed to bits, but nothing could break those teardrop crystals. He would never admit it, but I think he broke it on purpose. As a kind of consolation gift for my mom, he strung the crystals on my mobile so that she'd see them whenever she went in to check on us."

"I can see the two of you sharing a crib, with your chubby baby fingers reaching for those diamonds in the sky."

"Kari wasn't very interested in them. But I was. While Mama picked her up and rocked her to soothe her crying, I would sit for hours and hours watching those gems go round and round and round. Sometimes, I still think I can hear the tune of the music box in my head."

Kallista closed her eyes and hummed a few bars of a lullaby. She held the necklace out in front of her, slightly above her head.

Justin stepped closer to her and took the necklace from her. Then, on impulse, he clasped it around her neck. As his fingers touched the back of her neck, Kallista felt the skin prickle. The pulse at the base of her neck quickened as she held her breath.

"There," he said softly. "You can stop reaching. They're yours now."

"One of these days, they'll be the real thing."

"Is that what you want, Kallie? More stuff? More clutter? I thought you had everything you ever wanted. Good friends, a thriving business . . ."

"Not everything," Kallista admitted. She raised her eyes to look at him. The look was bold, open, and unashamed. "Not completely all mine."

Justin paused, taking in her expression and the expectant silence between them. And, in that instant, he knew what he had been wanting all along. He leaned forward slowly and brushed his lips across hers. Kallista sighed and closed her eyes. She swayed toward him and raised her arms to rest them comfortably behind his head. The back of his head was warm and smooth. Her fingers caressed the creases in his neck.

With a muted groan, Justin splayed his fingers against her back and pressed her to him. He backed her against the glass counter, pressing his hardness into her. Passion flared within him as his hunger crushed his reservation.

Kallista's response was instantaneous. It was as if someone had lit a match to the dry tinder which had been her heart.

Breathless, greedy, desperate to feel more of him, she tugged at his shirttails, jerking the tucked ends out of his pants as if they would burn him if she didn't free him. Justin pushed into her, his fingers working frantically, desperately to free her of the clothes. The bone-colored buttons down the front of her linen dress were no match for the fingers that blazed to undo them. Within seconds, the two halves of the dress lay open. He grasped her by the hips and lifted her onto the glass-topped display counter. His fingers massaged her dark thighs and trailed over and behind her knees.

Kallista lifted up as well, clasping her ankles behind him. She scooted closer to the edge of the counter, pressing the core of her desire next to him. Justin hooked his finger into the leg band of her underwear and tugged. She opened her mouth, trying to tell him how much she needed and craved his touch, but the words wouldn't come out. For once in her life, she was silent. Her responses were primal, pouring from a place in a soul where words had no place. They were too inadequate to truly express her feelings. It was all in the touch, all in the breath, and all in the glance. Kallista reached between them, grasping his manhood and easing it toward her. He clasped his hand over hers. Full contact was separated by the width of a small foil package.

"I think we're going to need more of these," Justin predicted as he unwrapped his last condom. Later, there would be time for tender touch and softly whispered words of sweet endearment. For now, there was the call of the flesh—and their answer to it.

"Kallie, do you know how long I've wanted to touch you like this?"

She shook her head, not sure whether she was answering his question or quickly forming a denial. She knew better than to make him answer this. She just might hear something she didn't want to hear. She didn't want to hear him try to make her believe that it was she that he wanted all along, and not the vibrant Karimah.

"Sh . . . don't tell me anything, Justin. Don't say a word. Just . . . just hold me. Touch me."

"You don't believe me?" His voice was raw. "A man can't fake a feeling like this, Kallie. You believe that, don't you?"

"How do I know that it's me?" she asked. "How do I know that you aren't settling for me because you can't have Karimah?" She needed him to quell her doubts, once and for all.

"I *can* have Karimah," Justin said tightly. "She made that very clear to me—even when she and Faizon were working things out. But I made my choice, sweetheart. It's you. It's always been you." He ended there. He didn't know what else to say. How could he show her that she was the one?

He reached for her hand and raised it to his lips. She didn't pull away, but she didn't respond, either—not like the way she'd responded moments before. She'd been so full of passion. Now, there was nothing but poison. He wanted to draw the poison from her, to squeeze out every last drop until there was nothing but pure love for her coursing through her veins.

"You have to believe me, Kallie. You're the one I want. Only you."

He drew a finger into his mouth, applying slow, steady suction, and moved it in and out of her mouth. Kallista thought she wanted to scream. But her throat was closed. All she could manage was a low, soundless sigh at sensations so pleasurable they were almost painful. She felt herself throbbing, pulsing, and wishing that the magic he was working on her hand would be shown to all parts of her body.

"Justin!" she cried out, pulling him toward her again.

"I know, Kallie, I know." He soothed her and rocked against her. This time, flesh met flesh. He stepped away for a brief moment. His skin was flushed, and his hands trembled slightly.

Kallista took the condom from him. She was surprisingly calm for someone who felt like she was going insane. With a slight dip of his knees, followed by a slow thrust forward, he was suddenly inside of her. Kallista gasped, her mind blown by the touch she had so often dreamed of but never imagined that she would experience.

Justin pulled his hips back and thrust again, this time deeper, sheathing more of himself within Kallista's deep recesses. She clutched his arms just above his elbows. She could feel the muscles in his arms bulging as he moved inside of her. Forward and back. Forward and back. He clutched the counter to steady himself as the tempo increased to match her throaty urgings. She looked up, her eyes only partially focusing on a spot beyond his head. She continued to caress him, holding his head at the juncture of her neck and shoulder as he continued to drive into her. Faster and deeper. Deeper and faster. Intensity building as the time lapse between each thrust shortened. She could feel him, thick and throbbing, slick and surreal. He grasped her derriere. Kallista didn't think it was possible, but the feeling intensified.

She rocked with him, lifting off the glass to meet him. Perspiration gathered along her bottom, causing her to slide against the case. Their scents mixed and filled the air with the smell of pure sensuality. She sniffed deeply as his unique male scent and her female scent blended together. It was more powerful than any manufactured scent, and Kallista wished she could distill its essence and keep it for all time.

"Kallie!" Justin cried out her name. He was too near the brink. He needed a lifeline to bring him back. On the other hand, he wanted to jump. He wanted to plunge and drown himself in her depths. Each time he buried himself within her, he wanted to stay there—but he couldn't. He had to keep moving; he had to keep surging into her. He wasn't sure why. He just knew that he couldn't stop, he wouldn't stop—even when he was sure that his heart was about to burst free from his chest, he would still take this woman and claim her for his own.

Chapter Eleven

"How much are you selling this piece for?" Justin asked. He was putting away some small figurines after their photo shoot and ran across one that he wouldn't mind having in his own collection. Kallista came up behind him, wrapping her arms around him.

"Oh, I don't know," she whispered seductively in his ear. "Maybe we can work out some kind of trade."

"You've got something worth trading?" he teased her.

"What do you think?" she asked, kissing him on the back of his neck. Justin moaned. She could feel the depth of his emotion rumble from his torso all the way up to his throat. He set the statue on the countertop, with the intention of picking Kallista up and carrying her to her office where he could show her exactly what he thought—and felt.

When the statue scraped against the glass top, the resulting screech caught Kallista's attention. She turned a curious gaze toward it.

"Where did you get that?" she asked.

Justin shrugged. "I found it over there somewhere by those Kwele masks. Why?"

"I don't recognize the piece."

"Kallista!" Justin laughed at her, then tapped her forehead. "You can't possibly keep track of every item in the store."

"Then what good am I as the store's security head?" Kallista remarked dryly. She released her grip on Justin and picked up the statue. "That's my job to know. I must need a break. For the past few weeks, more and more stuff like this has been happening to me."

"Stuff like what?"

She shrugged. "I don't know. Merchandise appearing out of place. Items I don't recognize showing up. At first I thought it was because Karimah had been dealing with the new artists since I started working with you. I thought she was just being Karimah, not keeping careful records and letting things slip through the cracks. So, I started going behind her to check her records—and it still doesn't add up."

"You have been working too hard."

"Maybe you're right." She placed the statue back in his hand. "You want it—it's yours. Consider it payment for services rendered."

"Go ahead. Make me feel like your boy toy," he called after her as she moved around the store preparing to close up shop.

She crooked her finger at him, smiling seductively before turning off the lights for the evening.

Flashing lights greeted Kallista as she pulled up to one of Karimah's boutiques on the south side of town. She'd arrived early to help Deandre open up. As she pulled into the drive, she couldn't see Deandre's car. Several marked cars bearing the logo of the Houston Police and the sheriff's department blocked the entrance.

"Now what?" she muttered. It couldn't be a routine pickup. Not with this kind of firepower. It couldn't be a break-in. If the silent alarm had been triggered, she would have been notified by the security company employed to monitor after hours.

She climbed out of the car, looking for someone in charge to give her some answers. Kallista recognized one of the officers from the substation who often answered her call to help her process shoplifters from their new store on the northeast side. Before she could wave him over, a female plainclothes officer started walking toward her. She wore a dark windbreaker with POLICE written in bright letters on the back, and she had a poker face that even Kallista would have difficulty duplicating. She strode over, flanked by two uniformed officers.

Kallista didn't know what was going on. It didn't take a genius to figure out that whatever the officer had to say wouldn't be good. She recognized the same no-nonsense look on the lady officer's face that Kallista used when she was about to confront suspected shoplifters.

Kallista stopped where she was, forcing the woman to come to her. "Can I help you?" Kallista called out, lifting her chin to stare into the woman's steely, blue eyes. "I'm Kallista Hart. My sister and I own this place."

"Ms. Hart, I'm Detective Morrissy. Can I have a moment with you please?"

"What's going on?" Kallista asked crisply. It was seven o'clock in the morning, and she didn't appreciate having her own detention tactics thrown back at her. Being faced with the same treatment, she resolved herself to appear more sympathetic the next time she addressed a customer sweating it in her command center. It was no fun being on the opposite end of law enforcement.

The detective held a piece of paper in front of her nose. "Ms. Hart, we have a search warrant for the premises."

"A search warrant? What are you looking for?" Kallista snatched it from her and scanned the contents. Her fingers convulsed around the paper. She didn't believe it. Even as she was reading it, she refused to believe that this was happening.

"Could you open the store please, ma'am?"

Kallista considered outright defiance. She wanted answers, not commands poorly disguised as pleasantries. Then again, what did she have to lose by refusing? She reached into her pocket and pulled out her keys. After deactivating the alarm, she gestured grandly, allowing Detective Morrissy and her team to pass inside.

From that moment, the surreal events playing out in front of her turned into a virtual nightmare. She watched as Detective Morrissy went into action, directing the flow of the search all around. The officers called orders to each other, efficiently dividing up the store into search quadrants to make sure every inch was covered.

"What are you looking for?" Kallista demanded. She walked behind one officer, then another, asking the same question. She watched as they rifled through racks of clothing.

"If it's a discount you're looking for, you're going about it the wrong way," Kallista said sarcastically. For a brief moment of imagined sanity, she thought that it wasn't a police raid at all. Maybe it was an elaborate burglary ring. She'd heard it could happen. Documents could be faked or forged. Uniforms could be duplicated or stolen. Kallista wouldn't mind the loss of the merchandise as long as she could report it to the true police later. Most of the inventory was cataloged or photographed. If thieves tried to fence it, it would be too hot to move. She'd get most of it back. Yet, this didn't have the sordid feel of thievery. Kallista knew what that felt like. This raid had a more sinister feel. It was too close to home—too much like reality.

"Wait a minute! What are you doing!" she called out when several officers returned to the front of the store, where Detective Morrissy stood overseeing the raid. They were carrying armloads of clothing in their arms.

"Load it up," Morrissy directed with a tilt of her head.

"I want answers—and I want them right now," Kallista demanded. She didn't raise her voice. She kept the same tightly controlled tone that Morrissy used on her team.

"Could you turn around please, ma'am?" Morrissy said. "Place your hands on the counter."

Kallista was too stunned to not comply. She turned around, allowing herself to submit to the type of search that she had often performed. When Morrissy reached for a pair of handcuffs, leaving no doubt about what she intended to do, Kallista felt a wave of panic sweep over her. *What are they doing? They can't treat me like this. What have I done to deserve this?*

"Will you at least tell me what the charge is?" Kallista demanded, twisting around to get a better look at Morrissy. She wanted to look into this woman's eyes. She wanted to confront her accuser face-to-face. They were about to arrest her! The least that they could do was look at her, not treat her like so much scum. Another officer moved into Kallista's field of vision, there to help subdue Kallista in case she got violent.

"Kallista Hart. You are under arrest for the possession and sale of counterfeit designer merchandise. You have the right to remain silent . . ."

Kallista closed her eyes and shut her ears while the officer read her rights. She didn't know how, but she must have answered when Morrissy asked if she understood her rights. The next thing she knew, they were ushering her into the back of a squad car. Like some sort of obscene blessing, Morrissy placed her hand on top of Kallista's head and guided her into the seat.

How could she understand her rights when she didn't clearly understand what was happening to her? How could she be arrested? What had she done? She'd always lived her life by a code of honor and ethics. She didn't lie. She didn't cheat. She didn't steal. Her code demanded that she deal fairly and decisively with everyone. This couldn't be happening to her. She supposed she should shut her mind down. Denying reality was easy enough if you drank enough, or snorted enough, or turned inward enough.

She couldn't check-out of reality now. Not when she had finally found it within herself to want something more out of life. She fervently held onto the belief this was a mistake that could be sorted out. Kallista wouldn't release that belief even as they took her to the police station for processing. Faith was the only thing that kept her calm.

In the holding cell, she didn't discuss her charges or her reason for being there with others who had been incarcerated. She was going to save her energy, her eloquence for those who could help her. When the time came for her one phone call, she was terse in her explanation to Karimah. With the embarrassment factor aside, all her sister needed to know was where she was and how much it would cost to bail her out.

Kallista surprised herself at how calm she was during her arraignment. With the support of family and friends behind her, she had no reason not to have the utmost faith in the ultimate triumph of justice over those silly, trumped-up charges. When she was brought before the judge and asked to enter a plea, it took every ounce of her strength to keep from shouting, "No!" She was not guilty, and she didn't understand how anyone could believe for one ludicrous moment that she was.

Kallista had been in a courtroom many times before. She'd stood ready, waiting to give her account of what was stolen from her, when, and by whom. She had always gone into the hearing confident that she was right. Now that *she* was the accused, she somehow had to hang on to that same sense that justice would prevail. Wrapping her dignity around her like a shroud, she stood silently. This time, her lawyer, Marti Barnett, would have to give an account of the truth.

When Marti Barnett called out in clear, crisp tones, "Not guilty, your honor," Kallista lifted her chin and stared back defiantly at the judge. If for any reason her picture appeared in the media, she didn't want it to give even the smallest suggestion that she had anything to hide. No hurried dashes through the courtroom halls. No hiding her face behind newspapers or coats. With head held high, she would remain proud until completely exonerated.

The prosecuting attorney tried to make her appear like a

flight risk, and he wanted to set her bail at a ridiculous amount. Kallista's composure almost broke—with laughter. She was such a workaholic. She couldn't remember the last time she had a vacation in a different state—let alone had the inclination to skip town. Again, Marti came to her defense. In a few short sentences, she summed up the essence of Kallista's life.

"Your honor, Kallista Hart is an upstanding member of her community. She has numerous ties to that community. She is a respected business entrepreneur, an active member of the church, a woman who's dedicated herself to curbing the very activities that she's being charged with. To suggest that she would be a flight risk is an insult. These very proceedings are an affront to independent, intelligent, African-American women everywhere."

The judge halted Marti just shy of flag-waving. She would be given the chance to preach during her closing statement if this case ever came to trial. Though Marti's statement had been cut short, something must have registered with the judge. He reduced Kallista's bail—enough to make Kallista believe that the world hadn't gone completely mad. Yet, it was still high enough so that, even with a bail bondsman, her family would have to scramble for the funds to free her.

As Kallista was led back to her holding cell, she scanned the crowd for familiar faces. They would be her lifeline. *Her family.* She certainly had enough of them to keep her hopes afloat. They'd come out en masse to support her. Her father and mother had flown in from Florida to be with her. Aunts, uncles, and cousins she'd rarely spoken to crowded into the courtroom. She was not surprised to see Karimah and Justin sitting as near to the front row as they could. Faizon was also there. Kallista hid a bittersweet smile. She figured a courtroom was the last place Faizon wanted to see. Kallista raised her eyebrows in surprise when she saw Miss Tansy push the doors open and walk as quickly as her wide girth would allow to a seat beside Faizon. She blew Kallista a kiss, letting her know that she was with her. Tears sprang into Kallista's eyes. This was too much. It was just too much.

As she was led away, her eyes fell on Deandre and Brandt and enough employees of all three boutiques to make her wonder with sweet sarcasm how they were going to raise the money to get her out of there if no one was minding the store. She turned her gaze forward again, and she thought she caught another familiar face in the crowd. She was surprised. Kallista didn't think her pitiful case caused that much of a stir. The knowledge of her arrest wouldn't have traveled far beyond the bounds of her community. If that were the case, what was *she* doing here?

CeCe was sitting in the rear of the courtroom. Kallista almost didn't recognize her. She'd cleaned up considerably since their chance meeting at the Artist's Alliance. Her hair now sported a fashionable, new cut. The gray-streaked blond strands were now dyed platinum. Her paint-splattered smock was replaced with a stylish Donna Karan suit. She was even wearing makeup. Kallista did a double-take to make sure she was not mistaken. Telling herself to memorize the faces to be able to thank them later for their support, Kallista stared hard for as long as she could at the crowd. Every familiar face, every name, was stamped onto her memory. If it took the rest of her life, she would have to thank them all.

After the bailiff led Kallista away, her family and friends filed out of the courtroom. "They can't do this!" Tranquility repeated. "They can't do this to my baby. Xavier, do something! I didn't carry my girls for nine, ankle-swelling, back-breaking, bean-sprout craving months to lose one now."

"The DA thinks he's got an airtight case against her," Faizon said glumly. "We can get her out on bail, but proving her innocence is not going to be easy. Trust me. When you're trying to prove yourself innocent, it seems as though the whole world is against you."

''We got her through diapers, pimples, and periods. We can get her through this,'' Xavier declared.

Justin paced up and down in the corridor, waiting for Marti Barnett to come and give them directions on how they should proceed.

''Sit down, Justin. You're wearing a groove in the floor,'' Faizon admonished.

''You're making me tired just watching you,'' Miss Tansy wheezed. She thanked Xavier as he gave his seat on the bench to her. Xavier wasn't sure what caused him to look up when he did. A feeling, maybe, or divine intervention. Up until now, he'd ignored the constant flow of traffic in and out of the courtroom. Those were other cases unrelated to his daughter. He had his own private pain to suffer through without caring about the pain of others. But, he did look up, and for a moment, he was transported back over thirty years. A face, much changed yet achingly familiar, stood out. There were a few more lines around the grayish eyes, and a little too much paint on the lips. But it was her.

Their eyes met. Recognition registered. For a moment, Xavier thought he saw a glimpse of a smile. Then, in an instant, it was gone. She was gone—swallowed by a press of bodies. Xavier took several steps away from his family. He craned his neck over the crowd.

''Xavier? Where are you going?'' Tranquility called out to him.

''Chasing ghosts,'' Xavier murmured to himself. He turned back to his wife, shaking his head and saying nothing. Why worry her? She had enough on her mind as it was. Why would he bring up the fact that he thought he'd just seen the woman who'd almost killed Tranquility and their twins? How could he come up with a gentle, polite way of saying that after all of these years, Chastity Cain had surfaced?

Chapter Twelve

She was going to get to the bottom of this. Kallista didn't know how, or when, or what it would take. But she was going to find out how those items got into her boutique if it was the last thing she ever did. She trusted Marti Barnett. When she'd met with Marti's private investigator, Kallista felt better about her prospects. Yet, she would never have true peace until she'd done what she always did—taken matters into her own hands.

The investigator seemed competent, but Kallista was familiar with the inner workings of her stores. She knew each employee by name and enough information about each of them to make them seem more like an extended family. Her employees knew her and trusted her. She could get them to do things that no outsider would be able to do, no matter how sincere the offer to help.

Piece by piece, item by item, Kallista called for an inventory of every article in all three boutiques. She had each store manager pull sales records from at least six months back. Since every item was scanned before it was sold, Kallista compared her records of items ordered against items sold.

Day and night, night and day, she and the private investigator poured over documents. Foregoing food and often sleep when she could, Kallista became obsessed with tracking down the gap in her system that had allowed so much contraband material to slip by her.

Justin could begin to see the strain wearing on Kallista. Her trial was in four weeks, and he didn't know if she would last that long. Because of the sleep and food deprivation, Kallista seemed to be wasting away before his very eyes. She'd beome a mere shadow of her former self.

"Kallie, baby. You've got to get some rest," he encouraged her. "You're going to make yourself ill." He wrapped his arms around her waist as she sat at her desk.

"You want to know what's making me sick?" she countered tightly. "All of the people who say they want to help but wind up cutting out in the end." At one o'clock in the morning, the private investigator had left for the night. Karimah had said that she'd be back after taking her parents home. But that had been two hours ago. Kallista suspected that she'd taken a detour to Faizon's house on the ride back—if she was even coming back. Only she and Justin remained to pore over the remaining documents.

Up until a definitive time period, Kallista's records had been perfect. Every item was accounted for. She compared photos of items that were confiscated from the store to descriptions of merchandise that she'd either commissioned from artists or bought from wholesale distributors. The first discrepancies in her record started right around . . . right around . . . she looked up from her notes, pinning Justin with a bleary-eyed stare.

"Valentine's Day," she thought aloud.

"What about it?" Justin asked, curiously flipping through sales records.

"That's when it all started."

"You mean us?" he suggested hopefully. He leaned forward, kissed her on top of her head, then took a stack of photos from her. He wasn't sure what he was looking for. She was the one who knew her store and her goods. He supposed that what he was looking for was a miracle.

"Besides that." Kallista smiled, despite herself. She wondered why he was still around. She'd become a stonehearted bitch since being arrested. Convinced that no one knew her pain, that she was walking alone in her shame, she'd tried to push everyone away. But Justin had hung in there. Responding to her sarcasm with sweetness, her tirades with tenderness, he held onto her hand, even as she did all she could to push him away.

"All of this started right around Valentine's Day," she said, pointing to a sale for a pair of Tommy Hilfiger shorts on a sales list. The shorts rang up two days after Valentine's Day but never appeared on any of her original inventory lists. They were tagged with a barcode, however, because the item scanned. To have a barcode, someone must have created the tag for it.

"I still don't see how all this stuff got in your store in the first place," Justin said distractedly. As he reviewed a photo, he tossed it onto the couch beside him.

"Most of it was in the South-side store, I guess I haven't been spending as much time in the other boutiques as I should have been."

"You can't be everywhere all the time, Kallie."

"Who says I can't?" she said toughly. "My problem is that I got a little distracted."

"Oh?" he said, raising an eyebrow at her.

"Um-hmm," She nodded her head. Propping her chin on her fist, she fixed him with a direct stare.

"Oh, you mean me?" he replied in mock innocence, pointing to himself. "Well, I suppose there are worse things to have on your mind."

Kallista shrugged nonchalantly. "You're probably right. But I can't seem to think of any right now."

"Maybe I should refresh your memory," he countered suggestively. Justin patted the couch next to him, indicating that Kallista should take a seat. She sighed heavily, as if he were disturbing her, then pretended to drag herself away from her work.

Instead of sitting on the couch next to him, she took two steps, then launched herself into his arms. Planting her knees into the couch on either side of him, Kallista wrapped her arms around Justin's neck.

"I'm so glad you're here, Justin," she murmured.

"I'm not going anywhere, Kallie."

"My life has been so crazy lately. I know I haven't been very nice to you—any of you. My mother thinks I need a double dose of Prozac. My father thinks I need a good colon cleansing. Karimah just wishes that I would stop harassing our employees."

"Way too much information on the family home front," Justin teased her. "I'm here to help you, but I'll let you figure out a way to make it up to them."

"And as far as you're concerned?" she prompted. "How can I make it up to you?"

"You're a creative woman. You will figure something out."

"How's this for starters?" Kallista offered. She lowered her head and caught Justin's lower lip between her teeth.

"Pleasant," Justin murmured blandly, pretending that having Kallista on his lap was something less than earth-shattering. "But conventional. Feel free to get as creative as you want to be."

"Karimah doesn't seem to think that I have an imaginative bone in my body," Kallista replied. Her tone was light and teasing. "What do you have to say to that?" She smoothed her hands over his shoulders and paused to massage his chest. Lower, across his torso, and lower still, she didn't stop until she'd reached the clasp of his belt.

"Keep touching me like that, and you will in a minute." Justin gasped aloud. "A very, very imaginative bone."

He squirmed under her, trying to relieve the sudden taut pressure of his slacks across his groin. When he placed his palms against her thighs and dug the heels of her hand into her bronze skin, Kallista laughed.

''Poor, neglected baby,'' she cooed. Then she arched her back, raising her hands above her head. Justin took that as an invitation to remove her T-shirt. He pulled the bright cotton material over her head. While her arms were pinned, caught at the elbows, he pressed his lips against the sheer, filigree lace material of her brassiere. He caught one dark, swollen nipple between his teeth and applied sweet, torturous suction.

Now it was Kallista's turn to squirm. Grasping the hem of her denim skirt, she raised it over her hips. With only a thin swatch of cloth separating her and the hardened heat emanating from the bulge in Justin's slacks, she welcomed the warm rush between her thighs that signaled that she was more than ready to accept him. Kallista snaked her arms around his waist, reaching for his wallet. With a small cry of triumph, she found the foil condom packet. The sound of the ripping packet coincided with the slippery hiss of Justin's zipper as he prepared the way for her.

She raised up on her knees, but only long enough to allow him to position her above him. With definitive, controlled force, he grasped her hips and pushed steadily downward while he rose up to meet her. Kallista paused, letting herself slowly adjust to him before starting the slow, sensuous dance of timed temptation. She rocked forward and back, squeezing and releasing, baiting and battering.

Justin allowed her to set the tempo. This was her time. As much as he'd wanted her while she had been conducting her own investigation, he did not push. Her mind was completely dedicated to finding out who had sabotaged her store. Justin didn't want to distract her from that goal, no matter how much his arms ached to hold her. He'd walked the thin tightrope of letting her go, giving her the space she needed, while at the same time letting her know that he would always be there for her.

Now she had chosen to close the gap between them. She

had initiated the contact. Who's to say how she would feel
when all was said and done? In the morning, she might revert
to her typical driven, obsessed behavior. He didn't want to think
about that now. He would take what she gave him willingly,
joyously, and then worry about tomorrow on tomorrow.

"Now!" Kallista murmured frantically in his ear. "Take me
away from here, Justin." She pleaded. "For now, I don't want
to think about stores and sabotage and jail cells. I don't want
to. I'm so tired of it all. So, so tired."

"Sh . . . don't worry about it, baby. Let me carry your burdens
for a while. Let me help you. Let me take you away from all
of this."

"Take me," she echoed. "Let it all go."

"All of it," he intoned. "All of me."

"I want all of you," Kallista cried out, clutching his shoulders.

Without severing contact, Justin spun Kallista around, pressing her into the cushions of the couch. His hands smoothed the
underside of her thighs. Kallista brought her legs up and around
him. She clasped her ankles just above the small of his back.
As he plunged into her, she matched him stride for stride, sigh
for sigh. Her moans of pleasure mingled with his until Kallista
couldn't be certain where her cries ended and his began. She
supposed it didn't matter. Wasn't that what union was supposed
to be about?

As a twin, she lived feeling part of a family, yet fragmented.
She was only one-half. With Justin, she could be herself—
whole and complete.

Drowsy and deliciously happy, Kallista lay in the crook of
Justin's arms. She wanted to stay like that forever. She wanted
to forget about all unpleasantness. If she could just steal a few
more moments of peace, she would never be unhappy again.
But she couldn't. There was enough stealing going on. She'd

faced it every day. It was always on her mind. And now, thanks to their frenzied lovemaking, it was all over the floor.

While Justin dozed, Kallista reached on the floor beside them and picked up a few, crumpled photographs. She reviewed them, shaking her head in mystified wonder. Some of the items confiscated from the store weren't even her taste. She would have never authorized their purchase. *Ugh!* She made a soft sound in the back of her throat in disgust. Somewhere, in his sleep, Justin registered her discomfort. He threw his arm around her, drawing her closer to him.

Some of the items she could see herself purchasing, even wearing herself. She paused at one photo. It contained half a yard of brightly colored cloth. A scarf maybe, or a wrap skirt. Kallista shook her head. No, it wasn't that. An African head wrap. That seemed more like its proper use to her. She could almost see herself in it—in Erykah Badu fashion.

Kallista suddenly sat up, startling Justin awake.

"What? What is it?" He looked around, confused.

"Justin, take a look at this," she pointed to the picture. Justin frowned. "A scarf. Not a very pretty one at that. Is that what you woke me up for?"

"You don't like it?"

"Not particularly," he said. He reached up and fingered one of her reddish-brown curls. "I like being able to touch your hair." He nuzzled her neck. "Especially when I'm just about to—" He whispered the rest of his statement in her ear, reminding her how eagerly he had grabbed handfuls of her tresses when he'd succumbed to the pleasures of her body.

"Could you focus on the picture, please?" she insisted. She couldn't afford to be distracted, not when she felt this close to resolving her problem.

Justin sighed again, then took the picture from her hand to study it. "I don't like it any more than when I saw it on Karimah."

"On Valentine's Day," she reiterated. "After we met her back at the boutique. She was wearing it."

"I know. I remember," Justin said, squinting at the photo. "She wasn't wearing it while we were meeting to discuss the web site. In fact, by the time you and I got back, she'd changed her entire outfit. For me, she was wearing this skimpy little two-piece with a slit up to . . . ," Justin's voice trailed off. "I'm not helping matters much."

"I'm glad to know you're so observant about what my sister was wearing. It might save my hide. She had this wrap on when she met us on the stairs, didn't she?"

"Why would she tell the police that she didn't know where it came from?" Justin asked.

"Maybe . . . maybe she didn't want to get someone into trouble," Kallista said hesitantly. Justin followed her train of thought as easily as if she'd painted road signs.

"You mean like Faizon." His mouth tightened into a disapproving line.

"They used to be close, Justin. When you two came into the store and they met up again, sparks were flying."

"But Faizon's on parole. He wouldn't fall back into that old line of work."

"Would he for Karimah?"

"She's your sister. Would she push him into it?" Justin countered.

"He has the connections, Justin. You know that."

"I know. I know. But, he's changed. He wants to go straight. He wants to do it for Miss Tansy and Chantal, and most of all, himself. Kallie, you should have seen the look in his eyes when Emeril almost took that necklace. He's not a thief anymore."

"But . . ."

"I don't buy it, baby. The police questioned your sister. She took a polygraph and passed it. She didn't know where any of that stuff came from."

"That doesn't mean anything. *I* failed it!" Kallista said miserably. "Calm, cool Kallista cracked under pressure."

"Don't worry about that, Kallie. We'll get it all straightened out. Come on. Let me take you home."

"Speaking of straightening, we'd better clean up this mess. I don't want the cleaning crew to come in, think it's trash, and dump it before we get back in the morning."

Kallista gathered up her clothes, then started to rearrange her documents.

"Where do these go?" Justin asked, pointing to a stack of bound invoices.

"I'll take them. We have a storage area at the back of the store with a vault."

"I'll finish up here."

She slid into her skirt and reached for her shirt. "You owe me another one." She shook the garmet at him. The rip in it from his overzealous removal could not be hidden or repaired.

"Here," he said, tossing her his own. Kallista buttoned a few of the buttons. Blowing him a kiss, she gathered the invoice binders and headed for the stairs.

Justin watched her progress though various monitors until she passed beyond a section of the store that would temporarily be in a blind spot until the cameras panned to that area once again. He saw her pass through a door and approach several, large floor-to-ceiling metal cabinets. After fumbling for a second while she located the proper key, she opened the doors and began to place the binders in their proper order.

Justin smiled to himself. This could take awhile. Kallista was efficient and thorough. She wouldn't leave until each binder was back in its place. He yawned and stretched. He might even be able to sneak in a few more winks before she got back upstairs. He wouldn't even be thinking about sleep if she hadn't awakened him to look at that awful scarf. Whatever possessed Karimah to wear such a thing?

It was the soft rustle of cloth, not paper, that drew Kallista's attention. "Couldn't wait for me to get back, huh?" she called out. Justin must have come after her. The man was insatiable! She didn't think she minded. It had been a long, dry spell for her, too. Incredible what the body will endure when the mind forced it to.

"Actually, I've been waiting longer than you think, sister dearest."

Kallista spun around to the sound of Karimah's voice, cold and mocking, coming from the shadows of the storeroom.

"When did you get back?" Kallista asked, trying to find her in the darkness. "I thought you'd be hooked up with Faizon for the rest of the night."

"You know, sister, I *thought* you might think that," Karimah mused. "Maybe it's true what they say about twins having that mental bonding connection thing."

When Karimah stepped closer to the light, Kallista's eyes zeroed in on two items—the elaborate wrap wound around her head, and the silver, ladies-choice 32-caliber weapon held unwaveringly between her fingers.

"What . . . what the hell is that?" Kallista gasped.

"My insurance policy."

"Your what?"

"Do me a favor, sister. Open up that cabinet and hand me those books again."

"What do you want these for?"

"Like Nike says, just do it." Karimah raised her hand and gestured at Kallista.

Kallista didn't want to turn her back. She suddenly didn't trust the flint-eyed woman watching her every move.

"Which ones do you want?" she said, stalling for time.

"Start pulling the invoices from around . . . oh, February fourteenth or so," Karimah suggested nastily.

"Why are you doing this, Kari?"

"For the smart sister, you certainly are full of questions. Here's one for you. Do you love me, Kallista?"

"What kind of question is that? Of course I love you, Karimah. You're my sister." She started toward Karimah, her arms outstretched.

Karimah made a rude sound like the buzzer for giving a

wrong answer on a game show. "Try again. You're only half right."

"I don't understand."

"Here's a hint for you. How about only a third right?"

"Kari, you're not making any sense. Just tell me what you want me to know!" Kallista snapped. Her patience was starting to wear thin. She was frightened and confused. Where was Justin? Was he part of Karimah's plan, too? Did he know about Faizon and Karimah all along?

"News flash for you, little Kallie," Karimah whispered harshly. "I'm not Karimah."

Chapter Thirteen

He wasn't sleepy. Not anymore. Who was he kidding? When he tried to climb back onto the couch, his stomach rumbled in protest. Four in the morning, and he was starving.

"Where is that woman?" he complained, checking his watch. He could sure go for some of Miss Tansy's cooking right now. But he didn't think she'd appreciate being awakened at this time of morning. They'd just have to settle for one of those all night restaurants. Steak and eggs? Pancakes and sausage? Right now, either combination sounded good to him.

He found his pants, slipped into his shoes, then checked the monitor to locate Kallista. She was probably sorting invoices by item, date, and color of paper. Of all the women in the world, he had to pick one more anal-retentive than he was. He saw her still standing by the cabinets. This time, she was removing the invoices.

"What?" he said in confusion. They'd be here all night and all the next day at this rate. "Come on, Kallie. Just leave them for tomorrow. Nobody's going to throw out your—"

He stopped short when he saw her turn to someone off

camera and hold the books out. Alarm bells went off in Justin's head. During this investigation, there was only one person Kallista trusted enough to hand over her books to. That was herself. She didn't trust Karimah with them, knowing that her sister didn't care nearly as much about organization and structure as she did. The private investigator could look at them and make copies, but the originals stayed with Kallista. Who could she possibly be talking to?

"What did you say?" Kallista croaked.

"Use your sisterly intuition. You know I'm not your sister Karimah. That going-back-to-Africa, wannabe-dressing, capitalistic slut doesn't have half my brains or my looks."

"Who . . . who are you?" Kallista could barely get the words out. She shared the face, but there the resemblance ended. The woman was right. Nothing in her mannerism suggested that she was Karimah Hart at all.

"Well," the woman paused dramatically. "I'm so versatile. I can be all women. I was Kallista on Valentine's Day when I came in behind your cleaning crew to get the access codes to your store. I was Karimah a few weeks ago when I authorized that shipment of knock-off designer clothes to your South-side store. When I made the call to the police to bust your ass, I was an irate elderly citizen, cheated out of my hard-earned cash by a pair of greedy, opportunistic, menace-to-society soul sisters."

"Who are you now?" Kallista insisted.

"I'm your prodigal sister," the woman said solemnly. "Coming home to claim what should have been shared with me."

"No," Kallista mouthed, shaking her head.

"Yes!" the woman snapped. "Up until a few weeks ago, I was happy doing my thing at the Artist's Alliance. Me and my mama were doing all right. At least, we thought we were doing all right. Then, you show up, bragging about your three big boutiques. You'd better believe that when mama saw you and talked to you, she was going to make sure that I got a piece of that action.''

"CeCe is your mother?" Kallista asked.

The woman laughed, for a moment, sounding very much like Karimah. "Everyone calls her CeCe, but her name is Chastity Cain," she supplied. "Resemblance is incredible, don't you think?"

What did she mean "resemblance?" Kallista wasn't sure if the woman was making a cruel joke or if she was mentally unstable. Did she honestly think that CeCe was her biological mother? How could she think that? She didn't bear any resemblance to CeCe. CeCe was blonde and blue-eyed. This woman was Kallista's twin. That meant she had two sisters, not one. Kallista's mind whirled with unanswered questions. All this time, why hadn't her parents mentioned a third daughter? Triplets? Did they know about her? Had they given her away? How did she come to call CeCe "Mother"? It didn't make any sense. What was even more confusing to her was why would her own sister threaten her?

"What's incredible is that you can come up in here and threaten me," Kallista snapped.

"Not threaten," the woman corrected. "Frame and blackmail. Let's get our felonies straight."

"What do you want from me?"

"A piece of your pie."

"Then get to a bakery," Kallista retorted.

"No? Then you can go to jail. Do not pass go. Do not collect two-hundred dollars. But before you go, I'll take those books from you."

"What do you want them for? They're no good to you."

"Is that why you're poring over them like your life depends on it? Maybe it does. With the invoices gone and you in jail, who's going to believe that an evil twin sister masterminded putting you away? Hmm? You try spouting that crap in prison, and they'll have you so far into a loony bin."

"What do you want? Just name your price, and I'll pay it. Anything you want as long as I can get you the hell out of my store."

"Not quite that easy. I'm not settling for a measly few thousand anymore. I will get what I deserve. I'll get a piece of this gold mine that you and our other sister dearest have going for you. But I'm not going to settle for shares. I want it all. When I take over the Hart empire, I don't want anyone suspecting that I did so with anything but the loving reunion of my precious family in mind."

"Go to hell," Kallista flung at her. She considered throwing the books, anything to cause a distraction, but she didn't. Books were no match for this woman's weapon. "Why'd you have to go through all of this trickery? Why didn't you just come to us? You're our sister, for God's sake. We would have welcomed you into our family."

"No offense, Kallie, but your family has a history of screwing mine. And I mean that in every sense of the word. My mother told me all about it. First, your father dumped my mother for Tranquility. Then, he didn't pay her for bringing you squalling brats into the world. Then you show up, ruining a perfectly good con. Do you know how much money was in that pot when you showed up at the Artist's Alliance?"

"Someone mentioned three hundred dollars, I think."

"Try three thousand. We'd been working that con all day. And then you had to come along."

"You're blaming me for CeCe's screw up?" Kallista said in derision.

"Just shut your trap, and give me those books."

Kallista threw them down on the floor and pointed a defiant finger at the woman. "No. You want them so bad, you come and get them."

"Girlfriend, don't you know I can pop a cap in you and take what I want?"

"Go ahead, if you're badass enough. Somebody will hear the shot and bust your little game right up. Come on. Come

on!'' Kallista egged her on. She wanted to draw the woman
out. She wanted Justin to be watching, to see her theatrics on
the camera. Once he realized what was going on, there would
be no more cat and mouse games.

Please, Justin! She silently pleaded. *You can't hear me, but
I know you can see me! See me!*

He was just going to have to go and get her. She'd been
down there for too long. He knew that she was talking to
someone. The cleaning crew, perhaps? Or Karimah? When he
saw Kallista throw the invoice books down in a fit of temper,
he made the decision to go after her. *Great.* She and Karimah
must be fighting again. What was it this time? He thought that
everything was cool between them.

Justin hunted for his shoes. One had slid under the couch,
and the other was stuffed between the cushions. Now, how did
that get there? In the heat of passion, he hadn't remembered
disrobing. Then again, when he was with Kallista, a lot of
things slipped through his memory. When he was with her, she
became his primary focus. It scared him, sometimes, how very
into her he was. Faizon teased him unmercifully and said that
he was whipped. Who was he to talk? When they were together,
Faizon couldn't stop talking about Karimah. Like a one-two
punch, those women had managed to bring two of the most
steadfast, confirmed bachelors this city had ever seen to their
knees.

Not a bad place to be, Justin thought in chagrin. Being down
there helped him to find his clothes that much faster. As soon
as Kallista was cleared of the counterfeit charges, he would go
to his knees once more—this time to slip the ring he'd been
holding for her onto her hand. She would be cleared. He had
all of the faith in the world. The good Lord wouldn't be so
cruel as to make him wait all this time to find a woman who
was his match in every way, only to lock her away from him.

He reached for his shirt, then remembered that Kallista had

taken it with her. He couldn't help but give a little grin of male pride. A store full of clothes—and she had to put on *his* shirt. Justin considered grabbing something off the racks when he went down to locate Kallista, then decided against it. He couldn't remember which zones she'd activated in the store security system. If he crossed the wrong beam and brought the police, he would just be adding to the awkwardness of her predicament.

Justin spun around as the door swung open.

"Hey, I thought you were—" Karimah ducked in, then ducked out again, covering her eyes. "Oh, geez. Put some clothes on!"

"I am dressed, mostly," Justin called through the open door. "Since when did you become a prude anyway?"

"Since you became my sister's man," she responded. Karimah pushed the door open again and leaned up against it. She folded her arms across her chest and regarded him speculatively. *Yes, Kallista has her brand all over him.* Still, she couldn't help but wonder about what might have been. Sighing, she resolved herself to eventually have him as part of the family. Vicarious lusting after his body was better than nothing at all.

"Have you two made up yet?" Justin asked, wishing for his shirt.

"What do you mean?" Karimah asked.

"I thought you two were having another argument. That last one was pretty nasty. It really had Kallie shaken up."

"Did that woman completely scramble your brains? What are you talking about, Justin? Kallista and I don't fight."

"Kari," he said, his tone slightly disapproving. "I thought you were going to rip her a new one that night I brought her back from the Ice House."

Karimah's face scrunched in confusion. "You know, Kallie said something about that night. Justin, I couldn't wait for you guys to get back. I called Faizon, and he took me home before you two got back. I didn't see Kallie until the next day."

''No, that's impossible,'' Justin said, shaking his head. ''You're not pulling my leg, are you?''

''Of course not. Even though you won't let me pull anything else,'' she teased him, bringing him back to their dinner banter that night.

Justin circled around the desk where he could get a better look at the closed-circuit security monitors. ''You weren't just down there in the storeroom with Kallie, arguing over those invoice books?'' Given what they had considered about Karimah and Faizon working together to supply the store with counterfeit designer labels, Justin wasn't sure he trusted Karimah's assertion. If she could fake out a polygraph test, would she be capable of looking him straight in the eyes and lying? She certainly had no reservations about sleeping with him, even in light of Faizon's feelings about her.

''I just got here,'' Karimah insisted. ''I figured Kallie would be cursing a blue streak now because I wasn't back when I said I would be.''

''If you weren't in the storeroom talking to Kallista, then who is she talking to?''

''You got me.'' She shrugged, then moved around the desk to join him. Together they watched Kallista gesture at someone they couldn't make out. They watched her back away from the books scattered on the floor. Too many unanswered questions for Justin. He didn't like what he was seeing. The look on Kallista's face, tight and angry, squeezed a tight note of apprehension in his own gut. He started to move past Karimah, but stopped abruptly when she clutched at his arm, pointed a shaking finger at the monitor.

''*Who the hell is that?*''

The knot in his gut mushroomed into a full-sized web of fear. He looked up into Karimah's face, then back at the monitor. He reacted immediately, though he feared in his heart that he could never move fast enough. The gun in the woman's hand didn't frighten him nearly as much as the look of deadly intention on the woman's face. That face, so precious to him, was now a source of gut-wrenching panic.

"Call the police!" he snapped, leaping across the desk and hurling himself at the door.

"Wait a minute! What are you going to do?" she screamed at him.

"Get my woman back," he said tersely, jerking the handle of the door toward him. He flung it open long enough to say, "Lock this. Stay here."

He took the stairs several at a time. Before he was halfway down, he stopped and kicked off his shoes. Justin wasn't exactly sure what was going on. Something told him that stealth was just as important as speed. He took the shortest route to the storeroom, hoping that he had triggered a hundred silent alarms along the way.

Pausing at the door, Justin listened carefully. He could hear two muted voices, similar in pitch and quality. Both were raised in a heated discussion. Taking several deep breaths to calm his nerves and steady his thinking, he grasped the door handle and pushed against it. "Kallie," he called out to her.

Keep the tone light. Keep it cool, he repeated to himself as he moved into the dim light. "Hey, baby. I thought you were going to be right back." He kept his eyes focused on her, pretending not to notice the woman who'd moved away from him.

"Justin!" Kallista started for him. But a subtle movement from her twin reminded her of the gun. She nodded her head in the woman's direction.

"Oh, hey, Kari." Justin waved to her. "What are you doing here? I thought you and Faizon were spending the night in Galveston?"

Kallista turned a curious gaze to Justin. Where had that come from? Kari was supposed to come back to the store to help them go through those cursed invoices.

Justin edged around the woman to get to Kallista. Still smiling, he wrapped his arms around Kallista's waist and nuzzled her neck. "What are you doing leaving me alone for so long, woman? You said you'd be right back."

"It couldn't be helped," Kallista said, wondering how he could have sex on his mind. Couldn't he feel the danger and tension in the air?

"Well, I'm here to fix that," he said. With not-so-subtle insistence, he started to lead her toward the exit. "You don't mind if me and my lady cut out, do you, Kari?" He grinned at the woman and raised his eyebrows comically. "It's late, and we have a date with a bottle of Chablis."

"Justin," Kallista protested. "This really isn't . . ."

"No, you go on," the woman said smoothly. "I'm sorry for barging in on you. What was I thinking?"

"Later days," Justin hailed her. "See you in the morning."

His grip on Kallista's waist was rib-crushing. Justin leaned down, presumably to whisper sweet nothings in her ear. "Move!" he said, harshly.

Kallista looked up to him with grateful eyes. He knew! If, by some cruel twist of fate, that woman decided not to let them leave, if she decided not to let them live, she would always treasure this moment. Her man, her protector, her lover had come to her rescue again.

"Wait a minute!" the woman's voice rang out. "Where do you think you're going?"

Glacier tendrils of fear crept up Kallista's spine. She missed a step.

"Keep moving," Justin directed. He turned, interjecting himself between the woman and Kallista's retreating figure. "What's the deal, Karimah?" Justin said. He had a hard time keeping his tone neutral.

"I need the keys to the other cabinet," she said. She wasn't going to leave until she'd gotten every shred of evidence that connected her to Kallista's incarceration. Given some time and some very creative—but broke—artists, she could have any document she needed duplicated and then altered to suit her needs.

Justin glanced back at Kallista. A few more steps, and she would be out the door. He needed to stall a few more seconds, give the police a chance to get there. He held his hand out to Kallista, communicating with his eyes not to argue. Just give him the keys.

She didn't hesitate, but tossed the ring into the air to him. He had asked her once if she trusted him. There was no question. She did so unconditionally.

As the keys sailed through the air, Justin reached them and snatched them into his hand. "Here you go." He turned back to the woman, swinging his arm as if he was going to complete the toss to her. In a moment too fast to see, Justin whipped his arm out, skidding the ring of keys into a darkened corner of the room. At the same time, he shouted at Kallista to get out.

Kallista didn't need to be told twice. She was through the door with Justin at her back before the keys had ceased their skid across the floor. He yanked the door toward him, wondering how he was going to lock that witch in without the keys.

When a shot rang out, barely missing him, he abandoned that idea. He grasped Kallista's hand and sprinted for the store exit. They were almost at the double-glass entrance, but then pulled up short when a face, pale and concerned, appeared pressed against the window.

CeCe! She must have heard the shot and had come running to rescue her child-prodigy partner in crime.

"Get back here, you bitch!" the woman screeched at her, pointing her gun at Kallista.

Justin shoved Kallista to one side as he dove for the other. When the gun spat fire once again, Kallista screamed in horror, watching as CeCe spun away from the door, covered in a shower of glass.

"No! Mama!"

The woman dropped the weapon, but not out of remorse for what she'd done. Her hands flew up as she convulsed, then collapsed to the floor moaning.

Kallista crawled over to Justin, clutching at him, "Kallie!" he hugged her into his chest. "Baby, are you all right?"

"I am now," she said, on an exhaled breath.

"Do I get a hug too?" Karimah suddenly called out. She popped up from the center of a rack of clothes where she'd taken cover when she'd heard the first shot. She waved in her hand a familiar device.

As Karimah peered over the body of the woman writhing and clutching her leg, she whispered, "I'm sorry. I'm so sorry. But I couldn't let you hurt my sister."

The woman glared up at her and croaked, "I *am* your sister."

Karimah turned a shocked gaze back to Kallista. "What is she talking about? Do you think I put too much juice on this thing? Do you think I scrambled her brains?"

"Where'd you get that?" Kallista asked.

"You're not the only one who can pack heat, baby sister." Karimah grinned at her, waving a taser at them.

Justin hung his head, shaking it in grudging admiration. "You women and your personal-security devices. I'm the one who needs the shock therapy for getting involved with the both of you."

"Involved with me and only me," Kallista said, cradling his face between her hands and planting a kiss on the tip of his nose. "And don't you ever forget it, or I will give you the shock of your life."

"Speaking of shocks, before I ask you something, I have to know, Kallie. You don't have any more sisters running around out there, do you?"

Kallista and Karimah exchanged glances.

"Maybe we should ask her." Kallista pointed through the shattered glass doors.

The sound of crunching glass as CeCe tried to stand drew their attention. Kallista's fears quickly drained away at the sight of CeCe's injuries. The woman who'd appeared so composed at the Artist's Alliance, so confident in the courtroom during Kallista's arraignment, was now contorted in pain. Her face was scratched from the shattered glass. She gripped her shoulder, trying to staunch the flow of blood. Yet, she seemed more concerned about the woman lying in the middle of the boutique floor than her own injuries. CeCe stumbled, and would have fallen herself, if Justin had not been there to catch her.

"Take it easy now," he said.

Kallista hestiated only a moment before taking CeCe's other arm to help her. "It's going to be all right," she soothed. She didn't know if CeCe heard her—or cared. All of her concern was on her lost sister. Biological mother or not, in that moment Kallista had no doubt that CeCe loved her sister as deeply as any mother could.

"I'll call 9-1-1," Karimah said quickly.

"Hurry up, Kari. She's bleeding pretty badly," Kallista urged. "And I don't know what damage you've done with that stun gun."

"Remind me not to make you Hart girls mad," Justin teased.

"Why'd you ask about other sisters?" Kallista asked.

"Besides the obvious reason," he said dryly, nodding at the woman on the floor. "Nothing makes a sister madder than not being asked to a wedding."

Kallista's resulting cry of delight was drowned out by the wail of police sirens filling the parking lot of Karimah's boutique.

Epilogue

Hand in hand, Kallista and Justin watched as CeCe and Keely were placed in separate ambulances. The paramedics were about to close the doors when Kallista called out.

"Wait! Wait a minute. I want to talk to her. She's . . . she's my sister." The paramedic didn't have to question. He could see the resemblance.

"One minute," he cautioned her.

Kallista ran to her estranged sister's side. Strapped in and cursing, Keely was issuing threats that no one cared to listen to.

"I just want to know one thing," Kallista began. "Well, maybe two."

Keely stared back with eyes as cold, flat, and hard as bricks. Kallista didn't know if she would answer, but she had to try. "Why?"

"The money," Keely croaked. "With three boutiques, you were probably rolling in money."

"And that was more important to you than family?"

"My family!" Keely spat. "My family gave me away. They sold me for drugs to CeCe."

"I don't believe you. Our parents would never—"

"*Your* parents," Keely interrupted. "The only mother I've ever known was CeCe."

The paramedic tapped Kallista on the shoulder. "I'm sorry, ma'am. You'll have to step back now."

"One last thing," Kallista called out as they were lifting Keely up to the rear of the ambulance. But before the doors shut completely, Kallista had the answer to her question.

She rejoined Justin at the entrance to the boutique. Her face was streaked with tears.

"Come here, baby," he said, drawing her into his arms once again. Justin's heart went out to her. He had seen so many of Kallista's emotional facets. He'd seen her spitting with anger, cool with jealousy. Amorous, tipsy, defiant, and obsessed. Never once had he seen her cry. He never wanted to see that look on her face again—if it was within his power to prevent.

"I have a sister," she snuffled into his shoulder. "Her name is Keely."

"You have a third sister. You mean to tell me that you're triplets! Lord help me, I had enough to try to understand with just the two of you." Justin exclaimed.

"I'm not sure if I understand it either. But somehow Chastity Cain got my sister to live with her."

"Or she took her away from your parents," Justin suggested.

"Those were such crazy times back then. Keely tried to tell me that my parents sold her to Chastity for drugs."

"Do you believe that?" Justin asked increduously.

Kallista shrugged. "I wouldn't believe that of them now."

"But all of this time and no one knew she existed?"

"They were living out on that commune. No one questioned the obvious lack of family resemblance. My folks wouldn't have gone out there. They gave up the hippie life. They became respectable so they could raise us girls. I guess it was just pure, dumb luck that I wound up out there. But you know what,

Justin, after all that's happened, I still feel hopeful. I have a sister. I have another sister!''

One more Hart sister. Justin didn't know if his heart could take it. Though the siblings had been split during conception and separated after birth, there was nothing diminished about them. They lived, worked, and loved with a double dose of sensuality, charm, wit, and devotion. He didn't know what he would have done if the third sister had been a part of their lives. What elements would she have brought to the trinity? He supposed now they would never know.

He closed his eyes, not wanting to think of what could have been. He already knew what was going to happen. Kallista would be his—his wife, his soul, his heart.

VALENTINE'S DAY

Adrienne Ellis Reeves

Chapter One

Johnetta Raymond counted the money again. The noise of the crowd distracted her. If only it hadn't rained so hard. Early February in Charleston was often rainy, but the sunshine of the past few days had given her hope that the moving sale she was conducting for the Websters could be held outside. She ran her fingers through her thick, brown curls, causing more disarray than usual. Wasn't the last count $982? She needed to bring in at least $1050 to secure her bonus of $150. She desperately needed that amount to meet the rent without drawing any more money from her scanty savings.

She was distracted again but not due to the hum of conversation from people looking at items who then decided not to buy after all. This was the feeling of being under scrutiny. Maybe one of her helpers needed her attention, but Don was in deep negotiation about the armoire, and Carol looked like she was finally getting a buyer for the mint-condition RCA Victrola. She could see Helen through the archway in the dining room, taking money for the smaller odds and ends of dishes, linens, and kitchenware. But Johnetta still felt like the subject of someone's attention. She deliberately looked all around the large room.

Then she saw him. He was standing in a far corner. A tall, brown-skinned man, his long hair smoothed straight back and held in a ponytail, looked relaxed yet gave the impression, she thought, of total alertness as their eyes met.

The angles of his strong face showed distinct pleasure as they looked at each other. "I've been waiting for you to see me," his look said, and Johnetta felt a jolt of recognition.

Surely she had seen him before. It hadn't been at a social event because she'd almost been a recluse this past year. Perhaps they'd passed each other on the street or she'd seen him in the library, where she spent countless hours researching her novels. She couldn't pinpoint it, but there was something familiar about him

"Johnetta, I sold the Victrola!" Carol's eyes were bright with triumph. "He wanted it for less but I held to the price, and here's the money." She handed Johnetta three one-hundred-dollar bills.

"Good work, Carol. You want to take a break?"

"No way. We only have a little over an hour to go, and I'm fired up to see if I can sell that Persian rug without coming down from our price."

"If you do, you'll get a bonus," Johnetta promised and watched her friend hurry away. Carol had always been able to outsell anyone else in the various fundraising events she and Johnetta had been associated with over the years.

Johnetta slipped the money in the desk drawer and locked it. Any other items that were sold would be icing on the cake, and she could give a bonus to her crew.

"Good afternoon." Johnetta heard a baritone voice with just a hint of a rough edge and knew before she looked up that it belonged to the strangely familiar man from across the room.

"Hello." Upon closer inspection, Johnetta saw that he had warm, dark eyes and a well-shaped mouth that looked as if it smiled easily. "You look so familiar. Have we met before?"

"Rafael Thorne." His hand enclosed hers for a brief, tingling moment. "We have now," he said, smiling into her eyes.

"Johnetta Raymond," she answered.

Don touched her arm. "Can I speak to you a moment?"

"Excuse me," Johnetta said, turning to Don. The man who had introduced himself as Rafael Thorne stepped away to look at some bookcases.

"I had to drop the price on the armoire twenty dollars," Don said as he handed Johnetta some bills. "It's getting late, and I thought I'd better take her offer. Is that all right?" His eyes were anxious.

"I know you did the best you could, Don, and time *is* running out." She locked the money away as a business card slid across her desk.

"I'm called Rafe," the man said as Johnetta looked up. The card said HOUSE RESTORATION and gave a local number. "Sorry I got here so late. Looks like you had some nice pieces. This your own moving sale?"

Please let her answer be no, Rafe thought. Rafe attended moving sales for the pleasure of seeing how people furnished the houses that he restored and dreamed of one day being a designer. Occasionally, he found items that spoke to him, usually pieces that needed care and came to life under his loving attention.

He'd seen the ad for this sale, but a morning trip to a nearby town and the rain had almost kept him from coming. How could he have known that when he saw the dark-eyed, curly-haired woman at the desk his heart would turn over? When she felt his gaze and looked at him, he knew that she was the woman he hadn't realized he'd even been seeking. She *couldn't* be leaving now that he'd found her.

"Heavens, no," said Johnetta, and Rafe felt himself breathe again as she smiled at him. "I'm just handling it for the Websters."

"They moving far?"

"To Seattle."

"That's far." They smiled at each other, making conversation so they could maintain eye contact.

"You live here in Charleston, Johnetta?" He eased the question in.

"Yes. Do you?"

"Moved here six months ago from Hartford, Connecticut." He'd better get down to business before she found a reason to politely move him along. "Could you take a few minutes to show me what you have left?"

Johnetta knew she should call Carol or Don, but she'd been at the desk nearly all day. The crowd was thinning out, and her crew could see her if they needed her. Making sure that the drawer key was in her pocket, she stood and found that, although she wasn't at eye level with Rafe, they were at a comfortable height to each other. She didn't stop to analyze what this errant observation meant but instead began to walk with Rafe and point out items.

By unspoken agreement, they stopped beside a charcoal rendering of a black man holding a young child. "Do you happen to know who drew this?" Rafe asked.

"Mrs. Webster said it was one of four she bought from the artist, a young black man living at the time in northern California."

"She didn't want to keep this one? It's very expressive."

"They wanted to keep all of their artwork, but they're going to a smaller house so they had to let some of it go."

"There's such tenderness in it," Rafe murmured. "You feel it also, don't you." It was more of a statement than a question. His hand sought hers.

"I do, yes." It seemed natural to Johnetta to stand there holding hands with Rafe.

"You've been to the Gibbes Museum?" Rafe asked.

"Many times."

"We'll have to go together some time," Rafe said. "I love museums. How people looked, how they dressed, what their buildings and furniture looked like, what they did for entertainment—it all fascinates me.''

"That's why I go." Johnetta started to add, *and to get materials for my books.* That thought stopped her cold. She loosened her hand from Rafe's warm grasp with the pretense of looking at her watch. What was she thinking of, risking her deepest secrets to a man she'd met only moments ago? Her writing was something that she rarely spoke of, except occasionally to her family and to her writing group.

I'm losing her, Rafe thought. "What are you asking for the picture?" He hoped that getting back on the business track would keep her by his side.

"One hundred is what we're asking."

"I know I'd like to have it," Rafe said, "but let me see what else is available. I didn't bring a lot of cash with me."

They passed a brown suede club chair, several tall plant tables, and two file cabinets. Then they stopped again.

The Victorian desk called out to Rafe, loud and clear. "What time did you open this morning? Wasn't it ten o'clock?"

Johnetta wondered what he was getting at. "People started lining up about nine-fifteen, so we opened the doors as soon as we had everything in place."

"It's three thirty-five now. Why hasn't this lovely piece sold?" *He's stroking it like it's a living thing,* Johnetta thought.

"A lot of people asked about it, but no one wanted to pay what it's worth, and we'd decided that for the Victrola, the mahogany dresser, and this, we weren't going to lower the price—even though a few small pieces of molding and two drawer pulls are missing."

"That is minor," Rafe said dismissively. "Easily taken care of by anyone who knows the business. This beauty was just waiting for me. What's the price that you're not going to lower?"

"Two hundred," she said.

"I think I have that much." He pulled out two fifties, three twenties, and two tens. "Here's one eighty." He handed the money to Johnetta, and then looked in another section of his wallet and his jeans pocket. When he couldn't find more money, Johnetta found his dismay almost comical.

"That's all I have," he muttered. His face cleared. "I can write you a check."

"I'm sorry, but we're not permitted to take checks."

"Credit cards?"

"No."

"But I've got to have that piece, and I also want the charcoal. So I owe you one-hundred-twenty dollars. Keep the money you have as the down payment, and I'll bring you the rest of the cash."

This was tricky business. Johnetta had worked many sales, and either the salesperson got the full price of the items, or the customer didn't get the merchandise.

But surely the circumstances here were a little different. First, the two items hadn't had a single buyer all day. Now, it was a half an hour until closing, and it was highly unlikely that a taker with the needed cash would show up. She actually had a buyer who wanted both pieces—at the full asking price—now. She already held in her hand most of the money for the secretary cabinet, and if she kept it and didn't let the merchandise out of her sight until the rest of the cash was also in her possession, then what could go wrong? These calculations sped through her mind in a matter of seconds.

"When will you have the money?" she asked.

"It will have to be tomorrow because I'm almost late now for my next appointment with a prospective client. You keep the money and put 'sold' on the charcoal and this piece. What time can I get them tomorrow?" Now Rafe hurried the negotiations along before Johnetta could change her mind. This situation gave him a bona fide reason to see her tomorrow. "You have my number on my card. It's my home phone, and I'll wait to hear from you. All right, Johnetta?"

"All right." *I do have his card, and the money, so there is nothing to worry about,* Johnetta thought as she and her crew closed down the sale. Except how glad she was that matters had worked out so that she would see him again tomorrow!

Johnetta opened the door to her one-bedroom apartment and locked it behind her with a sigh of relief. This had been one long, exhausting day. The rain had awakened her at four A.M. *Maybe it'll go away after awhile,* she had thought as she turned over and tried to go back to sleep. She awakened again at five and listened to the steady downpour. At six she gave up and turned on the weather, which reported "Rain throughout the morning with intermittent showers later in the day."

She pulled herself out of bed, and by seven-thirty had her team assembled at the Webster house. In two large rooms they rearranged what was supposed to be spread spaciously over the yard. Once the sale began, the hours had gone by quickly, leaving her too busy to eat.

She hung up her jacket, put the money box on the table, and opened the refrigerator. There was a baked yam, half a head of lettuce, a package of lunch meat, some milk, and three eggs. Nothing appealing. She then checked the cupboard: three cans of soup, crackers, half a jar of peanut butter, and—miracle of miracles—a handful of oatmeal cookies.

The chicken noodle soup was hot and comforting in her stomach. She followed it with a peanut butter-and-jelly sandwich, and for dessert she had coffee and two cookies.

With a sigh of contentment, she pushed the dishes aside and opened the money box. She counted the money one last time using her calculator. The total was $1898.25. When Rafe brought his money tomorrow the total for the sale would be $2018.25 Not bad for a rainy day!

If only she could be as successful at writing as she was at selling. She'd begun working at her family's clothing store while she was still in high school and had gradually learned how to turn a "just-looking" customer into a buying customer. She had enjoyed getting to know the customers' names and preferences, and when she worked at the store full-time during summers and holidays, people asked for her by name. She then went off to college to be a business major, but during her second year at the University of South Carolina, she and a friend had taken a creative-writing class. She'd written a short story based on an old man buying a dress for his wife. It won an award and was printed in the college paper.

Life-changing events are not always recognizable at the moment they happen, and Johnetta only realized later the significance of that story. She took all of the writing classes that were offered, and had written the greater part of a novel by the time she graduated.

It was clear to her from the beginning that she couldn't pursue a full-time writing career. Her parents had sacrificed too much in paying for her degree. As the eldest of three children, she'd been the first to graduate from college, and they were proud of her achievement. But, they also expected her to take her place in the family business.

She had fulfilled their expectations and contented herself by writing in her spare time. She had sold a few articles to magazines, but her dream was to publish novels. Her first one, completed a year after college, had been rejected. She took this in stride because she knew that she still had so much to learn. But, two novels and several short stories later, Johnetta felt that it was time to take stock of her situation.

Her father wanted her to take on more responsibility by running the store instead of just being their top salesclerk. She had always resisted this, leaving it instead to her parents and younger brother, Frank. She made no definite move except to promise herself that she'd spend more time writing now that she'd passed the big three-oh. In her off-and-on social life, she'd started seeing Harvey Wilkins, who'd entreated her to wear his ring.

In January, she'd run into Professor Darren, her old creative-writing teacher. She told him about working in the family business since high school.

"You haven't done any writing?" he asked.

"Yes, when I have time after work." She felt like this answer was inadequate.

"What have you written?"

"Two novels and several short stories."

"Did you send the novels out?"

"Yes. They came back without comment, just rejection form letters."

Professor Darren looked at Johnetta speculatively. He'd felt from the very beginning of class that she had talent. Nearly nine years later, she hadn't been successful. He decided that she needed a little help and perhaps a push.

"Would you like me to take a look at your latest work? Perhaps I can make some suggstions," he offered and was rewarded by her eagerness to send it to him promptly.

In early February, he returned her manuscript, which was about a black family homesteading in Oklahoma in the 1920s. His comments read: "As a reader, I have the impression I'm being given a history lesson, and, while the history is informative, the characters seem stilted and contrived. I don't experience them as living, breathing people. Find a way to bring your characters to life, Johnetta. It may be that you're not giving yourself enough time to explore them in depth. Think about it! Don't give up. I've always felt that you have the talent to be a writer, so do something serious with that talent!"

Until that letter, Johnetta had thought she *was* being serious about writing. She wrote every chance that she got after working and taking care of other obligations. What else could she do? She could make writing her full-time job, but what would she do for income? She had a modest savings, but it couldn't support her. What would her parents say? Wouldn't they feel that she was being ungrateful?

Johnetta thought of little else day and night. She awakened on a Sunday knowing that she had to talk to her parents.

She approached the subject head-on. "Mom, Dad, I need to

talk to you about my job. I'm giving notice so you can get someone to replace me.''

Ernest Raymond put down the Sunday paper. A deep frown furrowed his brow, and his heavy eyebrows shot up. "What do you mean?" he asked sharply.

"I mean that I have decided to see if I can make a living with my writing.''

"You're going to make a living by quitting a good job? I don't understand you." He looked at his wife. "Did you know about this?"

Emma Raymond wasn't as surprised as her husband at Johnetta's announcement, but her round face was still anxious. "This is the first I've heard, too. What is it exactly you want to do, dear?" she asked Johnetta.

Johnetta knew that the most important thing was to reassure her father that the business wouldn't suffer without her. "Dad, you know that Mable is a good salesperson. All you have to do is change her from part-time to full-time." She looked at her mother. "What I'm going to do is give myself a full year to write and prove that I can do it. You both know I've been spending a lot of time writing since I left college, but that's not good enough anymore. I've just turned thirty-two, and there's no reason for me *not* to take the time now and put an all-out effort into doing what I've always wanted to do.''

"I always thought the writing was just a hobby for you," her father grumbled. "Something to pass the time.''

"That's just it, Dad. Until now, that's the way I treated it— like a hobby, something I did when I had convenient spare time. I'm so glad you see it that way." She beamed at her father because he had given her the most cogent argument she could advance. "But now I'm going to give it a full-time commitment. It has priority, and everything else will just have to fit in around it." Johnetta's eyes gleamed.

Ernest looked at his wife for help, and she said, "But, baby, how will you live? You still have to pay your rent, your utilities, buy food. Your car is paid for, but you still have to buy gas.''

"I've thought all of that through, Mama. I have savings, and when I need more money, I'll get work from temporary agencies to tide me over."

Emma and Ernest looked at each other. "What're you going to do about Wilkins?" Ernest played his trump card. "He told me he wants to marry you."

"I'm going to tell him just what I've told you. I'm taking this year to write." Johnetta set her mouth in a stubborn line. "Besides, we're just friends."

"Do you think he'll agree to that, Johnetta?" Her mother's face showed apprehension and disappointment. Johnetta had anticipated this because she knew how pleased her mother had been about Harvey's serious courtship.

"We'll just have to see, won't we?" Johnetta put her hand on her mother's hands. "I know this is a disappointment for you, Mama, but I was hoping to make you both understand that I can't keep putting this off." She appealed to her parents.

She's been a good daughter, Ernest thought. *I don't know much about this business of her writing, but a year isn't so long and I guess she deserves a chance to try it.* He knew by the way Emma looked at him that she'd decided to support Johnetta—so he might as well give his approval.

"So when does this year begin?" he asked.

He knew that he'd pleased his wife and daughter by looking at their smiles.

"Today is the seventh. Let's say Valentine's Day," Johnetta answered.

"You'll let us know if you need some help during the year?" her mother asked.

"Yes, thanks, Mama." Johnetta appreciated the offer but knew she'd literally live on bread and water before she would ask for help.

Dealing with Harvey Wilkins had been another matter entirely. She'd known him all her life. They'd gone out together during high school, drifted apart during college, and drifted back together in the past year. Harvey was ready to settle down and begin a family now that he'd achieved the directorship of a large neighborhood clinic. He'd recently grown a mustache, and he had pulled on it as he listened to Johnetta's proposal— a sure sign that he was upset.

"What are you telling me, Johnetta? That we're through? That you don't want to see me anymore?" His eyes had darkened, and his voice was tight.

"Harvey, we're good friends. I don't think I'm ready for more right now. I need this whole year for writing. It might not make much sense to you, but it's very important to me." As soon as she said it, Johnetta had wished she'd put it a different way because she knew what Harvey's response would be.

"More important than our relationship?" Harvey was on his feet now. There was anger and hurt in his eyes.

Johnetta rose also and went to him. She pulled him down beside her on the couch. "Listen, honey," she pleaded. "Try to see what I'm saying. You know how long I've been working on writing. You know how badly I want to be a successful writer. But all these years since college, I've only been able to put a few hours a day on it—and it just hasn't been enough. That's why I've decided to take this year off from everything and work at it full-time to see if I have it in me to do this."

"What am I supposed to do while you're writing?"

"We'll still see each other. Maybe not as often," Johnetta said carefully.

Harvey's eyes were still hurt, but the anger was gone. He looked at Johnetta impassively. "I just hope you know what you're doing. A lot can happen in a year, Johnetta."

Chapter Two

Johnetta felt sunlight on her face when she awakened the morning after the sale. "Where were you when I needed you yesterday," she grumbled. It was still early enough to take a morning run before getting to the day's tasks. She slipped on her well-worn running clothes and shoes, got in the car, and drove to the Battery.

She loved running on the broad sidewalk that ran along the waters of Charleston harbor. Even at this early hour, there were already a number of other runners and walkers enjoying the crisp air, and there were small crafts already in the water. The run and the air energized her.

She still couldn't stop herself from worrying about the future. She was only two weeks away from her own deadline of Valentine's Day. Her hopes now were pinned to a contest for unpublished writers that she entered. She had submitted the required first three chapters and a synopsis of her newest novel. The work on it had been intensive, demanding, and constant. Johnetta felt like her heart and soul had been put into the telling of a story of her own slave great-grandmother and how a contemporary male descendant had discovered his history, thus transforming the life of the family.

When she'd completed the novel, she felt strange. Exaltation had swept through her, along with profound relief that the task was complete. In her bones, she knew she'd never written anything like this before. She wanted to laugh and cry and celebrate the achievement.

Her writing group had understood and congratulated her. Like her, they were eagerly awaiting a response from the contest. She'd been able to share some of her feelings with her mother, who periodically asked about her writing.

"I think I've done my best work on this one, Mama," Johnetta had said.

"What happens if you win the contest? Do you get some money or what?" Emma hadn't cared *what* Johnetta would get as far as money was concerned; she had wanted her daughter to win to confirm that her writing was good.

"No money. You win first, second, or third place. What it means is that the judges feel your work is good enough, with a little polishing, to be published. I don't know anyone here who's placed in one of these contests . . . but it surely raises confidence in one's ability."

"I'm sure you'll win something," Emma had said, patting Johnetta's arm. "You've worked so hard."

Johnetta began her final lap before returning to her car. Suppose her novel didn't place at all? What would she do? Hard work alone didn't guarantee anything. She didn't know what she'd do, but she decided that today she wouldn't worry about it.

The sale had gone well. She was feeling good, and she had met the most interesting man yesterday. As soon as she got home, she'd call him and arrange for him to get his merchandise. Just the thought of seeing him again made her smile.

It was only seven forty-five when she arrived home. Too early to call? *She* was up, so maybe he was too. He answered the phone on the first ring.

"Hello, Rafe. This is Johnetta."

"Good morning, Johnetta. You're up early."

"So are you for a Sunday."

"I've been up waiting for your call."

"Oh." *Maybe he has a lot to do today, and he wants to get this out of the way,* she thought. "You need to pick up the picture and the secretary early?"

"Not at all. I just wanted to talk with you again, Johnetta." Rafe had assumed from their conversation yesterday that Johnetta was single. "I'm not married, Johnetta. Are you?"

Johnetta blinked and looked at the phone. "No, but I was sort of seeing someone." She might as well say it because it was best to be totally honest about these things.

Rafe was silent then. "It's early, and I'm hungry. Why don't we meet somewhere for breakfast before dealing with business?"

Johnetta hesitated. Rafe was coming at her with such a rush that she didn't know what to say.

"Or lunch, or dinner," Rafe offered. His voice became persuasive and gentle. "Johnetta, I've nothing to do today except spend some time with you. Tell me what's convenient for you, but please don't say no."

She was tempted. No one had ever expressed such an intense interest in her from the first moment of meeting as Rafe was doing now. Even if another man had, it wouldn't have affected her like Rafe did. She wanted to spend time with him, too. She wanted to know more about him, sit across from him and drink him in. *There's danger here, Johnetta,* she told herself firmly. *Don't have a meal with him.*

"I have work to do this morning," she told him. "We could meet at the Webster house at noon so you can pick up your things, and then we can go on to lunch from there, if you'd like.''

''Thank you, Johnetta.'' He wasn't sure if she would go out with him, and he thought he should feel guilty about asking her, since she'd told him that she was ''sort of'' seeing someone. *But all is fair in love and war,* Rafe thought as he hung up the phone.

This is crazy, Johnetta told herself. She was supposed to go to a movie tomorrow with Harvey. How would she feel knowing that she'd spent this afternoon with another man? *I don't know how I'll feel, but I guess I'll find out,* she concluded as she began her work.

Her query to a regional magazine about an article on the Avery Research Center for African-American History and Culture was off to a good start. Two weeks of immersion in the history of the Center, which had been founded in 1868 as the only secondary school for blacks in Charleston, had given her ample material for thumbnail sketches of the Center and some of its outstanding graduates.

This morning she wrote about the school's glory days and the black community of the time. When she looked at the clock, she was surprised to see that it was after eleven.

Satisfied with her work, she stacked it neatly and got dressed. She decided that this was a day to wear red, and she put on a sassy, red sweater to wear with her black pants and red heels. She added red hoops to her ears, fluffed up her hair so the curls looked full and shiny, and went out to meet Rafael Thorne.

Rafe had eaten a light breakfast, read the Sunday paper, and thought about where to take Johnetta for lunch. He'd learned since coming to Charleston that most good restaurants specialized in a lavish Sunday brunch. He decided on one of the downtown hotels, where he knew they had booths as well as tables and where they could take all the time they wanted. He had just one change to make in their plans.

He arrived at the Webster house before twelve, and he was amused at how his normally cynical self was waiting to see a woman in whose company he'd been for barely thirty minutes yesterday but whose memory made his heart beat faster. He got out of his car, leaned against it, and watched for her car. When she pulled up, he was at her door to open it as soon as she stopped.

"Johnetta." Yes, she was as he remembered her, but the red she was wearing and the excitement in her eyes made him want to take her in his arms.

"You look wonderful!" Admiration echoed in his voice and eyes.

Johnetta flushed. No, she hadn't imagined the look in those dark eyes or the way his mouth curved up at the corners or the way his hair fell smoothly in a ponytail. He looked as intriguing as she'd remembered him. She hadn't imagined that she would respond this way because of the brief time they'd been together yesterday, but her heart was already beating faster.

"Thank you, Rafe." She couldn't stand here forever looking at him. "Where's your truck?"

"I'm not taking you to lunch in my dirty old pickup," he said, closing her door and taking her hand. "We'll come back for my things after lunch. Is that all right with you?" He led her to his Porsche, which was almost as old as his truck, but he'd kept it in excellent condition. He opened the door for her to slide in.

Johnetta thought that the car with its leather seats and a polished dashboard was as distinctive as its owner. "All right with me," she murmured, looking at the instruments and stroking the gleaming wood.

Rafe watched her and swallowed as he thought of her slender fingers stroking him. *Think of something else,* he commanded himself. "Were you satisfied with the outcome of your sale, Johnetta?" he asked as he pulled smoothly away from the curb.

"We never sell every single thing, but we were able to sell enough to make what the Websters wanted."

He told her about sales he'd been to in Connecticut, where the antiques brought in high prices. He wanted to know about her but didn't want to have that conversation until she was across the table where he could look at her. Their discussion about the differences between house sales in South Carolina and Connecticut lasted until they arrived at the hotel.

"I'm glad you chose this place," Johnetta said when they were seated. "It's a favorite of mine."

"I thought it might be."

"Why did you think that?" She was curious.

"Because I think we have a lot of similar tastes," he said. "Would you like the brunch, or would you prefer to order from the menu?"

"Order from the menu," she said. Sometimes she liked to select from the many dishes on display, but today she didn't want to move from the table. She had questions to ask Rafe, and she wanted to watch his face and eyes as he answered them.

"You prove my point," Rafe said. After the waiter took their order, Rafe looked across the table. "Did I tell you how wonderful you look, Johnetta?" His voice caressed her name.

Johnetta took a sip of her iced cranberry juice. She knew she should back away from Rafe, but she was too honest to deny the strong attraction between them. Since she had accepted his invitation, it would be coy to act as if she didn't want his attention.

"Tell me about yourself, Rafael Thorne," she said. "First, how did you get the name Rafael? Someone Italian in your family?"

"My grandfather was stationed in Italy during World War II and liked Italian names. He named my father Rafael, and Dad gave me the name. I was born in Chicago thirty-six years ago and went to school and college there. Have you ever been there?" he asked.

"Once for a weekend, when I was in college," she said.

"I have an older brother still there with my parents. My father is about to retire from his job within the school system and so is Lana, my mother. My brother, Randy, is a law clerk.

He's married to Martha, and they have a boy and girl, ten and twelve.''

He paused while the waiter set their food before them and filled their cups with hot coffee. "Is your food all right?" he asked Johnetta. At her assent, he nodded to the waiter.

He watched Johnetta sample her shrimp and grits. "Good?"

"It's wonderful," she said. "How about your eggs Benedict?"

"Just right," he said.

"What did you major in at college?" she asked.

"Mostly good times and partying, to be honest," he confessed.

"A lot of people do," she said. She could see him at college age with those looks. How the girls must have flocked around him!

"I finally decided I'd like to be an architect, but it was too late by then to do more than take a couple of courses in it before graduating."

"You didn't go to graduate school?"

"I should have but I got married instead."

The spoonful of fresh raspberries Johnetta had just raised to her mouth began to shake, and she hastily put the spoon back in the dish.

"You're married?" she repeated.

Rafe laid his fork down. This was more important than food. "I got married because I was so sure I was in love with Lucia. We were in college together, and we seemed to fit. But we didn't. That was perfectly clear after two-and-a-half years. We divorced, and I left Chicago."

"No children?"

"No children."

"You don't like children?"

"I love children, but Lucia said she wasn't ready for a family yet. Turned out she was right, so it's a good thing we didn't have any." Rafe waited to see what her next question would be.

She had another question that she had no right to ask. She wanted to know what the problem between them had been. Was it just immaturity? A mistaking of infatuation for love? She knew that could happen with young people just out of college.

Rafe watched these thoughts play themselves out on Johnetta's expressive face and was relieved when she raised her clear eyes to his. "What did you do then?"

He smothered a sigh of relief; he didn't want to talk about what had finally separated Lucia from him. He picked up his fork and resumed eating.

"I began traveling around, seeing the U.S. and a part of Europe, doing odd jobs mostly in something to do with houses. I figured that if I couldn't design them, I'd learn all I could about how to put them together, hands-on. I've also had my share of indoor jobs. Once I fell into advertising, another time into radio. I learned how to restore furniture." He gave a light shrug. "Jack-of-all-trades and a master of none."

Johnetta, fascinated by his spiel, picked up her spoonful of berries again. "You know what I think?" Her eyes gleamed with mischief.

"What do you think, Johnetta? And don't spare my feelings."

She swallowed the berries. "I think you're an adventurer at heart."

"You've found me out!" Rafe was delighted. "I love seeing new places and new people. That was very satisfying for years."

"It no longer satisfies you?" Her eyes were questioning.

"No, Johnetta. Now I find I have a different yearning. For the past year, I've had a strong desire to be settled. To be anchored." He held her gaze as the words echoed between them.

Rafe upbraided himself as the waiter appeared with the water pitcher. His emotions were driving him at a breakneck speed that could only lead to disaster if he didn't rein himself in.

"Your turn, Johnetta." He picked up his glass. "Tell me about yourself."

Johnetta took a deep breath. Maybe if she didn't look at Rafe all of the time she'd be able to keep her emotions steady. She made a business of eating as she told him about living in Charleston all of her thirty-two years, except when she went to the university in Columbia, about her parents, and about the family clothing store. "I have a brother, Frank. He's twenty-eight and works at the store. My sister, Donna, is twenty-five and works in the store part-time. She's studying to be a fashion designer."

Rafe sat quietly, listening and looking around the restaurant from time to time. When the waiter next came by, Rafe ordered hot croissants and honey. He seemed to have a hunger that couldn't be appeased.

When the fragrant bread arrived, he offered it to Johnetta. She took one absentmindedly. At least it was something to occupy her hands.

"What did you major in, Johnetta?"

"Business. The plan was for the oldest child to get training in business and then work in the store to help send the second child to college. Both would work to send the next child."

"Did it work out that way?" Somehow Rafe could not imagine Johnetta devoting her life to a business career.

"I'd worked in the store part-time since I was in high school, and full-time during the summer. As soon as I graduated from the university, I began working full-time." She buttered a piece of croissant.

"You've been there ever since?"

Something in his voice made Johnetta look at him. "Does that surprise you?"

He looked at her consideringly. "I can see you following your parents' wishes," he said, thinking it through, "especially in making it possible for the next child to have the same opportunity you had. But I can't envision you doing that permanently."

How does he know so much about me, she wondered. *Should I tell him about being a writer?* She took a bite of the croissant. She couldn't identify herself to Rafe nor anyone as a writer because she wasn't—not until she'd sold a novel. That was *her* definition of being a writer. Still, he was uncomfortably close to the truth about her.

"I can't see myself doing that the rest of my life, either," she admitted.

I was right, Rafe thought. *There's something more to her than running a store.* He waited to see what else that might be.

"I've taken a year off from the store," she said. "I've been doing a little of this and a little of that."

"Adventuring?" Rafe asked.

"You could say that," Johnetta agreed. "That's how you happened to see me yesterday. I enjoy moving sales. That's one of the jobs I've been hired to do."

"What else have you done?" he asked.

"Data processing, house cleaning, taking care of children at odd hours when their parents couldn't find anyone else. I do clerical work at home for agencies, and I've done some house-sitting and a few other things."

"Anything to break the routine of the store, it seems," Rafe said.

"Exactly."

He wondered if Johnetta would volunteer to tell him about the man she was seeing. He intended to find out about it, at least as much as she was willing to tell him.

Should I mention Harvey, Johnetta mused. *He probably isn't interested.*

The waiter returned to refill their coffee. Rafe and Johnetta politely declined, and Rafe accepted the check. He decided that he didn't want to hear Johnetta tell him about the man after all. Not now, when he was just getting acquainted with her.

"That was lovely," Johnetta said as Rafe helped her into the Porsche. "I'm so full, I don't think I'll eat again for a week."

"You don't mind if we stop at my place to get the pickup, do you?"

"Not at all." Johnetta was secretly glad to have a chance

to see where Rafe lived. She wasn't surprised when he pulled into the driveway of a small cottage that had been built as an auxiliary to a large-columned house on the front of the lot. It suited Rafe Thorne.

"I don't want to invite you in," Rafe said. "The place is a mess, I'm afraid, and I don't want to give you the wrong idea about my housekeeping." He opened the car door for her and walked her around to get into the pickup. "At least I cleaned this out to give you a place to sit."

"Don't tell me you're one of those people who keeps everything in his truck but the kitchen sink." She smiled at him.

"Who? Me? Only all my bills and correspondence," he answered jokingly.

Their mutual delight was palpable. The cab of the truck was small. In the Porsche, Johnetta had been able to sit close to the door and turn her body comfortably so that she faced Rafe while they talked. But this vehicle hadn't been designed for spaciousness.

Her awareness of Rafe had ebbed and flowed during their meal together. It had flowed at its fullest when he described his desire to be anchored, his eyes conveying a message that she was afraid to read.

Now the tide flowed again. She had the most errant desire to touch his face and his mouth. In her nervousness, she began telling Rafe about the Webster family and the other times she'd worked for them.

It was mindless chatter, and Rafe listened to it with only half his attention. He realized that Johnetta was reacting to the same tension he felt, and he was thankful that they only had a few more blocks to go. In the middle of one of her sentences, he murmured her name.

"Johnetta."

She looked at him. "Yes?"

"Nothing. Just 'Johnetta.' I love the sound of your name."

He put his right hand out, palm up. She laid her hand in his, and they rode the remaining blocks in contented silence.

Chapter Three

At the Webster house, Rafe put a tight curb on himself and accomplished his errand with such speed and silence that Johnetta began to think that she must have annoyed him in some way. With his money in her hand, she stood uncertainly by his truck as he arranged his furniture.

"Thanks again for the brunch," she said.

"Thank you for coming with me," he said gravely. He took a card and a pen from his jacket pocket. "I need your address and phone number, Johnetta."

"Do you think that's a good idea?" she asked.

"*You* have mine," he said with a lifted eyebrow.

"Yes, but that's different," she protested.

She is so sweet, Rafe thought. *If I don't get away from here, I'm going to kiss her until she begs me to stop.*

"What are you afraid of, Johnetta?"

"I'm not afraid of anything." Her chin came up.

"Tell me where you live, Johnetta, please," he repeated.

"One eighteen B Cutler Street," she said and followed it with her phone number.

Rafe put the card and pen in his pocket. He took her hands in his, leaned forward, kissed her on the cheek, and then opened her door.

She settled herself in her seat in a daze. He closed the door gently, waved at her, and waited until she drove away before going to his truck.

Rafe sat for a long moment thinking about how Johnetta's cheek had been so soft and how she had smelled like flowers. What had he gotten himself into?

That brief contact had only strengthened his hunger for her. His jaw tightened as he drove away from the curb. Johnetta's "friend" had better look to his mettle because Rafe intended to have Johnetta Raymond for his own.

Johnetta kept touching her cheek where Rafe's lips had been. When he'd leaned toward her, she'd expected him to kiss her on the mouth. Even though she knew she should not allow it, she'd been too excited to resist and had closed her eyes. His nearness made her shiver. Then she felt the tender caress as his lips lingered on her cheek.

The memory of the kiss stayed with Johnetta, infusing all that she did after returning home with a dreamy quality.

In the evening she decided to look through her writing magazines for contest notices and calls for manuscripts. Her Avery article was nearly ready to mail, and she needed another project to work on. She couldn't let the days of waiting go by without writing. Maybe she wouldn't hear about her entry by Valentine's Day. At the moment, she didn't care. She was tired of the suspense she'd been in for weeks.

The phone rang, and she suddenly remembered that she hadn't talked with her mother yet that day and that she was likely to get a loving reminder of that in a minute.

"Hello," she said, an apology ready.

"Johnetta, this is Rafe," the answering voice announced.

"Oh." Her voice was a breathless sigh.

"You sound surprised, Johnetta." *Was she expecting a call from the guy she said she'd been seeing?* he wondered.

"I thought it was my mother calling."

"Is this the time she calls? If so, I won't keep you long." He needed to hear her voice, to be in touch with her once more.

"No. I mean, we talk any time, but I haven't called her yet today, which is why I thought she was calling me." Johnetta flustered her way through the explanation.

Rafe smiled. She was fluttery, and he liked it because it meant she felt the same excitement he did.

"Are you doing another moving sale tomorrow, Johnetta?"

"No. Moving sales are always on weekends. Tomorrow I begin a week of work in the accounting department at the hospital."

"Which hospital?"

"The one near Willow Plaza. Do you know it?"

"The house I'm working on is about five mintues away from there. You know that little park across the street from the hospital? I usually go there to eat my lunch. Would you meet me there, Johnetta, please? I'll even bring an extra sandwich for you." Although his voice was light and easy, Johnetta could feel the insistence in it.

The thought of seeing Rafe again sent a thrill through Johnetta. *Maybe this time. No, don't even think it,* Johnetta thought.

"What time do you eat lunch, Rafe?"

"Any time. I'm my own boss. How about you?"

"I don't know. Part-timers fill in for regular employees, so I don't know from one day to the next."

"No problem. Call me when you do know." Rafe gave her his cell phone number. "I look forward to seeing you tomorrow, dear Johnetta." His voice caressed her name again.

The knowledge that she was getting in deeper and deeper didn't keep Johnetta from dressing with particular care the following morning. She knew that the two-piece, rose-colored outfit with matching earrings made her skin glow.

After her supervisor scheduled her lunch from twelve-thirty to one-fifteen, she called Rafe.

He answered immediately. "Johnetta?"

"Yes. Lunch is twelve-thirty to one-fifteen—"

She heard him draw a sharp breath. "I'll see you then!"

Johnetta watched Rafe walk across the grass to her, and she knew that she shouldn't have come. Her heart was beating so fast. Guilt warred in her, with the excitement of seeing him again winning. Heat suffused her, and her skin prickled. She couldn't take her eyes off of him. As he came closer, she had to fight the insane desire to throw herself into his arms.

"Johnetta." Her name was all that Rafe could say as he dropped onto the bench beside her. The need to take her in his arms was unbearable, but he knew this wasn't the time or the place. That thought faded into the background as Rafe saw the same desire that clawed at him in her eyes.

"Johnetta." Her name was both a caress and a plea. With a small sign of surrender, Johnetta swayed toward him.

"Johnetta." This time her name was a pledge and a vow, and he brought his mouth to hers in their first kiss.

It was all that Johnetta thought it would be. Rafe's lips were warm and firm and enticing, sending lovely, unfamiliar sensations through her. Instinctively, she moved closer and put her arms around his neck.

Rafe had known this would be different, but he hadn't suspected the intensity of his response, this wild need to shout hallelujah, to lift Johnetta in his arms and take her away to be his.

He pulled her closer and let his tongue tease her lips until she opened her mouth a little. She tasted like peaches and apples and sunlight. She tasted like everything he had ever hungered for, and his heart jolted within him.

Johnetta had forgotten where she was, but as Rafe tightened his hold and deepened his kisses she began to come to her senses. She pulled away gently; she didn't want to stop this heavenly delight but they were in a public park. She felt conspicuous and made small attempts to pat her curls into place. She couldn't meet Rafe's eyes as she shifted to put a little distance between them.

"Did I embarrass you, Johnetta?" Rafe asked. "I'm sorry, but I couldn't resist. I've been dreaming of kissing you ever since we met. Are you angry with me?" Rafe was still shaken and was babbling, saying anything to prevent Johnetta from getting up and walking away from him.

"How could I be angry?" Johnetta looked at him. "I was a willing partner." In an obvious effort to return matters to normalcy, she smiled at Rafe. "Did you bring me a sandwich as you promised?"

Rafe opened the paper bag he'd dropped on the bench. "Not one but three—so you could have a choice. Here's ham and cheese, chicken, and peanut butter and jelly." He laid them out, betting with himself that Johnetta would choose the peanut butter and jelly.

"My favorite," Johnetta said, taking the peanut butter and jelly. "Tell me about this house you're working on."

"The house was built between 1859 and 1860 by an attorney. It's one of those with twelve-foot ceilings. On the first floor, the rooms have wide cornices made of wood. Some sections needed replacing, so I have been doing that. Now I'm finished with that, and I'm working on the porch. Then there's a gazebo to repair to look like the original work, and then I'll be done. It's so fascinating to work on these old places and try to get inside of the minds of the people who designed them," Rafe said as he finished one sandwich and offered Johnetta half of the other. When she politely refused it, he began to eat while telling her about the marvelous examples in the Lowcountry of South Carolina of many kinds of architecture.

"Architecture is influenced by so many things, climate variations, available materials, economics, religious beliefs. Do you know what the early colonists in Charleston used to build walls with, Johnetta?''

"Logs, because there were so many trees.''

"Right. What do you think they filled the gaps between the logs with?''

Johnetta tried to recall what she'd read about this and couldn't, but Rafe had talked about available material. "Shells. I know shells were used.''

"Shells and straw and clay. This mixture was covered with plaster, and then the people had good, strong walls.''

"Since I've been here, I've driven through the Lowcountry and seen many remarkable examples of architectural design. You've seen Drayton Hall, of course.'' *How good it is,* he thought, *to talk to Johnetta about this.*

"On Ashley River Road. I was there several months ago.''

"Then you probably know it's considered the first true Palladian house in America. The two-story portico may be the first of its kind in this country.''

He loves this, Johnetta thought. *Architecture is what he should be doing. Maybe I can talk him into it.* She glanced at her watch. "I have to be going in a minute, Rafe. Thanks for lunch.''

"Johnetta. Would you please tell me about the man you said you were 'sort of' seeing?''

Johnetta was thankful that Rafe had brought up the subject. She would feel less deceitful if he knew about Harvey.

"His name is Harvey Wilkins,'' she said. "I've known him all my life. Our families are friends, and we went to the same school. He's the first boy my parents let me go out with when I was a junior in high school. When I was a senior, Harvey took me to the senior prom.''

Rafe imagined a very young Johnetta, fresh-faced and starry-eyed about going to her prom.

"Were you wearing your hair long then?'' He took her hand and played with her fingers as she told her story.

"Yes, and I had my first long dress. It was pale pink with

embroidered roses around the neckline and the hem.'' *How easy it is to talk to him,* Johnetta thought. She'd forgotten about that dress until now.

''Did you enjoy yourself?'' Rafe asked. He wondered if she'd fallen in love with Wilkins that night.

''It was fun until I caught my heel in my dress. I tried to save myself from falling and twisted my ankle. I was so humiliated.''

''I can imagine. What did Wilkins do?''

''Took me home. The prom wasn't over yet, and I told him to go back for the rest of it—so he did.''

Strike one, Rafe thought.

''When it came to colleges, I went to USC in Columbia, and Harvey went to Clemson, so we met other people and drifted apart.''

Strike two, Rafe counted.

''Last year we began seeing each other again . . .'' She paused a moment. ''He wants to give me a ring.''

Strike three. If Wilkins didn't have sense enough to marry you immediately, then he's out, Rafe decided.

Johnetta looked at her watch and jumped up. ''I've got to go, or I'll be late. Thanks again for lunch.''

She'd already begun to hurry across the grass when Rafe said, ''I'll call you.''

She waved a hand and broke into a jog. Rafe watched until she crossed the street and disappeared through a side door.

The lunch had been a success. He'd kissed Johnetta, and she'd kissed him back. The other man was now in the open, which was where he liked it. Fighting obstacles in the dark had never been his style.

When Johnetta got home that evening, she couldn't settle down. She cleaned the bathroom, reluctantly throwing out the latest bouquet she'd bought from the store, and tackled the writing corner in her bedroom. It seemed that every two or three days, she had to clean it or she would become smothered in paper. She lay on her couch in the living room to read the paper, but a slight dizziness gave her an excuse to put the paper down and close her eyes.

She awakened suddenly with a rolling stomach and made it to the bathroom just in time to lose all she'd eaten that day. It happened again in the next hour, even though her stomach was empty. Her stomach muscles ached, her head had drums beating in it, and she knew that she had the flu or a virus of some kind. Remembering that this was movie night with Harvey, she called to cancel the date—but he wasn't home.

"Harvey"—she said to the machine—"this is Johnetta. I think I've picked up some kind of virus. Don't come by because I don't want you to get it. Talk to you later."

She put the phone down and dragged herself to the medicine cabinet. She wondered where the Tylenol capsules she always took for headache were. Maybe she had put the bottle in her bag. She searched the bag and, thank goodness, there was the bottle. Empty. Now she recalled that the empty bottle was to remind her to replace it, but she'd even forgotten to do that.

Her throat was dry, and her tongue had the brassy taste that indicated fever. She decided to get some juice before she laid down again. The juice was gone too, as was the ginger ale she usually kept. She'd planned to do a little restocking tomorrow, now that she had not only the rent but an additional twenty-five dollars the Websters had told her to keep when she'd e-mailed them the previous day about the sale.

Johnetta settled for ice water, put a straw in it, and started back to the bed. The phone rang, but her head was hurting too badly to hurry. The machine came on and she heard Harvey say, "I got your message, Johnetta, and I'm sorry you're not feeling well. I'll check with you tomorrow, and I hope you'll feel better."

She took small sips of water from time to time, enough to wet her throat but not enough to cause more heaving.

When the phone rang again, she didn't open her eyes but reached out blindly for the receiver. "Hello?"

"Johnetta?" Rafe's voice was uncertain.

"It's me."

"It doesn't sound like you, Johnetta. What's wrong?" Rafe thought that her voice was a little slurred, as if she'd been drinking. Somehow, he thought that was unlikely.

"I'm sick."

"Sick! Was it the sandwich?" His voice was anxious.

"I think it's the stomach flu or some other virus."

"You're throwing up?"

"Umm, and have a blinding headache and a little fever."

"I'm so sorry, Johnetta, you must be miserable. What are you taking?"

"Nothing. Just lying down. I'm out of Tylenol and juice. I was going to the store tomorrow."

"I'll bring you some."

Johnetta tried to protest, but the line had been disconnected.

When the bell rang forty minutes later, Johnetta made her way slowly to the door. The combined stomach discomfort and headache overcame any concern she might have felt about her appearance as she opened the door to Rafe.

"You shouldn't have bothered," she said as he emptied his shopping bag.

Rafe was shocked at her change from the vivacious, lovely woman he'd seen earlier today into this Johnetta, with a drawn face and pain-filled eyes. *Why is she alone? Where is her family or Wilkins?* he thought. His anger rose as quickly as his need to do something to give her comfort. But as he started to speak, she clamped her hand over her mouth and hurried to the bathroom. He instinctively followed.

She knelt over the toilet. Nothing came up but water and bile, but still the retching continued, leaving her perspiring and too weak to care that it was Rafe who gave her a tissue to wipe

her mouth, assisted her back to bed where she'd been lying—
still fully dressed—and cooled her face with a damp cloth.
Then he took her temperature; the mercury shot right up to
101.5° and stayed there.

She frowned a little when he asked if she wanted him to call
her doctor. It hurt to shake her head, so she whispered, "No."

"How many Tylenol do you normally take?"

"Two."

Rafe brought her the capsules and supported her head while
she swallowed them with a little water.

"I hope they'll stay down," she said.

"I hope so, too."

Rafe looked around the room for the first time. Johnetta's
bed, which had a wooden headboard, was against the room's
back wall. The space on the far side had a window, her computer, a chair, and some books and paper. He recalled her saying
that she did clerical work at home for agencies. Next to him
was a lamp table, and against the wall behind him was a chest
of drawers, topped with a small television set. The door to a
walk-in closet was on one side of the dresser, and the bathroom
was across the hall.

Rafe moved noiselessly around the bed, picked up a chair,
and brought it to where he'd been standing. He eased into it
and stretched out his legs. He hoped that Johnetta would sleep.
Meanwhile, he indulged himself in a favorite pastime, which
was asking himself what a room could tell him about its occu-
pant.

She liked color. The matching bedspread and curtains had
vivid shades of blues and purple, with red flecks here and there.
The effect was one of warmth and movement, not gaudiness.
The floor was covered with a dark-blue carpet.

She didn't like clutter. Surfaces were free of knicknacks.
The bedside table held only a lamp and a clock radio. On the
dresser beside the television was a photograph of Johnetta with
her family, taken at her college graduation. There she was,
smiling, tall and straight in her academic robe, her mortarboard

tilted on her head. Her mother and father stood to her left, with her brother and sister on her right. They were all smiling proudly at the first person in the family to achieve that honor. *How young and vulnerable Johnetta looked,* he thought tenderly.

Johnetta didn't rely on cosmetics for her looks. Rafe couldn't recall seeing any in the bathroom, although there might have been some in a drawer. The counter around the sink held only a bottle of perfume.

Art spoke to her. On the wall opposite her bed hung a Jonathan Green print called *White Scarf.* In the picture, a young black girl, clutching a red book, looked over her shoulder, the long ends of her white head scarf blowing in the wind. Her round-collared white blouse had three buttons, and over it she wore a jumper or perhaps it was an apron of blue with large white dots. Behind her was a blue sky with white clouds. Rafe thought that the girl was anchored to the green earth on either side of her, but her thoughts and hopes were flying with the clouds.

Rafe wondered which one had come first: the colors for her bedroom or the print. The artist used blue and purple to show the highlights of the girl's dark skin. The fabrics echoed that same melding of purple and blue.

The thumping in Johnetta's head was diminishing as the medicine began to take effect. She opened her eyes a slit and saw Rafe sitting in a chair looking at the picture. That he was here in her bedroom after watching her throw up her insides was highly improper. Her parents would be scandalized. Especially since she'd just met him Saturday. *But I don't feel threatened by his presence at all,* Johnetta thought as she began drifting off to sleep. She felt secure.

* * *

Rafe kept his vigil as Johnetta slept. Pain had caused frown lines between her eyes, and he saw how those lines gradually smoothed out.

She'd said she took a year off from the store and he speculated it might be from stress, especially since she'd indicated she wasn't ready to make it her life's work.

He wondered if maybe that's why she had that particular picture on the wall. She had been anchored in the family business since high school, and now she was thirty-two. Where were the hopes and dreams in her universe? He knew she was looking for something more than the kinds of occupations she'd told him about, and more than just getting married to Wilkins, if that was what she'd eventually decided to do.

Perhaps her secret dream was to be an artist of some sort, although he hadn't seen any art materials around. He'd passed through the living room so quickly that he hadn't taken it in—but he'd notice next time. He'd seen her response to the charcoal piece he'd bought, and she said she went to the museum frequently. The more Rafe thought about it, the more certain he became that Johnetta was meant to do something with the creative arts. It fit with the little he knew of her factually and what he knew of her intuitively.

That was fine. They could make their lives match pretty well, because he certainly had interests in that area—with the exception of writing of course. *But that needn't concern us,* he thought.

The only thing that needed to concern them was that they belonged together. Rafe had spent time with other engaging women since the ending of his marriage. He'd had feelings for one or two but nothing compared to this. When he'd seen Johnetta, it had been like coming home when he'd been so far away that he'd almost forgotten what home was like. But his heart and his gut knew.

Johnetta was still sleeping at ten-thirty, and Rafe thought she might now sleep through the night. If it were up to him, he'd stay all night just to be sure—but that wouldn't be wise. He didn't want to put her into an embarrassing position. He left a note on her bedside table, replaced the chair, and turned off the lamp. He put the juice he'd brought in the refrigerator and left.

As Rafe left, Johnetta's front door gave a loud *clunk.* She woke up and tried to sit up fast but felt dizzy. Then she remembered that she was sick and Rafe had come over. She thought that maybe the noise she'd heard had been Rafe. She saw his note when she turned on the light.

> *"10:30* P.M. Dear Johnetta, You look like you're ready to sleep through the night. I hope you will and that by morning you'll feel better. Your juice is in the fridge if you get thirsty. I'll call you in the morning. Rafe."

It was ten thirty-five now. She wished she'd been awake to thank him. She put the deadbolt on the door, changed into her nightgown, and went to bed after taking two more Tylenol.

In the darkness, she thought of Rafe. Rafe whose eyes saw deeper than the surface of Johnetta. Rafe who listened about Harvey then ignored it. Rafe who had come at once when she said she was sick. Rafe who had seen her in the ultimate, undignified situation of throwing up and had still taken care of her as if he'd been doing it all his life. Rafe, whose kiss had burned through her like a flame.

Johnetta snuggled down in the bed. *Rafe,* she thought with a tender smile. *Rafe.*

Chapter Four

"Johnetta, this is Rafe. You better this morning?"

"The headache has subsided but it's still back there. I think it's really a virus because my stomach is still upset."

"Can I bring you something?"

"I called the doctor just before you called, and my sister's picking up a prescription for me. Rafe, thank you for last night. Coming over and taking care of me was very kind. I hope I didn't embarrass you."

"You didn't embarrass me at all, Johnetta. I was glad to be with you even though I didn't do much. I wish I could have done more. The doctor tell you to stay in bed?"

"He suggested that might be the best place for me for a while."

"You going to follow his orders?"

"I don't think I follow orders very well." For the first time, Rafe could hear a smile in her voice, and he felt himself smile in response.

"You want to get well, don't you?"

"Of course."

"Do what the doctor says then."

Johnetta said, "I have work to do, and it won't get done by my staying in bed."

"Work can always wait."

"No, it can't. The hospital expects me back tomorrow."

She wondered why she was arguing with Rafe about this. She knew the work could wait a day or so and she'd be back unless the virus took a sudden turn and kept her as sick as she had been last night, but that wasn't likely once she had the prescription.

"Surely it can wait at least another day."

"I don't think so."

"Johnetta, why are you being so stubborn about this? You're probably already dehydrated from yesterday, and if you get yourself to where you're throwing up again you will become seriously dehydrated. Then it's harder to get well. So why won't you use your brain and do what the doctor tells you?"

The exasperation in Rafe's voice was suddenly clear to both of them. Johnetta reacted to it with her own burst of temper.

"I'll use my mind to do what I think is best." Her voice was icily courteous. "Thank you for your concern," she said and hung up the phone.

Who does he think he is telling me to use my brain? I'll use it all right—and put this Johnny-come-lately right out of my mind, she thought. She'd only met him a couple of days ago, and he was already trying to tell her what to do. He was acting like he'd known her for years and that familiarity had given him the right to talk to her this way. Besides, she was hardly ever sick. There was that bad case of bronchitis she'd had last winter, but she'd survived it—and even Harvey hadn't bothered her about it like Rafe had with this sickness.

Johnetta had contemplated getting out of bed after talking to the doctor. Fueled by the adrenaline of her confrontation with Rafe, she swung out of bed and felt her head spin. She gritted her teeth against the movement in her stomach and stood motionless until her head and stomach were at ease. The phone rang. *That's Rafe,* she thought, and she let it ring while she made her way to the bathroom. An hour later she was ensconced on the couch in the living room, fully dressed, a glass of juice by her side and the article on the Avery Institute in her hand. She couldn't work at the computer, but she could edit what she'd written as long as her head and stomach were quiet.

Rafe had made himself wait until after nine o'clock to call Johnetta. He hoped she'd had a night of healing sleep, and he didn't want to interrupt it. He was relieved when she'd told him she'd talked with the doctor and was getting a prescription. She'd take the medicine and stay in bed at least for today so it could take its effect. By tomorrow, he figured that she should feel better, but some viruses held on for a long time, especially if you didn't give them proper attention at the beginning.

That's what he'd tried to tell Johnetta. *Why is she so hard-headed about her own health?* he wondered. *Doesn't she know the long-term effects that the virus can have?* Laying down his cell phone, he resumed hammering the nails on the porch planks he was putting in. He thought that it was just like a woman to be so sick that she could hardly hold her head up and so weak that all he wanted to do was to hold her and care for her until she was better. *I do the best I can,* he fumed, *and when I can't be there beside her, I want to be sure she is doing what the doctor said. But no, she is determined to go her own stubborn way.*

He wondered why she couldn't understand that he was only concerned for her own sake? It wasn't that he was trying to tell her what to do because he thought he knew better than she did.

He reached for another handful of nails. *Why did she hang up on me? Was it because of that remark about her intelligence?* he wondered. He hadn't meant to insult her. He had just been so anxious about her.

Rafe stared into space and questioned. Maybe she'd taken

it wrong. He'd better be sure. He dialed her number to explain himself. When she didn't answer, he knew she was offended. There was another way to apologize for his thoughtlessness, if she wouldn't talk to him. He picked up his cell phone and dialed again.

Trying to concentrate on her article had been harder than Johnetta expected. She wished Donna would arrive with her medicine. When the bell rang, she opened the door thankfully.

"Johnetta Raymond?" The delivery man handed her a large basket of flowers after she identified herself.

"Thank you." Johnetta accepted the flowers, which were arranged in a graceful white basket and tied with a white ribbon. *Harvey must have felt sorry for me last night,* she thought. *He doesn't usually send me flowers.* She put them on the table and opened the card, which said: "Forgive me. Rafe."

What am I going to do with this man, she wondered, admiring the mass of spring flowers artistically arranged in the large basket. *Is this a careless gesture on his part, or has he sensed that I have a passion for flowers?* Just looking at them made her feel better.

She was still bemused by Rafe's action when Donna arrived and the bell rang again.

"Sorry to be so long, but there was a line at the pharmacy"— Donna began, handing her sister the medicine bottle—"and the lady—Wow! Look at the flowers!" Donna's brown eyes opened wide, and her mouth turned down at the corners sardonically. "Don't tell me Mr. Wilkins spent his tightly held money on these gorgeous flowers. He must care more than I think he does."

Donna had never kept her scorn for Harvey secret. She thought that he wasn't worthy of her sister, and nothing the family could say kept her from expressing that opinion. Johnetta had given up trying to rein in her sister's remarks about Harvey. She simply ignored them.

Donna picked up the card. "Forgive me. Rafe," she read aloud. Johnetta couldn't keep from smiling at the pure shock on Donna's face.

"Rafe? Who is Rafe? Forgive him for what?" She made room for herself on the couch. "What's been happening with you, 'Net? Come on, now. Tell your sister everything."

Donna had respect for her older sister as well as love. The seven years between them had not stood in their way, even though Donna—gregarious, risky, and fun-loving—had tried Johnetta's patience like sisters do, especially during Donna's college years. When Donna had wanted to go into fashion design as a career, Johnetta's support had helped convince their parents that this was where Donna's true talent was. They agreed to pay for school as long as she worked in the family business part-time and kept her grades up. If she could prove that she was serious, then they would consider the next step.

Johnetta's decision to take a year off to write had impressed Donna. She hoped that, when it came time to strike out on her career on her own, she'd have the fortitude Johnetta had. She knew that Johnetta had made it on her own money due to the fact that she'd refused the small amounts Donna had offered her. What hadn't impressed Donna was Harvey hanging around and talking about marriage. In Donna's opinion, Johnetta had agreed to go out with him to please their mother. Because she was so intent on her writing, she hadn't paid much attention. If some man had finally made her pay attention, Donna was eager to know about him.

"Where did you meet this Rafe, 'Net?"

"At the moving sale I did for the Websters." She opened the medicine bottle, shook out two pills, and swallowed them.

"When was that? Several weeks ago?"

"No, that was another one. Webster's was this past Saturday."

"You just met him two days ago, and he's already sending you flowers and asking you to forgive you?" Donna wasn't sure what to think of this. Johnetta was smart and attractive but had a simplicity in her relationships with men that Donna was sure would be her undoing. *Look how it had landed her in this situation with Harvey,* she thought.

"It isn't what you think." Johnetta could feel herself blush. She told Donna about Rafe coming to the sale, about their conversation, and about his lack of enough money, which made it necessary to see him the next day. She also told Donna about how they had a meal together and a sandwich in the park yesterday and how she had gotten sick the previous night and how he brought Tylenol and juice and sat with her a little while. She skipped sharing the bathroom scene and the kisses in the park.

"While he was sitting with you in the bedroom, did he do something that you had to forgive him for, 'Net?"

"For heaven's sake, Donna, I'm not an idiot—nor is Rafe," Johnetta said.

"How do you know so much about a man you met two days ago?" Donna demanded.

"I just know," Johnetta said. "When he called this morning, we had a little argument and I hung up on him. The flowers and the note are his way of apologizing. That's all. *Now* are you satisfied?" She looked at her little sister defiantly.

"I sure am," Donna said. She got up and went over to the table to examine the flowers. She picked up the card and read it to herself again. Johnetta was wondering what was on her sister's mind when Donna pulled up a chair to sit opposite her.

"Let me get this straight," Donna said. "This man sees you at the sale on Saturday and lets you know that he's interested in you. He takes you out Sunday and tells you all about himself, even taking you to his apartment so you can see where he lives. The next day, you have lunch in the park. That evening when he hears you're sick, he finds out what it is you need and immediately brings it to you. This morning, he calls to see how you are, he disagrees with you about something, and then he sends you a beautiful, expensive basket of flowers as an apology. Have I got it right?"

"When you say it like that, it sounds impossible. Things like that don't happen to me," Johnetta said.

"Maybe it's too romantic?" Donna watched her sister's face. "Like one of your stories?"

"This kind of thing never happens in my stories," she said. "It's so sudden."

"But it is happening. To you," Donna said softly. "What does Rafe look like, 'Net?"

"He's tall. He's the color of coffee with a lot of cream in it. His face isn't exactly handsome, but it keeps drawing your attention because of its sharp angles. His eyes are brown. He has a nice mouth that fits his face, and he has long hair which he wears straight back and ties in a neat ponytail." Her eyes became dreamy as she catalogued Rafe's features. "His hands are big and strong with a few calluses from his work with houses."

I've never seen her go dreamy over Harvey, Donna thought, *so maybe there's hope yet.*

"Does Rafe know Harvey's intentions?"

"Yes. He told me he was single over the phone yesterday morning and asked about me, so I told him I had been seeing someone. In the park yesterday, he asked me about Harvey."

"What did he say when you told him?"

"Nothing. Just listened."

"You like him, 'Net?" This was a big question, and Donna didn't know if her sister knew the answer or would admit it if she did.

Johnetta hoped she wasn't blushing. "Rafe is a very interesting person," she heard herself say, ignoring the pull she felt toward him, the ease between them as if they'd been a part of each other for years. That might be fancifulness on her part. Or her reaction to his flattering attention. She'd had her share of male interest, especially in her college years, but nothing like this single-minded concern and solicitude from a fascinating man. There was no point in thinking too deeply about it.

All she wanted now was to get well.

Her mailbox rattled. Donna heard it, too, and jumped up. "I'll get your mail."

Johnetta sifted through the mail, but there was no letter from the contest. She put the mail on the table with a sigh of disappointment.

"What are you looking for, 'Net? Something about your writing?"

"A contest I entered for unpublished writers. I should have heard from them by now."

"What do you get if you win?"

After Johnetta's explanation, Donna was quiet for a moment. "Valentine's Day is getting closer, 'Net. What do you think you'll do?" She hated to see her sister fail, but the experiment didn't look promising at this point.

"I guess I won't know until that time. I'm taking each day as it comes, right now."

It was five-thirty when Harvey Wilkins left the clinic. Tuesdays were always busy days, and lately they seemed to get busier. So many new people had moved into the area that it was getting harder to find ways to provide efficient services. He'd had a conference this afternoon with the department heads to devise creative strategies for an insufficient budget.

Art Harris had come up with an idea about recycling, but Harvey didn't know how that would work out. However, it was a new idea, and Art was assigned to research it. They'd discussed scheduling changes, and someone had even suggested staffing cuts, but they already had the barest minimum of staff.

Harvey got in his Buick and pulled out of the parking lot. He thought about how lucky they'd been to acquire their latest staff member, Melina Williams, for the human resources department. She was easy to know and great to work with. They'd had lunch together several times as they talked about the clinic, and he'd been impressed with her insights. Today she suggested a way to use community people in nonprofessional jobs. She'd already spoken to some people who said they'd be happy to help, since it was their neighborhood clinic and they didn't want to see it close.

Harvey was suddenly reminded of Johnetta and how she'd been sick last night. He'd meant to call her from work to see how she was doing but had forgotten. He'd drop by after dinner, which would be better than a call anyway.

When he got out of his car in front of Johnetta's apartment later, he glanced at the classic Porsche across the street. That's the car he intended to have one day. He wondered idly who the owner of that one could be as he rang the bell.

Johnetta must have really been sick, he thought as he greeted her. She looked a little pale and weary around the eyes. Better not kiss her on the mouth. He didn't want to carry germs to the clinic. "How're you feeling, honey?" he asked as he kissed her on the cheek.

"I'm better today, Harvey." She closed the door behind him. That was when Harvey saw a strange man sitting in his favorite chair.

The man stood up as Johnetta said, "Harvey, I'd like you to meet Rafael Thorne. Rafe, this is Harvey Wilkins."

The two men were the same height, and they stared at each other without smiles as they shook hands briefly and repeated each other's name.

Johnetta sat back down on the couch where she'd been resting when Rafe had arrived half an hour ago, bringing her a bowl of fruit.

Harvey immediately moved to sit as close to her as he decently could, and Rafe returned to his chair.

Who is this guy and what's going on here, Harvey thought angrily. *Is he the one with the Porsche? Where'd Johnetta meet him?*

He turned to Johnetta. "What kind of sickness did you have, honey?" Maybe he could freeze the guy out by ignoring him.

"Upset stomach, terrible headache, throwing up."

"You called the doctor?"

"This morning, and Donna brought me over the prescription. The doctor said it was a flu-type virus that's going around."

"You didn't try to work today, did you?"

Johnetta slid a glance at Rafe and saw his amusement as she hedged. "I've been on this couch most of the day."

Rafe decided Wilkins had ignored his presence long enough. "The virus is going around. The families of two of my crew had it, then the fellows got it. It's apparently quite contagious. There was an article in the paper about it last week."

"What kind of work are you in, Thorne?" Harvey asked.

"House restoration," Rafe said pleasantly.

"That's how we happened to meet," Johnetta said. "Rafe came by one of my moving sales and looked at some furniture, then came by the next day and bought it."

And fell in love with her the moment I saw her. I'm sorry, Wilkins, but Johnetta belongs to me, thought Rafe.

"I find my best pieces from house sales. When I lived in Connecticut, I acquired some wonderful antiques that way."

"How long have you been in Charleston?" Harvey asked.

"Came six months ago from Hartford to do a couple of projects. This is the first time I've lived in the South. There's a lot about it I like. This your hometown, Wilkins?"

"The Wilkins family has been here for four generations," Harvey said with a touch of pride.

"Like my family, which I told you about, Johnetta. They've been in Chicago for four or five generations. That's why they think I should settle there."

"Will you go back, do you think?" Johnetta asked, keeping the conversation ball rolling and wishing one or both of the men would leave.

"I doubt it," Rafe said. "I like it right here." He looked at her steadily. The words were said without emphasis but their meaning was unmistakable to Johnetta. A quick glance at Harvey confirmed that he got the same meaning. What was Rafe thinking of to make a statement that Harvey could take as a challenge?

"You can stay here as long as you like"—Harvey stood up—"but you stay away from my girl!"

Rafe stood also. "Sorry, Wilkins, I'm afraid I can't do that."

Harvey clenched his fist. "What do you mean you can't do that?" He bit the words off.

Johnetta was on her feet, too, a hand on both men's arms. They ignored her completely.

"I mean I fell in love with Johnetta the moment I saw her. I can't just walk away without trying to win her. I'm sorry," he said again.

"I'll give you something to be sorry about." Rafe saw the blow coming and turned, so that Harvey's fist slid off of his jaw without connecting squarely.

"Stop it! Both of you!" Johnetta said.

"Stay out of this, Johnetta," the men said in unison, their eyes on each other.

"If we fight here, we're going to break up Johnetta's place, and she won't want either one of us," Rafe said, stepping back.

"What I want is for both of you to leave. Right now!" Johnetta opened the door and stood by it, not looking at either man.

Rafe took his jacket from the back of the chair and slipped it on. Harvey stood in the doorway, not moving an inch until Rafe was ready to walk out beside him.

"Forgive me again, please, Johnetta," Rafe said softly as he faced her. She made no reply, but he saw her eyes flicker as he left.

"What did you mean, 'forgive you again'? What was the first time for?" Harvey growled as they walked to their cars.

"I came down hard on her this morning on the phone when she said she wasn't going to do what the doctor said about staying in bed. She got angry and hung up the phone, so I sent her some flowers as an apology."

"I'm telling you again to watch your step, Thorne."

"I'm telling you I hear you, Wilkins," Rafe said.

Chapter Five

Johnetta had always considered herself a calm person, one not given to temperamental outbursts. Donna was the volatile one of the family, whereas she could always be counted on to be rational and composed. That was why her parents had been surprised at her determination to devote a year to writing. It didn't seem a reasonable thing to do—and Johnetta always did what was reasonable.

Johnetta felt anything but rational or reasonable now. She slammed the door behind Rafe and Harvey. She looked around for an object to fling against the door that would make a satisfying noise as it shattered. She picked up a vase and hefted it in her hand. This should do nicely.

It would also scar the door, and this was not her property. Reluctantly she replaced it on the table. What could she find to break? Maybe something in the kitchen.

On the top shelf of one of the cupboards over the stove she found three empty jars. She took them down one by one and threw them on the kitchen tile. They made a wonderfully loud crack as they flew into pieces.

It took her a long time to sweep up the glass. She went into every corner of the kitchen floor with the broom, then used the vacuum in an effort to find the remaining shards. Lastly, on her knees, she ran her hand over the floor until she was satisfied that all the glass was gone.

By the time she was done, the simmering rage had subsided. Harvey and Rafe had treated her as if she were an object, something of small value that they could quarrel over as it pleased their male egos: like two big dogs fighting over a bone that each wanted because the other had it.

''Stay out of this, Johnetta,'' they'd both said. Totally ignoring her. Not giving a thought to the fact that she was human, a living, breathing person. A woman with thoughts, feelings, and emotions like theirs.

Of course, she thought bitterly as she stepped into the shower, *a mere woman could never have the status of a man, even though the woman in this case was supposed to be deeply cared for—if she could believe the men.* One had asked her to marry him. The other had said he'd fallen in love with her the moment he'd seen her.

So what did that make her? Their love object? Not a woman who could fill them with sustaining love, steadfast devotion, loyalty, and tenderness. A woman who could create a home of warmth and companionship—a place a man would always want to return to and who would cherish the woman at its center. No, that kind of idea was beyond these two arrogant males.

They looked at her as an object, a toy, a plaything when they were ready to be amused, entertained, even pleasured. But when it came to the serious concerns between them, then the order was to step back, to stay out of this! As if it did not concern her.

As if it wasn't, in the end, about her. Not about which of them could choose her, take her, win her, say she belonged to one or the other. No. It was about which *she* would choose. If she chose either one of these two insensitive clods.

Neither Harvey nor Rafe was going to put her over a shoulder and carry her away to his cave! An errant smile quirked Johnetta's mouth at the image of herself slung over Rafe's shoulder or, for that matter, over Harvey's. How ridiculous!

As she embroidered that image into her mind, Johnetta found that she had worked through her anger. She still refused to answer the phone, although it rang four times. Rafe and Harvey would have to wait until she was ready to hear their apologies.

Rafe was disgusted with himself. At first he'd been glad when Wilkins showed up at Johnetta's. Not only was he curious about his opponent, he also wanted to make his own intentions clear to both Wilkins and to Johnetta. He believed in a fair fight, so Wilkins needed to know there was another man who wanted Johnetta.

His other concern was for Johnetta. Rafe didn't want her to have to conceal their relationship from Wilkins because that would only make her feel guilty. It would be a hindrance difficult to overcome.

Johnetta might not think they had what could be called a relationship since they'd only known each other a few days. He knew better. He'd been married to Lucia for two-and-a-half years, but he felt closer to Johnetta in a fundamental way. Love could not be measured by time.

Johnetta said she'd known Wilkins all her life. They'd dated in high school. But because they went to separate colleges they'd not continued dating, which told him it had been a matter of friendship in the first place. Even after college when they'd both returned to Charleston, they hadn't resumed any kind of relationship. It was just last year that they'd begun seeing each other again. That told Rafe that their arrangement was more the result of friendship and proximity than of love. They were at an age to think of starting a family and perhaps each was tired of the dating scene. He could understand that. They gravitated toward each other with a logical result. No surprises for either one. It was a convenient, comfortable arrangement—encouraged, no doubt, by their families.

Then he came into Johnetta's life. He knew she felt something for him. The current between them had switched on as soon as they had seen each other in the Webster house. Several minutes later, when they were looking at the charcoal sketch together, they'd had the need to touch by holding hands.

Johnetta had mentioned Harvey when he called the next morning. She was not the kind of person who took her responsibilities lightly, yet because of the attraction between them, she'd accepted his invitation to lunch. Throughout their hours together that day the current had grown stronger. She had tried to resist it when he asked for her address and phone but had given in.

The kisses in the park the next day were inevitable. He could see that her need was as strong as his for a communication more intimate than holding hands.

Rafe thought that intimacy had many aspects because, later that night when Johnetta had been sick, he'd felt a totally different intimacy when she was in the bathroom retching and he was beside her.

She'd not stopped him from being with her then and helping her to bed. She had obviously trusted him as he sat by her bed, and she had slipped into sleep.

Rafe's stomach tightened remembering how protective he'd felt, how much he'd wanted to care for her and to be there in the morning when she awakened. He thought Johnetta might not realize that, by letting him stay, she'd acknowledged the depth of her response to him as well as her confidence in him.

He'd scolded her a little about not taking time from work to get well, and they'd argued—but not seriously. Still he'd sent her flowers in apology. He took a bowl of fruit to her and had met Harvey Wilkins.

Wilkins seemed a nice enough fellow, but with all of his antennae out, Rafe had not been able to detect any deep emotion between Wilkins and Johnetta. So Rafe had deliberately made his position very clear, resulting in a predictable response from Wilkins.

That's when matters had gotten a little out of hand, ending

with Johnetta throwing them both out. Rafe couldn't blame her, and he knew he should have shown more restraint.

He dialed her number four times and let the phone ring each time. She was still mad, and he wasn't sure what to do about it. Flowers, fruit, or candy wouldn't do this time. Both of them had insulted her intelligence by telling her to stay out of their disagreement.

They were in her house and they'd been fighting over her, so she had a perfect right to intervene. But no—like a jackass, the level of his testosterone had pushed him to tell her, a woman, to stay out of this! How could he have done something so stupid?

Rafe was still grumbling to himself when he went to bed. He hoped by the time morning came he would have figured out how to get Johnetta to talk to him again.

As Harvey drove home, he wasn't sure what to make of what had happened. His relationship with Johnetta had always been so calm and easygoing. He'd thought there couldn't be any surprises in their relationship because they'd known each other forever. Their families were close, and thinking of marriage had seemed the right thing to do. Of course, Johnetta had this thing about trying to write and, although it put him out a little, he hadn't really minded when she asked him for more time. Better for her to do her experimenting *now* so she'd be ready to settle down later.

Now suddenly she was seeing another man, and she threw him out of the house! He didn't know what to think. He'd never seen her interested in anyone else. In fact, she didn't even show an enormous amount of personal interest in him. She was nice and she was sweet, of course, but always a little reserved, as if her mind was somewhere else.

He went to see how she was after she'd been sick, and there's this Thorne fellow sitting up there with her. Sitting in his chair.

He hadn't gotten around to mentioning it, but he had noticed that big basket of flowers, too.

How long did Johnetta say they'd known each other? Couldn't be long because she'd only had two moving sales that he could recall in the past few weeks. This sure was fast work on someone's part.

Apparently, there are some surprises in Johnetta, Harvey thought, as he parked his car and went into his house. They'd been seeing each other for more than a year, yet here she was entertaining Thorne. That just wasn't like the Johnetta *he* knew.

When Thorne decided he was going to stay in Charleston because he liked it here, Harvey had understood at once what he meant. No man worth his salt is going to stand for that, so naturally he'd told Thorne to stay as long as he liked but be sure to stay away from Johnetta.

Then Thorne had the gall to say he wouldn't. Laid down the challenge right there. It didn't leave Harvey anything to do except take a swing at him, to let both Thorne and Johnetta know he wasn't going to stand for that!

Johnetta should have been glad to see him standing up to a man who'd stated he was going to try to take her away from him. What had she expected him to do? Lay down and roll over?

Then she told them to leave. Both of them. One thing was for sure. It'd be a while before Johnetta Raymond heard from him again. He was going to give her plenty of time to calm down and be herself before he came by.

Johnetta worked overtime the next day, then spent the evening with her parents. Her visit with them was overdue, and she didn't want to listen to a ringing telephone that she didn't intend to answer.

The day after that, Donna picked her up for dinner. Then they went to a downtown gallery, which featured an exhibit of Jonathan Green's paintings.

"We don't have very long." Johnetta said as they hurried from the parking garage to the gallery. "The service in that restaurant was slow. Remind me not to go there again."

"At least the food was good—once they served it."

The gallery was full of people moving slowly from one painting to another, taking their time to absorb what they saw.

"This is hopeless," Johnetta complained. "We need to come another time."

"Wait a minute, don't be so impatient. Now that I'm here, I want to see at least a few of the paintings. I wonder if they have the one in your bedroom, *White Scarf.*" They began to inch along, murmuring their comments to each other about the vivid colors, especially the use of blues and reds as well as the ever-present white in fluffy clouds and in fabrics against hued skin.

Johnetta had to stop at a painting called *Corene,* fascinated by the rich blue, green, and yellow of the grass a woman in a white dress was standing in as she waved a tablecloth. As in all of Green's work, her head was covered, this time with a wide-brimmed, straw hat with ribbons blown by the same breeze as the banded skirt of her white dress.

"You can feel the sunshine, can't you," a quiet voice said next to her.

"You really can," Johnetta said.

I should have known Rafe would be here, she thought as she introduced him to Donna.

Johnetta was not surprised to see Rafe. The paintings displayed here represented the lives of the people who were inextricably mixed with the Lowcountry culture, its history, and the buildings Rafe was interested in.

"I'm so glad to meet you, Rafe," Donna said. *Johnetta hasn't done him justice,* she thought. Rafe was the kind of man you had to look at twice—at least. No wonder he'd captured the attention of her reserved sister. As they made small talk while still inching along the paintings, Donna decided she was rooting for Rafe all the way to the altar. She could feel the tension between Johnetta and Rafe—whereas with Harvey and Johnetta, she'd never felt anything.

Rafe had seen the article about the opening of the Jonathan Green exhibition and was immediately reminded of sitting in Johnetta's bedroom looking at her Green print. He decided at once to go. It was his first opportunity to see a number of the paintings, and he had the feeling that he might run into Johnetta. She wouldn't answer her phone, and he didn't want to sit in front of her house. He had no problem with doing whatever it took to get her to talk with him, but these were strange times and folks might accuse you of stalking or harassment.

He came early and had time to make a complete round of the gallery. The paintings were engrossing, and for brief periods of time he forgot to watch for Johnetta. He began to get worried when he realized how late it was, and then he saw her. His intuition hadn't let him down. The young woman with her was undoubtedly her sister, and they had come together—so he would have to figure out a way to get Johnetta to let him take her home. He hoped the sister would cooperate.

"May I take you home, Johnetta? I need to talk to you," he said as they came to the final two paintings. The room was emptying swiftly, and in another few minutes the gallery would close.

"Donna and I came together," Johnetta said.

Rafe looked at Donna, but before he could say anything she said, "We came in my car, so that's no problem."

It would be childish to protest Rafe's offer, Johnetta thought, *and anyway I can't continue to ignore his frequent phone calls.* She had to admit that she was curious to hear what he had to say.

"Did you park in the garage?" she asked Rafe.

"Yes."

"So did we. We can walk Donna to her car first."

"Of course." All the way to the garage Rafe's thoughts were on what he should say to Johnetta so she would understand

and forgive him. He wouldn't get a second chance, so this one had to be right.

He waited until they were out of the downtown traffic to begin his apology. "Johnetta, you had every right to be angry at me the other night, and I apologize. Will you forgive me?" He stole a glance at her. She was still looking straight ahead, but her face was relaxed. Rafe began to hope.

"I'm listening," Johnetta said. She realized that she was ready to forgive him; otherwise, she would have refused to ride with him. But she didn't want to wave the flag of peace *too* easily. Let him explain himself first while she tried to armor herself against the current that always connected them when they were together.

"To be honest, Johnetta, I was glad to meet Wilkins and to have a chance to tell him where I stand. I don't like going behind someone's back. My feelings for you are strong, and I didn't want to be deceitful about them by ignoring the fact that Wilkins is in your life. It was only fair that he should know about me."

"It didn't occur to you that if anyone told Harvey, it should be me?" Now she was facing him. Johnetta wanted to see his reaction.

"I acknowledge that it was your right, Johnetta." He was walking on eggshells again trying to put his action in a perspective that she would accept and forgive so that they could move on.

"Johnetta, honey, I certainly don't want us to quarrel. You don't know how desperately I've been wanting to see you and talk to you. The point is that, when I saw Wilkins, I just had to let him know that he had a challenger, that I was going to try my best to win you away from him. Can you put yourself in my place and see my point of view?"

Johnetta saw his point of view. She appreciated Rafe's sense of honesty and fairness, his willingness to be open—even if it meant trouble. *These are admirable qualities,* she thought, and to be strictly honest with herself, it was thrilling to hear Rafe state his need to let Harvey know he had a challenger for her. But there was still one point to clear up between them.

"Since you and Harvey were talking of your feelings for me, I don't see how you could think it didn't concern me. Then you *ordered* me to stay out of the discussion!" The idea still rankled despite Rafe's explanation.

"I can't expect you to understand because it was wrong," Rafe said. "It was a stupid thing to say even in the heat of the moment and of course you found it offensive." His eyes pleaded with her. "I apologize, Johnetta. I'm hoping we can get past this."

The uncertainty in his voice told Johnetta that Rafe had some idea of how she'd felt and he wasn't sure she was ready to accept his apology.

After studying him for a moment, Johnetta realized she was ready to let go of her resentment. It stood in the way of the next step and she was anxious to discover what the next step would be.

Chapter Six

Rafe had driven as slowly as possible to postpone this moment, but they were already in front of Johnetta's apartment. He didn't want to press his luck by asking if he could come in. He turned off the ignition and turned so he could face Johnetta.

He extended his hands to her. "Forgive me, Johnetta?"

Johnetta put her hands in his. "I forgive you, Rafe. Be sure not to let it happen again," she said in an effort to lighten the intense emotion she felt.

His hands tightened on hers. Was she saying that there was a future for them, or had she said the phrase carelessly? All he knew was that he was touching her again and her sweet mouth was close to his.

"Let me kiss you, sweetheart," he whispered, pulling her gently toward him with their linked hands, warning himself to be slow and careful.

Johnetta surrendered to the sensations building inside her and leaned forward. Ah, yes, this was what she remembered. The way his lips felt on hers, the way they moved, delicately exploring until she could no longer prevent him access to her mouth. One part of her noted how different his kisses were to Harvey's kisses. Maybe that was why the response Rafe evoked was so different, causing her to be assaulted by unfamiliar urges.

Through the blood pounding in his head, Rafe began to sense Johnetta's situation and eased back, ending his kisses with a gentle peck on her forehead. He had to get some air or he would explode. Rafe lowered his window and gratefully inhaled the slightly chilly night air.

The air was welcome to Johnetta, too. Maybe if she let it pass over her for a few minutes she'd be able to pull herself together enough to get out of the car.

"I need to go in," she murmured, breaking the silence.

"There's one more thing before you leave," Rafe said.

Johnetta made no move to leave but turned her head to meet Rafe's eyes. She was limp as a blade of grass, but she wanted to hear what Rafe's "one more thing" was.

"Do you believe in my feelings for you, Johnetta, and that I truly do want to win you for my own?" The grip of his hand was as uncompromising as the look with which he held her.

She was held captive by what she saw in Rafe's eyes. Yet how could that be true? She'd never seen that look in Harvey's eyes, and she'd known him for years. She'd only known Rafe for a few days, so how could he give her what his eyes promised of caring and passion? She could feel a pulse beating in her throat, and she closed her eyes against the intensity she felt from Rafe.

"You've only known me a few days," she finally said.

"Time doesn't matter when it comes to the heart, Johnetta." He had to make her accept this emotion between them if he was to have any chance with her. "You've known me the same few days, but you have feelings about me, don't you, sweetheart?" He pressed the matter because it was urgent.

"Look at me, Johnetta, and tell me."

An upsurge of emotion filled Johnetta, overcoming her

embarrassment at her response to Rafe's kisses. She was afraid to declare the strength of her feelings for him, but the desire to do so betrayed her, and she opened her eyes.

"Yes, I have feelings for you," she said and felt the heat rise in her face. The happiness that suffused Rafe's features made her catch her breath. A great longing to throw herself into his arms seized her, but if she gave into it, she knew there'd be no turning back. She opened the car door.

"I have to go in."

The walk up to her door was silent but once there, Rafe said, "May I hold you, sweetheart?"

Johnetta moved to him and laid her head on his chest as his arms came around her.

Rafe kissed her hair and murmured something she didn't understand because her heart was beating so heavily.

"I'd better go," Rafe said. "Goodnight, sweetheart." He raised her face and kissed her with a hunger that left her weak and trembling as she stepped inside and closed the door.

Johnetta felt like she was adrift in an unknown sea. Her familiar moorings had vanished, and she couldn't control the emotions that were carrying her along. She had to get back to shore, find solid ground so she could decide what her direction should be. Meanwhile she would let herself float for a while longer in the delicious sensation of Rafe's kisses.

She'd had her first encounter with love when she met Michael Carter in her third year at the university. She could remember even now how giddy with excitement she'd been and the bubbling happiness that carried her along during the heavy months of their romance. Her refusal to become his lover and his lack of interest in commitment and marriage had ended the relationship. The devastation Johnetta had felt kept her from any serious emotional investment in the intervening years.

After college, her life had settled into a routine of work at the store and writing at home. She had been a part of several weddings as her friends began to get married but had found no one to interest her among the men she dated from time to time. Then Harvey sought her out at a dance and had suggested they go together to see a movie everyone was talking about.

The evening had been pleasant, and the movie date became a habit. They gradually slid into the habit of seeing each other at least once a week for dinner, a movie, or whatever social event was taking place. There was always something to talk about because of their long history together. Johnetta listened to Harvey talk about the clinic but spoke little about her writing after her first attempts had been met with patient politeness from Harvey.

One night after a particularly enjoyable evening at a dinner dance, Harvey's usual goodnight kiss had turned into something different that left Johnetta breathless and surprised. "Why don't we get married, Johnetta?" he'd said. "We get along so well together. We almost act like an old married couple already, so why don't we make it legal?"

Johnetta was even more surprised when Harvey produced a ring and took her hand to slip it on her finger. Johnetta instinctively pulled her hand out of his grasp. Harvey had gone very still. "What's the matter, Johnetta?" She wondered the same thing. "I'm not quite ready for this." That's where matters stood until Rafe entered the picture.

Johnetta looked at her calendar to figure out exactly how many days had elapsed since Rafe walked into her life. She had the Webster moving sale marked on the preceding Saturday, and this was only Thursday. That was only six days. Surely it was longer than that because Rafe was now indelibly imprinted on her consciousness.

She listed the times they'd seen each other: at the sale, brunch at the hotel, lunch in the park, her place when she was sick, her place when he and Harvey were there, tonight at the gallery. Six times, plus a few phone calls. That was a pitifully small number of times to have as a basis for a committed relationship. Yet Rafe had said he wanted to win her for his own. He hadn't actually said the word "marriage," but surely that's what he had in mind from other comments he'd made. *Married to Rafe*. Clear images of marriage to Rafe flooded Johnetta's imagination: The home they would make together, the children they would have together, the trips they would take together. The constant joy and stimulation they would find in each other. She would write better novels, and he would realize his dream of becoming an architect. What a wonderful life they would have!

What was she doing? Johnetta jumped up from the chair where she'd been indulging in her daydream and went to the bedroom. She took herself severely to task as she showered. Because Rafe made her feel like a young college girl again didn't mean that she should turn her world upside down.

Michael Carter had done that—and look how that had turned out. What kind of trust could you put into such intense emotions, especially when you'd known the person only a short time? Convinced that she had stabilized her emotions into a rational space, Johnetta went to bed.

At his house, Rafe started to pick up the phone just to hear Johnetta's voice again. Then he replaced it. It was too late, and he'd wait until tomorrow.

It was hard to control his feelings, but he'd done it. He'd made the breakthrough with his darling Johnetta.

He'd found her at the gallery, she'd let him drive her home, and she'd accepted his apology. Emboldened by her acquiescence, he'd asked her to accept the fact of his feelings for her. She'd protested about the shortness of time that he'd known her, but his senses had told him that she was ready to meet him halfway.

The current was vibrant and strong between them, forcing her almost against her will to acknowledge that she returned his feelings. The kisses they'd shared had testified to those feelings. When he'd held her against him for the first time at her door, he'd been shaken by the strength of the fire that had ripped through him.

The strongest feelings he'd had for other women were pale imitations of what he felt for Johnetta. Marriage had never been an option before—but marriage with Johnetta? He could imagine what that would be like: a home, children, travel. Taking a lifetime to explore all the joys each could give the other!

Tomorrow he would get the ring.

Harvey Wilkins didn't believe in astrology, but as he drove to work he found himself wondering if somehow the signs in the heavens were aligned against him—because he was certainly going through a strange time.

He still couldn't understand what had happened at Johnetta's the other night. He'd never seen her angry like that. The statement Thorne had made about falling in love with Johnetta the moment he'd seen her puzzled him, also. Johnetta was attractive enough, but she was definitely not the kind of woman men fell in love with immediately.

Harvey knew he'd done the right thing in trying to protect Johnetta and their relationship from Thorne, so why was he feeling uneasy about it? It was always there in the back of his mind. As if that weren't enough, today at the clinic was bound to be a headache.

The clinic had a board of directors who visited on a quarterly basis to look it over and make recommendations. The staff dreaded the visit—no matter how prepared they were, some of the directors invariably found something to criticize.

Today was no exception, and Harvey found his prediction to be accurate. The clinic had been cleaned and polished to perfection. The directors decided to interrogate the executive staff about their budget recommendations.

Two of the five directors targeted Melina Williams' idea about using community volunteers to assist in nonprofessional jobs. How could they find the right caliber of people to do the work? Melina gave examples of the volunteers who were already lined up including retired professional people. How would they be trained? By the department heads to insure quality training. But they protested that would take away valuable time from what the department heads had been hired to do.

Melina remained composed and pleasant throughout, but Harvey saw the effort it took. He intervened as often as he could, but when it was over and the directors had gone, he was shaking with the anger he hadn't allowed himself to feel during the meeting. Couldn't those people see how Melina's idea was going to save the clinic money and at the same time get the community more heavily invested in it? They shouldn't have jumped on her.

Melina had stayed behind. She told Harvey that she was sorry her idea had generated such criticism. She didn't want anything that she did to distress him. He was feeling protective of her, and she was concerned about him. As she stood before him, Harvey felt like he was seeing Melina for the first time. Something happened inside him that made the air shimmer as they gazed at each other.

Melina gave him an uncertain smile and left the room. That was wise—because Harvey's instinctive thought was to reach for her, to touch her in some way.

All the way home he thought about Melina, the way she looked, the way she moved, the sound of her voice, the way her eyes smiled at him when he said something that amused him. He didn't realize that he had noticed those things about her. It was as if they were filed in his subconscious, ready to come forward when he called for them. She had an endearing little habit of running the tip of her tongue over her upper lip when she was concentrating. And when they were in the same room together, her glance was always just sliding away when he looked at her.

Harvey's career had occupied the majority of his interest

since leaving college. His only romantic investment had been with Johnetta, and it had been neither complicated nor exciting but rather effortless and relaxed. How had it all changed? Suddenly there was complication with Johnetta and excitement with Melina.

A wayward thought that what he was experiencing about Melina was what Thorne had experienced about Johnetta struck him.

But that was ridiculous, wasn't it?

The one fact Johnetta was sure of at the end of her work day was that she needed to see Harvey. The other facts that had run through her mind all day didn't seem to stay in place.

By the time she arrived home, the idea of a serious relationship with Rafael Thorne still hung in the balance—but Harvey was quite another matter.

She dialed his number and got a busy signal. She counted off a minute, then dialed him again. This time he answered.

"Harvey, this is Johnetta."

He sounded surprised. "I just got through calling you, and your line was busy."

"That was me calling you. Could you come over?"

"That's what I was going to tell you. I'll come right away."

That's a good start, Johnetta said to herself. He didn't sound like his usual self. But when she opened the door to him ten minutes later, she thought he looked anxious.

"Harvey, I'm sorry for the way I acted the other night," Johnetta said after they sat down.

"It's okay, Johnetta. I shouldn't have done what I did either, but I got a little upset."

"I've had time to think about the whole thing, Harvey, in these last few days." She leaned forward, her eyes on him. "I don't want to hurt your feelings, Harvey, but I know now that my feelings for you will never include marriage. I wanted to tell you so there won't be any misunderstanding.'' She didn't know how Harvey would take this.

He asked, ''Is it Thorne?''

''Harvey, we have known each other too long for me to be anything but honest with you,'' Johnetta said. ''At this moment I'm not sure how I feel about Rafe, except to say there's something happening between us and I have to see how it's going to turn out.''

Harvey said, ''I appreciate your telling me how you feel, Johnetta.'' He stood up and took her hand. ''We'll still be friends like always?''

''Of course,'' Johnetta said and kissed him on the cheek, thinking that Harvey almost looked relieved. She wouldn't be surprised if he was. It had become obvious that they were not meant for each other.

Harvey felt uncharacteristically lighthearted. He was supposed to feel hurt and resentful. But all he could think about was how Johnetta's explanation echoed in his heart.

''There's something happening between us and I have to see how it's going to turn out.'' Between Melina Williams and Harvey Wilkins.

Did he have Melina's telephone number? He'd have to look it up when he got home.

Chapter Seven

Johnetta closed the door behind Harvey with a sigh. Harvey was a good friend, and they should have had the sense to keep it that way and not try to mold it into something more. She didn't think it would take long for an eligible man like Harvey to find a woman he truly cared for and who cared for him.

Johnetta warmed up spaghetti and meatballs, fixed a slice of garlic bread, and sat down to dinner. The feeling of freedom— of relief from a burden—was extremely pleasant. *That* was the reasonable Johnetta.

The other Johnetta that she was seeing more of lately said it was like a mountain off her back, and she was getting happier about it by the minute!

That Johnetta freely admitted that now she could think about Rafe. There were no obstacles between them. There was no reason now not to be brutally honest and confess that she was falling in love with him.

True, she'd met him only seven days ago but—as he said— love can't be measured by time. She had been drawn to him with an immediacy and intensity that was totally new to her. She had found it irresistible.

Johnetta pushed her plate away and gave herself over to thinking about Rafe. He was a complex individual. He could be both gentle and demanding, cooperative and firm, thoughtful and careless, arrogant and humble, generous and intemperate. Life with Rafael Thorne would never be dull.

She knew there was a difference between the headiness of a courtship that, by its very nature, was brief, and the endurance of a marriage. But Rafe had said he yearned to be anchored, and she suspected that his passionate nature would not only survive the courtship phase but find its fullest outlet in the long-term commitment of marriage.

But could she be sure? He had already tried marriage once, and it had lasted only two-and-a-half years. He'd never talked about the reason the marriage had failed. What had he said about it being clear they didn't fit? That could mean any number of things. She wanted to know what he meant because it would give her added insight into his character. Would he volunteer the information, or would she have to ask him? She hoped he would volunteer it.

If Rafe asked her to marry him, and *if* she said yes, then it would be urgent to know that their union wouldn't be jeopardized by whatever had caused Rafe's first marriage to break up.

Johnetta got up from the table. *I'm borrowing trouble,* she chided herself. *I don't know that Rafe is going to ask me to marry him—and if he does, I don't know if I'll say yes. Yet here I am anticipating problems related to Rafe's first marriage. It's his second marriage that should concern me now!*

I wonder if Donna told Mama and Dad about Rafe? I guess they'll be disappointed because I settled things with Harvey, but I hope they'll like Rafe once they have a chance to know him.

Each time the phone rang that evening, Johnetta expected it to be Rafe. First it was Donna, then two offers of work and two telephone marketers offering rewards for consenting to look at vacation condos. She wondered why Rafe didn't call. She longed to hear his voice and to feel the current that made her tingle with excitement and anticipation. Especially now that she was no longer bound to Harvey and free to let her feelings for Rafe flow. Rafe, who with one look could make her tremble, who with a brush of his lips on hers could make her knees weak, whose arms about her made her feel cherished, feminine, and desired.

Rafe had spent the day in Spartanburg where the Masterson family who owned the house he was working on were presently living. Two of the Masterson brothers had been down to Charleston several times to see the work and had invited him to their corporate offices for an interview. To Rafe's surprise, they had offered him a lucrative contract to restore five other properties they owned around the state.

"We like your work," Tom, the older brother, had said, rocking back on his heels. "You're the best we've found."

"We'll show you the property that's nearest here," Clarence announced, grabbing his hat and ushering Rafe ahead of him.

It was that house, aging well as it passed its century mark, its graceful Palladian lines bathed in the late afternoon sun, that spoke to Rafe. The photographs and written descriptions of the others had been informative and interesting, but this house captured his heart. He agreed to study the offer and to give them an answer within a week.

He was later leaving the upstate city than expected. His intention had been to see Johnetta by eight at the latest, but it was closer to ten o'clock by the time he was a few blocks from her apartment. He was hungry to see her, to touch her, to hear her say his name, to find out what her eyes were telling him about her feelings for him.

When he'd taken her home from the gallery, he'd tried to make her understand that he cared for her, but she'd never said she believed him. That was before she confessed to having feelings about him and before they'd embraced. Had that helped his case, he wondered? What would convince her? A ring? He didn't think so, not yet. Although he'd seen several he liked in the jewelry store in Spartanburg this morning, he thought he'd have a wider selection in Charleston.

Rafe glanced at his watch. It was probably too late too call her. He dialed her number, and she answered immediately.

"Johnetta, it's Rafe. Honey, I know it's late, but I'm almost at your door. I've just arrived back from Spartanburg. Could I please stop by for a moment? I promise not to stay long."

"I'll look for you." *So that's why I haven't heard from him,* Johnetta thought, giving her hair a quick brush then going to the door as his knock sounded.

Rafe came quickly through the door and closed it behind him, aware only of Johnetta, welcoming and waiting.

"Would you like to sit down?" Johnetta murmured politely. The words slipped out, leaving no trace in the atmosphere. Rafe was vivid before her, as if this were her first time seeing him: a tall man with angular features, assured, attractive, and ardent, his dark eyes mesmerizing her with their heat.

Rafe reached for her instinctively, and she went into his arms.

"I've missed you so, Johnetta," he said, placing soft kisses on her hair, her ear, her forehead, her cheek, and her neck.

Johnetta put her arms around him. "All day I've thought of you," she whispered. "Only you."

The fire flamed in Rafe. He pulled her closer. His mouth on her was hard and hot. The taste of her drove him wild, but he reined in his hunger. Letting himself get out of control would be disastrous. He gentled his caresses while his breathing returned to normal.

Johnetta laid her hands on each side of his face. The tenderness of her caress made Rafe humble with gratitude. He kissed her hands, which were slim, soft, and smooth.

"I've something to tell you, Rafe. I've settled things with Harvey."

"Johnetta?" His head shot up and his grip on her hand tightened.

She scarcely breathed under his piercing gaze. "It wasn't fair to him."

"Why not?"

"Because of how I feel about you." All of the words that she had told herself in describing those feelings were locked inside of her. Now that the moment had come, they remained in her heart.

Rafe saw them in her eyes. "Sweetheart, you're killing me by slow degrees," he said. "Let me hear you. I'll say it first."

What was he going to say first? Johnetta was afraid to blink or breathe.

"I love you, Johnetta. With all of my heart."

She could breathe again as a flood of joy engulfed her, sweeping away her hesitation and anxiety. "I love you, Rafe," she said.

"Sweetheart. My Johnetta." In his intense happiness, Rafe could only crush Johnetta to him. Her name was a paean of triumph that he said over and over. "Kiss me, please, Johnetta."

Johnetta's hands caressed the back of Rafe's head as she put her lips on his. Her response to Rafe's request quickly changed its nature as electricity jolted through her. She needed to get closer, and she burrowed into Rafe while the kiss deepened and her breathing thickened.

Johnetta pulled back. She'd faint if she didn't get some air.

They held onto each other, drawing air into their lungs and regaining their balance. It was time to leave; Rafe had promised to stay only a short time, but time had lost its meaning since he'd held Johnetta.

"I promised not to stay long, Johnetta, so I'm going. I'll see you after work tomorrow, but before I go, tell me again."

Johnetta saw the need for reassurance in Rafe's eyes, and her heart swelled with tenderness. She held his face and looked into his eyes. "I love you, Rafe. Truly I do."

''Thank you, sweetheart. I promise that you'll never regret it.''

Rafe was only able to sleep because he was tired from the Spartanburg trip. All he could think about as he went to bed was that Johnetta had not only dismissed Wilkins but had admitted that she loved him. Johnetta loved *him,* not Wilkins!

He'd meant to tell her about the offer he'd received in Spartanburg, but he had forgotten all about it. He couldn't think of anything after she had said she loved him. He could no longer imagine life without Johnetta by his side. He would urge her to wed him as soon as possible.

The wedding. Rafe replayed his conversation with Johnetta in his head. He hadn't even said ''marriage,'' much less ''wedding.'' He hadn't asked her to marry him in any formal sense. All he'd done was tell her he loved her. What does she think? He sat up and reached for the phone, automatically noting the time. It was nearly midnight. Reluctantly, he decided that a marriage proposal would be the first order of business when he saw her tomorrow.

His face brightened as he thought about how well that would work out because tomorrow he would buy the ring, and when she said yes, he would put his ring on Johnetta's finger. A contented smile curved his lips. His engagement ring would mark their anniversary. Tomorrow would be exactly one week since they'd met.

Johnetta had one more day at the hospital. On this last day, she was culling files and color-coding them. It was busy work that kept her hands occupied but left her mind free to dwell on more important matters—like Rafe.

He loved her. He said he did, and she believed him, even though it seemed like a miracle. She loved him, which was even harder to believe, yet every fiber of her being told her it was true.

How strange that she'd been trying to write about love for the past ten years but was only now experiencing it! Her writing had drawn on her imagination and fantasies as well as an expansion of what she'd felt for Michael Carter so many years ago. Had her depiction been lacking in some critical way, and was that a contributing factor to the rejection of the novels?

Perhaps not, but there were two things for certain: The novels had been sent back, and what she felt for Rafael Thorne bore little resemblance in essence to what she'd felt before for anyone, including Michael.

What she felt for Rafe was life changing. No matter what happened in the future, she'd never be the same Johnetta. The world around her was not the same. She marveled at how knowing that she loved and was loved sharpened all of her senses. Sounds that she heard were keener, sights had greater clarity, smells were stronger, her food had a more distinctive flavor, and even the files she was working with seemed to have a different texture.

It's strange how I feel like I can take on anything and conquer it now, she thought. *Knowing Rafe loves me makes me stronger within myself. I can do whatever I want to do, and what I want to do is sell my novel and help Rafe become an architect.*

She ticked off the things she wanted to do in preparation for Rafe coming over tonight. First, make an apple pie, then straighten up the living room. The first time Rafe had come to the apartment, he'd brought her medicine and juice. The second time he brought her fruit. This time when he came she wanted to do something for him. Her pies were pretty good, and she thought he'd appreciate the fact that she made one just for him. He could take it home after they'd sampled it.

The more she thought of seeing him in a few hours, the more excited she became. She wanted to wear something special for their evening together. Mentally she reviewed her moderate wardrobe, but nothing appealed to her until she remembered the flame jumpsuit she'd bought in an unguarded moment but hadn't yet worn. It was just the right outfit because it fit like a second skin and made her feel alluringly feminine.

She stopped at the market for Granny Smith apples. At her door, she juggled the shopping bag, her purse and the handful of magazines and junk mail from her mailbox. She first went to the kitchen to empty the shopping bag, then to the bedroom for a quick change into jeans and a T-shirt. On the way to the kitchen, she stopped to look at the mail she'd dropped on the table.

There were two letters asking for donations, a library notice for an overdue book, a magazine on health, and the weekly ads from the stores inside a tabloid folder. She tossed this aside to look at later, but it slid off the table, spilling its contents.

Johnetta bent to scoop up the ads. Her breath caught when she saw the large manila envelope she'd enclosed with her contest entry. She put the pile of ads on the table and used a letter opener to carefully slice the top of the envelope. Then she sat down on the couch and pulled out the letter with trembling fingers.

Dear Author,

The winners in the historical novel category are: Cynthia Roper, First place; Dora McCall, Second place; and Marguerite Berg, Third place. Our thanks to all who submitted manuscripts. We hope that you will continue your efforts to become a published writer.

Johnetta looked disbelievingly at the letter. She hadn't placed at all, not even third. She was unaware of her tears until they began to fall on the page. She threw the letter down and buried her face in the couch. Hopelessness welled in her. Deep sobs tore at her chest and wrenched her stomach muscles. All the months she'd worked so hard, all she'd given up to have time for the novel, all the hours she'd felt she was finally achieving good solid work—all for nothing.

How had she ever deluded herself into thinking she could become a published writer? It was obvious that she was a barely competent hack who could write an article or perhaps a short story but never a novel. That was beyond her capabilities no matter how hard she tried. She'd been trying for ten years and four novels and this letter proved it. She could write her best and it still wasn't—would never be—good enough.

Despair ate at her guts, and she clutched her stomach as the sobs kept coming. What was she going to do now? Writing was what gave meaning to her life, gave her the greatest pleasure, made her someone of value who could express herself creatively. This was the image of Johnetta Raymond she'd nurtured since college. Who would she be now?

She wished that she could stop crying. It must be the stress of the past year releasing itself, the year she'd strained to make ends meet so she could write the novel and meet her Valentine's Day deadline. So she could prove to her mother and father that she could be a success in her chosen field. Now she'd have to face them with the bitter truth of her failure.

A desolation that was so deep she didn't hear the knock at the door some time later engulfed Johnetta. The knock grew louder, and she heard a voice call her name.

"Johnetta, are you in there? Johnetta?"

Moving like a robot, she went to the door. She pulled it open just as Rafe raised his hand to knock again.

Chapter Eight

"Johnetta?"

This woman can't be Johnetta, Rafe thought when he first looked at her. Her eyes were red and puffy, her skin splotchy, her hair tangled, and her face drawn in such devastation that Rafe felt his heart plummet.

"Johnetta, what's happened?"

She looked at him dully and moved aside as he came in and closed the door behind him. *Maybe there's been a sudden death in the family,* he thought as he took her hand and led her to the couch so he could sit beside her. She still hadn't spoken when he gently pulled her into the curve of his arm. He pillowed her head on his chest and stroked her back.

He thought she was in shock and decided to find a blanket to cover her with while he made her some hot tea. Then, he heard her say his name.

"Rafe."

"Yes, Johnetta." His voice was quiet and soothing.

"I'm glad you're here."

"So am I." He continued stroking her and could feel her relax slightly.

"You comfort me," she said with a deep sigh.

"As soon as you can, sweetheart, you must tell me what happened." Rafe was trying to figure out what could have brought Johnetta to such a state since he'd seen her last night, when they were both giddy with joy. It had to be news that was received very recently because otherwise she'd have probably told him. Whatever it was it had knocked the props right out from under her. It must have been a death. He had to know.

"Was it a death in your family, honey?"

"No."

Thank God for that, Rafe thought as he breathed a sigh of relief. He could now afford to wait until she felt able to talk, and he could deal with whatever it was. He continued holding her and stroking her back. Something crinkled under him, and then he remembered seeing some papers on the couch. He shifted and pulled a single crumpled sheet out from under him.

Johnetta saw him pick up the letter. She took a deep breath and hoped that she could confide in Rafe without crying again. She held out her hand for the letter and smoothed it out as he watched her curiously.

She handed him the letter. "I got this in the mail when I got home," she said, as if that explained everything.

Rafe took the sheet eagerly and quickly read the few paragraphs. Johnetta saw the bewilderment on his face. He read the letter through again, slowly this time. "I don't understand. What has this to do with you?" he asked.

"I entered the contest by sending in the chapters and synopsis of my novel. I thought the work was good, and I'd hoped to place in the top three. But I'm not."

Rafe heard Johnetta's words but he couldn't take them in. He looked at her so strangely that Johnetta felt the need to elaborate.

"This is the first time I've entered that contest. I thought my writing had improved enough to win a place in the historical fiction category. I've been waiting for weeks to hear the results.''

"You're a writer?'' Rafe felt like he'd been hit with a large club. This couldn't be happening, not to him. Not again.

"I started writing in college, and I've been writing ever since,'' she explained.

"All the times we've talked you never mentioned it,'' Rafe said. "You talked about the other things you did, like the store and the moving sales, but you never said anything about writing.'' Rafe heard the accusatory tone in his voice, but he couldn't help himself. He moved back from Johnetta involuntarily. Johnetta responded with a little frown as she tried again to explain herself to Rafe.

"I don't talk much about my writing, Rafe. I've published a few short stories and several articles—but that's all. I always figured I couldn't call myself a writer until I was good enough to sell a novel.''

"That's why you took off from the store,'' Rafe said with sudden insight.

Johnetta, pleased that he was beginning to understand, agreed. "Yes, that's why. I saw my old college professor last year, and he asked to see my work. He encouraged me to continue but said I had to be more committed if I wanted to be successful. That's when I decided to take the year off and work full-time on the novel.''

"All of your family knows?''

"Yes, of course.''

"Did Wilkins know?''

Johnetta was puzzled by this line of questioning. Why was this so difficult for Rafe to comprehend? "Harvey knows I write. He never paid much attention to it.''

"In other words, everyone knew except me.'' The rising resentment in Rafe's voice began to register with Johnetta.

"You make it sound as if I deliberately held something back from you.''

"Didn't you? I told you all about me, how I'm working on

houses now but what I'd really like to be is an architect. But did you at any time tell me that what you really wanted to be is a writer, that it's important to you?'' Rafe's anger was so intense now that he had to get up from the couch and away from her.

What is the matter with him? Is this jealousy? she wondered. That didn't make any sense to her, but in the back of her head was the thought that if Rafe got this jealous over what she considered a small thing, how jealous would he get over a legitimate cause?

"I'm waiting for an answer, Johnetta," Rafe said grimly.

When Rafe had first arrived, Johnetta had been full of her own grief and he had not pressed her for conversation. His main concern had been to comfort her. Now he was experiencing some distress that she couldn't identify, and it was her turn to be patient until she could find out what the problem was.

"Rafe, you're right. You told me about wanting to be an architect, but I didn't tell you about wanting to be a writer. But I don't understand why that is so important. You know it now. There's nothing illegal or terrible about it.''

Rafe leaned against the table, his hands fisted in his pockets as he looked at her. "I'll tell you what's terrible about it, Johnetta. My ex-wife, Lucia, was a writer. She took writing all through college and was convinced she had talent. I don't know about the talent but she had the drive. We both had jobs the first year of our marriage. Four days out of seven, she spent her free time writing. When I objected, she said she'd make it up to me as soon as she sold her first novel. I was so much in love I gave in because I thought at least she had a goal and I'd missed mine. Then she decided to work part-time so she could spend more hours writing.''

Johnetta listened avidly. She'd wanted to know the details of his marriage, and now he was telling her. She'd never suspected that his wife had been a writer. How strange for him to become attracted to another writer without even knowing it.

"We spent less and less time together. All she focused on

was her writing. I felt I was an object in the house, not a husband, so I spent time away from the house with my buddies. I'd tried to get her interested in starting a family, but that didn't work. Just about the time I got to the end of my patience, she sold her novel. I was happy for her—and glad for me. I thought that maybe now we could resurrect our marriage, but the next thing I knew she wanted a divorce.''

"A divorce? But why?"

"Her exact words were, 'I know now I can sell my novels, so I don't need you any longer, Rafe'."

Without thinking, Johnetta jumped up and went to Rafe. "What a cruel thing to say, Rafe. I'm so sorry."

Rafe stepped back to keep her hands from touching him. "That's what you say now, but you'll be just as cruel."

Johnetta stood still. "I don't see how you can say that. I could never be that selfish and thoughtless about you."

"You don't think so? You said you loved me, yet you kept from me the part of your life that was so important you gave up a whole year to work on it exclusively. It was so vital to you that all of your hopes were on the contest, but did you share that with me?'' Rafe's voice was cold. *Maybe the frost will keep my heart from breaking,* he thought, his fingers clutching the ring box in his pocket.

"This was supposed to be our night, Johnetta, but what did I find when I got here? A woman so distraught I could hardly recognize her. So devastated she couldn't even say hello. I thought you were grief stricken over a death in the family but no, it was only that you hadn't won some writing contest."

Now he leaned his face closer to Johnetta. "You forgot about me, didn't you, Johnetta?" He spit the words out between his teeth. "You forgot I was coming over. All you thought about was yourself and your book."

"But I've put a whole year of my life in that book," she cried. "I'd worked harder on it than anything I've ever done. I thought it was good work. Can't you see that?"

"Oh, yes, I see it. I've heard it all before." His anger had subsided, and he was weary to the bone.

Johnetta fought the guilt caused by Rafe's accusations. There was too much truth in his words for her to make a defense against them. She hadn't told him about her writing earlier; habit had betrayed her, but she would have gotten around to it. She scrambled for what she could say that could salvage something for their future.

"Please listen to me, Rafe. Not telling you about my writing was not a deliberate act of shutting you out. You must believe me. I just met you a week ago today, and I'm used to keeping that part of my life to myself." She realized she was digging the pit deeper. Rafe's face confirmed it. His eyes were icy, his face set in hard lines.

She tried again. "Rafe, it was just yesterday that I realized I'm in love with you. Then this letter I've been waiting for arrived—and it was a shock. But it has nothing to do with my love for you. I'm not like your ex-wife."

"You're only fooling yourself, Johnetta."

"I'm not!" She wasn't getting through to him. "I know what I feel for you, Rafe, and it's something deep and powerful that I've never felt before for *any* man."

"God knows I want to believe you. I just can't."

The resignation in his voice made Johnetta go to him, even though he had stepped away. She gripped his arm.

"But last night you said you loved me, Rafe. You told me you loved me with all of your heart."

"Why do you think this is killing me, Johnetta?" The bitterness in his look seared Johnetta, and she dropped her hands from him.

"I went through this hell once. I can't go through it again."

"Rafe, please don't go."

He turned at the door. He wanted to hurt her as deeply as he was hurting.

"Don't worry, Johnetta. You have your writing for comfort. You won't miss me."

Chapter Nine

Sunday was gray and chilly. Winds from the northeast blew down the coast, dropping temperatures by twenty degrees in an hour. Rafe was glad. He pulled his hood up over his head and hunkered down in the biting wind on Folly Beach.

The beach had earlier held a sizable group of walkers but now he encountered only a few as he strode along. *They can't take it,* he thought, but he gloried in fighting the gusts of wind that had driven people out of the choppy water.

The element suited his mood and his need to be in the open air after a sleepless night. He had never been in such pain before. He thought that the suffering he endured after Lucia had been bad. He'd learned several painful lessons from it. But in these sleepless hours, he realized that this was different. He'd met Lucia when he was nineteen, married her at twenty-three, and at twenty-five was divorced. He had been disappointed in her, and the love he'd started out with began to fade away. In the end, they were only two people sharing the same living space. Rafe had vowed to never again put himself in that position.

While it was true that the fact she married him for financial support had been a blow to his pride and his ego, his heart and soul had never been at risk as they were now.

His heart had recognized Johnetta at first glance for its own reasons. Rafe had acknowledged the recognition and cherished her from that moment on. As he grew to know her, he'd been drawn by her genuineness, her innate dignity, her unassuming competence—and by the slowly blossoming quality of her response to him. There was so much more to learn about her, which he'd eagerly looked forward to.

He had known with absolute certainty that Johnetta was destined for him. It was only a matter of time until she came to the same conclusion. Rafe didn't think it was because he was a better man than Wilkins. It was a deep, almost mystical, connection that he and Johnetta shared.

He couldn't explain his ignorance about her writing. He should have picked up on it somehow. He knew she was meant for something creative, and he should have followed up on that intuition by asking her.

How was he ever going to get her out of his system? He didn't want to let her go. He began to run, pounding his feet on the sand and taking in gulps of air. If he'd known this at the beginning, he'd have walked away. It would still have hurt—but not like this.

She was so precious to him. She was to be his beloved wife, the mother of the children he'd always wanted. Now she was gone. Rafe ran faster and faster into the wind, not caring whether the moisture on his face was from the wind or his tears.

Johnetta had found sanctuary in a hotel room in Columbia. She hadn't been able to sleep at all Saturday night. The confrontation with Rafe played itself over and over in her head. By the time dawn came, she knew she had to get out of the apartment and out of Charleston. She made a reservation at a small hotel she'd stayed in several times, and by seven she was on the road after leaving a brief message with Donna. She didn't want her family calling the police when they couldn't reach her.

Johnetta felt like she had fallen into a Carolina swamp. She couldn't find firm ground anywhere she turned—mentally or emotionally. All of her decisions had been wrong ones, and—one by one—their erosion had set in. The year off to devote to writing had resulted in failure. She'd built on a false foundation with Harvey. She had met the love of her life and had quickly lost him. The deadline of Valentine's Day was fast approaching, and she had nothing to show to herself and her parents—just a wasted year, a rejected novel, scant finances, and lost love.

The lost love truly was not her fault. How could she have known that Rafe didn't like writers just because Lucia had treated him badly. Why should he think she'd be like Lucia? The circumstances were entirely different, and he had no reason to get so angry with her. She wouldn't ignore him if they were married. All of these years she hadn't ignored her job or her family, so that proved she wasn't as narrow-minded and selfish as Lucia.

The image of Rafe's face, alight with tenderness, filled her mind. Her heart swelled with grief. She blinked rapidly to keep the tears from obscuring her vision. Sheer misery made her pull off the road and lay her head on the steering wheel, mourning her loss. Rafe—her love—was gone. His arms, his kisses— gone. Her life with him—gone. The family she wanted with him—gone.

There was a knock on her window. She looked up at a man and a woman who had pulled off the road. "Do you need help?" the woman asked.

Johnetta wiped her eyes and lowered the window a little. She shook her head. "I'm okay. Thanks just the same."

"You sure?" The man didn't seem to be convinced.

"I'm sure." Johnetta managed a smile, and the couple walked away. She combed her hair and repaired her makeup as best she could, then carefully pulled onto the highway.

In Columbia, she unpacked her overnight bag in her room, then went out for breakfast. She was glad to have brought her warmest jacket and a knit cap. Warm, sunny weather would not have fit her mood like this gray, blustery day.

She ordered juice, hotcakes with bacon, and coffee, but when it came she found she could only tolerate the beverages. Her stomach roiled at the smell of the bacon, and she pushed the plate aside. She sipped the juice, then the coffee. *What I need,* she thought, *is to run. Maybe that will clear my head.*

Columbia was a busy city and, although it lacked the beauty and history of Charleston, it had the distinction of being the state capital, housing government buildings, the capitol building, a fine arts center, the state university, and several other colleges.

Johnetta drove around until she found a park that suited her needs. She left her heavy jacket and cap in the car and began a slow run. Gradually, she increased her speed until she felt her muscles become limber and well oiled. Sweat began to pour from her body, and the misery that had troubled her floated away.

After she returned to her room, she stepped under a warm shower. She put on her robe and then stretched out on the bed, relaxing. When she awakened later, she was pleased to realize that she had taken a short nap. Getting out of bed, she glanced at the clock-radio in disbelief. She'd slept three hours.

For the moment, her mind was empty and clear. She looked at the Sunday paper she'd picked up. Several churches were having afternoon concerts. If she hurried, she could catch the one at AME Zion.

The large audience had just settled down to hear the opening number when she found her seat. The young adult choir was hosting its counterpart from a sister church in Gaffney. The guest choir sang four songs, then the host choir had its turn. Some of the songs were familiar to Johnetta. The music swirled around her, filling the air with soaring sound. As she listened, she thought that, if she could open herself to it, she might find healing and peace, a way out of the morass she was in, and a clue about what to do next.

The choirs merged for the final selection, and an expressive solo voice prayed, "Lord, here I am. Guide Thou me."

Johnetta's hands were tightly clasped in her lap and her head was bowed as quiet tears slid down her face.

Johnetta awakened again to gray skies on Monday morning. The wind had subsided, and cold seemed to have thinned when she walked out to find a coffee shop. The two blocks that she walked before finding one that caught her fancy increased her energy. She enjoyed her juice, bagel, and coffee, then was off for a brisk walk that covered six blocks.

She'd gone to bed still pondering the question of what to do next, and now the answer was crystal clear: First, cleanse her mind of blame for either Rafe or herself. She didn't want to dwell on what happened, and she had to let it go because, if she held on, it would exact a crippling emotional toll and become a stumbling block to regaining her balance.

Second, she needed to read the rest of the contents of the manila envelope. She'd read only the letter but knew there should be something from the people who judged each entry.

She made herself comfortable at the square table in front of the window and took everything out of the envelope: the letter, her three chapters, the synopsis, three pages from the judge. The first two pages contained detailed scoring items, while page three was a typed commentary. She resisted the temptation to read it first and concentrated on the one-to-five scores given on setting, dialogue, characterization, conflict, and motivation, as well as several other categories.

Johnetta was surprised to see that, with one as the lowest and five as the highest score, many of her scores were fours, with an occasional three and several fives.

The judges had given her a three for a good balance of action and description, but for her story's conflict between the hero and heroine, she was given a four. The fact that her secondary characters weren't well established got a score of three, but because her heroine had a distinctive voice, she got a four. Johnetta read through each of the nine categories, including the synopsis. So many of the sixty listed items had received fours she began to wonder why she hadn't earned at least a third place showing. Then she understood when she read the commentary:

> *This is a fascinating story, and I like your approach. I can see the places you write about. The opening hook is good, and the leading characters are vividly displayed. The main problem in the three chapters and in the synopsis is a lack of tightness, a tendency to wander and to leave loose ends. Look at your book from first to last page, with an eye on integration and balance. That shouldn't be difficult for a writer of your talent. I look forward to seeing this fine story in print. Don't disappoint me.*

Johnetta looked at the phrase again. The judge had written that she had talent and expected Johnetta to get the book in shape for publishing. No one had ever told her that before, except Professor Darren. In the final paragraph, the judge had listed questions a reader might have, as an example of the need for tighter construction.

Why hadn't she read all of this when she first opened the envelope instead of just the letter? She knew why. She hadn't been able to acknowledge it to herself. She had egotistically thought her work was deserving simply because she'd spent so much time and effort on it. But what did she know of the many other entries and their quality? She got a lot of fours, but how many entries got mostly fives? She had let herself fall into the same trap that a lot of aspiring writers stumbled into, and she had paid the penality for it. Had she read the whole packet with the right spirit, perhaps the evening with Rafe would have turned out differently.

Johnetta got to her feet and went to gaze out the window. People and cars passed by, but they didn't register in her mind. She saw Rafe's face, cold and bitter, as he rejected her touch. Perhaps nothing would have changed the outcome; at some point during the evening, she would have mentioned the writing and his prejudice against it because of Lucia would have become an issue. Misery stirred in her, and she had to remind herself of the decision to let it go.

Still on her feet, she picked up the papers and read them again. She began to have new ideas as she considered the story from the reader's point of view. She sat down and made notes, but after an hour, she knew she had to get home to her computer. She checked out, and, two hours later, had her manuscript spread out on the bed so that she could review it chapter by chapter.

Rafe found a flat tire when he went to get in his truck Monday morning. He was late to work, only to be informed that the materials he'd ordered for a gazebo were unavailable. *So it's going to be this kind of day or maybe week,* Rafe thought. He wasn't surprised. After Saturday's fiasco, nothing could surprise him. Any person who could make the huge mistake of falling in love with Johnetta and ruining his whole life couldn't be trusted to get anything right.

If he'd known from the beginning that she was a writer, maybe this heartache could have been avoided. But maybe not. Sometimes destiny stepped in, and nothing he did could change it.

Weary and frustrated, he tried to decide if he was hungry enough to prepare a meal when he got home that evening. His stomach felt hollow, but he wasn't sure if food could satisfy him. The phone rang, providing a welcome distraction.

"Rafe? This is Morgan. I thought you were going to keep in touch."

"Hey, Morgan. You know how time slips by, buddy. How's everything?" Rafe welcomed the jovial voice of his friend from college days and wished that Morgan was in Charleston instead of Hartfort, Connecticut. He needed a friend to discuss his present dilemma with.

"All is well, and that's one of the reasons I'm calling you." Morgan was a dean for the University of Connecticut and had frequently urged Rafe to study for a degree in architecture there. "The applications for next year are beginning to pour in, and I want you to apply. You're been putting it off for too long, Rafe. You've got to get started."

"I just can't see myself competing with all those kids, Morgan."

"You've got the wrong idea, Rafe. You're making that tired excuse because you're scared or you're lazy, or you don't want to be an architect at all." Morgan's voice lost its joviality. "Now, which one is it?"

"I *do* want to be an architect," Rafe protested. "You know that, Morgan."

"If you do, this is what can happen. You have years of practical experience, and I know you're widely read on theory and practice. That means you can take exams for some of the requirements. If you pass—and I'm sure you will—you won't have to take the class. Also, Rafe, get that notion of competing out of your mind. The only competition is against yourself, no one else."

Morgan's voice was stern, and Rafe absorbed all he was saying. If he didn't have to sit in boring classes about subjects he already knew, it might not be so bad. Maybe now was the time to take Morgan up on the offer. What did he have to lose, other than time? *There is nothing to keep me here now, once my current project is completed,* Rafe thought, trying to ignore the flash of pain that came with the thought.

"Morgan, you're making sense to me for the first time."

"You mean you're *listening* for the first time."

"That deal about the exams instead of classes. Do other colleges do that?"

"Most have some kind of arrangement. Why?"

"I received this offer to work on five other properties owned by the brothers who also own the house in Charleston I'm working on. They like what I've done and have offered me a contract."

"Does that mean you won't be coming back to Hartford?" There was disappointment in Morgan's voice.

"I haven't given them an answer. I was thinking that, if there's a college near them, maybe I could do both at the same time."

"You could do that here, Rafe. Your work is well known, and it wouldn't be hard for you to get the same opportunity here," he said persuasively. "I can begin making inquiries once I receive your application."

"I don't know about that. The deal here is already in the works."

"You have another reason for staying in South Carolina, Rafe. Did you meet a woman?" When he was answered by silence, Morgan's voice changed. "Seriously, Rafe, have you finally met someone you don't want to leave?"

"Met her, fell in love with her, bought her a ring, and lost her," Rafe said soberly.

"Man, that's awful! What happened?"

Rafe slumped down in his chair and told Morgan the whole story, answering all of Morgan's questions. He felt the first stirring of comfort. This felt like the old days, when the two friends saw each other frequently and always knew what was happening with each other.

"How do you feel about all this?" Morgan asked.

"At first, all I felt was hurt and anger and betrayal. Then frustration, sadness and grief. Right now, I feel like I've ruined my whole life because I'd begun to build everything around Johnetta and me being together."

Rafe heard Morgan take a deep breath. "Rafe, I love you like the brother I never had. But I've got to tell you the truth. You're crazy—and you're wrong."

Rafe sat up straight. "What do you mean?" he asked indignantly.

"One woman has nothing to do with the other. Lucia never loved you, and she deliberately used you. I think that Johnetta loves you. She made sure everything was clear with this other man as soon as she understood her feelings for you, and, from what you've said, she's not a shallow woman who would do this easily. She explained her actions to you, but you refused to listen in the same way you haven't listened to me about college—until today. The most important thing to remember is that you allowed Lucia to use you, and you've got to face that."

"How can you—"

"Rafe, I'm going to give you two things to think about before I go because you've got a lot at stake here." His voice was quiet and serious.

"One is that you finally have to acknowledge you didn't do what you should have done about Lucia. The other is about the happiness you and your Johnetta could have. Don't throw it away because of your problem about what she does for a living."

Chapter Ten

There were twenty-three chapters in Johnetta's book. She scanned each one, keeping in mind the commentary on better integration and tighter construction. She began to see loose ends in the narrative where an action or a character's reaction lacked sufficient or appropriate motivation and resolution. In the third chapter, Cynthia, the female protagonist, promises to tell her older child a particular incident in the life of his great-grandmother, who was a slave. Johnetta looked for the mention of the storytelling but never found it. Later, Cynthia decides, after a long inner struggle, to confront her husband, Rollo, with her suspicion that he has another woman. Johnetta searched for that confrontation but found that, because of subsequent events, it had apparently been dismissed in Cynthia's mind. Yet there was no direct reference to it.

Johnetta shook her head in wonder. How could she have missed that? She couldn't believe that she had the nerve to think *her* entry was superior. Her lips tightened in shame. By the time she finished reviewing the entire manuscript, she had two pages of notes plus several sketches of reworked events that would fit better than the original ones.

Immersion in the work made her forget to eat or to look at the time, but when her stomach growled, she realized that it was after eight o'clock. She made an omelet and ate it with toast and coffee.

She wondered what Rafe was eating and how he'd made it through the day. Did he miss her like she missed him? She'd told herself to once again let it go, and she found that she could think of it now without blame on either side. What had happened was a result of their past experiences and couldn't have been prevented.

Johnetta felt the stab of loss deep inside. She wanted to be with Rafe. She'd arrived at the realization that he was her other half. Together, they created the wholeness she always wanted. It was only through Rafe that she understood what she had been missing in her relationship with Harvey: the feelings of oneness, of being understood, of being cherished, of the desire and readiness for intimacy, of the exaltation of loving and being loved.

She finished her meal and thought about how often she'd heard the saying that art imitated life. She'd written about love—its joy and pain. For her, life was now imitating art. She was experiencing the reality of love's pain and joy for the first time.

The phone rang, and she quickly grabbed it, hoping it was Rafe.

"Hello?" she asked breathlessly.

"I'm glad you're home," Donna said. "Why did you go to Columbia? Are you okay?"

"I'm not okay, but I'm better." *Donna has called at the right time,* Johnetta thought. She felt like she could talk to Donna because she'd met Rafe and knew about the relationship.

"What do you mean, 'Net? I bet it's got something to do with Rafe. Did you break up with him when he took you home from the gallery?"

"No, it was just the opposite, and the next day I told Harvey I could never marry him."

Donna didn't even try to repress her whoop of joy. "Thank goodness you finally saw the light. You two *never* belonged together."

"I see that now. That's the only good news. Now for the bad." Johnetta told Donna about the contest letter, how it made her feel, Rafe's arrival, and the resulting separation after he learned about her writing.

"I don't believe this," Donna said indignantly. "He walked away just because you write like his ex-wife did? If he has no better sense than that, you're lucky to be rid of him."

The vehemence of her loyalty is so characteristic of Donna, Johnetta mused as her sister went on to delineate exactly how she felt about Rafe's betrayal.

"But that doesn't make you feel any better, does it?" Donna asked as she wound down. Her voice became sympathetic. "You hurting, honey?"

"Yes, I am now, but I guess I'll get over it eventually. The good news at the moment is about the novel. I read the judges' notes, and they were very encouraging. I've begun the revisions according to the critique, and I'm excited about getting it right this time."

"That's good, 'Net. Have you talked to Mom and Dad yet?"

"No, but I probably will tomorrow."

"You know Valentine's Day is Friday, only four days away. They'll want to know what you're going to do."

"Friday?" Johnetta had lost track of the days. "I'll have an answer to give them," she promised. *And to give myself,* she thought.

At six-thirty the next morning, Johnetta circled her block twice, running hard to clear away the effects of a troubled night that had been filled with thoughts and dreams in which she and Rafe were tangled with the family in her novel. Going to sleep with her characters in mind was normal, but she'd never before been mixed in with them. *It must be the Rafe effect,* she thought wryly.

After a shower and breakfast, she began working on chapter one. As she worked steadily throughout the day and into the evening, she experienced a new flow of insight into her characters, and the words that appeared on the paper seemed to come out effortlessly.

After she stopped, she spoke with her parents and made it clear that there would be nothing but friendship between her and Harvey because he wasn't the right man for her. She told them about the outcome of the contest and how she was revising the book. She assured them that she was fine and would contact them as soon as she finished the revision. That night she slept dreamlessly.

Johnetta had always known that she had a good story and strong characters in *The Road To Ravenal.* She'd felt inspired by certain scenes when she'd done the version for the contest. But no writing she had ever done felt like this. She always had a clear picture of what had happened, was happening now, and would happen in the future—and why. This realization was stunning. It seemed that what she was now producing had the dynamics of a solid, salable piece of work.

There were times when she found herself thinking that she'd like to read this part to Rafe. At night, her longing for Rafe was acute. She'd never been able to share her work with anyone which whom she was on an intimate basis. She yearned for that closeness. She longed for his touch. She needed to tell him that she loved him, to watch the intense happiness bloom in his face. How could they have been so foolish to allow the breakup?

For a week, Rafe pondered Morgan's opinion that he was partly responsible for the way Lucia had acted. He tried for the first time to look at his previous marriage objectively and without resentment. What had he done to stand up for himself and the marriage? He could honestly say that initially he'd talked to Lucia when she left him alone evening after evening to go to the office she'd made in the smaller bedroom. Eventually, she'd agree to go out with him to a movie, a club, or to see friends. When people occasionally dropped by, she would sometimes come out of the office. That's where he had made the first mistake. He could now see that he should have insisted on some equable arrangement of her time—and when she didn't honor it, to confront her. That would have been more honest.

When Lucia changed to part-time work, he should have seen where it was leading. There should have once again been an honest discussion of her time. If she no longer cared, the truth would have come out. *It is ridiculous that such an argument had been needed after only a year of marriage,* Rafe thought. It was due to his own immaturity and pride that he was prevented from seeing the truth of Lucia's feelings. Instead, he had begun to sulk and spend his time with friends or alone. He'd felt sorry for himself and blamed it on her.

When he finally decided to have it out with her, he found out that her novel had been accepted. He was initially glad that he hadn't confronted her because now they could get back to being married. This was yet another error in judgment. He remembered how Morgan and other friends used to chastize him, saying, "Man, how can you put up with that?"

He'd thought that he was being unselfish and was a loving husband. But there were more things to making a marriage work. There had to be sharing, a partnership, an understanding of common goals based on open communication, friendship, and love. Lucia had a single goal—to be a published writer—and she was willing to sacrifice the marriage to reach that goal. His goal was to be married to Lucia, with a vaguely perceived idea of an eventual family life together.

By Thursday night, Rafe had concluded that he and Lucia shared reasons for the failure of their marriage that had nothing to do with her writing. Anything could have been the singular focus that diverted Lucia's attention away from the marriage.

As soon as he realized these things, Rafe was relieved. He wanted to shout, "It wasn't the writing!" How blind he had been. Now he was free, and his love for Johnetta was also free again.

He had to see Johnetta. He had to let her know how wrong he had been. Most of all, he had to tell her how much he loved and needed her. That wouldn't be easy to do, not after walking away from her and rejecting her love.

Rafe pounded a fist into the palm of his hand in frustration. Why would she even listen to him after the way he acted? How could he get her to realize that he had changed? He knew better than to simply show up at her door, so he had to come up with some strategy that would convince her to see him *and* give him the opportunity to put his ring on her finger.

Johnetta was up at six on Friday morning. She found the name of an editor whom she'd met at a writer's conference last year and who had expressed interest in seeing her completed novel. As she typed the single-page cover letter, she was grateful once again that she had not submitted it earlier. She turned the pages one by one to be certain that everything was in order. She took the packet to a mailing center at eight o'clock and sent it off by Federal Express. *This is well worth the expense,* she thought.

She also knew that she wanted to continue writing. She would not go back to the family business. She had made it through the year, proving that she could support herself. Perhaps she would take a permanent part-time job, so that income would be more consistent. But no matter what it took, she would continue to write.

She treated herself to breakfast at Rita's Coffee Shop, a favorite place for her to go. She felt at peace finishing *The Road to Ravenal* and making the decision for her future.

As she watched people come and go, she wondered if she would ever fill the emptiness left in her by losing Rafe. If only she could have him as well as her writing. If somehow she could have the opportunity to convince him that he too was her passion. She needed both.

Johnetta was reluctant to go back to her apartment. The day was sunny, and she'd been cooped up all week long. She walked around downtown, enjoying watching the tourists in shorts and sandals who would return to places with snow and ice. She spent a leisurely hour strolling through The Market, looking at the many crafts and talking to the sweetgrass basket weavers whose art was so impressive. She did a little window shopping until—thinking she had indulged herself sufficiently—she drove home, arriving at two-thirty.

When she got to her doorway she stopped, looking down in utter surprise. There sat six identical vases, each holding two red roses and each bearing an envelope.

Johnetta unlocked her door and brought the vases inside, making sure to place them in the same order. Her heart was beating fast because she knew the roses could only have come from Rafe. Perhaps her prayers were being answered. She read the first card: "Please forgive me, sweetheart. Rafe." The next one said, "I was wrong, and I apologize. Rafe." Number three said, "Dearest Johnetta, I love you with all of my heart. Rafe."

She didn't know what the other three cards said, but these first three went to the heart of the matter. Rafe understood he had been wrong in treating her like Lucia, and he still loved her. Johnetta sank into a chair and read the first three cards again. Happiness filled her heart.

She reached for number four, thinking that Rafe must have sent a vase each hour. "I have missed you so much. Rafe." *As I've missed you,* she thought. "I understand now that it wasn't the writing. Rafe." Card five mentioned and card six contained an invitation. "Will you have dinner with me tonight? Rafe." *Yes, I will,* she thought.

At three o'clock the seventh vase arrived. It said, "I'll be by at six. Rafe." The four o'clock card said, "I am deeply sorry for any pain I've caused you, Rafe." "I love you, I need you, and I ache to hold you again," said the one at five, which sent Johnetta into shivers. *I know, dearest, for I feel the same way,* she thought.

She was dressed to perfection in a jumpsuit by five forty-five. The house had been cleaned, and she'd washed her hair and done her nails. She was in a fever of anticipation, glancing out the window every few minutes. She couldn't bear to sit still and so instead paced around.

When she saw Rafe's car pull up, she opened the door to see him the instant he got out of the car. In his arms were more roses and a box of candy.

Their eyes were fixed on each other. She held the door open, and he stepped inside and closed it, setting the flowers and the box on the table and opening his arms. There were no words. They clung together in deep thanksgiving and happiness, then exchanged a kiss of love, longing, and commitment.

"Can you forgive me, Johnetta?" he asked.

"We'll forgive each other and go on from there," she said.

"You look absolutely stunning," Rafe said as they sat on the couch. "Every man in the place will envy me."

Johnetta had wanted to be beautiful for him. She thought the happiness that she felt must glow through her—and that was part of what Rafe saw.

"Johnetta, I need to explain something," Rafe said, holding her hand as he looked at her. "What happened with Lucia was partly my fault, and with my hurt pride, I transferred all of the blame onto you. I now understand why I carried all of that resentment for so long. I'm telling you so that you won't have to worry about it happening again. I matured a lot this past week," he said deprecatingly, but his eyes were serious.

"You understand that it could have been *anything* that she was doing that could have taken her away from the marriage?" Johnetta asked.

"I see that. The other thing I want to say is that I don't want you to give up your writing just because your novel didn't get the result you hoped for. You *must* keep trying, Johnetta. Would you please tell me about it over dinner? I'd love to hear it.''

Johnetta could hear his anxiety. She raised their clasped hands and held them to her heart. ''Oh, Rafe, I want to talk with you about it. I revised it completely and sent it off just this morning, but the whole time I wished I could discuss it with you. It's a part of me that I've never shared with anyone—but I want to share it with you because you're so close to my heart.''

''Sweetheart, I don't deserve you, but I've loved you since the moment I saw you. My heart knew you were the one for me. Will you marry me, please, Johnetta?'' Rafe felt the world stand still as he waited for her answer.

''I know you're the one for me, Rafe. Yes, I'll marry you.''

Rafe knew he'd never seen such beauty as what he saw in Johnetta when he placed his ring on her finger. The marquise diamond sparkled as she admired it.

''It's lovely, Rafe.''

''Not half as lovely as you.''

Johnetta looked at the ring again. ''May I ask you something?''

''Anything at all.''

''Did you have this with you last Saturday?''

''Of course.''

''I'm so glad you brought it back to me tonight. I haven't thanked you for the roses, Rafe, and the lovely cards. I was out, and six of them were at the door when I came home.''

''Who did you think sent them to you?''

''I knew they were from you as soon as I saw them. When I read the cards, I could see you had given them a lot of thought. By the time I read the first three, I wanted you to walk through my door.''

''I brought four more to complete the dozen and a Valentine's Day box of candy for my very own, sweetest heart.'' He kissed her and asked, "This is your deadline day, isn't it? What did you decide?"

"To marry this attractive man who says he's in love with me."

"Correction. Who does love you."

Johnetta had been nestled close to Rafe. Now she sat so she could look into his eyes. "Rafe, I can't give up the writing, and I can't give you up. But I can promise I'll never let the writing come between us."

"I believe you, sweetheart. I promise I'll never let your writing interfere with my love for you and my commitment to our marriage."

They looked at each other and, satisfied with what they saw and felt, knew they'd set the seal on their future.

"How soon will you marry me?" Rafe asked, drawing her close to him.

"I haven't even told my parents about you, Rafe. Have you told yours?"

"No, but we've both been gone a long time, Johnetta. So how soon?" He nibbled on her earlobe.

"I can't think when you do that, Rafe."

"That's the idea," he murmured. "Just name an early date."

"In six weeks?"

"Too long. Try again."

"Four weeks. Any sooner wouldn't be decent. There'll be scandal enough for me since everyone thinks I'm still seeing Harvey."

"When will you tell your parents?"

"I'll take you to meet them tomorrow. Okay?" She moved out of his arms. She didn't want to, but the temperature was rising dangerously fast.

"I'll be glad to meet them and your brother. I hope they'll approve."

"They will. I've already told them about breaking up with Harvey. Where will we live, Rafe? It should be where you can finish your architectural degree."

"That gives us two choices." Rafe explained about Spartanburg and Hartford. He was anxious to hear what she said.

Johnetta didn't hesitate. "Hartford seems to be the best choice because you're certain of the school situation there. You may or may not find that advantage here. And as Morgan pointed out, you can find enough work there because your work is well known."

"But what about you? Would you leave your family to move to a strange place? Could you write there?" Rafe was not sure how she felt about this.

"Whither thou goest . . . ," she murmured. "Right now, you're the most important part of my family. I'll be glad to see another part of the country, and I can write anywhere. The main things are you and school."

"Johnetta, I love you so much, I can't even begin to tell you. We'll never forget this Valentine's Day."

"No, because it brought us together. We'll have a wonderful partnership," she said dreamily as he held her.

"How do you mean?"

"You'll design the houses, and I'll write the stories about the people who live in them."

"And we'll always want each other," Rafe said softly, turning her face up for his kiss.

"Always."

ALL BECAUSE OF YOU

Mildred Riley

Chapter One

"If I hadn't decided on a degree in nursing," Anika Wayne explained to Drew Dawson, "I would have opted for a career as a jazz pianist."

"Really?"

"Sure would've. I love jazz, but my mom said that playing piano in a jazz band was not what she wanted for her daughter, and I'd better find something else to help me make a decent living."

"And you're happy with nursing?" Drew wanted to know.

"Yes, I am. I've always liked people, and if I can make their lives better, that's what I want to do."

Drew Dawson had joined her at a lunch table in the university cafeteria, where she sat alone. When he approached her table and asked if he could sit down, she'd nodded, unable to take her eyes away from him. Tall, with copper-bronzed skin, he had sculpted, well-developed muscles that were clearly defined beneath a white tank top and navy jeans.

She felt her face grow warm as he scraped back a chair and threw his long, lean leg over it to sit down.

He put a mug of hot coffee and a tuna sandwich on the table, then turned to place the tray on an empty table. She noticed that his movements were easy and fluid.

"Thanks for sharing your table," he smiled. "I'm Drew Dawson."

Anika's heart lurched unevenly, and she hoped he hadn't noticed her sudden tension.

"Anika Wayne," she said.

"So, Anika," he began, "you're in nursing school?" He'd glanced at the heavy textbooks on the table.

She'd swallowed some iced tea before answering. "Yes, I am, and I find it exciting to be learning new things."

"And for fun," he questioned, "what interests you?"

"I like to fly . . . and playing jazz piano gives me a lot of satisfaction."

"You fly a plane?" He sputtered.

"Since I was sixteen."

"Wow! I've never known a girl who could fly a plane! I'm impressed!" His dark eyes flashed with admiration.

"What about you? What are you studying, and what do you do for fun?"

She'd wanted to sound calm and matter-of-fact because she was really quite affected by this young man she'd just met.

"I'm in communications and advertising. And as for fun— well, basketball is my passion. I really enjoy most sports. I did play basketball in high school, and we were state champions my senior year. But . . . I'm not tall enough nor good enough for a professional basketball career."

"You still play?"

"Whenever I can."

"Like one-on-one, shooting baskets?"

"Anika"—he smiled at her, and her heart flip-flopped again—"there's nothing like the great workout you get from a fast paced, one-on-one game."

"What about track? You look like a track guy to me," she said, eyeing his well-honed body.

He noticed and grinned, demonstrating his prowess by flexing the bicep in his right arm.

Laughing at her stare of admiration, he said, "Never did much in track and field, but what I liked—besides basketball—was boxing."

"Boxing?" This time *her* eyes widened.

"Yep, boxing. I never played it much, but I want to tell you—contrary to public opinion—*there's* a sport that requires skill. Sizing up your opponent quickly, figuring out what skills he brings to the fight, how to use your own ability to your advantage . . . plus, a boxer needs a lot of courage and self-confidence to believe he can beat his opponent. There's only two men in the ring other than the referee, but only one can win."

"I never thought of it like that. Isn't boxing risky? Brain damage, that sort of thing?" She was beginning to find Drew Dawson interesting.

"Oh, sure," he agreed. "There's plenty of risk. You've got to make sure you're up to it. That's why training is so important, and that's why the referee always tells the combatants to 'protect yourselves at all times.' Guess I got to appreciate the sport because my dad liked it. We spent many an evening when I was growing up watching the fights on TV."

"My dad and I spent a lot of time flying together. I always wanted to be the son my dad never had," she admitted.

"Well, from where I sit, he's got one fantastic daughter."

"Flatterer! But, if you trust me, I'll take you up some day."

"With my life, my girl, you know that." He grinned at her and pushed his empty sandwich plate aside.

"So, you're not too scared to put your life into the hands of a girl?" She raised her eyebrows and peered into his face, emboldened by her feeling of one-upmanship.

"Not one bit. If the state of Massachusetts gave you a license to fly, that's good enough for me."

"All right then, we'll make a date."

"And I'll look forward to it," he answered quickly. "Finished your lunch?"

She nodded, and he placed their dishes on a tray. Together they walked to the retrieval carousel.

As they left the cafeteria, Anika realized how tall Drew Dawson really was. Since she was a little over five-feet-four, the top of her head barely reached his shoulder. *He must be well over six-feet tall,* she thought. There it was again, her heart doing those crazy, erratic beats. And even more than that, a strange sensation came over her whole body. *Get a grip on, girl,* she reprimanded herself. *This is not the first guy you've ever met.*

"So," she asked as they walked out into the bright, early fall sunshine, "how do you like going to college here in the North? You're from Atlanta, you said?"

"Right. Born and bred." He took her arm as they walked down the building's front steps. "It's just fine with me, especially now that I've found you."

"Found me?" she shot back. "I wasn't lost, and I've always known where I was and where I was going, thank you."

They stood facing each other on the sidewalk.

Drew knew he was already attracted to this sprite of a girl who could fly a plane, play a jazz piano, and was entering a field to care for others and save lives. He raised his shoulders in a gesture of surrender. His fingers itched to touch her smooth— almost translucent—soft, brown skin. And her elfin face with its delicate features unnerved him. Her hair was glistening black and cut short, giving her a sleek, waiflike appearance. But he had already noticed her strong sense of self. He had to get to know her better.

"Don't mince words, do you?" he said softly.

Her chin shot up. "Not my style, my friend. Say what I mean, and mean what I say," she said slowly. "I figure that's the honest way to be. Saves time and prevents misunderstandings."

"Can't quarrel with that," he conceded. "Will I see you later today, after class? I'd like to."

"I'm not sure. I have to check my schedule."

He scribbled on an envelope and gave it to her.

"Here's my phone number and my pager number. Please call me if you're free, okay?"

"If I have some free time, yes."

"I'd really like to get together, Anika." He gave her a quick peck on the cheek. She could smell distinctive aftershave lotion. As she walked away from him, she placed her fingers on the spot where his gentle, warm lips had touched her.

Chapter Two

A few days later, Anika and Drew bumped into each other at the campus bookstore in Kenmore Square.

"Still buying more books? Those look heavy!" Drew said to a preoccupied Anika.

She looked up at him and placed a credit card back into her wallet. "Oh, hello, Drew. How're you doing?"

"I'm fine. But I thought you were going to give me a call, so we could get together." He frowned at her as he reached for her bag of books. Disappointment clouded his face.

She *had* thought of Drew often since meeting him, but she dared not let him know. After all, they'd just met and their friendship seemed to be developing rather quickly. She hoped her inner feelings wouldn't betray her true sentiment. She answered quickly, happy that she did have a valid reason for not calling him.

"I've been bogged down with classes. Plus, our professors have been familiarizing us to some of the medical facilities in the area . . . field trips, that sort of thing."

"Are they trying to make you a nurse overnight?"

"Not that, but I guess it's a good way to separate the wheat from the chaff. A number of students have already dropped out—even in this, our senior year."

"Not what they expected, eh?"

"Guess not."

"But you're doing fine, right?"

"I'm giving it my best shot. I'm in it for the long haul and not about to give up!"

"Good."

They walked out of the bookstore, with Drew carrying her bag of books, and he suggested, "How would you feel about going out Friday night? Doing anything special?"

"I've got a project that's due, but I think I can take some time off on Friday. What have you got in mind?"

"A Japanese jazz pianist is appearing at eight at the Berklee Performance Center. Interested?"

He watched her face expectantly and was pleased when she smiled and said, "I'd like that very much."

"Good. Look, my car is parked around the corner. Why don't we put your books in it, lock it up, and grab a snack. Then I'll drive you back to your dorm on campus."

"You have a car?" she asked.

"It's a minivan. I told my folks that I needed some wheels, so they let me lease one."

"You'll have to be careful around here. Boston's streets are tricky," she warned him as they walked to his car.

He laughed. "So I've discovered. They were originally cow paths, or so I'm told."

"That's right, and—believe me, Drew—there's no rhyme or reason to the way they were laid out."

He opened the door of a silver-white minivan. "I wanted something that I could use to drive to Atlanta when I go home on vacation."

"This is nice and will certainly do well for traveling, but my original offer stands. I'd be happy to fly you home to Atlanta anytime you want to go."

He slapped his forehead with his left hand. "That's right. I forgot you were a 'fly lady,' Anika. You're pretty amazing, you know that?"

"Don't know 'bout that," she said modestly. She watched him load her books into the rear of the van, then cover them with a shabby blanket.

"Don't want to tempt thieves," he said.

"Can't be too careful. Come on, there's a great pizza place near here."

He ordered a large pizza—with everything—a garden salad for each of them, and then asked her what she wanted to drink.

"I'd like a large glass of water with lemon, if you don't mind," she told the waiter.

"Drink a lot of water, do you?"

"Yes, I do."

"That's why your skin is so beautiful, so flawless. You're beautiful, you know, Anika."

"Drew, with lines like that, I'll bet you have girls lined up all over Atlanta. And we've known each other less than a week."

"I can't help it, Anika. Doesn't the Bible say, 'The truth is the light, and the fullness thereof'? Let's eat this while it's hot," Drew said. He gave Anika a generous slice of pizza that was served within minutes of their order. "Umm, good. I didn't know I was so hungry." They were silent until after they finished their lunch.

Drew had always been around a lot of girls. His mother was involved in a great many of Atlanta's social circles, and her friends' daughters were constantly being introduced to the Dawson boy. That was one reason why he opted for college in Boston. Sitting at the table with him now was one of the most attractive, appealing young women he had ever met. He ached to know her better. There was something so fresh, so new, so direct about her. She regarded him with a look that was not bold, yet it made him feel that she was truly interested in him, that she cared, and that she was willing to be a friend. He didn't sense that she wanted anything from him, not like some of the many young women he knew back home. *But then,* he thought, *perhaps I am the one who has changed.*

"So, Miss Anika Wayne"—Drew leaned back in his chair—"tell me about yourself. All about you. Don't leave a thing out." He smiled.

"Nothing much to tell. I'm an only child, live with my folks in a small town on the south shore, graduated from high school, got accepted at BU's School of Nursing . . . and here I am."

"From where I sit, I believe there's a lot more to you than those few sentences. What do you want out of life?"

"God, Drew, you're something else! From pepperoni pizza to philosophy in twenty minutes. What do *I* want from life? Like everybody else, I want to be happy! Now, tell me what *you* want out of life?"

"The same, I guess," he said sheepishly, looking somewhat subdued. "I want to be happy, too, but I do want to make a name for myself. Like you, I'm an only child . . . and I feel that I have to live up to my parents' expectations."

"What about your own goals?" she asked.

"Well, I'm interested in television."

"In front of the camera or behind it?" She raised her eyebrows perceptively.

"You go right to the heart of the matter, don't you. I think I would like to have my own television show," he told her.

"If that's what *you* want, then I say go for it, Drew. Nothing beats a trial but a failure, *I've* always heard." She smiled at him.

The effect of her smile shook Drew. He wasn't prepared, and he felt as if someone had hit him with a solo punch. Although he'd only known her for a short time, she was already very important to him. He was glad that she'd agreed to go out with him—their first true date.

Anika prepared to leave. He left some bills on the table for the waiter, and together they walked to his car. As soon as they were settled in, Drew drove Anika home.

"I'm looking forward to Friday night, Anika. I hope you'll enjoy it," he said.

"I will. If it's jazz, I'll be happy. I understand that some Asian musicians are really taken with jazz. Something about it appeals to them, maybe because they are used to a five-tone scale, I think."

"We'll have a good time. I know I will, because I'll be with *you,* pretty lady. I'll pick you up at seven."

He retrieved her books from the back of the van and carried them to the elevator of her building. After another quick peck on Anika's cheek, he left. She picked up her bag and entered the elevator to her third-floor apartment, which she shared with two roommates. *How is this handsome, personable young man going to figure in my life?* she wondered as she went into her room.

Chapter Three

Anika had decided to wear a green silk pantsuit for her Friday date with Drew. She had chosen an ivory satin blouse to wear beneath the single-button jacket. A strand of pearls and small pearl earrings given to her by her mother were her only jewelry. Black, high-heeled strap sandals, a black clutch bag, and a lacy, black knit shawl—in case of a chilly evening—were her accessories.

When Drew saw her, he gave a low whistle of admiration. "Lookin' good, Miss Wayne, lookin' mighty good," he said.

"You look rather elegant yourself, Drew."

His outfit made him look very sleek and trim. He was wearing a slate-gray suit with a black silk turtleneck sweater. The color combination enhanced the healthy vigor of his marvelous bronze skin. As he helped her step into the van, she noticed his black tassel loafers.

"Don't get your heel caught," he warned her.

"I'm fine," she reassured him. She settled into her seat and fastened her seat belt.

He got into the driver's seat and turned to grin at her. "I believe we make a right good-looking couple, don't you?"

"Umm, maybe," she answered. She was reluctant to admit, even to herself, how comfortable and secure she was beginning to feel around this Drew Dawson from Atlanta.

They joined an excited, festive crowd entering the large Berklee Performance Center, and Anika could feel her own expectations for an exciting evening begin to rise. She followed Drew to their seats. *These are very good seats,* she thought. *Drew must have paid a lot of money.*

Drew squeezed her hand, and the curtain rose to reveal a magnificent baby grand piano, center stage. Moments later, the pianist took his seat in front of the piano. The emotions that he summoned from the piano were felt by every member of the audience. Everyone was totally engrossed.

Drew noted how attentive Anika had become. It made him happy to realize that she was sharing and enjoying every nuance, every delicate jazz shading that the pianist presented to the audience. Then he began to realize that, more than anything in the world, he wanted to make this slip of a girl happy. *When did I fall in love with her?* he wondered. *How does she feel about me?* An eternal optimist, he allowed a bubble of happiness to rise within his body. He wanted her—more than that—he needed her. She was beautiful, enticing, strong, and very certain of herself.

As he watched her, he knew he wanted his parents to meet her. Perhaps he could persuade Anika to go to Atlanta with him during the Thanksgiving holiday. Realizing that he had a tentative plan in place, he settled back into his seat to enjoy the concert.

After the concert, they stopped at a nearby bar and grill for a quick meal.

"Drew," Anika said, "I can't tell you how much I enjoyed myself tonight."

"It was my pleasure," he said as they drove to her dorm.

"You were really into it. Seemed to me that you were almost itching to get up on stage and join the guy."

"Didn't you love the way he used his left hand? And improvising! He really knows his jazz," she said. "He was great. I wonder if he has recorded anything?"

"I believe I saw something in his bio notes about a few CDs he's made," Drew said. "I'll check it out for you."

"You don't have to do that. I can do it myself."

"Now, I said *I* would, Anika. Don't deny me that pleasure."

"It was enough that you took me out tonight to hear him. Those seats we had must have cost you plenty."

"What's money for anyway," he bantered, "if you can't have something that you want? By the way, I have something I want to share with you."

"What's that?" She turned in her seat to look at him. He stared straight ahead, his eyes on the surrounding traffic. Both of his hands gripped the steering wheel, and Anika sensed that he was serious about whatever he had on his mind.

"Something wrong, Drew?" she asked.

"Only if you say no."

"Say no to what?"

"I'm getting to be very fond of you, Anika, and I'd like for us to start dating. What do you think?"

"Well . . . ," She hesitated, not certain if she was ready to make a commitment, although she did like him.

"Please, Anika"—he glanced over at her—"don't say 'well,' say 'yes.' "

"We've only known each other a short time. I . . . I suppose we can give it a try, to see how it goes."

"Yahoo!" he yelled. "I'm already dying to take you home for Thanksgiving, so my folks can meet you—"

She interrupted him. "Hey, not so fast! I'm planning to spend the holiday with my own folks. They'd be happy if you came."

"Well, ordinarily I would. I'm so crazy about you, Anika.

And I want my folks to meet you as soon as possible. I can hardly wait.''

''Well, you'll have to wait,'' she said simply.

There it is, he thought. *That obvious streak of self-assurance that has attracted me to her.* Then, her next words shocked him.

''Tell you what, Drew,'' she spoke quietly and thoughtfully. ''You go home and have Thanksgiving with your folks, but I'll be with my folks for the holiday—''

''But—''

''I'm not finished with my proposal yet,'' she interrupted. ''Here's what I'm thinking. Classes don't start again 'til Monday. Why don't I fly down to Atlanta on Saturday, and we can fly back together on Sunday? That way, I *can* meet your folks.''

He stopped the car in front of her dorm and turned to stare at her.

''You can do that?''

''Sure. Piece of cake. I've flown to Atlanta and Florida many times.''

He turned off the ignition and shook his head, grinning in amazement.

''Girl, you never cease to amaze me! Imagine that—a little thing like you flying all over God's Creation.''

''You'll have to foot the bill if you want me to do it,'' she said.

''Of course, of course! Wouldn't have it any other way. Just let me know how much.''

''The plane rental and the gas . . . won't charge you for my services.'' She tilted her head to one side. ''You interested?'' she teased.

''You bet I am! It's a deal. Anika, whatever got you interested in flying?'' he asked, a serious look on his face.

''Well, as I told you, I've always loved my dad. Not that I don't love my mother, but my father has always been special to me, and I think it's because he has always been special to my mom. Anyway, I was a bit of a tomboy and loved doing things with him . . . going to ball games, track meets, fishing. Guy things, you know. The naval air station was nearby, and when I became interested in planes, my dad encouraged me. As a result of *my* interest, both of my folks have pilot licenses, believe it or not.''

''Wow! Isn't that unusual?''

''Not at all. We've met quite a number of 'flying families.' ''

''Remarkable. That's all I've got to say.''

''Drew''—Anika was serious as they walked to the lobby of her dorm—''I've always believed that life is to be lived the best way you know how. I believe that you should do your best, live every day to the fullest, and accept what it offers. I also think you should know what you want from life and go after it. Do you agree with that?'' she asked.

Drew placed both hands on her shoulders and looked directly into her eyes. ''I agree wholeheartedly with what you say, Anika, and—more than that—I want you to know that I have deep admiration for you. You are becoming very, very special to me.''

He leaned forward and kissed her lips lightly. The zesty scent of his aftershave provoked a strong urge in her to respond to his caress, but she held back. Caution was almost her middle name. She would not rush into a relationship with Drew, although her body was telling her otherwise.

Chapter Four

Five years later

The helicopter whirred through black skies toward a rescue mission on Cape Cod, eighty miles away from Boston.

Sitting directly behind the pilot, Anika Wayne adjusted her flight helmet. She was glad that her hair was short and sleek, making the cumbersome helmet bearable. She adjusted her seat belt and checked to see that her emergency medical kit was properly stowed.

The throbbing roar of the rotor blades made conversation difficult. As team leader, she was already aware that the victim they were going to med-flight back to Boston had wrapped his Jaguar around a tree. As she settled into her seat, she breathed a silent prayer: *Let everything go well.*

Anika was the leader of the four-member flight crew, which included the pilot, Grady Simpson, and the other nurses, Marie Frost and Tony Jenkins. The rescue call to boarding took less than four minutes. The team worked well together and had been together for two years, despite some reluctance to have

Anika, an African-American, as team leader. But, she had an advantage. Not only did she have a master's degree in nursing, she was also certified in emergency nursing and was a licensed pilot. This was an asset because she could fly fixed-wing aircraft should the need arise.

It was while growing up in Weymouth, near a naval air station, that the jets that flew over her house had intrigued Anika. One day, she had told her father about her dream to become a pilot.

"Dad, I've got to learn to fly!"

Fred Wayne saw the excitement in his only child's face. "Honey, if that's what you want, go for it."

Not only had she received her pilot's license when she was sixteen, but her enthusiasm for flying touched her father.

"Rachel," he had told his wife, "I can't let Anika go flying all over creation all alone. She's only sixteen, for God's sake. Doesn't even have a driver's license yet . . . ."

"And you plan to do *what* about it?"

"I think I have to take up flying myself."

Rachel Wayne watched as the father-daughter relationship solidified with a shared love of flying. She had made her own plans, which she did not discuss with either of them.

One day, Fred mentioned that Anika's high-school graduation was approaching.

"I'd like to do something special for her, Rachel. She's always been a wonderful daughter, a good student . . . never given us any worry."

Rachel had just placed a freshly made corn pudding in the oven, and, with her face flushed from the heat, she sat down at the kitchen table across from her husband. They had been married nearly twenty years and adored each other. Fred was the 'light of my life,' Rachel always told friends.

Although his hair was gray at the temples, his smooth brown

face was unlined. Slight crinkles appeared around his eyes as she smiled affectionately, and he reached for his wife's hands.

"I've got an idea. We can rent a Cessna, a four-seater, down at the Plymouth airport. Why don't we do that and take Anika someplace, have a nice lunch, and fly back? Think she'd like that?"

"It's a great idea, Fred. How 'bout Maine? She loves lobster." She smiled.

Fred smiled back. "That's what we'll do. Shall we keep it a surprise?" He winked at her, his love for her clearly expressed in his eyes. She winked back at him. They hugged like conspiratorial playmates excited with their plans.

When the day finally arrived, Anika was beside herself after she realized that they were heading to the Plymouth airport, where she had taken her flying lessons. Open-mouthed, she watched her dad pick up a set of keys from the airport office.

"Follow me," he grinned and led Anika and her mother out onto the tarmac, where a sleek blue-and-white Cessna sat.

"Dad! She's a beauty! Are we taking off in this?"

"She's ours for the whole day, honey. Your mother and I wanted to do something special for your graduation. How would you like to have some Maine lobster for lunch?" he asked, delighted by her reaction.

"We're flying to Maine?"

"Right now." He turned to his wife. "OK, Mother, in you go." He helped her board the plane.

"Let me try this on for size," Rachel grinned as she settled into the pilot's seat. "You've both talked so much about flying, I believe I could to it."

"I do, too, honey," Anika's father answered. "All you'd need would be a license."

His wife reached into her jacket pocket and pulled out a folded envelope. "Like this?" She waved the envelope in front of her husband's nose.

"What's this?" he asked. Then he saw COMMONWEALTH OF MASSACHUSETTS in the left-hand corner.

"Rachel Wayne!" he boomed. "What have you been up to?" He opened the envelope. "Why, you vixen! When did you get this?" He turned to Anika, who was adjusting her seat belt in the passenger backseat.

"Anika, your mother has been sneaking out on us while you were in school and I was at work . . . she's been taking flying lessons! Know what this is? *Her* pilot's license!"

"Mother!" Anika yelled. "And you never said a word!"

"Well"—Rachel grinned—"haven't you both teased me about the great big, blue, beautiful sky out yonder? Didn't think I was going to let you guys have all the fun, did you?"

"Rachel," Anika's father said softly, "you never cease to amaze me. No wonder I love you so much."

Flying in the copter during the dark night, Anika remembered how she hoped for that same kind of love if she fell in love with Drew Dawson.

The pilot's voice interrupted her reverie.

"Estimated time of arrival—ten minutes," he announced into their headphones. "The police have cleared a landing area for us on Route 6."

Anika looked down on a brilliantly lit scene. Spotlights and police search beams illuminated the accident area. Police cars, fire trucks, and ambulances crowded the scene. She and the two other nurses prepared to exit the helicopter. Once on the ground, they raced to the scene with their equipment and a transport litter.

At first the scene appeared to be controlled chaos, but after a quick assessment of the situation, the flight team took over.

The police reported that the victim had been identified as a "twenty-seven-year-old African-American male—a television host from Atlanta."

Anika gasped when she saw the victim's face. Marie heard the sharp intake of breath and saw the odd look on Anika's face.

"You know this guy?"

"I think I've seen him on TV," Anika lied.

Hurriedly, she started an intravenous infusion as Tony took the patient's vital signs. The paramedics had already immobilized the victim on a backboard and he was quickly transferred to the helicopter.

She worked feverishly because the victim was having difficulty breathing, was in and out of consciousness, and might have chest injuries or other internal injuries. His right leg appeared to have been fractured and had already been immobilized.

Pushing errant thoughts to the back of her mind, Anika steeled herself to use her professional skills to the task at hand. She had not seen Drew Dawson for five years.

Until now.

Suddenly, the only man she had ever loved was back in her life . . . or was he?

Chapter Five

Drew was standing in front of a pair of ornately decorated elevator doors. Anika saw him as soon as she entered the hotel lobby.

Her heart took an unexpected lurch, and she felt her knees shaking. Why were her palms wet? God, he was still a very handsome man, despite an injured left arm in a sling and a black sock covering the plaster cast on his right foot. He was leaning on a cane.

He evidently heard her heels echo across the marble lobby floor because he looked in her direction as she approached. He waved his cane at her.

"Anika! Over here!" he said. "Good to see you, girl. How are you?" He kissed her cheek.

She moved back a few paces as if to check him over.

"*I'm* fine, and I'm delighted to see that you look a whole lot better than when I saw you last. Two weeks ago, was it?"

"Just about."

"And you're making a smooth recovery?"

"Better believe it. The hotel staff has been very kind to me, and the nurses and physical therapists that come in to help have been wonderful.''

"Good. I'm glad, Drew.''

"They seem to think that I can go home in another week to ten days. Look,'' he said, "let's not stand here talking. We do have reservations in the dining room.'' He waved off her attempts to assist him, so she watched him manage the cane and make his way gingerly on his walking cast. The waiter directed them to a window table.

"What about your TV show, Drew?'' she asked as the waiter seated her and gave them menus.

Drew took his seat with the waiter's help and placed his cane on the floor beside the window before he answered.

"Since my unfortunate accident, the producers have shown reruns, and they have used guest hosts, but now that I can walk, I'll be able to get back in front of the camera.''

"That's good news.''

"And I owe it all to you.'' He reached across the table for her hand, pulled it toward him, and kissed her palm. When his warm lips touched her hand, she was not prepared for the sensations that flooded her body. She had considered herself to be well over their long-ago relationship. His next words shook her even more.

"You know you saved my life, Anika. To me it means we forget the past. We are destined to be together, I truly believe that. I've always loved you—you know that.''

She glared at him and picked up the menu. She knew her face was flushed, and she was angry. How dare he be so presumptive! She pulled her hand away.

"Drew Dawson, you're crazy! We stopped being a couple when you left for Atlanta. You know that''—she looked at him, her eyes sober—"and I must tell you, if I'd known it was *you* we were going to med-flight to Boston, I'd have refused the assignment. Good thing they never identify the patient, only the location. It's never easy to come upon an accident and discover it's someone you know.''

"I'm sure," he said. He leaned forward, as if to press his case. "Anika, when they pulled me out of that car, and I was drifting in and out, somehow I heard your voice, sensed your presence, and realized that it was *your* voice I heard reassuring me, and it was *your* hands working on me. I tell you, 'Nika, I couldn't believe it! I knew then that I was safe . . . was going to make it."

Anxious to get past the emotional moment, Anika responded in her most matter-of-fact tone. "Well, Drew, for your information, we weren't sure you'd make it. Your vital signs were way below normal."

"Really?"

"Yes, and you had difficulty breathing due to your chest injury, despite your car's air bag. We knew you needed to be intubated, probably had a collapsed lung, and you kept fading in and out of consciousness. Your condition did not rule out internal injuries. We did all we could do to keep you alive on that flight to Boston."

"It's all a blur to me."

"I expect as much, Drew. You know, I never told anyone on the flight crew that I knew you. Kept reminding myself to do my job and try to help save your life. I couldn't have done it otherwise. I put my mind on automatic and focused on my responsibility." Then she gave him a direct look. "What happened, anyway, Drew? You were always a careful driver."

"Guess I was just so tired. I had been making TV guest appearances all over that day, and I was trying to get to a flight out of Green Airport in Providence. Fell asleep at the wheel. Dumb, wasn't it?"

She agreed. "I would say that it was really dumb." She picked up her menu again to decide what she would order. Drew did likewise, although he continued to watch her face for a reaction to his proposal that they pick up where they left off in their previous relationship.

"Order whatever you like, Anika. I'm so glad you agreed to meet me for dinner tonight. It's like old times," he ventured.

She peered at him over the menu. "A lot has happened to us since those 'old times,' as you put it, Drew."

"Don't say that, Anika. You know how I felt about you—still do—and there's so much I want for us. I truly believe that I can't let this second chance go by. And I do owe you so much."

He reached for her hand again.

"I *have* to say it, Anika. I really mean it. I'd like for us to get together again."

His jet-black eyes were solemn as he wound the fingers of his uninjured right hand around hers and squeezed gently. "And I think we were brought together for that very purpose, to start over and make up for lost time," he continued. "Think of it—a second chance."

He waited for her response, remembered how captivated he had always been by her elfin face. Her smooth, cocoa-brown skin was like a delicate rose petal that could be easily bruised. But he knew, too, that Anika Wayne possessed an innate strength of character beneath all that delicate softness. It was not going to be easy to win her again, not after he had hurt her so badly the first time. He looked at her. She was more beautiful, more serene, than ever. Her dark brown eyes, set deep above her chiseled cheekbones, always reminded him of the stunningly beautiful Egyptian queen, Nefertiti.

Aware that Drew was waiting for her to respond, Anika studied his face for a few more moments before she spoke. "You do know, Drew, as I said, that a lot of water has gone under the bridge since you left. I don't know how you can think that we can pick up where we left off. *You* were the one to leave, remember?"

"I remember," he said contritely. "It was selfish of me, but there was some force, some unknown element, that pushed me into believing that it was okay to go and take that job in Atlanta. I figured that we would be together once I got settled in my job, that we'd get married . . . you know, like we planned to in September."

Anika took a sip of wine and then sighed deeply. "I know *you* got married."

"God, Anika, to this very day, I don't know how or why I made such a dreadful mistake." His face reddened, mirroring his distress as he continued his sober apology. "Guess I wasn't prepared for the onslaught of flattery and adulation that I got from her—and her overbearing mother—before I knew it . . ."

He could see that Anika was paying attention to this embarrassing confession of weakness, and hoping that she *did* understand, he plunged ahead.

"Even my mother warned me, but I'd completely lost my senses, would listen to no one. Within the first month of marriage, I realized what a fool I'd been! Can you find it in your heart to forgive me? Please, give me a chance to show you how much I really love you—and only you. Please, I'm begging now—because Anika, you are my life!"

Anika looked around the opulent dining room that was comfortably filled with elegantly dressed diners seated at tables decorated with fresh flowers and linens of muted pastels, and softly glowing candles, and she remembered how often Drew used to say, "Someday, Anika, we'll go to the most exclusive places."

That "someday" had never come. She couldn't even say that it had come tonight because they had always planned to reach those days as a couple. Tonight, only Drew had selected their meeting place. It had not been a place that they had decided upon as a pair, together, and . . . in love. *But,* she thought, *it is typical of Drew to select the most expensive venue in Boston.* She realized he wanted to impress her, or at least as he had said when he phoned to invite her to dinner, "to catch up on the past, make amends, and start over."

Angry thoughts raced through her mind. *How dare Drew think he can just walk back into my life with a few mea culpas, and all will be well? Doesn't he know how much pain he is causing me?* The hurt, the disappointment, the feeling of being cast aside—a feeling that threatened to shatter her self-esteem—all those feelings and more washed over her. *Can what I believe to be true love between us ever become real again?*

She began to pay attention to the salad in front of her, alert to the fact that Drew was waiting for some sign of understanding from her. She decided that he would wait a while longer. After all, it *had* been five years.

She *was* hungry, and if she ate perhaps she could choke back her angry disappointment at this man who she had once loved with all her heart.

Cool, crisp salad greens, cherry-red tomatoes, bits of jewel-like green and red peppers, and slices of snow-white mushrooms were gently bathed in a succulent, creamy, rich dressing. She concentrated on her food. It was not at all in her nature to be vindictive, but she couldn't help it. *Once burned, twice shy,* she thought.

As if willing to give her time, Drew started to speak. His voice was solemn and quiet. "I was very sorry, Anika, to learn of your mother's death. I was in the middle of that stupid divorce, and I couldn't get up here to attend the funeral services."

"I understand, Drew. The wreath you sent was beautiful."

"It was the least I could do. I always loved your mother. She was a wonderful woman, and I'm lucky to have known her."

"Thanks, Drew. It's kind of you to say that."

"I mean it sincerely, 'Nika. And your Dad?"

"Dad relocated to California. He wanted me to go with him, but I'd already decided to work on my master's degree in nursing and was committed to that. When I finally got my degree, the offer to join the medical flight crew came up, so I took it—"

"Lucky for me," Drew interjected.

"Maybe," Anika said. "But I do have a career change planned."

"What?" His eyes widened. "What are you talking about, a 'change in plans'?"

"I'm leaving this area."

"What do you mean, 'leaving this area'?"

At that moment, the waiter arrived with their entrées. Anika had ordered broiled salmon, and Drew's plate contained a magnificent sirloin steak.

"Will there be anything else, sir?" the waiter asked.

Drew brushed him aside quickly. "No, not at the moment, thanks." He could hardly wait for the man to leave before he blurted out, "Leave, Anika? To go where?"

"I'm going to Barbados."

Chapter Six

Those Sunday mornings with Drew were memories that Anika had not wanted to forget. Drew would always accompany her to early Mass, after which they would go to their favorite coffee shop for fresh orange juice, muffins and jam, and huge cups of coffee. Then, armed with the Sunday papers, they would go back to her house to read and discuss the current news.

Drew's eagerness to begin his career in television journalism was never more evident than during those Sunday mornings. His enthusiasm showed in his face and his body language as he leaned toward Anika and read news items to her and discussed their importance.

"Listen to this, Anika. Says here that a prominent black sociologist is doing a research paper on what it means to be black in America. What do you think of that?"

"I'll bet he'll never really find out," she said. "There'll be as many answers as the different number of interviews he makes. Everyone will have a different opinion, depending on their individual experiences."

"You're probably right, hon. Take the two of us for example."

"Right. You were born and raised in the South. Me—I've always lived in the North. Our experiences are not alike at all," Anika contended.

"Well, my sweet one, how would you feel about sharing our lives together?"

She looked at him and realized that he was serious. He lowered the newspaper to the floor and joined her on the sofa surrounded by newspaper sections. Drew brushed the papers aside and took both of her hands in his. She felt an intense warmth emanate from his body, and the serious look on his face alerted her to be prepared for a stunning announcement. She already knew her own feelings.

"Anika, you know how I feel about you. Since I first met you, I've walked a little straighter, thought a lot more clearly, have seen the whole world as a wonderful place . . . all because of you. You have such a calming manner and make everything seem so much better. There is so much to love about you that I'm desperate"—he hesitated for a moment—"Like I said a few moments ago, I want *our* lives to be alike from now on. I want to marry you. Please say you'll be my wife"—he sighed deeply—"Please?"

Anika thought, *I was happy with my life, but I know now that this man has brought such wonderful magic to me. I can't imagine going through life without him.*

Glistening pools of tears formed in her eyes, and she gave Drew a wobbly smile halfway between a sob and a grin. Her voice was quiet and tremulous. "Yes, Drew, I will marry you," she whispered.

There was a special warmth to their kiss at that moment. Nothing at all like the kisses they had exchanged many times before.

"Oh, Anika, my darling, I'm so blessed to have you in my life," Drew murmured as he trailed kisses over her mouth, her cheeks, her eyes, her hair. He couldn't get enough of her.

Anika moaned his name, felt the hunger for him. A hunger that she had tried to deny for so long. This was real.

On Valentine's Day, a few days later, Anika received a dozen red roses from Drew. On a lacy pink-and-white card, he had handwritten:

> Roses are red, violets are blue,
> Their colors seem brighter since I've met you.
> The whole world is delightful, and that's a good sign.
> Please, love me, my darling. Be my Valentine.
> Please???
>
> Love, Drew

Chapter Seven

Sitting in the dining room of one of Boston's most elegant hotels, Anika's mind drifted back to the night the glorious world of love began to crumble. Drew had come to her apartment that evening with a rental car, and they drove out of the city to one of their favorite spots. Nantasket was a beach park on the Atlantic, with amusement rides, inline skating areas, and sea-food take-out spots. The ocean waves pounded hungrily against the sea wall. Drew found quickly an available spot that faced the dark ocean.

Anika had noticed that he seemed more preoccupied than usual—he was not his normal, eager, enthusiastic self. She watched as he set the car's emergency brake.

"Well, here we are," he said, staring out the car's windshield at the ocean. Usually he would reach for her for a loving kiss, and then he would start to talk, eager to share his day's events with her—new techniques of television or journalism that he'd had in class that day. His usual spontaneity was missing. *What's wrong?* she wondered.

She had taken a closer look at him. The only light in the car came from the spring full moon riding high in the heavens, reflecting brightly on the crashing waves. She saw his jaw tighten, as if he was facing a momentous decision. She could see faint flints of moisture beaded on his upper lip.

"What's wrong, Drew?"

"Something . . . I have to tell you."

"What? What is it?"

He started to speak, but his voice was husky and he cleared his throat several times. "An offer for a job in Atlanta came today."

She grabbed his hands and kissed him. "But, Drew," she exclaimed excitedly, "that's wonderful news! It's what you wanted, isn't it? I don't understand why you're so upset."

"I'm upset because they want me to come down right away. Right after my graduation in June."

"Well, you can certainly make *that* commitment, can't you? You're lucky to be able to start your career so soon after graduation." She peered into his face. "Oh, Drew, a real, true job to do something you've worked and planned for. It's awesome!"

"Anika, with you in my corner, how can I fail? But I hate the thought of leaving right after graduation. I had hoped to take you to Atlanta with me, as my bride. I was willing to wait until you graduated in August."

"I know it's awful, but the school of nursing always had a different graduation than the rest of the university. It's because the students need time for clinical experience—"

"But," he interrupted, "we can still plan for our September wedding, can't we? I don't want anything to interfere . . . "

"Oh." Anika was trying to sound cheerful. "Drew, you silly thing! I'll miss you like crazy, but there's no reason you can't come back to Boston in September, a willing bridegroom," she teased him. "It happens every day."

"Anika, girl, how am I going to live a *minute* without you, having you a thousand miles away?" Drew's face mirrored his anxiety.

"I can visit you, and you can visit me. We'll just have a long-distance relationship. It'll only be a few months. Like I said, it happens every day. And we can go ahead with our plans for our September wedding. It'll work out fine—you'll see."

"Oh, God, I hope so. Honey, you're just too special to me." He reached for her. "Come here, love."

He pulled her close. When he kissed her, his firm mouth on hers validated her love for him all over again. He was relieved that she had been pliant and understanding, and he began to kiss her with a hunger, and ardor, that neither had felt before.

Anika clasped Drew's head with both hands as if she were a starving fledgling. The scent of his aftershave excited her, and his tongue sought to caress hers. She hungered for the taste of him and began to run her hands along the sides of his face, the tips of her fingers lightly caressing the whorls and crevices of his ears. His response to her caresses was a throaty growl that said he ached to share more of himself with her. At that moment, she knew it was what she wanted as well. The idea that they could soon be distances apart swizzled through her brain. She made a decision.

"Drew"—she panted in a coarse whisper—"take me home, please."

"Oh, yes, babe, I'll take you home." Since he had first met her, he'd longed to hear that invitation. He held her hand as he drove through the dark streets to her Boston apartment. No words were needed because they both knew they were ready for the next step.

Arm in arm, they climbed the stairs to her second-floor apartment. As usual, Anika's radio was playing, tuned to a jazz station. She hated coming into a quiet house, and this night, appropriately, they both heard the passionate voice of Lionel Richie crooning a sensitive ballad. The music washed over them, increasing the emotional and physical tension they both felt.

Drew threw the bolt as the door closed behind them, and he

saw the wide-eyed longing and anticipation in his beloved's face.

"Baby"—he moaned and drew her close—"I want you so much . . . so much . . ." his voice trailed off.

Her response reassured him. "I'll always be yours, Drew, always."

She was wearing a light-blue twin sweater set with a white skirt, and its color was reflected from the black brilliance of her eyes. She concentrated on his face, using the soft light of the one table lamp in the room. What she saw confirmed her emotions, and she knew she wanted to feel his warm, golden-bronze skin next to hers, feel his noble heart racing in tandem with hers. She watched him watching her and knew they could not turn back.

Wordlessly, they began to undress each other, fingers working frantically at zippers and buttons. They stepped away from the pool of clothing left on the floor, and he picked her up. She clung to him, her slender arms soft and warm around his neck. He found her willing lips again as he carried her into the bedroom. He never removed his lips from hers, gently depositing her on the bed.

The same full moon that had ridden over the dark ocean stirred up the emotions that led them to the present moment and now cast a silvery, soft luminescence over everything in the room. It seemed like the glorious interior of a fairy-tale castle.

"Honey," he murmured into her ear as he leaned over her, "you are the most beautiful, most desirable woman in the whole world. I love you. I've wanted you for so long."

He left her side abruptly, then returned just as quickly. She saw the silver foil packet in his hand. She felt that he wanted to protect her and that he really cared.

"It's all right, 'Nika. It's really all right because we love each other." He pulled a folded coverlet from the foot of the bed to cover their naked bodies because he knew she was modest. There was no chill between them, only the heat of increasing passion. She sighed and allowed him to caress her soft, smooth skin. His fingers moved lightly, as if memorizing and claiming every curve, every juncture, every limb, and every pulsating swell that he touched. She responded with soft, purring sounds, and he continued to stimulate every pore, every nerve, every inch of her body. She never imagined that she could feel such exquisite ecstasy. Drew's love for her was like magic. She would never be happy without this loving, sensitive man in her life. Her body arched and hot blood surged through her veins, propelling her toward complete fulfillment.

She thought that she would lose her senses when Drew tasted her round, roseate breast, moaning as he loved it with his tongue. His hands continued to explore her arms, thighs, and then the soft mound that hid the secret treasure he sought. She touched him then, and he raised his head to look into her smoldering eyes. As her fingers closed gently around him, his sibilant breath made him sound like he was in pain.

She knew that neither her body nor her mind would have any peace if she did not go where this moment was taking her. She only wanted to have Drew love her, and she wanted to love him, now and forever. There was no turning back. He was her life.

She caressed him gently and moved seductively against him. When had her body learned to behave like this? How had it learned these secrets?

She shook her head from side to side, and the agony and longing that she felt was also shared by Drew. The moment of fulfillment for their love had been reached together. They were about to cross the threshold into a new world that would be uniquely theirs.

"Anika!" Drew cried out her name as they rode tumultuous, pulsating waves and soared high toward a pinnacle of wonder.

Anika held on, her arms and legs twined around Drew's body as he carried her with fantastic rhythms to breathtaking glory.

Fully spent after the most rocketing experience she had ever shared with another person, Anika found Drew's mouth and kissed him, grateful for the love in her heart. With their arms still wrapped around each other, they lay quietly. She whispered, her lips forming the words like a silent code right onto his mouth, "Drew Dawson, I love you."

Jolted from her sensitive memories, Anika was brought back to the tension-laden moment. Drew was questioning her again.

"What do you mean, 'going to Barbados'? You've got to give our relationship a second chance. You know we could be happy," he pleaded. His face was flushed with intense anxiety as he searched for understanding from her.

Anika pushed her half-eaten entrée aside, her appetite gone. The emotional memories of their sexual past kept nibbling around her consciousness, and she knew that she had to let him know how much he had wounded her. She looked at him directly, realizing that this was possibly the last time she would see him.

"Drew," her voice was soft, but controlled, "you hurt me deeply. Even after my graduation in August, you had still agreed on our wedding plans. So, can you imagine how I felt when you sent your wedding announcement . . ."

Drew's face reddened with shame. "I'm sorry for what I did to you. It was cowardly of me not to call and tell you."

"It was *more* than cowardly! It was unfeeling and cruel. You can't know how dreadfully painful it was for me to stare every day at a plastic-wrapped wedding dress, knowing that I wasn't going to wear it. Or to be the one—alone—to have to tell friends and family that the wedding was off . . . that you didn't love me, after all."

"But that's just it. I *did* always love you. Still do. I made a mistake, a dreadful one. I admit it. But . . . and . . . yes . . . well, the fault was mine"—he searched her face for some sign of merciful forgiveness—"Please forgive me, and give me a second chance. If you can't, I'll try to accept it, but not without trying to win you back. No matter what you do, or where you go, I'm going to try to recapture what we had. I really do love you and want you in my life, by my side. Don't tell me it's too late for us. Remember that Valentine I sent you that said, "the whole world is brighter because you are in my life"? It always will be. Please, Anika."

"Hah!" Anika snorted. "Are you trying to sell me the Brooklyn Bridge, Drew?"

"No, no, no. I'm not trying to sell you anything, except now that I've found you, it's more important than ever that we start over—to be together for life."

Anika shook her head. "At one time, you *were* the most important person in my life, and I truly expected that you always would be. But now—after what you did to me—why should I give you any consideration?"

Drew could see seething, palpable anger move over her face. *She hates me,* he thought. He watched as she threw her napkin down on the table. She pushed her chair back and stood up, still glaring at him. "Thanks for the meal, Drew. I hope that you'll make a speedy recovery and that you can get back to work. Good night!"

Drew tried to rise from the seat before she strode away, her lithe frame erect, her head held high as the soft lighting in the room reflected off her glistening hair. He knew then that he had lost her for the second time, and he watched until she disappeared through the hotel lobby and into the night.

He did not realize it, but Anika could hardly see where she was going. Her eyes were full of tears as she waited for the parking valet to retrieve her car. Her mind was on the memories of the many loving moments they had shared, plus the realization that she still loved him, wanted him . . . more than ever.

As she drove back to her apartment—where she had first tasted love—she thought, *if he loved me so much, how could he let himself be seduced by a brainless vixen? How could he?*

Chapter Eight

As the plane flew over Grantley Adams International Airport in Bridgetown, Barbados, Anika viewed the scene from below her window. The azure blue of the Caribbean flanking the soft green of the island beckoned to her. *What a beautiful spot,* she thought.

A voice came over the intercom, informing the passengers that the plane was about to land. With a sprightly, clipped, accent the flight attendant welcomed the passengers to the former British colony.

"Ladies and gentlemen, we are preparing to land in a few moments. Be sure that your seats are in an upright position and your tray tables are safely stored away. Welcome to Barbados. The weather today is clear and sunny, with the temperature at twenty-six degrees Celsius, or seventy-nine degrees Fahrenheit. Today the exchange rate is two hundred and eight Barbadian dollars for one hundred U.S. dollars, so your shopping tours should be delightful. We will be on the ground in five minutes. Enjoy your stay in Barbados, and thank you for flying with us."

After safely passing through customs, Anika walked outside to where cars and taxis were lined up. She was scheduled to be picked up by someone from the Medical Education Institute. Within a few minutes, she was approached by a young man holding a placard that read BARBADOS M.E.I. WELCOMES MS. ANIKA WAYNE.

"I'm Anika Wayne."

The young man smiled and said, "Welcome, Ms. Wayne. I'm Reginald Holland. I'm to escort you to the Institute. These are your bags, eh?"

Anika nodded and Reginald deposited her suitcase and valet bag in the trunk of a small car. Printed on the door panel was the name of the Institute and an address in Christ Church, as well as a telephone and fax number.

"You had a pleasant flight, Miss?"

"Yes, Reginald, I did."

"First time in Barbados, Miss?"

"Indeed, it is my first visit."

"Well"—he looked back at her from the front seat—"I guarantee it won't be your last. We want you to fall in love here . . . with our country, that is." He smiled.

"I see that you drive on the left side of the road," Anika observed. "That will take some getting used to for me."

"Oh, yes, ma'am. We do here in Barbados like they do in the mother country, merry old England. Some say"—he laughed, his strong white teeth gleaming—"some folks say we 'Bajans' are more British than the British are. We even have our own Trafalgar Square with Lord Nelson's statue in it."

"Really?"

"Right in the middle of our capital, Bridgetown, down by the careenage. I'm certain you'll get to see it, and all the other attractions we have. You know tourism is our number-one business. All visitors are our privileged guests. Their happiness and well being are our main concern."

Anika's mind wandered as they rode from the airport to the

parish of Christ Church. Would she be able to get on with her life, to free herself from the image of Drew that insisted they go back to the way they were? Would this relocation to a new place and a new job help her forget her past with Drew? It had been five years, surely by now ... She looked out the car window at colorful trees with brilliant flowers. Even the shrubbery around the houses and buildings was thick, lush, and glossy. She noticed that, although it was warm, she could see trees swaying delicately with the slight breeze.

"Ms. Wayne"—Reginald broke into her reverie—"I'm to take you to the Institute, then later you'll be escorted to your living quarters. Your luggage will be quite safe, I can assure you."

"Fine. That will be fine."

"And here we are." He pulled up in front of a low two-story, white stucco building. Large windows on both sides of a wide portico welcomed Anika with their brightness. Large ceramic pots of croton, rose, and pink hibiscus lined the walkway to the front door.

Anika had not expected to meet the director of the Institute so soon after arriving, so she hoped that she didn't appear too grubby in her navy pantsuit. After all, Dr. Cyril Roberts, the director, must know she had just landed after a four-and-a-half hour flight from Boston. Thank God she'd had enough sense to freshen her makeup in the car.

She heard a booming voice as she entered the building. "Aha, here you are!" A dark-skinned man moved toward her, his white coat swirling around his large frame like a sail in full gale. He extended a giant hand.

"Welcome, welcome, Ms. Wayne! I'm Cyril Roberts, director of the Barbados M.E.I."

Anika felt small, but the hand that grasped hers was warm and friendly. Surprisingly, she felt safe and secure. She steadied herself, feeling as if she'd known this man for a long time.

His 'hail-fellow, well-met' attitude lessened any tension she had anticipated. His hair was black and closely cropped to his noble head, with slight wings of white at the temples. Anika looked into his eyes, which seemed incongruous with his skin coloring. They were soft brown with faint glints of amber. He had a muscular physique and she wondered if he had ever played football, or was it rugby, the English game?

From her first impression, she thought, *I'm sure his staff works well with him. He seems like a favorite honey-bear of a man.*

"Welcome to Barbados Medical Education Institute, Ms. Wayne. Come, come into my office. This way, please."

They walked down to the end of a short corridor into a sunny suite of rooms.

"This"—Dr. Roberts waved his hand about—"is the center of my little kingdom. I'll only keep you a few minutes, just to sign some forms, and then Reginald will whisk you off to the apartment we've secured for you. I hope it will be satisfactory."

Anika nodded in agreement and took the seat he had pulled up beside his desk.

"I'm certain it will be."

"We found a place within walking distance, but if you decide you'd like to move farther away, we can place a car at your disposal."

He smiled warmly at her and opened a file. "I know you have already signed the contract we forwarded to you . . . here it is, and the only other papers are insurance and nurse liability forms. I suggest that you take them with you and look them over. You can bring them back, and we can have you sign them and have them witnessed. Now"—he sprang to his feet— "let's get you on your way. Get a good night's rest," he advised, "and we'll see you tomorrow morning."

"At what time?" Anika asked.

"Eleven will do. You can meet the other staff members then. Welcome again, Ms. Wayne. I'm looking forward to having you with us."

As the affable Reginald drove to her apartment on the Institute's grounds, Anika thought about what she had done. It was

September, and she was over two-thousand miles away from Boston, from the familiar fall colors of the trees, the sharp, biting winds of cold winter days, the sparkle of snow on the trees, and the soft, gentle blush of a New England spring. She had signed a contract to stay on the island for one semester. What had she done? Was Drew's magnetism so strong that it made her move to another hemisphere? She wondered if the six-month contract that she had signed would give her enough time and . . . was she far away enough to forget . . . and face reality? She could not love a man who had hurt her so deeply. Was she really that weak, that vulnerable? She hoped not, but . . . here she was, about to embark on a strange new life. Would it be what she wanted?

Chapter Nine

Anika arrived at the Institute's administration building at the scheduled time the following morning. She was escorted by Dr. Roberts into a large, sunny conference room. Already seated around a large table were several men and women. Some wore street clothes, while others wore white coats. All, she noticed, wore name tags.

"Everyone! Good morning!" The doctor's resonant voice encompassed each of them.

"Good morning, sir," the voices responded collectively.

He picked up a folder from the table. "I'm pleased to introduce to you the newest member of our staff." He nodded at Anika. "This is Ms. Anika Wayne, from Boston. She is a registered nurse with a B.S. degree. She also holds a master's in nursing education. She has many years of experience as a trauma, emergency and med-flight nurse, and"—he turned again to look directly at Anika—"she is a licensed pilot, as well."

Anika heard comments like "Hear, hear," as well as welcoming applause and smiles.

Cyril Roberts continued, "I would very much like for each of you to introduce yourself to Ms. Wayne and let her know what your responsibilities are here at the Institute. Let's start with you, Nigel." He nodded to a middle-aged man seated at the opposite end of the table.

"I'm Nigel Cutthbert, assistant director."

Anika acknowledged him with a nod, knowing that she would not remember everyone's name.

At the conclusion of all the introductions, Dr. Roberts thanked everyone and said, "I know that each of you will help Ms. Wayne to settle in and get things sorted out. As I have advised her, tourism is our largest industry here, and we want our visitors to have top-notch medical care if ever they need it while visiting. We must educate and train our medical staff in the newest procedures and techniques that are available anywhere in the medical world. That is the true mission of M.E.I."

Murmurs of consent and agreement followed the director's statements. She sensed that the staff worked as a team, which made her feel even more comfortable. She liked working within a team.

Her first month went quite smoothly. During the day, she was busy teaching nurses, both undergraduate and graduate, but her evenings were usually spent on lesson plans as well as studying British law and the history of Barbados.

Because the days were different than what she was accustomed to, they required some minor adjustment on her part.

"You mean I start work at seven-thirty?" she had asked Angie Simmons, the secretary assigned to her.

"Yes, ma'am, seven-thirty. Then at nine, breakfast is served in the cafeteria."

"Breakfast! I usually have breakfast at home before I come to work."

"As I said, ma'am, it's different here than in the States.

There is a half hour for breakfast, then you may go home at one for lunch. It's quite hot here about that time of day, so everyone takes a siesta after lunch. Then we return to work at three-thirty and work until six-thirty. You'll get used to it.''

Angie gave her a big smile. ''It seems to me that you Yankees are always rushing about, like when I was in New York.'' She smiled. ''Always in a hurry.''

Anika conceded. ''Perhaps you're right. Guess I can get accustomed to a slower pace. I might even live longer.'' She grinned at the secretary.

''I do believe so, Miss.''

While on her way to her last afternoon class later that afternoon, Cyril Roberts fell into step with her along the crushed-stone path to the classroom building.

''Ah, so, Ms. Wayne, everything is going first-rate, I hope.''

''Just fine, I think. You haven't heard anything to the contrary, have you?'' she asked.

''Oh, no, not at all. In fact, most everyone remarks on how well you have settled in.''

''That's good. I really like it here, especially the lovely weather, the beauty of the place, and the people. So warm and friendly.''

''We pride ourselves on being a friendly island,'' he said as he held the door for her. ''But I must tell you, Ms. Wayne, that I do feel you have been neglected . . . short-changed . . .''

''What do you mean, short-changed? My salary?''

He threw back his head with a hearty roar of laughter. ''Oh, no, my dear, not that! I've been busy getting this fall term started, but now I must make up for it. You see, you haven't been given a tour of the island, and one reason that I wanted to speak with you today was to invite you to take a tour with me on Sunday coming. Would you like to do that?''

He looked at her, his auburn eyes focusing on her face as he waited for an answer.

"I'd like that very much, Doctor."

He clapped his large hands together and smiled broadly.

" 'Tis done and done, then, my dear. I shall pick you up at nine, and we shall have a grand day! You'll see. And it's Cyril, my dear."

With a whirl of his voluminous white coat, he turned and left her.

Anika smiled. For such a mountain of a man, he could surely move quickly.

Serena Battison, the staff social worker, told Anika that Dr. Roberts' specialty was cardiac surgery.

"I believe," she told her, "that his patients have confidence in him and his large, capable hands. They all worship 'Dr. Cyril,' as they call him. You should see him in the OR. Never a wasted motion or gesture," she added, "or so I've been told by those who work with him."

Sunday bloomed bright and beautiful, and Cyril picked up Anika promptly at nine, as promised.

Anika had fretted over what to wear, finally settling on black cotton slacks, a white, mock turtleneck silk blouse, and a black-and-white striped linen jacket. She wore white, flat-heeled sandals and a white visored cap to shield her face from the sun. She already realized how much hotter the Barbados sun was than the same rays back home.

"You look lovely, Ms. Wayne. I hope you'll be comfortable in my little sports car."

She noticed that the steering wheel was on the right and that he was leading her to the passenger seat on the left side of the vehicle.

"I wonder if I'm going to be able to learn to drive on the left side of the road," she said.

"Oh, you will, you will. As a matter of fact, I'll teach you. You'll get the hang of it in no time."

"I don't know . . . seems wrong to me, somehow."

"Not to worry, you'll catch on quickly."

As they drove away from Christ Church through other parishes, Anika marveled at the beauty she saw around her. Casuarina trees waved gracefully in the breeze. She saw wide fields of sugarcane and tidy houses along the way, some with tin roofs, others with blue shutters and tile roofs. The road followed the curve of the ocean, which she could see from time to time.

"Our first stop will be Sam Lord's Castle," he told her. "It is a very popular, elegant resort now, but it was once the home of Sam Lord, a notorious pirate who lured ships into the harbor at night and then plundered them."

"My goodness," Anika murmured.

They stopped for a delightful seafood lunch around noon at one of the seaport towns.

"I know you are accustomed to fresh seafood up there in Boston, but you're in for the treat of your life when you taste *our* seafood specialties," he warned her. His smile was all encompassing, and Anika relaxed. She felt cared for and valued. *This is a nice feeling,* she thought as her tensions melted away.

By mid-November, Anika and Cyril were spending almost every weekend together.

"I want to show you everything our delightful island has to offer," he said to her one Sunday. They were on their way to visit one of the oldest Anglican churches in Barbados.

Anika was impressed by what she saw. "I've never visited a church with tombs inside," she said. "It makes me feel strange."

"I know," Cyril answered, "me, too. But I guess you get accustomed to it."

Anika found herself entranced by Cyril's clipped accent, and she asked him about it.

"Right, Anika. I was born here in Christ Church parish and

went to elementary school here, but my parents shipped me off to England for my formal education. Then I went to med school in Edinburgh. You know," he laughed, "they say we 'Bajans' are more British than the British are."

"So I've been told, Cyril, and I do love to hear you speak. It sounds so exotic and colorful."

He gave her a broad smile, his eyes cheerfully bright, and he bowed to her. "I'll always want to please you in any way I can. I think you know that, my dear."

Anika nodded silently. Indeed, she was aware of his interest in her. But was *she* ready for a new relationship?

Chapter Ten

Within two weeks of her arrival in Barbados, Anika received an unexpected letter from Drew.

My dearest Anika,

When you walked away from me that night at the hotel, I knew that somehow I had to convince you that the love I feel for you is real and will always be, until the day I die. I admit that I was stupid and foolish. I also admit that I know how deeply I hurt you. But I'm begging you to be generous and please put my transgression in the past.

Hope you're well and enjoying your new job. Want to know how I found you? The Center for Disease Control is here in Atlanta . . . and I do have sources. (grin.)

Anika, I will always love you.

Yours, Drew.

She was not prepared for her reaction to the letter held in her shaking hands. Suddenly, her eyes grew blurry, and she could even smell the scent of his aftershave. Memories of his gentle hands on her face, holding her tenderly as he kissed her, stimulated a hunger within her. She felt a painful need to feel his strong arms around her body. It all came surging back into her consciousness. She couldn't push it back into the past. She slipped into an armchair, pulled her knees up to her chest, and let the hot tears fall. "Oh, Drew," she moaned.

She recalled the way he looked that night when she left the table. His eyes were clouded in disappointment and he had tried to get to his feet to prevent her from leaving, but because of his injuries, he couldn't move quickly enough. She could still hear his ragged, "Don't go! Anika! Please!"

She dropped the letter to the floor and wiped her eyes with the heel of her hand as she relived the moment. How *had* she been able to walk away? Was it anger, pain, the feeling of betrayal? *Probably all three,* she decided.

She got up and walked over to the window in the living room of her one-bedroom apartment. She looked out at a peaceful scene. Soft green grass, white-stone paths, gloriously colored flowers, and the well-kept grounds of the Institute appealed to her and offered a calming solace. But the truth was that even a thousand miles away, Drew still affected her.

She still loved him. Dare she admit it to herself?

Then, a dozen roses came on her birthday in October. Three letters had preceded them in the weeks prior. Finally, Anika decided that she had to reply.

She wrote to tell him about her work, the staff members she had come to know, the island, its marvelous weather, its culture, and how friendly she had found the people. She signed her brief note with, *Thanks for remembering my birthday. The roses were beautiful. As ever, Anika.*

She hoped her 'just-friends' attitude would work. It did not deter him, however. He continued to write every week. He wrote about his television programs, the famous guests he'd interviewed, such as the secretary-general of the United Nations, and some famous celebrities, such as sports figures like Michael Jordan. His enthusiasm for his work was evident, and it seemed that he was becoming a skilled interviewer. He reported that he was making a steady recovery from his near-fatal accident, reminding her, *Honey, you're my angel,* and he always signed with his declaration of love. *Anika, I'll always love you.*

Cyril Roberts, cheerful and confident that their relationship was progressing smoothly, had no idea that Anika was attempting to recover from a failed relationship.

His boundless energy, unwavering optimism, and infectious good humor often punctuated by a hearty laugh eased her anxiety a little. She found herself becoming more relaxed in his presence. She began to compare the two men: Cyril was dependable, tolerant, friendly, and warm like a soft, cuddly teddy bear. Drew, on the other hand, was intense, curious about life, and eager to try new experiences. He was more like a thoroughbred racehorse, dynamic and quick.

She realized that Cyril was becoming fond of her . . . and she *did* like him. He made her feel secure and cared for. Drew, however, always made her feel alive. He always had—since the day he sat at her table in the cafeteria. From that instant, her life had changed. What had he done to her?

One day, Cyril appeared in Anika's office.

"Busy?"

She looked up and smiled. "Not too busy. Reviewing some test papers."

"Everything is going well, Anika. You have adjusted beautifully to life here in the Caribbean." He waved his hands in an encompassing gesture.

"You've made it easy—all of you," she answered.

"I'm glad." He took a seat beside her desk, and she moved some papers aside to give him her attention. "As you know, the holiday season is approaching.'' He smiled broadly. ''And I want to make your first Barbadian Christmas a memorable one. You *do* plan to spend the holidays here, eh? You have made no other plans?'' His eyebrows rose like twin question marks.

''I . . . I was planning to stay. My dad's in California. There's no one else.''

''That does it, then. You'll be here for the holidays.''

''It will be different, I'm sure,'' Anika told him. ''No ice, snow . . .''

''Forget ice and snow. You must not think of cold, blustery days and nights that you all bother yourselves with up there in Boston. Instead, m'dear, you must concentrate on our lovely sunny weather and gentle breezes. Forget that nasty weather.'' He laughed.

It turned out to be a Christmas like none other she had ever experienced. The students were given vacation, to return after New Year's Day.

Despite what Cyril said, Anika did miss her New England Christmas. It seemed so strange to shop for gifts with no snow on the ground, no biting winds, no sleeting rain. She could hardly summon a holiday feeling, even though the stores and shops displayed Christmas decorations. Santa Claus and his reindeer seemed out of place. Hoping to get into the spirit, she finally did some shopping. She bought her father some colorful ties and an English light-wool vest. The soft beige color would go well with his smooth, tobacco-brown skin. She missed him a great deal, but she knew from his letters that he had made an adjustment to his new life in southern California. She was aware of the loneliness he had felt since her mother's death, but was proud of the way he had forged a new life for himself. She wondered if she had inherited this strength of character.

She bought a small cloisonné pin for Angie and a pair of silver filigree earrings for Serena Battison, the staff social worker who had been so supportive when she first arrived.

But Cyril was a problem for her. She spotted a wood carving of a flying fish that she knew to be a symbol of the island. She did not want anything that could be considered too personal.

"Could you gift wrap this, please?" she asked a salesclerk.

"Certainly, madam," the young woman said. "Would you like to select the wrapping?"

Anika picked out black-and-white, glossy paper and a black satin ribbon. She didn't want her gift to be too Christmasy, yet she wanted it to be in good taste.

She purchased a small ceramic Christmas tree to put on her coffee table.

"Well," she said as she surveyed it. "I guess you're it! Mighty puny, but there you are."

"My, you look lovely tonight," Cyril said as he kissed her on the cheek. He helped her get in and closed the car door.

"Thanks, Cyril."

She had decided that because it was Christmas she'd wear something that would reflect the season. Her white silk pantsuit had gold threads woven into it. She thought it looked quite festive. Small gold earrings and a simple gold necklace were the only pieces of jewelry she wore.

"Yes, you really do look very nice. As always," he added. "But to tell you about tonight, the Hilton hotel chain is so pleased with our efforts to make tourists safe and healthy that they have given us one of their most elegant conference rooms for our holiday bash."

"How nice. Back in the States, we call that 'networking.' One hand washes the other, and both parties do well in a viable partnership."

"I agree one-hundred percent. Sometimes, it seems that, by ourselves, we can do little. But together we can do so much."

"You must be proud of the Institute and the contribution it is making in the tourism industry," she said.

"Indeed. I must admit, in my most modest way, that I'm

very proud.'' He looked at her. ''Did you know that other countries that are also heavily involved in the tourism industry are interested in our success?''

''Really?''

''We get many inquiries. And some are sending representatives to come and get a firsthand look at us. I'm seriously considering holding a seminar.''

''And that can be another link in your relationship with the Hilton. No doubt guests will stay there.''

''I plan to meet with the hotel staff and see what we can come up with. And''—he squeezed her knee—''I'm hoping you'll be a part of that.''

Anika's spine prickled at the intimate gesture. She liked Cyril very much. He was kind, considerate, thoughtful—but was he the one she wanted to start a new relationship with?

Cyril's little sports car purred along the coastline as he drove to the beachfront Hilton. The hotel's portico lights were blazing with a holiday welcome. Cyril handed his keys to a valet.

''Here we are, my dear,'' he said as he helped her out of the car. The night air was soft and warm, and the black-velvet sky sparkled with stars like diamonds in a heaven different from the one Anika knew. She reminded herself that she was living in the Southern Hemisphere, and even the night skies were different. She paused for a moment before they went into the hotel. Cyril stood beside her, a questioning look on his face. ''What is it?''

''The ocean. I've never heard ocean sounds quite like this. It's a constant rushing, roaring, demanding force that you can't ignore.''

''There's something else that I don't want you to ignore,'' he said. She did not miss the serious note in his voice and tried to prepare herself for his next words.

''Please forgive me for being impatient, but I want you to know that I'm falling in love with you.''

Chapter Eleven

The music was festive. The steel-drum band played everything from Christmas carols to reggae music to calpyso. The food was almost overpowering. Mounds of peas and rice, platters of golden-fried fish, beautifully delicate, crispy fried chicken, and huge bowls of fresh salads were placed where they could be easily reached.

Even though Cyril was at her elbow, urging her to sample everything, Anika was unwilling. Her mind was on his latest declaration. Suddenly, it all seemed too much for her. The abundant table, the lavish setting, and the intoxicating music all made her feel uneasy. Her stability had been disturbed, and she did not welcome the sensation.

She tried to get into the happy spirit of the evening, but her mind kept thinking about her future. What was she going to do? She liked Cyril Roberts, but she knew that she did not love him. Perhaps she'd return to the States and get a place to stay and a new job. Should she go live with her father in California? Could she find work there?

"Having a good time?" Cyril's voice broke into her thoughts.

"Oh, yes, I am," she lied. "You were right. It's like no other Christmas I've ever experienced."

A few days later she felt she needed to get some exercise. She had awakened early and decided that a brisk jog would help her think. It was quiet and calm as she jogged around the grounds. Her thoughts were interrupted by the drone of a single-engine plane, a familiar sound. She looked up and spotted a plane disappearing in and out of soft clouds in a magnificently tranquil, blue sky. At that moment, she knew what she needed.

She hopped out of the car and gave a bright smile to Reginald, who smiled back.

"OK, Miss?"

"Oh, yes, Reginald. And thanks so much for the ride. Are you sure you can pick me up later? I can always taxi back to the Institute."

"No problem a'tall, Miss. I shall be here at six on the dot."

"Thanks so much!"

"Have a good flight," he said as he drove off.

Anika walked toward the small concrete-block building at the edge of the airfield. She could scarcely believe her good luck. She had located an owner of private planes who was willing to rent one to her for a few hours.

As she approached the open door, a red-bearded man with tanned, leathery skin came outside. He extended his hand.

"Sam Goodridge," he said.

"How do you do, Mr. Goodridge?"

"Call me Goody, please. Everybody else does."

"I'm Anika Wayne, Mr . . . Goody. I called about renting a plane."

His cobalt-blue eyes winked with friendly good humor, and

Anika recognized a fellow pilot who loved to fly. She could tell by the way he welcomed her.

"So, ye're from the States, eh?"

Anika thought it seemed strange to hear the clipped accent coming from the white man's lips. He sounded just like a native Barbadian.

But she answered quickly. "Yes, I'm from Boston."

"Ah, yes, that's where they lose their r's and say 'pak the cah'."

Anika laughed. "Afraid that's it, sir."

"That where ye learned to fly?"

"Not exactly. I took my lessons in Plymouth."

"So now"—he peered at her, his blue eyes making a quick assessment—"guess ye're wantin' to be aloft."

"Can't wait," she told him.

"Come on in, then. I have some papers . . ."

She followed him into a cluttered office, and he pointed to a chair beside his desk.

After he checked her pilot's license, she signed other required forms and gave him a check for the entire rental fee, and then he took her out on to the tarmac. A small, sleek, single-engine plane with a light-blue body and yellow tail fins stood ready. Anika could not hide her joy at seeing such a beautiful aircraft.

"Oh, Mr . . . Goody! She's just like my favorite plane back home. She's gorgeous!"

He grinned happily, waving his hand. "She's all yours. Set to go. I know you'll have a nice little spin."

"Oh, I will, I will!"

Anika took the clipboard he handed her and completed the inspection check, delighted to be involved in an activity that she loved so much. She hadn't realized how much she had missed flying. But today—at last—she could indulge in her favorite pastime—flying.

Chapter Twelve

The little plane proved to be perfect. It responded to Anika's touch on the controls as if to say, "Lady, where have you been! 'Bout time you showed up. Let's go!"

Eager to be aloft, Anika grinned to herself and taxied down the runway. The earth sped beneath the plane's wings with a quickening acceleration, and as she reached for the sky, her mind shed the tension and anxiety that she had accumulated. *Oh, God,* she thought, *this is what I needed.* She soared into the clean, bright sky. Earthly problems could wait. Freedom, solitude, no restraints—for her this experience was a much needed renewal. She knew that it would give her an expected, cleansing relief, and she was delighted that her expectations were not denied.

She viewed the island below. It seemed cool and placid surrounded by the azure sea. It appeared to float like an emerald jewel reflected by the brilliant tropical sun. But she realized that she could not allow the island's tranquil beauty to seduce her. Somehow, she had come to another crossroad in her life.

Would she allow Drew back into her life, or would she accept Cyril? Could she learn to love him?

As she continued her flight, her thoughts turned to her father. When they flew together, her father would often use those special, private moments to share some thoughts with his only child. One spring morning, they had been on their way to Connecticut to look at a used plane.

"Don't ever be a hussy, honey. Be truthful, especially in dealings with the opposite sex," her father had said to her.

"What do you mean, Dad?"

He looked at her from the pilot's seat and touched her cheek lightly.

"What I mean is this, 'Nika. You see, a man's psyche is different. He is more vulnerable during certain circumstances, you see. He can't help it. Nature made him that way."

"What way?" Anika questioned.

"Maybe I'm not sayin' it right, but a man is easy prey to the wiles and tricks of a beautiful woman. He's like a bee drawn to a beautiful flower. I wouldn't want you ever to deceive a man . . . or lead him on."

As she remembered that conversation, she began to wonder. Had that happened to Drew, with that quick marriage? The "hussy" had led him on. Was Anika guilty of the same behavior with Cyril? Was she leading him on when, she had to admit, she still had feelings for Drew? Even five years and thousands of miles had not extinguished her love for him.

Then, what made her turn away from the man she loved? Never had her emotions been so tormented. When she had first learned of Drew's infidelity, her feelings ranged from despair to disbelief, hate, and anger. Then, she realized that what she truly felt was loss. She had lost Drew's affection, and she had lost the important position she held in his life. Did she want to reclaim what was once hers?

Her allotted flying time went by quickly, but she landed the plane feeling invigorated. One thing was certain: She had been restored by the activity that she loved. She would be back to Goody's to fly again soon.

"Nice flight, Miss?"

"Reginald, it was wonderful!" She climbed into the car, threw her head onto the back of the headrest, puffed out her cheeks, and exhaled forcefully.

"Whew! It was great! Have you ever flown, Reggie?"

"Indeed, yes, ma'am, I have. But I never thought to fly a plane myself. 'Tis a good feeling?"

"The best, Reggie. Simply the best. You should try it. I guarantee you will love it. I think part of the feeling comes from feeling free and part comes from being in complete control. There's nothing quite like it in this world."

"You make it sound exciting. You will be going back to the airport again?"

"Whenever I can, Reggie, whenever I can."

After she got into her apartment, she turned on the television set. Sometimes she would catch a rerun from the States. She dashed into the shower before she relaxed in front of the TV.

She came out of the shower, toweling her hair, when a male voice filtered into her consciousness.

"Ladies and gentlemen, welcome to 'The Awesome Dawson Show,' featuring Drew Dawson!"

She turned and stared at the television as Drew bounded through black-velvet curtains and onto the stage. Music flared up to the wild applause of the studio audience.

She stared at his face. He had not changed at all. The opening segment was a complete blur, and she slowly sank down onto the sofa. Drew walked over to his desk on the stage, and she noticed that he walked quite well, without any trace of his old injury. She began to listen to his patter. His talk was frequently interrupted by laughs and applause from the audience: He had them eating out of his hand. He was good, and she was happy for him. *Is he happy?* she wondered.

She watched and listened, and she realized that her body was suddenly aflame as she looked at the hands, which had stroked her so tenderly a lifetime ago, it seemed. She noticed his arms, which had cradled her with love, and his mouth, which had tantalized hers. The physical longing that she sensed almost took her breath away. She realized with regret that the man she was watching on television could still affect her so strongly. She would never love another man the way she loved him. Her thoughts, feelings, and memories kept plaguing her— those heady, wonderful days and nights she'd shared with him. Because her mind was so filled, she did not hear Drew's plan to broadcast from various locations. She did not hear him mention the Caribbean. All she heard was his deep, warm voice washing over her, leaving her more vulnerable than ever.

Chapter Thirteen

Anika was not prepared for the anger she saw on Cyril's face when he strode into her office the next day. Despite the confrontational attitude he presented, she greeted him in a normal fashion.

"Good morning, Cyril. How are you?"

"It's not a good mornin', not a'tall," he thundered. He leaned on her desk with both hands. With his face inches from hers, he demanded, "What's this I hear about you taking off in a plane and flyin' off into the wild blue yonder?"

"I had a lovely flight yesterday. Yes, I did," she answered agreeably.

"Well, you can't to that!"

"What do you mean, 'I can't do that'?" She bristled at him.

"It's too dangerous, and I can't have my staff in danger. It's too risky."

"You must be crazy! There's nothing in my contract that says I can't pursue my own interests! Flying happens to be one of them."

"Don't you see, Anika, I don't want *you* to be in hazardous

situations, ever! I care about you ... your safety, your welfare—''

She glared at him, interrupting his litany, ''If you care about
my welfare, then you'll let me live *my* life in my *own* way,
Cyril.'' She sat down behind her desk and indicated that he
take the opposite chair. Still glowering at her, but somewhat
deflated because she had not backed down, he puffed out his
cheeks with a deep sigh.

''Cyril, I've been a licensed pilot since I was sixteen, over
ten years now. It is one of my most enjoyable activities. It's
part of what I do, who I am,'' she explained.

''I know, but you could get hurt.''

''I can get hurt right here on the grounds, walking to class.
Even in my apartment, I might slip in the shower. Anything
can happen, anytime, anyplace. I believe I'm a fatalist. What's
meant to be, will be.''

Cyril's voice lost its edge when he responded, ''It's just that
I care ...''

''And I thank you for caring, but I'm a big girl. I know what
I'm doing, and I am cautious. I'm not a silly airhead. I consider
myself a very responsible person.''

''But,'' he persisted, ''suppose something did happen ...
you became incapacitated, unable to teach your classes, what
then? Don't you think you owe it to your job not to put yourself
in a dangerous situation?''

Anika would not back down. ''It's like this, Cyril,'' she
explained, measuring each word in a slow, controlled voice.
''I have always been my own person. I take responsibility for
my own actions and my personal activities, as well as my
professional duties. Now, listen to me. My contract to teach
here at the Institute was for one semester, which concludes at
the end of January. I will not renew my contract. You have
made it impossible for me to stay.''

''But I ... I don't want you to leave,'' he sputtered. ''I just
want you to stop flying.''

"Out of the question!" she snapped. "You're asking me to stop breathing."

An unexpected memory of Drew flashed into her brain as she spoke. *He* had been proud of her accomplishments and had once remarked, "You're a girl after my own heart, 'Nika. You are willing to live life to the fullest, go where it leads you. That's what I love about you. You'll never back away from life."

She faced Cyril, who stood in front of her desk now.

Anxiety clouded his usually calm countenance. She saw smoldering anger in his eyes and realized that an impasse had been reached in their relationship.

"I will compromise with you, Cyril. I will not fly while I'm a staff member. But I will still leave at the end of January."

"You don't mean that . . ."

"Yes, I *do* mean just that."

She managed to get through her daily work with only fleeting thoughts of the change in her situation. She would have to make new plans. She'd have to look into a flight back to Boston and then find a new apartment there. And, most importantly, find a new job. Her previous position with the med-flight team had surely been filled. But, she wouldn't starve: She had some money put aside, and per diem work was always available for nurses. She realized that she had to work quickly. Her time at the Institute was fast coming to a close.

As she opened the door to her apartment, her thoughts were filled with the next step in her future.

She had to admit that she had been happy in Barbados. It had provided a welcome respite from her rejection of Drew and his plea for a reconciliation. In her mind she began to once again compare the two men.

Cyril was predictable, dependable, and serious in his need to control. Drew, on the other hand, was exciting, intense, and eager to try new things. Life with Cyril would be slow, measured, and parochial. It would be just the opposite with Drew. There would be challenges, changing vistas, and excitement. She could no longer hide her feelings from herself. She still loved Drew.

She walked into the dark apartment. Night fell quickly in the Southern Hemisphere. It was only seven-thirty. The small light on her living-room table barely filtered into the room's dark corners.

Suddenly, she felt lonely. Tears flooded her eyes. She pulled off her lab coat, threw it down on a nearby chair, kicked off her sandals, and fell onto the sofa.

Then, the bravado she had exhibited to Cyril, the self-assured positive note she had tried to present to him, drained away. She covered her face with both hands and let the tears fall.

As she reached for a tissue from the box on the coffee table, she was suddenly aware that there was someone in the room. She caught a whiff of a familiar aftershave. Was she hallucinating? She switched on the table lamp. Then she saw him.

"Don't cry, babe, I'm here." He walked toward her.

"Drew! How did you get in here?"

"Easily. I lied, telling your accommodating landlady that I was your fiancé, visiting from the States, and she let me in. Simple as that."

Chapter Fourteen

"How come you're in Barbados?" she asked, as Drew's nearness caused waves of emotions to flicker over her body. Her palms were wet, and not only from her tears. She felt her heart beating so rapidly that she thought she would choke. She wanted to fling herself at him, to strike out at him, to make him feel some of the painful, almost physical, emotions she had endured.

He sat down on the sofa beside her and took her hands in his. His hands were warm and comforting. She still wanted to hit him. As if he knew and could sense her turmoil, he spoke quietly and gently.

" 'Nika, the letters you sent to me were welcome, but I said to myself, 'Drew Dawson, this will never do. If you want to win 'Nika, you'll have to go to her. Cards, letters, and flowers won't cut it!' This calls for *mano a mano,* a hand to hand, face to face meeting. I love you, and I truly believe that you still love me. Don't you?"

She looked at him. Tears clouded her eyes, and she could not speak, merely nod.

She *was* tired, tired of being brave, of being alone, of being denied the love from the man she wanted.

He took her silence for assent and gently lowered his mouth to hers. She melted against him. Her lips quivered as she tried to control her gulping sobs.

"Don't cry, babe. Please, don't cry."

He kissed her wet eyes and her cheeks as she lay against him, feeling as if her strength had evaporated. She was willing to be cared for and . . . loved.

His kisses began to demand more from her than she was able to give, and she needed some answers. She pushed him back.

"Tell me, really. Why are you here in Barbados?"

" 'Nika, I had to come! I couldn't stand having you an ocean away from me . . . and I told my producer that if it meant leaving the show, I was coming to Barbados to convince you that I love you. As I've said before, you are my life, and all that matters to me is loving you. So, it was his suggestion that we bring the whole show down and call it the 'Awesome Dawson Show on Tour.' We are staying at the Barbados Hilton. As soon as I was able to drop off my luggage, I caught a taxi over here. Girl, I thought you'd never get home." He reached for her again.

She could hardly believe that Drew was really beside her, his arms encircling her. It wasn't a dream or hallucination. He was here—was real—and as she pulled his face toward hers, it was right. It felt as it had in the beginning. She loved him and always would.

"Oh, God," Drew moaned as he sealed her lips with his own. "It's been so long, so long . . ."

"Don't talk, Drew. Just love me." She moved her mouth to his ear, speaking with an urgency that met his own.

" 'Nika, 'Nika, 'Nika. It's all I ever wanted to do—to love you, my precious . . . love you for the rest of our lives."

For her the epiphany came rushing . . . he wanted her. It seemed as if his loveless marriage had made the bond between them stronger than before. The bond had come through fire, had been tested, and had not been found wanting.

More questions arose in her mind about his sudden reappearance in her life, but the moment for new discovery was now. Every query, every doubt vanished from her mind. Nothing and no one mattered. Not anymore. Her hunger for him was so strong that she was acting like a wild woman. She pulled and tugged frantically, pulling his jersey over his head. She had to see and feel his chest, the sculpted muscles of the sleek bronze body that she had glimpsed so long ago. She spread her fingers over his firm flesh, letting them trail lightly as she outlined his rock-hard muscles.

He opened the buttons on the shoulders of her sleeveless denim jumper and pulled the straps down, exposing her bra. She gasped as he unfastened her bra and caressed each sensitive breast. With his mouth on one and his fingers gently stroking the other, she felt herself melting into nothingness. She held his head close as her whole body began to heat to almost a white-hot fever pitch. Her breathing began to come in explosive pants, and she thought she was going to die.

"Drew, oh Drew, please love me," she whimpered.

He stood up, released his belt, and took off his jeans and shorts. They joined his shirt and her clothing on the floor. His mouth fused to hers. Naked, he carried her into the bedroom. Swiftly and tenderly, he raised her hips to peel her half-slip and panties down her legs. He stared at her body as if he had to memorize every curve, every contour, every pulsing beat of her heart.

" 'Nika, you're so beautiful. I've wanted you for so long. I promise here and now that I will always love you and be your rock, your soulmate. I will love you more tomorrow than I do tonight." She nodded and through tear-filled eyes saw that he was already protectively sheathed.

He was not selfish, even in this heated moment of passion, and he wanted to keep her safe. Wearing sexual protection meant that he really cared about her. She knew that she was right. She would always be safe with Drew, the man she loved.

Silently, slowly, with moist kisses, he explored her whole body: her legs, the soft mound, her stomach, her breasts, her cheeks, eyes, and mouth. The trail of kisses seemed to brand her flesh. She began to writhe with intense feeling. She pulled him close and whispered in his ear, "I've missed you so much. You're the missing piece of my life's puzzle. But now you're here . . ."

"To stay, forever, my sweet. Forever."

When he kissed her this time, his tongue danced crazily, caressing the inner soft recesses of her mouth. Her tongue joined his in a wild frenzy as they clung to each other. Anika felt as if her body was on fire. She needed quick release from the torrid flames that tormented her. As if he understood her hunger, Drew closed his mouth over her aroused nipple and reached for the secret treasure between her smooth, slender thighs. She moved her body seductively, welcoming the promise of fulfillment that he offered. Leaving the world behind, they soared with an overpowering, dizzying ascent to reach the singular moment that came swiftly and surely. After they caught their breaths, Drew shuddered with passionate emotion. His voice crackled hoarsely in the quiet room.

"Never, never doubt my love for you, my sweet. I'm in your life for keeps." He threaded his fingers through her short, tousled hair, forming it into a sleek cap molded around her head. "You're *my* love and always will be. You know that, don't you?" He kissed her love-swollen lips with a force that almost took her breath away.

Her eyes filled with bright tears as she gasped her answer. "Yes, yes, Drew. I know that."

She lay cradled in his arms, listening to the wondrous thrumming of his heart. She was where she belonged and where she wanted to be.

Drew began to sleep soundly, his arms tucked securely around her. She couldn't help but think about the day's events.

What a day it had been. The morning had brought resentment, disapproval, and annoyance from Cyril—forcing her to consider changes in her life. But now, at the end of the day, Drew had brought a calm, loving peace that would be with her to the end of her days. She drifted off to a peaceful sleep.

She awoke to the tantalizing smell of freshly brewed coffee. After questioning her senses for a bewildering moment, it all flooded back—the most memorable night of her life. Drew!

Savoring this astounding revelation, she stretched languidly. The man she had always loved was nearby. She turned to face an empty spot in the bed, and the crackle of paper when she touched the pillow made her sit up.

My dearest one, Drew had written, *your breakfast is ready. Had to leave. We start taping today. Will see you this evening. I will always love you. Drew.*

She lay still for a moment, clutching the note. She was not accustomed to the new feeling that came over her. She was being cared for, comforted, and loved.

Tears squeezed from beneath her closed eyes as she realized what she had missed. Struggling alone and refusing to allow Drew to come back into her life had been inane and fruitless. Thank God she'd had sense enough to listen to her heart—not her ego. The grief over the early loss of Drew was gone and was replaced by unrestrained joy. *He loves me and I love him,* she thought. She ran her hands down her body, remembering the miracle of love she had experienced last night. *The puzzle of life is complete,* she thought. *Today—this morning—I am truly a whole woman. I am loved.*

Chapter Fifteen

A few days later, Drew and Anika were in her small kitchen, having a quick snack at the bar.

"There's no reason why you can't come straight to Atlanta when you leave here, is there?" Drew asked.

She gave him a glass of iced tea to go with the tuna sandwich she had prepared. Taking a bite of her own sandwich, she nodded her head in agreement. "Don't believe I'd have a problem finding a job. My nursing license covers all the states . . ."

"I'm not talking about a job. I just want you with me as soon as you can make it. But knowing you, as independent and as career oriented at you are"—he sipped some of his iced tea—"Um-m, this is very good. What did you put in it?"

"Some lemon and lime juice."

"Tastes great."

"Glad you like it. But about work . . . I *have* to be busy. I thrive on activity. I'm also glad that I can contribute something."

He smiled at her and put his arm around her to pull her close. He kissed her forehead.

"Can't wait, my sweet. Can't wait to get married and have you all to myself, and to have all your 'contributions' for *my* welfare. Selfish, aren't I?" He grinned at her, a small, impish grin that tugged at her heart.

"Now," he continued, "promise me you'll let this job-hunting business wait for a little while."

She nudged his shoulder playfully. "Guess it would make sense. I should get to know what opportunities are available. So, yes, m'dear," she teased, "I can put my employment search on hold."

"Perfect! Boy, am I glad you decided not to renew your contract."

"I am, too. I thought once that I would stay here for a few years. I enjoyed the work and the people . . . and the climate. Still, I find a parochial—rather insular—attitude down here." Cyril's distressed face flashed through her mind. She shook her head as if to rid herself of the image. "The people are still quite loyal to Mother England," she added.

"I've noticed that about some of the employees at the studio. They do seem to have a lot of pride. Have to admire that."

"It's an admirable quality in anyone," she agreed.

He nodded, finished his sandwich, pushed his plate aside, and drained the last of his iced tea. "Gotta go. Tell me, honey, have you made your plans for leaving here?"

"I'll be flying to Atlanta on February first. Already booked my flight."

"A girl after my own heart! I can hardly wait. I want to get married as soon as you get there."

"Gosh, Drew, I'll need some time . . . to plan . . ."

"Two weeks. That's all I'm going to give you. Two weeks. And I know my mother will help. You know"—his eyes twinkled—"I have faith that you two women can do anything. Move mountains! Where's a calendar? Let's decide now."

She pointed to a calendar held on the refrigerator by a colorful magnet. Quickly, he checked the month of February.

"February fourteenth—two weeks—is Valentine's Day!" he said excitedly. He jabbed his finger on the date. "That's it! That will be our wedding day. Oh, honey, say it's okay."

Inwardly delighted by his exuberance, she walked over to stand beside him in front of the refrigerator.

"It's okay, Drew. Valentine's Day will be perfect."

He groaned softly and bent to claim her lips with his own. "Oh, baby, I don't know how I'm going back to Atlanta without you! I've waited so long. Too long. Even a day without you by my side seems like a lifetime." He moaned as he kissed the side of her neck, nuzzled into her collarbone, and held her close. His kisses continued to roam over her eyes and cheeks, finally claiming her lips.

Reluctantly, she pushed him back, then held his face with both hands. She smiled gently. "You'd better hightail it back to the studio, or we'll both be jobless and there'll be no wedding."

"It'll never happen! Don't forget—I'm the star, 'Awesome Dawson'."

"Well, get goin' 'Awesome,' and drive carefully."

She had not forgotten the accident that nearly claimed his life five years ago. She shuddered thinking that she could have lost him for the second time. She would not have been able to experience the promise of happiness that lay ahead.

Anika arrived at Atlanta International Airport at three in the afternoon. She was exhausted and tired, but when she saw Drew waiting to greet her, she flew into his arms and her weariness vanished. He swept her up, spinning her around.

"Babe! God, do you look great!"

He kissed her repeatedly until she gasped for breath.

"Drew! Everyone's staring at us!"

"Let 'em. I want the whole world to know you're mine!"

*   *   *

Leia Dawson yelled to her husband Benjamin, who was reading the paper in the den. "Come on, Ben! They're here! I just heard Drew's car pull up in the drive."

"I'm coming! Be right there." He heard his wife's cordial voice receiving the couple.

"Come in, come in. So nice to see you!" Drew's mother gave Anika a warm hug. "And here's Dad to help welcome our daughter-in-law to be!"

She stepped aside so that her husband could embrace the newcomer.

"Here she is, folks!" Drew beamed as he pulled Anika close, pride and confidence surging in his voice.

"Welcome to the Dawson family, my dear," Drew's father said.

"Thank you," Anika answered. Benjamin was originally from New Orleans, evidenced by the signs of creole ancestry that he had: light gray eyes set in a full face, skin the color of burnt sugar. His smile, very much like Drew's, made her feel welcome. His handshake was firm and warm. His posture was rather military-like, and she was not surprised. Drew had already told her, "My dad's a retired deputy police chief, hon. But he's a lot of bark with very little bite. And you know, he's my best friend. I've already asked him to be my best man."

She could sense the rapport between the two men, but it was his mother that Drew most resembled. She was tall and stately in appearance. Anika saw at once that Drew had inherited his smooth bronze coloring from his mother. Her eyes were beautiful, a sparkling dark brown. Her love for her only child was apparent. The chemistry they felt circled around everyone as Leia led the way into the living room.

"You must think of this as your home," she told Anika. "We are so happy to have you in our son's life." She looked up at her son from the sofa where she and Anika sat. "Drew?"

"Yes, Mom?"

"I believe you got it right *this* time."

"Mother! Please!"

"It's all right, son. Anika and I understand each other, don't we, dear?" She patted Anika's hand, aware of the mischief she was causing.

"*Anika,*" Benjamin said, anxious to move past the awkward moment. His wife always spoke her mind. "Anika is a very beautiful name."

Drew spoke quickly, glad that his father had moved them away from the subject of his prior, painful, and brief marriage.

"It's African, Dad, and means 'very beautiful.' And she is, isn't she?" he said proudly.

"You have a lovely home," Anika said, waving her hand about.

The living room was decorated with floral draperies and lots of cushioned chairs. The sofa was large and comfortable, with many colorful pillows. The walls were a creamy white with opulent gold sconces on either side of a formal white-and-gold fireplace. Fresh flowers were arranged on a low white-and-gold coffee table. The furniture seemed to have been specially designed for the elegant room. At the opposite end was a book-filled wall with its own ladder for reaching the upper shelves. Anika recognized it as a room she could feel comfortable in.

"Let me show you the rest of the house, then you can relax. You might want to freshen up." Leia said, then she advised the two men, "Please take Anika's luggage to the guest room. I'm going to show her the rest of the house, then I will have a light lunch ready."

She linked her arm in Anika's and led her away. The two men watched them leave, then Drew spoke to his father, a wide grin on his face.

"Perfect, eh, Dad?"

"Perfect, son," his father agreed.

They each picked up a piece of luggage and went up the wide stairs to the guest room.

Chapter Sixteen

"I shouldn't have teased my child like that," Leia Dawson confessed, "but I couldn't help it. I was so upset when he took up with that airhead hussy. Well, *nothing* I said could make him see her for what she was. But, thank God, he came to his senses and, at last, you've come into our lives."

She showed Anika the dining room, a large room with a huge bay window overlooking a well-manicured lawn with dogwood, magnolia trees, and richly colored azalea bushes along the border.

"Such a pleasant room," Anika said.

"I like it," Drew's mother said as she steered Anika into a large, well-equipped kitchen. "This"—she pointed out—"is my domain."

"You like to cook?"

"Indeed I do. But now that we're senior citizens, I have to cut back."

"You both look fine to me."

"We try to stay healthy. We want to be able to be here for

our grandchildren. Come out to the backyard. Let me show you one of my hobbies."

She led Anika out to a beautiful patio. Comfortable chairs and a large umbrella over a round glass table made for an inviting place to sit. On the other side was a large hammock. Anika could feel it calling to her. Her parents had one when she was a child. Some of her favorite moments were spent swinging back and forth, daydreaming.

"Come, my dear."

Leia took Anika past the swimming pool to a small greenhouse tucked in a far corner.

"You must see my babies." She smiled.

Orchids. It seemed as if hundreds of them, all with different colors, shapes, and sizes, greeted Anika's eyes.

"Since I retired as school principal after forty years, I had to do something, so now I'm an 'orchidholic.' I love them."

"They are beautiful! Just beautiful! I've never seen so many varieties. Do you propagate them?"

"Oh, yes, I do. I'm planning on a new one that I'm going to name 'Anika.' " She smiled broadly at her future daughter-in-law, and then she hugged her when she saw the tears in Anika's eyes.

"Don't cry. We'll have to see what it looks like."

"It'll sure be a first for me."

"Shucks, girl, don't you know I owe you?"

Leia's words jolted Anika, and, with tears still shining in her eyes, she asked, "You *owe* me?"

"Yes, I owe *you*. You've saved my son's life. Saved it twice, as a matter of fact."

"I don't understand."

"When he had that car accident, you were the flight nurse on the team that flew him to the hospital."

"One of the nurses, yes, ma'am."

"No matter. You were there. And the second time is now, by marrying him and making him happy. It's all his father and

I have ever wanted for him. I've never seen him so happy. *Never.''*

"I love him," Anika said. "I've loved your son for a long time."

They hugged each other silently—they had bonded, and a relationship between them had been forged.

Leia took Anika up to the guest room, which had been placed at the far end of the upstairs area. It was bright yellow, with a small area in front of a large bay window. A white, wicker chaise lounge with colorful pink-and-white chintz padding had been placed in front of the window. The afternoon sun poured in on a small round table set with a plate of fresh fruit. A portable television completed the area. "I love to sit up here in the afternoon," Drew's mother said. "I hope you will, too."

"Looks lovely."

"And"—she indicated the rest of the bedroom—"use the chest for your clothes—there's plenty of space. And your own bathroom is right here."

She showed Anika a well-appointed bathroom of blue and white, as fresh as an ocean breeze, which added a crisp, clean, restful atmosphere to the room. A delicate orchid spray, curled in a ceramic container, had been placed on the lavatory's white-and-chrome counter top.

"Now, take your time, my dear. Whenever you're ready, come down and we'll have a light lunch."

"Thank you. I'll be down shortly."

Leia Dawson served lobster newberg on toast points with a crisp green salad, and Benjamin poured white wine. Dessert was fresh fruit: strawberries, melon balls, and slices of kiwi.

"I know that Drew is planning to take you to dinner tonight, so this will just be enough to take the edge off your hunger."

"Everything is great, Mother," Drew said.

"Glad you like it, honey."

"You didn't know it, of course, Mrs. Dawson, but lobster is one of my favorite foods," Anika told her.

"Really? I'm glad that I've served something you like for your first meal with us."

Drew's father proposed a toast. "To Anika and Drew, our children. May all your days be filled with happiness and all your problems be little ones."

They clinked glasses. "Thanks, Dad," Drew said. He raised his glass again in Anika's direction. "Here's to my beautiful bride!"

After dinner at one of his favorite restaurants, Drew had taken Anika on a tour of the city. Anika had recognized some of the names and places: Peachtree Street and the birthplace of Martin Luther King, Jr., his gravesite, and the Ebenezer Baptist Church where the slain martyr preached.

"There's so much to show you, 'Nika, but I don't want to overwhelm you on your first night here. Tomorrow is another day. We do have some things to plan for our wedding."

"I would like it to be a small wedding, Drew. Perhaps something here at your parents' home."

They were sitting in the family room, having a glass of sherry for a nightcap. Drew explained, "It's been a long day for you, and I want you to get a good night's rest."

"I'll sleep well. No reason why I shouldn't in that beautiful, white sleigh bed. But really, Drew, please, let's keep it small. My mother's not here to see me get married, and I don't have a lot of close relatives, so right here in your home would be perfect. My Dad plans to come."

"That's wonderful, hon. And whatever you want is what we'll do. You may get some opposition from my mother. I think she has an idea of a big bash."

"We don't have time for any of that," she persisted, "and if you want me to marry you, we'll do it my way or . . .''

Drew threw up his hands in a quick surrender. "We'll do it *your* way. Don't even mention any 'ors'."

"I *would* appreciate your mother's help in helping me select an outfit."

" 'Nika, she'd be thrilled."

"I know one thing, that's for sure."

"What's that?"

"She has impeccable taste. And I know I can depend on her to help me."

"She will, she will, and will be happy to do it. Well, I can see you're tired. Want to go up to bed?"

"I think maybe I should. It's been a long, eventful day."

"It's not over yet."

He walked over to where she was sitting and got down on one knee. He took her glass from her hand and placed it on a nearby table. Then he took a small, black-velvet box from his pocket and placed it in her hands.

"Anika Wayne, I love you with all my heart. You are everything to me, and I want to be with you the rest of my life. I don't know how or why God sent you to me, but thank God He did. Will you marry me on Valentine's Day?"

She gasped when she opened the box to see a beautiful, sparkling marquise diamond set in white gold.

"Drew Dawson, it's perfect. And, yes, you bet I will marry you on Valentine's Day."

Chapter Seventeen

Drew's mother did try to talk Anika into a church wedding.

"I'm really proud of you, my dear, and I want my friends to meet the smart, beautiful, intelligent young woman my son has chosen. I have so many friends here in Atlanta. And I'll admit I'm selfish—I want to show you off."

"I'm sorry, Mrs. Dawson, but I don't want anything like that. I just want to marry your son in a simple ceremony here in your home. I'm an only child. My mother has passed away . . . ," Her voice cracked slightly.

"I'm sorry," Leia said softly.

"Thanks. I'll have my Dad and my college roommate, Chantal, who will be my maid of honor. That's about it."

"We'll do as you wish. Ben is going to be Drew's best man, and the other guests will be family: my sister, her husband, and Ben's brother and his wife, also my mother—who is over eighty—and Ben's father. My father-in-law is in his nineties, but he can get around nicely. A few of Drew's close first cousins, and that will be it. That will be about a dozen or so."

"That will be fine."

They discussed a few more details, and Anika laid out more wishes for her wedding.

"Mrs. Dawson, I don't want a formal, white wedding gown. I . . . I had purchased one . . . before, and I don't want to bother with that nonsense again."

"I understand perfectly. What exactly do you have in mind?"

"I am considering something to go along with the Valentine's Day theme."

"Red and white are Valentine colors, but you don't fancy red, do you?" she asked.

"Don't think so. The 'Bride Wore Red' . . . no, that won't do." They both laughed at the idea.

"How about a very pale petal pink?"

"Think we can perhaps find a simple silk suit of that color? Then my bridal bouquet can be white roses. Chantal, my maid of honor . . . oh, on second thought, I can wear a white silk suit, carry the white roses, and Chantal can wear red or pink and carry red roses. I think I should call her tonight, touch base with her, see what she thinks."

"I'm sure she'll be agreeable. You've known her a long time?" Leia wanted to know.

"Since college. We were in the nursing program together. You know, Mrs. Dawson, there's something about nursing that forms a strong bond between students. Probably because it is such an intense experience that we go through together."

"I'm sure it is. And Drew tells me that you have had many different types of nursing careers. I think that's wonderful. We're delighted to have you come into our family. By the way, since your wedding is less than two weeks away, when are you going to stop calling me 'Mrs. Dawson'?" She raised her eyebrows.

"I really haven't thought . . . but I guess it does seem awkward."

"Yes, it does, my dear, particularly when you will soon be the 'other' Mrs. Dawson."

"Well"—Anika smiled and tilted her head to see how the

older woman would take her suggestion—"how about 'Mama D'?"

"I like that. And if anyone asks, we can say it means 'Mama Dawson' or 'Mama Dearest.' How 'bout that?"

" 'Mama D' it is, then. So, are we going on a shopping trip tomorrow?"

"First thing in the morning," Leia said. "Anika," she continued, apparently still thinking about her own social status in the community. "I respect your wishes to have a small ceremony here at home, but would you have any objections to a reception when you get back from your honeymoon?"

Because Atlanta had always been considered a highly socially conscious city, Anika understood how important a reception would be for Drew's mother. Probably due to the many colleges in the area, as well as the Dawsons' standing in the community. Ben Dawson was a retired deputy police chief, Leia was a retired school official, and their only child was a famous television personality. She had to be fair and agreeable.

"Of course, Mama D, it would be very nice to have a reception when we get back."

She was rewarded by a smile and a warm hug.

"Thanks, my dear, for being so understanding. I'll start planning right after the wedding! Now, let's get you and my son married first!"

Later, Leia spoke with Drew about some of the plans.

"I must say, Drew, that this child has a mind of her own. I could not talk her into a church wedding. And you *know* I tried. I'm usually pretty persuasive when I want to be, but . . ."

"But this time you met your match, eh, Mother?" He laughed and hugged her.

"Sure did. However, she did agree to a reception when you two get home."

"So it's okay with you and Dad to have the ceremony here?"

"If it's what you and Anika want, it's perfectly fine with Ben and me. We want you to be happy."

"Thanks, Mother. I'm so happy now, I can hardly wait for Valentine's Day to arrive."

The two women went to several very elegant specialty shops before Anika found what she really wanted. It was a two-piece dress of white silk faille. The jacket was a fitted tuxedo, with two large pearl buttons at the fitted waist. The accompanying sheath dress was strapless and fit Anika's size-eight body perfectly. She purchased white silk pumps with stiletto heels. "So I can at least get up to Drew's shoulder," she told Leia.

"You look very beautiful, Anika. That's the perfect dress. My son is going to be speechless when he sees you on your wedding day," Leia said when Anika modeled the outfit.

The dress was carefully wrapped in tissue paper and a large box, and the shoes were boxed as well. As the two women made their way to Leia's Lexus, Anika asked, "What do you think I should wear on my head?"

"Perhaps a chin-length veil. Tulle, I think, held in place with jewel clips."

"Since I wear my hair short, that should do nicely. Thanks so much for your help."

"*Thank you* for letting me help," Leia replied.

Chapter Eighteen

Anika spotted her father first. He strode confidently toward her, looking fit and healthy. Her heart thumped wildly as she ran into his arms.

"Dad!"

" 'Nika, baby! How's my girl?" He hugged her as if he couldn't hold her close enough.

"Dad, I'm so glad you're here."

"Wouldn't miss your wedding for the world. Drew!" He grasped Drew's hand with a firm handshake, still holding his other arm around his daughter's shoulder.

"Good to see you, Mr. Wayne, sir. It's been some years. Did you have a good flight?"

"First rate, very nice." He gave Anika another squeeze and a brief kiss on her forehead.

She looked up at him. "Ready to give me away, Dad?"

"No, not really. No father is ever ready to give away his child, but all any dad wants is his daughter's happiness. I am ready to give you to Drew because I know that will make *you* happy. Right, Drew?"

"Mr. Wayne, I promise you that's what I want to do. My goal in life is to make Anika happy. I love her, and, for the first time in my life, I feel complete. She has made me whole, and everything is perfect now that she's willing to share my life."

They had reached the baggage carousel and Fred Wayne's bag appeared within a few minutes. As they walked to Drew's car, Anika's father asked, "Were you able to reserve a restaurant for the rehearsal dinner?"

"Yes, sir, I sure did. Everything's all set. Like you requested, I found a soul-food place. I think you'll be pleased."

Anika and Drew made a second trip to the airport to meet her previous roommate, Chantal Grier.

"Chantal, I hope I haven't asked too much of you—to be in my wedding on such short notice. Two weeks is not too much time, I know," Anika said.

Chantal scoffed at Anika's notion. "Sister-girl, I would have been real upset with you if you'd gotten married without me!"

Anika shrugged her shoulders and smiled happily. "Would have been in big trouble, eh?"

"Right. Big trouble. And wait 'til you see what I've brought for you and Drew."

"What?"

"You'll see. Just wait," she said.

Leia Dawson greeted Chantal warmly. "I'm delighted to meet you, my dear. Welcome to Atlanta."

Anika was eager to see what Chantal had brought and also eager to catch up on her friend's latest activities. Chantal had always been the instigator, the rebel in their class. Excitement and change usually followed in her wake wherever she went. Anika was glad that the big sleigh bed would accommodate both of them. She led her friend up to the room they would share.

"Okay now! Tell me everything. Who's the man in your life—don't tell me there's no one! And what did you bring?"

"Hey, hey, patience, my girl, all in good time. But first I want to tell you how happy I am to see *you* happy. *I* know how much you have always loved Drew, and I'm glad that you two are finally getting married. And I know something else, too. That man just worships you! I could see it in his eyes the minute I saw you two at the airport. I always said that there's nothing like the love of a good man. And Drew is a good man."

"I know he is, Chantal. I can't deny that. And believe it or not, we're very much alike, our goals and dreams, our hopes for the future. And I do believe that the trials and tribulations that we weathered are past us and we're stronger, more in love with each other than ever before."

They talked long into the night, catching up, until Chantal pleaded that even though she wasn't the bride and only the maid of honor, she had to look her best, which meant getting some sleep. Reluctantly, Anika concurred.

The wedding day arrived, bright and sunny. The ceremony was scheduled for noon, and a catered luncheon had been planned by Leia. After spending time with relatives and friends, the bride and groom would be off to Paris and the French Riviera for their honeymoon.

When Anika finally awoke, Chantal was gone. *That girl is something else,* she thought. *Probably chit-chatting with Mrs. Dawson.* She swung her legs out of bed and headed for the bathroom. Suddenly, she realized that this was her wedding day. Valentine's Day. After today, her life would change. She would no longer be Anika Wayne—nurse, pilot, teacher, daughter. She would be a wife, maybe someday a mother. Mother! Thoughts of her own mother circled the edges of her mind. Usually she would push the memories back, tamp down the painful embers until they were gone. But today she allowed her mother's voice to reach her. She could see her mother's smile, smell her favorite perfume, and hear her gentle voice. "You're going to be happy, child. Drew loves you and only you."

"Oh, Mom, I wish you were here," she said out loud, tears cascading from her eyes. She heard a knock on the bedroom door. "Just a minute," she said and grabbed her terrycloth robe. Those few seconds gave her time to pull herself together.

"Come in."

"Happy Valentine's Day!" Leia and Chantal chimed together as they brought in a breakfast tray. "Every bride deserves to have breakfast in bed on her wedding day," Leia added, smiling.

Chantal brought in a tray table and set it up beside the chaise lounge. Leia put the tray on the table, and then Chantal waved toward the tray. "Your breakfast awaits!"

"Thank you. You're both spoiling me."

"Spoil nothing!" Leia said. "The most important thing in this world is my son's happiness. And I tell you, since you're the one that's going to make him happy, I'd walk on glass to give you anything. Breakfast in bed is a small thing!"

"You're still spoiling me."

"That's all right, honey. I'm doing it for your mother, too," she said softly. She hugged Anika then, who let the tears fall freely.

"Hey, come on! Food's getting cold," Chantal urged. "I'm hungry. Let's eat!"

They all laughed, and the sad moment passed. Anika was pleased that Leia understood how much she missed her own mother.

The Dawsons had spared no expense in decorating the house. Flowers were everywhere. White folding chairs for the guests had been placed facing the flower bedecked fireplace. A center aisle had been created, wide enough for the wedding party to walk toward the fireplace where the ceremony would take place. Small white-and-pink bouquets caught with white tulle had been fixed to the stairway banister.

Leia had hired a string quartet to provide wedding music. They were all former students at her high school who earned extra money performing at functions. Dressed in formal attire, the four young women and men were delighted with this gig. After all, their ratings would go up after having played at the wedding of 'Awesome Dawson,' the television star.

At precisely eleven forty-five, Fred Wayne knocked on his daughter's bedroom door. Chantal, tall and slender and dressed in a soft-pink chiffon dress, answered.

"Mr. Wayne! Tah dah!" She stepped back so he could see his daughter.

"Oh, honey, you look beautiful."

He kissed her and stepped back again to take another look. "Picture perfect, that's what you are. Are you ready?"

"Oh, yes, Dad, I'm ready!"

They started down the stairs, Chantal leading the way to the familiar strains of the traditional wedding march.

As she walked through the double doors from the hall into the living room, Anika did not see anyone—her eyes were fixed only on Drew. He wore an elegant black tuxedo with satin lapels. His white shirt contrasted starkly against his bronze skin, and he wore a soft-gray satin tie. His welcoming smile was all that she needed as she walked toward her future.

He whispered, "You're beautiful."

She took her place beside him, and they faced the minister. The man's voice was somber and dignified. "Brothers and sisters," he began. "We are gathered here today to witness the marriage vows of Drew and Anika." He turned to Drew. "Do you, Drew Alexander Dawson, take Anika Rachel Wayne to be your lawfully wedded wife? Please answer 'I do'."

"I do." Drew's voice was firm.

Then the minister turned to Anika and asked, "Do you, Anika Rachel Wayne, take Drew Alexander Dawson as your lawfully wedded husband? Please answer 'I do'."

"I do."

Drew squeezed her hand as she spoke.

"The ring, please."

Drew's father moved forward to place the wedding rings in the minister's hand.

"Please turn and face one another."

As they did, he gave Drew the ring for Anika.

"Repeat after me. 'With this ring, I thee wed.' "

Drew placed the ring on Anika's finger, and then she put his ring on his finger, repeating the words that the minister intoned.

"Now," the minister said, "you may make your personal vows to each other. Drew?"

Drew looked intently into Anika's face. His voice was clear and solemn. "Anika, with you in my life, at last I feel complete, and I vow to you this day in front of these witnesses that you need worry about nothing else in this life. I will be your rock, your shield, your protector. I will always love you. *This* is my solemn vow."

"Drew"—Anika blinked and took a deep breath before she could continue—"Drew, you are the missing piece in my life. You are the anchor that steadies me, the star that glows to show me the way. I promise to love you more tomorrow than I do today. *This* is my solemn vow."

The minister announced, "Since Drew and Anika have exchanged rings and given their vows, by the power vested in me by the church and the State of Georgia, I pronounce that you are man and wife." He said to Drew, "You may kiss your bride."

A generous, hearty applause greeted the couple as they walked out into the hall. In the doorway lay a small floral-decorated broom. Anika laughed when she saw it—Chantal's "surprise."

"Will you jump, 'Nika?" Drew challenged. "We're together now, forever." He held her hand, and they both jumped over the broom in the African tradition of sweeping away the past and starting a new life together.

He kissed her soundly. "Our first act as a married couple."

Family and friends gathered around to offer congratulations as the guests made their way to the tent-covered patio at the back of the house. As soon as everyone was seated, the musicians—this time a saxophonist, a drummer, a trumpet player, and a young woman with a synthesizer—provided the music.

"John Anthony," Leia Dawson said to the young man who was the announcer on Drew's show. "I think we're ready to get started." She plucked at his sleeve and pointed to the newlyweds standing at the entrance.

"Oh, yes, right away, Mrs. Dawson."

As the master of ceremonies, he took the microphone from one of the musicians.

"Honored guests, it is my distinct pleasure to introduce to you for the first time, Mr. and Mrs. Drew Alexander Dawson!"

As Anika walked in, clutching her husband's hand, her heart was beating so fast she thought she might pass out. Never had she felt so much excitement, so much emotion. She looked at Drew, who pulled her close to kiss her. *He loves me and that's all I care about,* she thought.

"I thought the afternoon would never end," Drew complained later as they drove to the airport.

"It did seem like a long time, but I thought it was quite a day, wasn't it?"

"The best, honey, the best day of my life."

He glanced over at his bride. She was wearing a cerise-colored pantsuit that complemented her cocoa-brown coloring. Diamond-stud earrings—his wedding gift to her—sparkled in her ears. She had changed her hair from the sleek cap to softly curled tendrils that danced around her lovely face. This beautiful woman, his wife, enchanted and delighted him. He could hardly wait to start their life together.

Previously, while discussing their honeymoon plans, Anika mentioned that she had always wanted a European holiday.

"My mother had just died, and it became unthinkable to take a trip then, but I've always wanted to see Paris," she told Drew.

"It will be as you wish, my sweet."

"But what about your show?"

"You probably wondered why I haven't been around much. We've been taping shows. So, you and I are all set—free for ten days."

"Oh, Drew, that's wonderful! You're wonderful!"

"I hope and pray you'll always believe that," he said soberly.

By nine o'clock, they were on their flight to Paris. Dinner had been served, they had wine with their meal, and it seemed that the day's events were finally catching up to them.

"Drew, I'm so sleepy, I can hardly keep my eyes open," Anika complained.

"Don't fight it, love. Here, put your head on my shoulder. But before you drift off and this wonderful day is over, I've something I want to give you."

"What is it?" She stirred herself, stretching to fight back the weariness.

"This." He handed her an envelope that he took out from his inner pocket. "I've carried it close to my heart all day."

Anika opened the envelope and took out a sheet of paper. Written in delicate calligraphy, illuminated with gold foil and pastel flowers along the edge was:

To my darling Anika on our wedding day:

> Roses are red
> violets are blue,

I want you to know
that I'll always love you.

With you by my side,
knowing that you are mine,
life's good, God's in His Heaven,
you're my valentine.

Love, Drew

"Drew! It's beautiful! I'll keep it forever. No wonder they call you 'Awesome' Dawson."

He turned off the overhead light and pulled her close. "The best is yet to come, 'Nika. Trust me, it's yet to come." He moaned in her ear.

His promise to her was sealed by a kiss. She found herself responding hungrily as she held his head, her fingers kneading and caressing because she couldn't get him close enough.

She knew what glorious happiness lay ahead with the man she loved. She could hardly wait and willed the plane to move faster and faster toward their future. It had been so long in coming. The love she felt for this man coursed all through her body, and she knew release could come only by sharing her life with him.

"Drew Dawson, I love you," she murmured into his mouth.

"I love you, too, 'Nika, with all my heart," he said softly.

She snuggled into his strong shoulder, his chin resting on the top of her head. They slept, with the drone of the plane a calming promise of lasting love.

ARABESQUE

The Soul of Romance